I0761573

I DID NOT KILL MY HUSBAND

BOOKS BY LINDA KEIR

The Swing of Things

Drowning with Others

The Three Mrs. Wrights

The Royal Game

I Did Not Kill My Husband

BOOKS BY KEIR GRAFF

STANDALONE NOVELS

My Fellow Americans

One Nation, Under God

The Price of Liberty

ANTHOLOGIES

A Million Acres: Montana Writers Reflect on Land and Open Space (editor)

Montana Noir (editor, with James Grady)

NONFICTION

Chicago's Fine Arts Building: Music, Magic, and Murder

BOOKS FOR YOUNG READERS

The Other Felix

The Matchstick Castle

The Phantom Tower

The Tiny Mansion

MK'S DETECTIVE CLUB SERIES (WITH JAMES PATTERSON)

The Poison Puzzle

The Double Trouble Puzzle

BOOKS BY LINDA JOFFE HULL

STANDALONE NOVELS

The Big Bang

THE MRS. FRUGALICIOUS MYSTERY SERIES

Eternally 21

Black Thursday

Sweetheart Deal

THE SUNNY ST. CLAIR ROMANTIC COMEDIES

Frog Kisses

Over the Moon

I DID NOT KILL MY HUSBAND

LINDA KEIR

Published in 2026 by Blackstone Publishing
Cover and book design by Alenka Linaschke

Printed in the United States of America

First edition: 2026
ISBN 979-8-228-31006-3
Fiction / Thrillers / General

Version 1

Blackstone Publishing
31 Mistletoe Rd.
Ashland, OR 97520

www.BlackstonePublishing.com

This marriage needs revamping, so we're going glamping!
#Glamp #HappyMarriage #GourmetSmores #WhatHappensInTheWoodsStaysInTheWoods

—@carasloveisgold

ONE

CARA CAMPBELL

Can't wait for the Housebitches of Chowchilla!
—@aREALNJhousewife14

Feeling as dull and dirty as the stucco sprawl of the Los Angeles she'd left behind forever, Cara Campbell stared through wire mesh and tinted glass as the van rolled past fields of strawberries and avocados, and hillsides covered with orange groves she'd never see again. She was handcuffed and shackled. The chain around her waist, which bound her wrists to her ankles, clanked against her metal bench seat with every bump and swerve.

She willed herself not to cry. If she started, she'd never stop.

"This drive is taking forever," said LaDonna from in front of her. "I feel like I'm in the longest line to get on the worst roller coaster ever."

One of two other transportees in the grubby, dated, ten-passenger California Department of Corrections and Rehabilitation van, LaDonna was round-faced, plus-sized, and appeared to be in her early thirties.

Cara had to look at least fifty. A lifetime had passed in the two-and-a-half weeks since she'd been led out of the packed courtroom in handcuffs, strip-searched, and delivered to the California Institute for Women for processing. This morning she was issued a scratchy orange jumpsuit and matching fake Crocs that reeked of the previous owner's feet. Their yeasty cheese odor was nothing compared to the ungodly stench of the crowded holding cell where she awaited transport to the Central California Women's Facility.

To a fate sealed by the jury forewoman's single, devastating word: *Guilty.*

As the CDCR officers piloted the van out of the northeast San Fernando Valley and onto I-5, LaDonna and the other front-row occupant, Eve—Latina and pretty despite the shooting star tattooed across her forehead—chatted about the highlights of the state prison menu (strawberry Pop-Tarts on special days and a surprisingly generous selection of hot sauce) and took turns trying to figure out who Cara was.

I definitely seen you around.

You ever do time in Orange County?

Seriously, you look familiar.

Cara shrugged and wished they'd move on to any other subject. If she'd learned anything during her horrifying odyssey, it was that she intended to live out the rest of her *life without possibility of parole* attracting as little attention as possible.

If only she could sink through the floor and let the prison van's wheels roll over her. Cara suppressed a sob by coughing hard but fooled no one.

"Girlfriend's got a bad case of the first-timer terrors," LaDonna observed.

"I was in County with that actress who paid for her kid to get into college or whatever it was," Eve said. "She was one scared little rabbit, even with all the special treatment she got."

"Can't imagine that went over well with gen pop."

"She got all kinds of special treatment. We even did a thing where we all coughed and scratched whenever she was around. Actress Karen got so freaked out, thinking she picked up TB *and* scabies, that she got herself sent to medical and talked her way into an early release."

"Figures," LaDonna said, eyeing Cara's hair, which she'd only been allowed to wash twice at Chino and hadn't bothered to brush. "I'm sure they'll bend rules for you, too. Maybe even let you keep them blond extensions for a while."

"Already too janky," Eve said with a grimace.

LaDonna shrugged. "Nothing a little body lotion mixed with a melted Jolly Rancher and warm water can't fix."

"Really?" Cara asked, despite herself. Her on-the-go makeup tutorial—"Five Minutes to Look Like a Million Bucks"—had been removed from all platforms as soon as she was arrested.

"Can't get much in the way of real makeup from commissary, and what there is, is crazy expensive," said LaDonna. "Crushed colored pencil and baby powder works almost as well as drugstore eye shadow."

"So does a little bit of coffee mixed with face cream for foundation," added Eve. "Although you're pretty white. No offense."

Prison cosmetics would suit Cara just fine. In the year since Karl's death, she hadn't cared enough about her appearance to bother touching up her Botox or fillers, even in her rapidly deflating lips. The only reason she'd fixed up her hair and had her nails manicured was her lawyer's insistence that she look presentable in court.

It hadn't made a difference.

As far as the jury of her "peers" was concerned, she was guilty as charged from the moment they saw her. Living her truth had only made everyone believe she was a liar.

The corrections officer in the passenger seat turned around. Cara glimpsed his name badge through the security grate but could only make out the first three letters. Voz-something.

"Bet neither of you woke up today thinking you'd be teaching Chowchilla's newest celeb all the tricks of the inmate trade," he said with a grin.

LaDonna whooped. "I knew it was you! Gold-digger Karen, right? I'll bet you're gonna be the first-ever, real-life influencer in the state pen. I think we should nickname you Goldie. Kinda of like *Gold Is the New Black*."

At least it wasn't Grave-Digger Karen.

"You ever watch that prison show?" Eve asked.

"Nah," said LaDonna. "Figure I've been there. Going there again."

"Don't do the crime and you won't do the time," Corrections Officer Poff lectured from behind the wheel.

The two women rolled their eyes, but Cara didn't bother. There was no point in proclaiming her innocence to anyone on the inside—even in the van on the way. Given how she'd been treated as Public Enemy Number One during her trial, Cara was a little bit surprised that the van carrying her to prison looked and sounded decades old. Not that she expected a private car . . . or maybe she did?

A support beneath LaDonna's metal bench seat squeaked as she shifted from one butt cheek to the other. "Seriously, Goldie, you should score us a reality show."

"It'll never get canceled—I mean, you are a lifer," Eve added. "We can do season after season after *season*."

LaDonna and Eve proceeded to spitball *the best ever* prison reality show, starring Cara, who would commit newbie no-nos like asking fellow inmates what they were doing time for and sitting on other women's bunks without asking. Entertaining hijinks would include Cara getting her first prison tattoo and contracting amputation-grade foot fungus after showering barefoot.

"You've got connections to make the show happen, right, Goldie?" asked Eve.

There was indeed a time when Cara's status as a top-tier influencer enabled her to casually pitch an idea to the movie producer who lived at the end of her cul-de-sac. As the wife of a prominent plastic surgeon, she could also have discreetly circumvented HIPAA laws to approach any of the celebrities her husband, Karl, had nipped or tucked. She even had a friend whose sister had married a highly placed TV executive.

She doubted any of her contacts would accept a collect call from the state penitentiary.

Certainly not one from her.

"I'll have to think on that," she said.

Energized by their big idea, LaDonna and Eve began listing people they knew—or were related to, or were friends of friends—who were famous.

My second cousin's kid was on a football team Snoop Dogg coached . . .

I know someone who went to high school with Kendrick Lamar . . .

This girl on The Bachelor *was born in Inglewood and knows my sister . . .*

Met Doja Cat once . . .

Oscar De La Hoya was at this picnic I was at . . .

While they played Six Degrees of Separation, Cara leaned her head against the side of the van and dozed until she was awakened by the crackle of the van's radio. They were now traveling along a divided highway between railroad tracks and palm trees, in the city limits of Who Cares.

CalFire activity just north of Fresno. Be aware of a detour ahead.

"Great, just what we need," muttered Poff.

"We're stopping in Fresno for food, right?" LaDonna asked.

"I'm *so* thirsty," said Eve.

"We need a bathroom break, too."

Their liquids had been limited for the drive, and Cara was thirsty and hungry, too—her body was, anyway. Personally, she didn't care if she ever ate, drank, or went to the bathroom again.

In the aftermath of Karl's murder, Cara had begun to stress eat. Sugar, carbs, dairy, In-N-Out—anything and everything she'd denied herself since she finally shed that thirty pounds of "baby fat" in her early twenties. She couldn't stop overeating during the trial, either, and her growing roundness had been noted in increasingly hurtful posts headlined *Gluttonous for Punishment*, *Prisonly Plump*, and worse. A wellness spa had even reached out, asking her to participate in and promote their thirty-day detox program *if and when* she was acquitted of all charges.

And then she was convicted.

"Excuse me, Mr. Corrections Officer, I really need to go to the bathroom," LaDonna insisted. "And it's not just number one!"

"That explains the nasty-ass smell back here," Eve said.

"Squeeze your cheeks together, ladies," said Poff. "We're making a scheduled stop, and we're almost there."

Ten minutes later, they pulled up to a small sheriff substation, where they were unloaded from the van at gunpoint so they could shuffle into a restroom on the side of the building. Poff watched them closely as Vozenilek—which Cara could now read on his name tag—took the keys from his belt, unlocked each woman's right wrist, and quickly locked them into a windowless bathroom with a single toilet and an eye-watering smell of ammonia.

"Transport bathroom breaks are the worst," Eve said resignedly.

"Dibs," LaDonna said.

As Eve provided a free hand to help with the buttons on LaDonna's jumpsuit, Cara turned away to give them privacy.

"Don't worry, Goldie, you'll get used to it," LaDonna said.

Cara doubted that, especially as LaDonna began to loudly and unselfconsciously empty her bowels. She thought longingly of the TOTO bidet toilet with the heated seat in the primary bathroom of what used to be her home. Did state prison toilets even have seats, or were they all filthy, metal, wall-mounted horrors like those in processing?

After LaDonna flushed, Eve sat and pooped as well.

"Your turn," she told Cara when she was done.

"I don't think I need to go."

LaDonna washed and rinsed in the rust-ringed sink using what was possibly the last powdered-soap dispenser in existence. "No telling how long it'll be before we get there and how long they'll make you wait once we do. Do yourself a favor and force out whatever you can."

Neither woman had squatted or put toilet paper on the seat, so Cara didn't either, not wanting to give them more fodder for their make-believe reality show. She tried not to think about the superbugs hitching a ride as she popped the snaps on her jumpsuit and sat directly on the seat—something she had never done before on any public toilet.

Concentrating all of her willpower, she produced a small trickle of pee.

"This reminds me," Eve said. "We've gotta do an episode on going to the bathroom in prison."

"And the brutal constipation Goldie is going to have until she learns to poop on command!"

Cara wasn't about to tell them how hard it had been even while sequestered, due to her notoriety, in her own cell.

The two of them laughed their heads off until they were interrupted by the rap of a gun butt on the door.

"Let's go. Now!"

Back in the van, she discovered they'd been joined by a fourth transportee, a rail-thin girl with bleached-white hair, acne scars, and a sullen expression. She had taken LaDonna's first-row seat on the driver's side.

"She's even whiter than you, Goldie," cracked LaDonna as she took the empty bench across from Cara and behind Eve.

"She can play your assistant on the show," Eve added.

The new arrival didn't ask what they were talking about. Cara noted that LaDonna hadn't reacted at all to losing her seat—apparently, there was no pecking order in transport-van seating.

They turned onto a side road and quickly slowed to a crawl. For the first time in her life, Cara was thankful to be in bumper-to-bumper, destiny-delaying traffic. From her cage, she saw the cars ahead of them making U-turns. When the van reached a roadblock where two sheriff's deputies were directing traffic, Poff pounded the steering wheel in frustration and then rolled down his window.

"Where are you headed?" asked the nearest deputy.

"Chowchilla," said Poff. "These ladies have a date with the warden. We just need to get back to 99."

"Cal Fire just closed this road due to a brushfire. You'll need to keep going up 41."

"Highway 41? That adds—"

"A hundred miles," groaned Vozenilek.

"Why can't we just turn around and cut over on Avenue 12?" said Poff, looking at the map on the dashboard screen.

The deputy was impatient, ready to end the conversation. "This thing's blowing up fast around Irrigosa, between Fresno and Madera. Cal Fire wants to reroute everyone as far away as possible so they can fight it."

Cara smelled a hint of smoke through the open window.

"No way to sneak through?" asked Poff.

The deputy raised his palms, nothing left to say.

Everyone fell silent and watched the hazy sky in the distance as Poff turned the van around.

During closing arguments in the chilly, utilitarian courtroom, the prosecutor had swung the murder weapon thirteen times as if hammering an invisible spike. He ran his fingers along its sharp claw as he claimed Cara had raked it across Karl's right cheek before "tapping" herself on the head to "pretend" she was a victim, too.

She wanted you to believe this was the work of a fictional stalker, he told the jury. *Not the money- and fame-thirsty trophy wife who realized her financial tap was running dry.*

All of it was news to her.

Every piece of so-called evidence also argued for reasonable doubt, and yet here she was, listening to LaDonna and Eve resume their complaints about hunger. They grew more and more insistent until Vozenilek finally produced some Costco mini water bottles and MREs he claimed were "for emergency use only."

"And you didn't think this qualified until now?" said LaDonna, as the battlefield rations were passed out.

"Bon appétit," said Poff.

Cara noticed the COs didn't take any, even though they had to be hungry, too.

Each box contained a squeeze packet of chili mac, a kippered beef snack, processed cheese as orange as their jumpsuits, applesauce, and a bag of Skittles. After her experience in the bathroom, Cara couldn't imagine trying the chili mac, and anyway, it seemed impossible to eat with her hands cuffed close to her stomach. Eve simply squeezed the packet between her palms, bent forward, and tore it open with her teeth before sucking down the chunky lava.

LaDonna tore open her kippered beef stick and the cheese. The new girl ignored her food altogether.

Cara didn't dare to try even the applesauce, which was two years past its best-by date, but the Skittles seemed safe enough. Pouring a few into her hand, she decided to savor each flavor by picking them up one at a time with her tongue.

First a crunchy, chewy purple. Basic grape.

Then a delicious, lemony yellow.

She had just captured and begun to chew on a green one, the sweet but tangy lime flavor spreading across her tongue, when the van swerved so sharply the remaining Skittles flew out of her hand and rattled against the window like hailstones.

Poff swore and Vozenilek screamed. Her head jerked violently, and suddenly they were sideways on the road with two trucks bearing down on them.

Cara's vision blurred as the van collapsed in a cacophony of crunching metal and shattering glass. Then they were spinning, whiplash fast, gravity simultaneously pinning her to her seat and trying to free her body from her chains.

Strangely, it wasn't her own life she saw ending, but Karl's. His voice shouting her name as her skull flooded with blinding pain. His voice growing garbled and strange as he seemed to fight back and her vision went black. Coming to and discovering his body, heavy and cold, his arms and legs splayed stiff as she tried and failed to pick him up. Her tears falling on his face. Her clothes soaked with his dark blood as she raced back down the path for help.

"Goldie! Cara Campbell! Wake up!"

Cara wasn't sure she was still inside her body. Her hearing was muffled, and she couldn't tell if she was upside down or right side up.

"Open. Your. Eyes!"

It wasn't God, an angel, or even one of Satan's little helpers who had come to take her away, but LaDonna, who was trapped by a twisted steel cage that had been part of the rear security door.

The actual back doors hung open, one of them off its hinges.

When Cara looked for the guards, she couldn't see the front half of the van at all. Only asphalt. Broken glass, crumpled plastic, and torn metal littered the highway.

Her stomach twisted and brought her back to her body.

She dry-heaved.

"You have to get us out of here," said LaDonna insistently.

As she looked down, checking to see if she was still in one piece, her bench wobbled. It was then that she noticed Eve, who'd been seated on the first-row passenger side, was lying half in and half out of the van. Her head was sitting on her body wrong. All Cara could see of the new girl was her bleached hair, which was now red and gray. Blood and . . . brains?

Cara vomited rainbow-colored bile onto her orange jumpsuit.

LaDonna's voice was tight but calm as she coached her. "I'm stuck, so you have to get both of us free. Find the COs and grab their keys."

Below them, something popped and started hissing.

Cara's seat support had loosened from the floor, and the right side of her bellyband was pinned beneath it. If she lifted her bench and pulled the chain out from under it, she would still be shackled—but free.

"*Hurry!*"

The bench seemed to weigh a thousand pounds. It was awkward to lift, but she somehow did it. LaDonna groaned as Cara climbed over her and stumbled out of the back of the van.

Cara fell to her knees, then stood up into a scene of utter devastation. A mangled pickup truck rested on the center stripe. Beyond it, a jackknifed semitruck lay on its side. The front half of the transport van was in the ditch on the opposite side of the road.

Cara stumbled across the asphalt, her steps clipped by her shackles, smelling gas and an unfamiliar chemical smell. The two COs were still buckled into their seats, but the front part of the van was face down in the weeds, all of its window glass destroyed. She climbed awkwardly into the ditch on the passenger side and pulled the door handle. It fell open toward her.

Officer Vozenilek had been decapitated. His head lay in the footwell. Officer Poff was intact but unmoving.

If she had had anything left in her stomach, she would have vomited again.

She held her breath as she reached for Vozenilek's belt.

"I'm sorry," she whispered as she unclipped his bloody key ring.

Crouching in the rocky ditch, she tried every key until she found the one that unlocked her restraints. Without pausing to rub her aching wrists, examine the red rings around her ankles, or consider how good it felt to be free, she recrossed the road.

And was nearly hit by a car. A red sedan with a gray hood veered onto the shoulder and accelerated past the wreck without stopping.

"Thanks for helping!" LaDonna pressed her wrists against the damaged cage as Cara reached her. "Do my handcuffs and give me the keys, Goldie. I'll do the rest."

Cara's hands shook as she fumbled to get the key into the lock. The cuffs finally opened with a satisfying click.

LaDonna was bleeding from her forehead and her arm but didn't seem to notice as she unlocked her shackles. Then she kicked the metal grate out of the way like a bona fide superhero and quickly climbed out of the van.

"As much fun as it would be to costar in your reality show, I've got three kids, and I plan to see them again," she said.

"You're leaving?"

"When the Lord giveth a miracle, who are we to turn him down?" LaDonna said.

"Aren't you afraid they'll catch you?"

"If they do, I'll say I had shock or amnesia. Both, probably."

With that, LaDonna jogged across the highway, climbed over a sagging barbed-wire fence, and headed into the dry, brown grass. After a moment, all Cara could see were her head and shoulders. Then they, too, disappeared.

For a second, Cara wondered if LaDonna might have allowed her to tag along. But then she surveyed the tangled metal and smoking mess around her. Eve, New Girl, Poff, and Vozenilek were all dead, but there were two more vehicles. If anyone was alive in them, there was no one but her to help. The pickup truck in the middle of the highway was closer, so she made her way there first.

It looked like a tin can crushed with a brick. Through the open driver's-side window, she saw a freckle-faced teen no older than seventeen pinned between the steering wheel and the compressed roof of the cab. She looked hopelessly trapped.

Dear God.

Trembling all over, Cara reached inside and brushed the girl's lavender-tinted hair away from her blood-streaked face. She seemed only half conscious. Her eyes stared, unfocused, as she took rapid, shallow breaths.

"Everything's going to be . . ."

She couldn't finish. Because it wasn't.

In what LaDonna would surely have pronounced another miracle, Cara spotted a phone in a purple sparkly case on the asphalt near the truck. She picked it up, turned it over, and saw a half-written text on the spiderwebbed screen.

Don't worry Bree happy! it read. *See u soo*

Cara dialed 911.

"911, what's your emergency?"

"There's been a bad accident on . . . I don't know where I am," she said, the words rushing out. "We were just outside Fresno when we detoured from the fire. I think it's Highway 41. People are dead, and there's a teenager badly injured. Send help."

She hung up before the operator could ask her to stay on the line.

"Help is on the way, Bree," she told the girl.

Bree might have nodded. Or it might have been a spasm. Bloody bubbles were forming on her lips.

Cara thought about the Lord giving and taking. She'd always considered herself spiritual, plugged in to the universe at least, but the past year had certainly challenged her belief that everything happened for a reason. Yet here she was, still alive when a half-dozen people around her had died. She'd been praying for justice every day since her arrest but had let go of hope after the crushing verdict. Wasn't that exactly when manifestations *manifested*?

Bree's breaths, still shallow, were growing raspy.

Cara moved closer, gently rubbing the girl's arm.

The tears she had managed to hold back for the entire ride from LA finally began to pour down her cheeks. Her body convulsed in racking sobs.

Karl, she thought. *Oh, Karl. I'm so sorry. I miss you so much.*

Then the freckle-faced, lavender-haired girl stopped breathing.

Cara expected to see a mystical vapor or to feel a cold rush as the girl's spirit left her body. Instead, a white-and-gold sedan pulling a trailer slowed and pulled onto the shoulder of the two-lane highway and stopped beside the overturned semi. She watched, screened by the wreckage of the pickup, as the elderly couple cautiously emerged from their vehicle. Urged on by his wife, the husband looked into the cab and turned away, his face drained of all color. He seemed to steel himself before heading toward Bree's truck.

Why couldn't Cara claim she was in shock or had amnesia and simply wandered off, too? Even if no one believed it, what could they do to her? She already had a life sentence. If she ran, she'd be caught quickly, she was sure—she had no idea how to survive on the run—but shouldn't she at least seize a few hours of justice in the meantime?

Cara leaned in and tenderly moved some hair from the girl's face.

Then she ran.

TWO
JORDAN BURKE

Guilty! Guilty! Guil-tay!
—@Memphismom14

Madera County Sheriff Jordan Burke braked to a halt at the end of the gravel driveway as two people suddenly emerged from the bushes. When they began hammering on his windows with their hands, he instinctively shifted into reverse, dropped his hand to his hip, and unsnapped his holstered Glock.

After a second look at the man and woman attacking his car, he sighed and shifted into park. He had been surprised by tweakers and crazies in the backwoods before, but none of them had been wearing Lululemon and Patagonia. COVID-19 and the ensuing work-from-anywhere revolution had brought with it a bougie invasion he suspected he'd never really get used to.

Lifting his handset, he addressed them through the PA of his Ford Police Interceptor Utility: "I'm coming out. Please step away from the vehicle."

The man at the passenger-side window jumped back in alarm when he heard Jordan's amplified voice. The woman on his side—wearing yoga pants and a puffer vest over a hot-pink crop top that read *100% THAT BITCH*—folded her arms. When he opened his door, she stepped back just far enough for Jordan to swing it open.

He stepped out and surveyed the scene. He was parked next to a brand-new Tesla X, behind a new home with a green metal roof and red cedar trim. The door to the house was wide open.

The woman pursed her artificially bee-stung lips, her panic seeming to have evaporated since his arrival. "It took you long enough."

Jordan knew from long experience there was no point in telling her how far he'd come or how fast he'd driven. He'd been dealing with folks like this more and more often; job number one was to calm them down and assess the situation. All he knew was that Gracia, his sixtyish, grandmotherly dispatcher, had relayed a near-hysterical 911 call from two Airbnb renters about an intruder.

"What seems to be the problem?" he asked.

The man came around the hood and stood next to his wife, breathing heavily.

"I'm Dan Cashmore," he began, his voice rising. Catching himself, he found a lower register and continued. "We were setting out lunch on the deck, going in and out of the house. Lena wanted to eat outside so she could get a picture—"

"He must have come from the woods," interrupted Lena. "We left the sliding doors open all morning because we were trying to let out a *bat* that flew in last night."

Dan chuckled awkwardly. "The trees come right up to the deck, which is one of the reasons we chose this place, but the listing didn't say anything about bats coming into the house, let alone bears. I was bringing out the salad when I saw him. Then he decided to come inside, so we ran out here."

"There is a *bear* in our *house*," said Lena. "A *bear*."

While they were talking, Jordan sidled closer to the house, climbed the steps, and looked inside. Down a short hall, the place opened up into a great room lined by tall windows that offered stunning forest views. A medium-sized black bear was standing on two hind legs at the kitchen island, snout deep in an impressive slab of smoked salmon.

"Now get him out, please," said Lena behind him, sounding like a guest who had discovered a stain on her sheets at a five-star hotel.

Jordan led them back to the driveway before answering. "You said the deck doors are open, too? I'll wait with you until the bear leaves and then you can close up the house."

"Can't you shoot it?" asked Dan, a little too eagerly.

"Not unless it's necessary for our protection. If it comes out on this side, I recommend you climb inside your car for safety."

Lena looked like she was thinking about asking to speak with Jordan's supervisor. "Well, can't you at least call animal services?"

"They're pretty much limited to dogs and cats. If he comes back enough times to become a nuisance, you can file a report with Fish and Wildlife, and they'll see if he needs to be relocated. But black bears usually aren't dangerous unless they feel threatened."

"But what if it chews up our stuff?" Lena persisted. "The food I can deal with, but I have an open suitcase in there with two thousand dollars' worth of new outdoor clothing inside. Not to mention all of Dan's electronics."

"Look, this won't be like *Goldilocks and the Three Bears*. The bear might eat your lunch, but it's not going to play with your iPad and try on your clothes."

After eating all their salmon, the bear probably would get sleepy—unless they had also left a pile of cocaine on the kitchen table.

"But what if the bear . . . comes back?" asked Dan.

Jordan nodded. "He most likely will. Bears love salmon. And you pretty much invited him to lunch by leaving your door open."

Tires popped gravel behind them. Jordan turned and saw a gleaming orange Ford Bronco fully equipped with roll bars, a winch, and a snorkel, ready to churn mud and ford rivers in the jungle, should jungle ever overtake the foothills of the Sierras.

Unfortunately, he recognized the car.

"I texted the Airbnb owner right after we called 911," said Lena, sounding proud of her resourcefulness.

Jordan tried to never let his guard down in front of civilians, but he could have spit and sworn as he watched Troy Silverman—the owner of this and a dozen other local Airbnbs—check his gray but luxuriant locks in his ridiculous rig's rearview mirror. The real estate speculator had left Montecito the previous year to establish residency in Yosemite Lakes—the reason for the move becoming clear when he announced his candidacy for Jordan's seat in next month's sheriff's election.

Jordan had been a deputy for twelve years and sheriff for five, landing in the job only after his father, the sheriff before him, died at sixty-four of COPD and heart disease. Jordan's grandfather had held the job, too. Burkes had maintained safety in Madera County for seventy years, give or take. And while the job itself could be exhausting—he sometimes daydreamed about what it would be like to live life without being on call twenty-four seven—he was proud to serve his community and knew he would never stop feeling responsible for the place he'd lived every year of his life.

It was hard to say which way the election would go. Jordan hadn't thought there was much appetite for a self-promoting slickster from SoCal, but these days, a lot of people wanted change for change's sake. And Silverman had spent plenty on his effort to get elected, even hiring a campaign manager, media consultants, and a team of so-called volunteers, all of whom did their best to make Jordan sound like an out-of-touch good ol' boy who didn't believe Black and Brown lives mattered. Which couldn't have been further from the truth. While his grandpa, Chester, and his dad, Jerry, may have done their jobs like the other White sheriffs of their times, Madera was about 60 percent Latino. Spanish speakers formed the core of Jordan's constituency. They weren't just good, hard-working people—they were his friends.

Jordan suspected the real reason behind Silverman's sudden interest in the job was to expand and protect his real estate holdings, but so far Jordan had been forced to play defense. He'd been too busy being sheriff to run much of a campaign.

Troy Silverman's slogan? *The Burke Stops Here.*

Ignoring Jordan, the lanky Troy unfolded himself from his Bronco and aimed a smile at his renters. "I heard you're having a little bear trouble."

Lena and Dan perked up, perhaps sensing that Troy was one of their own, someone who would be just as alarmed as they were about what the bear was doing to their salmon and mixed-green salad at that very moment. Maybe they were from Montecito, too.

"The *bear* is still *in* there," Lena told him. "And this *man* says we just have to *wait* until it *leaves*. It's not even that *big*."

"It's Sheriff Burke, ma'am," said Jordan wearily. "And even small bears can be dangerous if they're spooked."

"We just don't know what kind of damage it's doing to our stuff—or to your place," Dan told Troy, clearly no stranger to the art of negotiation.

Troy turned to Jordan. "Sheriff Burke, are you going to stand by and let taxpayers' property get torn up by local wildlife?"

"I'm sworn to protect the lives of anyone in my county, whether they pay taxes here or not," said Jordan. "As for your property, I suggest you take it up with your insurance company."

For once, the Cashmores didn't weigh in, but instead watched Troy to see what he would do next.

"As someone who pays your salary, I find that answer disappointing," he told Jordan. "But I don't intend to employ you much longer."

He winked at his renters. "Watch this," he said, and strode into the house.

Jordan could feel the eyes of the Cashmores on him, their continued silence suggesting a disappointment that he hadn't resisted Troy's challenge to his authority. A bear encounter *and* a fistfight would have been an even better story to tell their friends. But even though what Troy was doing was stupid, there was no law against it.

Pans banged inside the house as Troy shouted, "GO ON, GET OUT OF HERE! GO ON, GIT!"

The country twang was a nice touch.

There was more banging, a few heavy thumps, a moan of distress—Jordan was pretty sure it was the bear—and the clatter of a thrown chair. Then a muted crunch.

Shedding crumbs of safety glass, the bear scrambled over the railing of the back porch, performed an ungainly belly flop into the bushes, and quickly disappeared into the trees.

Troy emerged triumphantly from the back door and casually chucked the frying pans onto the porch like a gunslinger tossing his smoking pistols.

"See?" he said, arching an eyebrow at Jordan. "No big deal."

"I'm glad you're safe," said Jordan through gritted teeth. "I'm also glad I don't have to radio for an ambulance. That could have gone another way."

"If I *were* a local voter, I know who I'd want for sheriff," said Lena, as Troy almost visibly swelled with pride.

"Just remember it's not all chasing bears out of rentals," Jordan told him. "Next time it could be a tweaker with a gun."

"Or even worse for you, it could be a raccoon!" chuckled Troy.

As Troy, Dan, and Lena all yukked it up, Jordan searched his mind for a comeback. He had never been particularly quick with words.

Then his radio crackled with a call from dispatch.

"Sheriff, there's been a multivehicle accident on Highway 41 with probable fatalities," said Gracia. "Sending other units, but you're the closest."

Jordan was behind the wheel before she finished. The Airbnb trio shrank in his windshield as he floored it in reverse. He was sorry he couldn't stay to watch Lena's face as she realized the bear had plowed through the closed side of the sliding doors. All kinds of forest creatures were likely to come in.

Actually, that was guaranteed.

THREE
CARA

That woman's so fake, she's got Botox in her DNA.
—@defpoetryslamama

Cara climbed over the sagging barbed-wire fence, snagging the sleeve of her jumpsuit, and jogged into the dry, brown grass. She had no idea whether she was headed north or south, east or west, but it didn't really matter as long as she got far away, as fast as possible, from the acrid smell of burning oil and rubber, and the sight of twisted metal, shattered glass, and broken bodies. She felt awful that the elderly couple who'd been decent enough to stop would see such gore but was thankful poor Bree wouldn't leave this earth alone.

Realizing she couldn't run inland because she'd end up in the front yard of a farmhouse, she sprinted parallel to the highway, moving from one sparse stand of trees to another in side-cramping bursts. Once past the house, she turned away from the road and jogged until she reached a rocky rise surrounded by dense brush. Panting and thirsty, she crouched to catch her breath.

Sirens blared nearby. More sounded in the distance.

Pushing on, Cara bushwhacked until her progress was stopped by a steep drop-off. She couldn't scramble up the rocky hillside or she'd be plainly visible. There was no time to turn back and head in a different direction. The only viable option was to drop down twelve feet or so—she hoped it was only that far—into the streambed below.

Cara refreshed the phone so it wouldn't lock up and tucked it into her uncomfortably small, prison-issue white bra. She bent over, and before she could think too hard about it, grasped an exposed tree root. She hoped her flimsy resin slip-ons would provide some traction as she found footholds on her way down.

They didn't.

Thankfully, the tree root held when the rock gave way, cracking only after she dropped into murky, ankle-deep water. Shock waves radiated up her ankles, but she landed on her feet.

Cara shook off the pain and sloshed along the gully, glad her otherwise useless footwear had holes that drained the water. She was well shielded by shrubbery until a small bridge appeared out of nowhere and crossed the streambed.

She moved closer until she could see it was part of a gravel driveway leading to a beautiful modern home perched atop a nearby rise. Movable glass walls—much like those in her Beverly Hills kitchen—opened onto a deck spanning the length of the house, affording an unobstructed view of the meadow before her.

Was anyone watching from behind those windows?

Cara crouched, scurried under the bridge, and dove into a field filled with feather reed ornamental grass. She knew the variety because she'd once bought bunches of it at the farmers' market to mix in with an arrangement of limelight hydrangeas. She'd spent the rest of that day styling a country-themed dinner-on-the-patio post, complete with metal buckets full of sunflowers, fresh herbs, recycled glassware, and gold flatware. Her Instagram story, *Before the Fall,* had gotten a few hundred thousand likes. *The Fall of Cara Campbell*—a photo of her scampering through golden grass, wearing the color of marigolds—would get millions.

Her chest tightened so quickly she began gasping for breath.

Forcing herself to breathe deeply and slowly, she tried to calm her panic with meditation. Her go-to mantra—*I create my own path and walk it with confidence*—was both too on the nose and no longer true.

What the fuck am I going to do next? was sure to make things worse. Instead, she zeroed in on the thrum of insects, birds, and the gentle breeze.

Be still and listen, she told herself, over and over, until she could.

She watched as a black-and-white-tailed hawk swooped down, disappeared briefly, and took off again with a field mouse in its talons. It was surely a sign—if not of her ultimate fate—of how many disgusting, sharp-toothed little rodents were scrambling through the grass along with her.

The hawk had spotted its prey with ease. She would be just as easy to spot via helicopter, drone, or the less expansive deck of yet another house she noticed just along the hillside from the first. How long could she possibly last out here? She was doomed to either quick recapture and a life sentence imposed by the State of California or the death penalty carried out by Mother Nature.

There was no calming her monkey mind.

Just focus on the task in front of you.

She spotted a cluster of boulders half a football field away.

Wiping the sweat from her forehead, Cara began to army-crawl across the field. She'd once beaten her fit-for-any-age husband in the mud crawl section of a Tough Mudder competition, surprising both of them. On race day, Karl motivated himself through the "Block Ness Monster" and "Everest" sections by whispering, Obama style, *Yes! We! Can!* while she propelled herself across the finish line by obsessing over snarky comments from Instagram trolls.

Daddy complex much?

You're nothing but a parasite in Prada.

If he doesn't cheat on you, he really should.

Ah, the lament of the trophy wife, Karl would say with a dimpled smile when she mentioned the haters and their inability to understand that she was just trying to normalize and destigmatize the very construct of gold digging, using their loving relationship as an example.

The kiss that followed always dulled the sting.

But now, as grass stalks whipped her face and pebbles dug into her elbows and knees, she had a whole trial's worth of indignities to work with. The prosecutor's smugness as he tricked Cara into confirming her height at five feet, eight and a half inches before asserting the killer was "approximately five-nine, based on Karl's head wounds." The mini-mart security video of a "raging argument" she'd had with Karl on the day of his death when they were only ribbing each other over his compulsive need to top off the tank and her tendency to drive on fumes. The hippy-dippy front desk clerk at the glampground testifying to a "weird, you know, vibe when I checked them in." The white-haired fitness freak who claimed Cara had been flirting with him in the saltwater pool, even though she'd reached for a towel the moment he pulled off his sweatshirt to reveal his leathery abs.

Even Cara's own heartfelt social media posts had been blown up to poster size and mounted on foam-core boards to be used as exhibits against her: *Release your emotions, even when they're scary* and *Sometimes true love hurts.*

The worst insult of all took her completely by surprise. The prosecution's forensic accountant took the stand and "went off script" by testifying that Karl "had millions less than he claimed and was deeply strapped for cash due to being overleveraged on the construction of Campbell Cosmetic."

Karl had never even hinted that finances were tight. Before his death, after the big groundbreaking ceremony for his all-in-one surgical suite and five-star recovery facility, Karl was in great spirits about his investment and its profitability. There was no reason to believe otherwise, considering that a generous chunk of money appeared in her spending account on the first of every month without fail. Yes, he was an optimist who never dwelled on failure, but why hadn't he said anything about delays, unexpected costs, or other complications with the project? Did he feel he couldn't be honest because their lifestyle was so crucial to her brand? That thought was the most painful.

Cara seemed to be nearing the end of the field, but it was hard to tell. At Tough Mudder, the finish line had been clear enough, with cheering friends, photographers, snack stations, and a beer tent. What she would give right now for a beer . . .

What she would give to be running for sport—for bruises that gave her bragging rights—and not for her life.

As Karl would have put it, she was *seizing an unexpected opportunity.*

Seeing a break in the tall grass ahead, she decided to ignore the heat, the pain, and the dust filling her nose and mouth. Instead, she focused on embodying Karl's can-do attitude—even if it was all an act.

"Sure, it would be nice to belly-crawl over sharp rocks through vermin-filled grass in moisture-wicking T-shirts and leggings like I had when I was sponsored by Alo," she said aloud to her fellow field mice and God knew what else, if only to make sure the various creepy-crawlies steered clear. "But this prison jumpsuit is a lot more durable."

Attagirl, she imagined Karl saying.

Had their *always be honest* promise to each other been a sham? What else didn't she know?

When the stand of boulders was close enough, she stood and sprinted over to a ten-foot-tall slab. She slid between it and a squat rock, peering back at the field she'd just traversed. She saw no movement and heard no sirens.

Scanning the route ahead, she thought she saw water about a hundred yards ahead. Lake water wasn't generally drinkable, but it had to be safer than the stagnant muck she'd just trodden through. She wasn't really thirsty yet, but everyone knew refilling your Stanley bottle throughout the day was the key to hydration. If she kept to the woods, she thought she could get there without being seen.

Cara pulled up her baggy pant legs and took off toward where the trees were thickest. As she did, songs from the 1970s rock anthems on Karl's treadmill playlist streamed inside her head.

Free Bird.

Why couldn't she live anonymously and free?

Dream On.

Universe willing, maybe she could figure out how to prove her innocence.

She was loping through the forest to the tune of *You Ain't Seen Nothin' Yet* when she tripped over a rock.

The cell phone flew from her cleavage, hit a tree, and landed with an ominous crack.

She landed even harder.

FOUR
JORDAN

Innocent is as innocent does!
—@cutiepiefromcali

Jordan found the wreck just north of the small town of Coarsegold, where the highway climbed through the hills toward Oakhurst.

At first, all he could see was the overturned, jackknifed semi blocking both lanes of the highway. Driving past a line of stopped northbound cars, he eased onto the shoulder and went around the big rig. As he did, he looked into the sideways cab and saw the staring, vacant eyes below the driver's bloodied forehead. An accident he would have likely survived in his mammoth vehicle if only he'd been wearing his seat belt.

Jordan's breath caught in his throat when he reached the other side.

A silver Dodge Ram 1500 with an oversized grille guard had come to rest on the center stripe, its cab nearly crushed. Ahead of him, the back half of a white transit van rested on the shoulder, opened like a tin can. Its front half was in the ditch on the opposite side of the road. The driver's-side door had an eight-pointed star showing it was from the California Department of Corrections and Rehabilitation. His scalp prickled. There was no reason a prison van should have been traveling on this road—except for the detour on 99.

Dimly aware of an older couple standing beside a Toyota Avalon pulling a teardrop trailer—apparently unscathed—Jordan thumbed his transmitter as he rolled slowly through the wreckage.

"Gracia, I'm about three miles north of Coarsegold. We have a head-on collision involving at least three vehicles: a semi, a pickup, and a CDCR van. We're going to need fire, ambulances, and wreckers. All hands on deck, including the coroner. Reroute traffic as quickly as you can. This road's going to be closed for hours."

"Understood, Sheriff," Gracia answered.

Leaving his flashers on, he pulled his vehicle across both lanes to block the northern approach. In the old days, he would have tossed flares, but given the fire outside Fresno and the constant fire danger in general, he had instructed his department to make do with triangle reflectors. He'd have to drop a few after he checked for survivors.

Jordan took deep breaths as he stepped onto the asphalt. He had arrived at the scenes of hundreds of accidents, but this was the worst one he'd ever seen. He summoned the words of his dad, and his granddad before him, the mantra that had allowed three generations of Burkes to keep functioning enough to do their jobs in the aftermath of murder, rape, battery, child abuse, farm accidents, and countless overdoses.

When the shit goes down, you're not a man. You're the goddamn sheriff.

It was the kind of macho bullshit that usually made his skin crawl. But it worked.

"Sheriff?" called the elderly male onlooker in a quavering voice. "I looked, but I don't think—"

"Please remain by your vehicle," Jordan instructed him.

He headed for the pickup, which was closest. His throat tickled as he realized he recognized it—that it had, in fact, been parked in his driveway as recently as last week.

When he looked inside the mangled driver's-side window, its safety glass nearly gone, he tried to swallow and couldn't. The bloodied, freckled face belonged to Bree McDaniel, his sixteen-year-old daughter's best friend. Her head was almost all he could see because the cab had crumpled around her, pinning her in place. He yanked the door handle with both hands, but it didn't budge. Reaching inside, he put two fingers to her neck. Her skin was warm, but her pulse was weak. They'd need the

Jaws of Life to get her out. His vision blurred. It didn't look like anybody else was with her, but it was hard to tell. He didn't want to leave her side, but he had to keep looking for other survivors. There was nothing he could do until the fire trucks arrived.

Not a man. The goddamn sheriff.

He walked unsteadily to the front half of the prison van, face down in the weeds. This driver was dead, a halo of blood ringing his head on the deflated airbag. Open, surprised-seeming eyes looked up at him from the footwell of the passenger seat. But the uniformed guard's body was still belted into the passenger seat. Both men still had their guns.

Three dead, one barely alive. So far.

The goddamn sheriff.

He crossed the road again. A Hispanic woman wearing an orange jumpsuit and shackled hands and feet was lying half in and half out of the back of the van. Her injuries were not immediately apparent, but she wasn't moving. Jordan lingered with her, checking in vain for signs of life but not finding any. It was possible she'd been killed on impact by blunt force trauma. The crash had happened so recently that he could still feel the heat from the hot tailpipes coming through the floor.

Four dead.

He circled the van, peering inside, calling out in the hope that someone could hear him, but no one answered. Where the damage was the worst, he glimpsed orange fabric, red blood, and a few wisps of white hair. Squeezing in for a better look, he recognized Molly Bailey, a meth dealer he'd known was headed back to the pen for multiple convictions. His simple decision to schedule her transfer for today had sealed her fate.

Five.

Jordan walked over to the couple, finally taking them in. The husband was a bald man wearing shorts and white knee-high compression socks, and his wife had highlighted, chestnut hair at odds with her deeply creased face. Judging from their trailer, they were most likely on their way to Yosemite.

"Did you see this happen?"

"We got here after it happened," said the old man, his hands tremoring. "Right after, I think."

"Not that we know first aid," said the woman.

"Did you see anyone leaving the scene?" Jordan asked, wondering if any other vehicles might have been involved.

"Yes," said the man, nodding.

"What did the car look like?"

His wife shook her head firmly. "She wasn't driving. She was jogging."

"What was she wearing?"

"Orange . . . you know, prison clothes."

"Which way did she go?"

"That way," said the husband, pointing toward a partially downed barbed-wire fence and the trees beyond.

Jordan swore silently.

"Stay here until my deputies can take your statement," he told the couple.

He radioed Gracia as he walked back to Bree's truck. "We have five fatalities and one girl with life-threatening injuries. Notify CDCR they have two corrections officers and two prisoners deceased, plus one on the loose."

"Will do, Sheriff. Beto is about two minutes out. The fire department is right behind him."

He reached inside to check Bree's pulse again. Nothing. He pressed his fingertips harder into her neck and found a heartbeat, agonizingly faint.

"Hang on, Bree. Help is coming."

As if on cue, he heard sirens.

FIVE
CARA

I used to follow her advice on fun adventures.
That is, until she killed her husband on one of them.
—@livelovelaugh47

Cara's palms burned and her knee throbbed from breaking her fall. At least she hadn't hit her head, although a concussion might have given her a break from her current reality. Lifting herself into a sitting position, she pulled aside the torn and blood-soaked fabric of her jumpsuit to see how badly she'd banged herself up. It didn't look great.

The phone still seemed to work, but there was no service. In the past, Cara had wasted countless hours scrolling her For You pages, looking for the best fragrances, hottest makeup dupes, and the latest home decor ideas. In all that time, only one of the online astrologers she followed had actually foretold *upcoming difficulty*, and even that one had failed to pinpoint imprisonment or this sudden turn as a fugitive. Now here she was, in need of first aid, and all she knew was not to swab her bloody knee with a leaf that could turn out to be poison oak.

Making matters even worse, the bottom of her right fake Croc had a rock wedged in the arch and its rubber was split open. She may have had no idea how to treat a wound, but she'd seen enough hacks to try and fix her broken shoe. In her former life as an influencer, Cara might even have reapplied lipstick, set up her phone and ring light, and recorded what she thought of as one of her "relatable" posts: *First, pry the jagged rock from the sole. Then grab a handful of small pebbles, which you will use to rejoin one side to the other by inserting them into the rubber along the cracked sole. Press the two sides together, and voila!*

The first pebble was too dull and wouldn't go in. The second gouged a bigger hole than the one she already had. And while she managed to insert the third pebble into both sides and press them together, they didn't stay that way for long. She let the fourth pebble fall from her hand, knowing this was a true #DIYfail.

Cara hobbled toward the lake, her knee aching and her good leg hampered by the broken shoe. She could only put weight on her toes and the usable front part while the heel and strap flopped flaccidly behind. She wasn't really hurt, but the setback from the minor fall was enough to fill her eyes with dusty tears.

Tears that kept coming.

For months, she had cried herself to sleep picturing Karl's mangled, bludgeoned body, with dried blood darkening his gray hair and beard, at the bottom of the ravine below Johnson's Point. When and where she'd ever sleep again, she had no idea, but she knew that ghastly image would now be accompanied by those of Eve, New Girl, Poff, and Vozenilek's severed head. Bree's dying moments would haunt her for the rest of her own life.

She was still ugly-crying as she rounded a bend and saw a glint of metal.

Panic stopped her tears. She froze until she realized the sunlight was not reflecting off the wheel rim of a police cruiser, as she had feared, but a Portofino Blue Range Rover SE.

Cara knew the car because she drove one.

Or used to, anyway.

She'd settled for Hakuba Silver, her second-favorite color, because she was too impatient to wait three to six months for a blue one with the illuminated metal treadplates and cabin air purification she just had to have. She knew everything about the vehicle, from how to use the automatic-access height feature to the cornering brake control—and she would park it in a safe place, to be reclaimed by its rightful owner, just as soon as she was done using it.

So it wouldn't be stealing, not really.

The Portofino Blue Range Rover—now, more than ever, the car of her dreams—was parked beside a lakeside picnic table. Cara spotted a yellow-and-blue striped beach towel on the bench just as she heard splashing in the distance. Climbing a few steps up a nearby hill, she hid behind a cottonwood tree to assess the situation.

The serene lake was bathed in afternoon sun. On the other side of the picnic area, down a tree-lined path, was a small cove, where she could just barely see a seemingly nude couple frolicking in the water. The scene was so on-brand for @carasloveisgold the hashtags wrote themselves: *#Romance #GetawaysAreGold, #AfternoonDip, #LovingMyLife, #SunAndSwim.*

#AboutToHaveMyCarStolen.

With luck, the twosome would remain blissfully unaware that the FBI's soon-to-be-most-wanted fugitive was about to relieve them of their transportation.

That is, if they'd left the vehicle unlocked.

Cara crept toward the passenger side of the car. Its windows were tinted, but she could still make out the outline of a cooler, a grocery store jug of water, and tote bags containing assorted supplies. This couple came prepared. Certainly, they were the type of people who would have the optional Range Rover First Aid Kit tucked into the cargo area. She was all set, so long as the vehicle was open and they'd left the keys inside—which seemed possible. All she had to do was slide in from the passenger side, climb into the driver's seat, and start the engine. She'd be halfway down the gravel road before the owners swam to shore.

She reached for the passenger-side door handle.

It was locked.

Cara's next impulse was to pick up a rock and break the back window, car alarm be damned. Thinking better of it, she sneaked over to the picnic table to see if they'd left the key fob underneath the towel.

There were no keys there.

There were, however, a white chocolate macadamia Clif bar and a pair of Golden Goose Super-Star sneakers.

Her stomach growled at the sight of food while her feet practically shouted with relief at the prospect of real shoes.

The splashing at the shore had stopped. Hurrying, Cara slipped off her fake Crocs, pulled her extra-long pant legs down over her the heels and arches of her size-seven-and-a-half feet in order to avoid blisters, and slipped on one of the decidedly larger shoes. She had tied and double-knotted it, and was about to start on the other, when she heard a voice.

"Hey!"

The man—huskier than she'd imagined the male half of her fashionista couple to be—stood halfway up the path from the cove, the other yellow-and-blue towel knotted loosely around his waist.

"What's going on?" called a woman's voice from behind him.

"No fucking idea," he told her. "Stay there."

Cara didn't stop to consider whether the command was for the other woman or for her. Grabbing the Clif bar and the beach towel, and holding the second shoe, she dove behind a bushy clump of sagebrush.

"You're stealing our *shoes*?" he said incredulously as he rushed toward the Range Rover, undoubtedly for his own shoes, and possibly a gun.

As he did, his towel dropped to the ground.

He was also less manscaped than she'd imagined.

As he fumbled to cover himself up, Cara stopped to put on and tie the second shoe, then trotted, knee pain and all, toward a ridge. No way the man was going to catch her barefoot *and* almost naked.

Before she disappeared over the crest, she stopped and shouted down to him, "I'm sorry and thank you! I really, *really* needed these."

SIX
JORDAN

Secluded rustic A-frame near Yosemite. 2 beds, 1 bath. Great weekend getaway or seasonal rental. Dogs welcome!
—Airbnb listing #1239485 (3.25 stars)

As burly firemen lugged their hydraulic cutters and spreaders toward him, Jordan touched Bree's cheek and told her he'd see her soon. He desperately hoped it was true. But he could do nothing for her and had an escaped prisoner to catch.

Jordan jogged over to Beto—Alberto Soto, his chief deputy—who was standing in the patchy weeds along the shoulder by the back half of the prison van.

Beto held up an empty set of shackles. "She can't have gotten far on foot."

"Do we have any idea who she is?"

"I'm working on it."

Judging by the number of incoming sirens, Gracia had sent every available unit and then some.

"I'll go," Jordan told him. "You direct traffic."

Beto nodded. "Go get her, Sheriff."

Behind the wheel, Jordan rolled north, away from the crash site, figuring the runner would flee from the first responders. But she would not be far from the road, and she would not want to get lost in the forest. Most offenders were neither criminal masterminds nor survivalists—they were opportunists. An escaped prisoner would look for civilian clothes and a car. He had to find her before she got mobile and left the area.

The first place he passed was a rundown prefab ringed by weather-beaten outbuildings. The compound was inside a climbable chain-link fence. When he slowed and rolled down his window, though, he heard the woofing of at least three or four big dogs. Even though he couldn't see them, he knew the sound would be enough to deter an escapee.

He lowered the rest of his windows and gunned it, swiveling his head as he watched for movement. If she was smart, even if she was following the road, she would stay off it as much as possible. Again, he hadn't met that many smart ones.

The next driveway was blocked with a cattle gate between two stone pillars, easy enough to climb over. Spotting an intercom, he pulled over and pressed the button.

"Yes?" The voice was female, a housekeeper if he had to guess.

"This is the sheriff. There is an escaped prisoner in the area, probably still wearing an orange jumpsuit. Have you seen anyone on your property?"

"N-no. I don't see anything."

"Lock your doors, and if you have dogs, let them out. If you see anything at all unusual, call 911."

He pulled out faster than he meant to, fishtailing on the dirt before his tires grabbed the asphalt.

The prisoner would be looking for a house with no signs of life. But Jordan was already reaching the limit of how far she could have run in the time since the crash.

The next turn was an unmarked dirt track on the left side of the road. He drove down it, branches whipping the sides of his SUV. Two hundred yards in, there was an old A-frame that looked like it had been built in the 1970s and hadn't seen a lick of paint since. There were no cars, no dogs, no signs of life. The curtains were all closed. If Jordan were the one running, this would have been exactly what he wanted.

He felt the seconds ticking as he scanned the weedy yard.

Then he realized the porch light was on. It was just an old-fashioned incandescent bulb, hard to tell in the sunlight. Someone unfamiliar with the light switch array could easily have flipped it by accident without realizing.

Just in case she was watching, Jordan shifted into reverse and backed up until he couldn't see the house. Then he turned off the car and got out.

Slipping into the scrubby trees, he headed toward the house again, walking in a wide semicircle until he could approach it from the hill behind. When he looked down, he saw where a pane of glass had been punched out of the rusted steel door, right above the doorknob.

Going alone into a house where an escaped prisoner was hiding was unnecessarily risky. It was also just plain stupid. Jordan knew he would be furious with any of his deputies boneheaded enough to try it. Both official procedure and common sense demanded he call for backup so they could surround the house and order the escapee to come out with her hands in plain sight. For all he knew, she was a cold-blooded killer.

But he didn't want to call even a single deputy away from the highway as long as there was a chance Bree might come out of the wreck alive. The road would need to be cleared, and the ambulance would need an escort. He was pretty sure he had the element of surprise.

And the only one who could reprimand him if this went wrong was his wife, Amber. Because Jordan was the goddamn sheriff.

He just hoped the homeowner didn't leave loaded firearms lying around.

Drawing his own gun, he approached the house, zigzagging from tree to tree. On the porch, he saw the small stick of kindling that had been used to break the glass.

The door's handle turned easily. Shielding himself behind the heavy wooden doorjamb, he swung it inward, waited for a response, then risked a quick look inside.

The place looked like a weekend home or a rental. He saw cast-off furniture, magazines with curling pages, dust spinning in the shaft of light from the doorway.

He slipped inside, careful not to frame himself against the light, and put his back to the wall as he swept the room.

He heard water running. A shower.

When he heard her singing, he almost laughed with relief.

Crossing to a bedroom door, he saw a dresser with drawers askew and a closet with its door hanging open. The prisoner's selections were lying on the bed next to a dirty orange jumpsuit marked with a crimson streak of blood.

Don't go chasin' waterfalls, she sang. *Do do do do do-do do de dah dah dah dah-dah-dah.*

Jordan hesitated. His suspect was cornered and completely defenseless. She was also naked, which added an unwanted degree of complexity. It was the kind of story that went viral: *Couldn't he let her get dressed?? Cop cuffs naked suspect!!* Like the average idiot with two thumbs and a YouTube account had ever been in the line of fire.

Before he could decide, his radio crackled. Beto giving Gracia an update. He heard a voice from the shower as he fumbled to mute it.

"Oh, *shit*!"

No time. He kicked open the door. "This is the sheriff. Put your hands in the air!"

Two hands appeared above the shower rod. She was Black, he noted.

"Officer, I am *not* coming out naked!"

The water continued to run as he kept his gun barrel locked on what he guessed was center mass. What now? There were situations no amount of training could prepare you for.

With his left hand, he grabbed a towel and threw it into the shower. "Dry yourself off."

There was movement behind the shower curtain as she turned off the water and started to dry herself off.

"I need another towel for my hair."

"Do the best you can," he told her, backing up through the doorway to remain out of reach. "And remember, I've got a gun on you."

"All the more reason to give me an extra towel. When you get a look at this fine body, that gun in your hand is liable to go off."

"Ma'am, I'm married and I have a teenage daughter. They tie up the bathroom every day, and I haven't shot either one of them yet."

Jordan eased his finger off the trigger anyway.

SEVEN
CARA

Like they say, grief is just love with nowhere to go. I am lost without my beloved Karl, but I will find my way. Grief is now part of my journey—my story still untold.
—@carasloveisgold

You shouldnt have killed him then
—@Justice0983465

Cara tried on Golden Goose sneakers every time she shopped at Nordstrom. The $500-plus price tag wasn't a problem—or so she'd assumed—but she just couldn't get herself to fork over that much money for shoes that came scuffed on purpose. But now, having scrambled halfway up a ridge, through bushes and brambles and around a boulder field, they were legit scraped and dirty. The pink stars were even missing a few sparkles.

#FashionVictim #AStealAtAnyPrice

Was it too much to hope that the skinny-dippers accepted her thanks and let the theft go, simply moving their camping getaway to a safer spot? Doubtful. If she and Karl had been the victims, he'd have driven directly to the closest police station. Cara would have taken it a step further, blasting the incident all over her social media—crowdsourcing her cry for justice among the amateur sleuths who lived for murder and mayhem.

As she'd done on her own behalf.

I would never, ever hurt my husband, she posted to her followers, whose numbers had mushroomed to eleven million after her initial booking and subsequent release on a million-dollar bond. *Please, I beg all of you to help me find Karl's killer.*

The Facts:

The killer knew we were staying in Ojai and that we'd hiked up to Johnson's Point for dinner.

I was unconscious when Karl died. I heard him shout my name and saw him fighting with someone before I blacked out.

Whoever killed my husband stole his rare, vintage watch. It has not been recovered.

Cara read all of the responses that poured in. Among the DMs from amateur sleuths, finger-pointing accusers, and the occasional sympathetic believer was a note from Roy Abel—one of the three criminal attorneys she'd interviewed to represent her.

Mrs. Campbell, he wrote, *I strongly advise against pleading your case on social media.*

People need to know the facts, she wrote back.

Facts are far less important than appearances and public opinion.

I happen to be innocent.

Unfortunately, your online persona as a gold digger suggests otherwise. Disappear from social media until you're exonerated and then you can talk to everyone who will listen.

Wearing her ankle monitor, she drove to his Century City office the next day to pay his retainer.

In person, Roy Abel was shorter and slighter than she'd imagined, but he exuded the confidence of an A-list celebrity. As the go-to criminal attorney for at least two cable news outlets, he sort of was. Cara's faith in him was boosted by the fact that he had taken the time to research her online presence and didn't seem to simply accept what was being written and said about her by others.

"I do all the talking from here on out," he said, offering a firm handshake. "Got it?"

If the framed photographs lining the hallway to his suite were any indicator, he'd successfully defended an impressive number of clients—many of whom were hugging and even kissing him.

Cara didn't post or respond to anything from that moment on, not even the painful taunts from her stepdaughter, Taylor, whose TikTok video described Roy Abel as *the best lawyer my father Karl Campbell's money could buy*, Cara as the *Mrs. Universe of Wicked Stepmothers*, and the home where Cara lived as *for sale the second they put her away.*

But she couldn't bring herself to delete her accounts. She followed her own story obsessively, even listening to true crime podcasts (the host of *California Death Trip* was one of the few who believed she could be innocent) and forwarding any potentially exculpatory leads to Abel. He built the case for her defense and pleaded her cause to the media. His sophisticated showmanship and graying-at-the-temples gravitas seemed to play better with the public than her sweaty desperation and panic.

Now that she was on the lam, Abel would definitely be back on the news, communicating on her behalf.

Cara labored upward, breathing hard, wondering why she still tasted the scorched smoke of the crash in her throat when she was so far away. Then she finally reached the top of the ridge and learned the answer: plumes of light gray smoke rose in the distance. The incessant wail of sirens couldn't only be for her.

Out of breath and starving, she collapsed onto the rocky ground. She hadn't allowed herself to eat, telling herself it was the same as intermittent fasting. But she couldn't take it anymore. She tore open the wrapper of the Clif bar and took a ravenous bite. As she chewed it into a dry, white chocolaty paste, she knew she needed something even more than food: water.

She was so thirsty.

EIGHT
JORDAN

Big accident on 41. No way anyone survived.
—@madera_watchdawg

The prisoner's name was LaDonna Williams, which she spelled for him, stressing the capital D, as she got dressed in the A-frame's bedroom. She managed to preserve her modesty by facing away from him and using the towel to cover her torso while putting her orange jumpsuit back on. As Jordan cuffed her, he saw her look longingly at the civilian clothes she'd picked out, still stacked neatly on the bed.

"I wasn't paying attention, you know, because I wasn't *driving*," she told him after he had walked her up the dirt driveway and settled her in the caged rear seat of his vehicle. "It all happened so fast."

"What do you remember?"

"Just this pickup truck coming right at us—in our lane!"

"Did you get a look at the driver?"

"I think it was a girl. She must have had a death wish or something. This is going to add to my time, isn't it?"

Jordan looked to his left and then pulled onto the highway. "You didn't think to stay at the crash site?"

"The gas tanks were probably about to explode or something. I was afraid for my *life*."

"You can save that story for the prosecutor. It's not my call whether they charge you or not."

"Can you put in a word for me, though?" she pleaded.

"I will testify that you did not resist recapture and that you surrendered peaceably."

His answer seemed to satisfy LaDonna, who leaned back in her seat. "That's right. I'm about the most peaceable bitch you will ever hope to meet."

Traffic was now backed up almost half a mile before the wreck, so Jordan turned on his flashers and drove in the empty left-hand lane, scaring several gawkers back into their cars with whoops from his siren. When he reached the wreck site, it was swarming with first responders. He parked and got out.

"Sit tight," he told LaDonna.

She batted her eyelashes. "I'll be good, officer."

Jordan counted one fire rescue truck, two ambulances, a half-dozen sheriff's vehicles identical to his, and a county wrecker. Everyone was busy, and distant sirens signaled even more help was incoming. Nodding at the new kid on traffic duty, Jordan headed for Beto, who was straddling the center line with his arms folded. Beto may have looked still as a statue, but Jordan knew he was watching everything and running the show.

Bree's truck had been opened like a tin can, and the cab was bloody but empty. When Jordan reached Beto, he tilted his head toward it.

"Did the pickup driver make it?"

"They're taking her to Valley Children's. The EMTs got her breathing, but they didn't look too hopeful."

Jordan's chest felt heavy. He looked down. The blood streaking his fingers was Bree's. "She's a friend of Sydney's."

His chief deputy groaned. "Goddamn it. I'm sorry."

"It was probably her fault. LaDonna says she was in the wrong lane."

"LaDonna?"

"The prisoner. I picked her up about a mile north."

"I have no idea how anyone was able to walk away from this, let alone run." The afternoon sun glinted off Beto's mirrored aviators, but

Jordan could picture his brown eyes roving over the scene. "Prison van was northbound, the pickup was southbound with the semi close behind. Judging from the tire marks, debris, and position of the vehicles, I'd say the pickup drifted across the center line on the curve, and the van driver was just trying to get the hell out of the way. Skids are short so nobody hit the brakes until the last second. They were going full speed."

Listening to the sounds of voices, radios, engines, and approaching sirens, Jordan looked up and saw a red-tailed hawk circling slowly above. There were going to be a lot of broken hearts by nightfall. He would have to call Bree's family, and his own, before news started spreading on social media.

"Bet she was texting," said Beto. "Whoever invented the smartphone sure has a lot to answer for. Know what your prisoner's in for?"

"No idea. All I care about is getting her where she belongs."

Down the road, the elderly couple was still waiting obediently for someone to speak with them. Their legs had gotten tired, though. The man was sitting in the open doorway of the trailer, and his wife was sitting across from him in a camp chair. Both of them were drinking coffee they had poured from a thermos.

"You interview the witnesses?" Jordan asked.

"Was just about to."

"I'll do it."

As Jordan walked away, he wondered, not for the first time, why Beto had never run for sheriff. The man had been his father's chief deputy, too, and likely could have done the job as well as all three Burkes combined. In the old days, a Latino name might have disqualified him from elected office in rural California, but not now. Beto could probably beat both Jordan and Troy Silverman handily.

Maybe he was smarter than Jordan by not taking the job. Maybe he just liked the job he already had. Or maybe he figured he was too close to retirement to put up with the headaches that came with leading the department.

Whatever the reason, Jordan was damn glad to have his help.

When he reached the teardrop trailer, he extended his hand first to the woman and then to the man. "I'm sorry I didn't get your names earlier. Sheriff Jordan Burke."

"August Fetz. This is my wife, Lolly."

"Can you please follow me? I'd like you to confirm that the woman I captured is the person you saw running away."

"Is she dangerous?" asked August.

"Of course we'll do it," said Lolly, already out of her chair.

When they reached Jordan's vehicle, they peered at LaDonna in the back seat, her brown face framed by shoulder-length, straightened, raven-black hair.

"Well, she's wearing orange," said August, as if that sealed it.

Lolly scoffed. "That's not her. The one we saw was definitely blond."

Jordan's gut lurched. He hadn't even considered a second prisoner. Who could easily be two miles away by now if she was traveling on foot. Or disappearing down the road in a car.

He wrenched open the back door.

"You never said someone else survived," he accused LaDonna.

"You never asked."

"I thought you wanted to be peaceable and cooperative."

She seemed to think about it. Maybe she had been buying time for a friend. Or maybe she just didn't want to be a snitch.

"Fine," she said, with a toss of her head. "But I have no idea what happened to that fancy Beverly Hills Instagram bitch who killed her husband."

Jordan stared at her with a sinking feeling. "Do you know her name?"

"Cara Cotton Candy or something. I don't know. We started calling her Goldie on the ride, but that was kind of an in-joke."

Jordan wasn't interested in her nickname. But he thought he knew who LaDonna had escaped with. "Tell me exactly what you saw before you called 911."

"I didn't call 911! I was worried about those gas tanks exploding, like I told you. I just wanted the hell out of there."

Jordan wished he had escorted the Fetzes back to their car before questioning LaDonna. Though they had backed away, they'd obviously overheard the exchange and were now talking to each other. Whatever they knew would probably be on Facebook as soon as they stopped for lunch in the next town.

He closed the door and hurried back to Beto, who was watching two deputies tramp around in the brush off the shoulder of the road by the back half of the prison van. Smoke was rising, but Jordan couldn't tell where it was coming from.

"LaDonna says she didn't call 911," he said. "Did we recover all the phones from the victims?"

"No idea, but I'll find out."

"Contact CDCR and get the names of everyone who was in that van. And issue an APB for the second escaped prisoner, Cara something. She's famous."

As Beto tilted his head and began speaking into the handset clipped onto his shoulder, Jordan heard shouts. His deputies stumbled back as flames erupted from the dry brush.

"And alert Cal Fire. We need water tenders and fire engines now!"

NINE
CARA

Deer me! Love you, deer! Oh my deer!
—@thedeerestwildlife

The shadows had grown longer, the temperature was dropping, and the sweat on Cara's neck was drying more quickly. She needed to get to a lower altitude before nightfall. She also desperately needed water. There *had* to be something drinkable somewhere—half the bottled water she'd ever bought was named High Sierra, Sierra Blue, or Sierra something-or-other.

She weaved her way downhill in the waning light, keeping close to trees and shrubbery for cover and longing for the convenience of, well, a convenience store. As she stopped and crouched to retie her shoe, a trio of deer ambled into the small clearing in front of her. They stopped so close that she could nearly touch the coarse brown fur on the flank of the largest one, a doe. A white-spotted yearling and a spindly-legged fawn stood beside her, nibbling shoots growing at the base of a nearby tree. For an exhilarating moment, Cara didn't move a muscle and just watched while the large doe foraged and crunched contentedly.

The magic of being in such close proximity to such beautiful wild creatures was broken when the yearling twitched her ears and grunted, and the doe responded with a loud snort.

Cara had barely allowed herself to breathe, but the yearling must have smelled her and sent a warning to her mother, probably, *Don't look behind you . . .*

In an instant, they loped away uphill.

I'm nice. I swear, she almost called after them.

She sensed movement across the clearing. Almost before she understood what she was seeing, a mountain lion—tawny brown with a whitish belly and a long, whipping tail—catapulted past her in the direction of the deer.

She covered her ears in a futile attempt to block out the growling, snorts, and high-pitched squeals that accompanied the thrashing in the brush just above her.

And then, as quickly as it had started, the forest quieted, resuming its eerily peaceful hum.

Cara forced her trembling legs downhill.

No matter where she went, death was following.

TEN
JORDAN

Unconfirmed reports say convicted murderer Cara Campbell was involved in a California Department of Corrections and Rehabilitation transport accident in Madera County.

—KALZ FM

Jordan knew he should wait until morning to restart his search with a full array of resources. The K9 unit had been tied up all day, assisting with the search for a missing toddler in Dairyland—fortunately, they found the kid—and the handler told him the dogs would be useless without a good night's sleep. The helicopter he'd requested was needed for wildfire spotting: the Irrigosa Fire now covered a thousand acres and was only 40 percent contained, while the Coarsegold Fire was a hundred acres and growing. While he had no idea how much the latter would limit access to the search area, tomorrow he would be able to borrow warm bodies from a handful of agencies, including the US Marshals Fugitive Task Force, who had already been in touch to offer their assistance if the prisoner was not recaptured.

So why was he out here? Cara Campbell—Gracia, who had followed the trial as a former fan, came up with her full name—was a wealthy woman who snapped and killed her husband. It wasn't like he had the Zodiac Killer on the loose.

One possibility that Jordan would not have admitted to anyone, maybe even Amber, was that it had to do with his Troy Silverman encounter earlier that day. Single-handedly capturing the fugitive would be the only advertisement his campaign needed—and would play even better, now that he knew the fugitive was famous.

Another possibility was the fact that he wasn't quite ready to face Sydney. The last time he called in, Bree had been in her fifth hour of surgery to repair massive internal bleeding from a fractured skull, a broken back, and a host of other injuries. If she didn't make it, how was he going to explain to his daughter that her best friend, the girl who had talked a blue streak through the family's Monopoly game last Friday night, would never come to the house, or school, or anywhere, ever again?

Maybe both possibilities were true. He wasn't proud of either one.

Nailed to a lodgepole pine up ahead were two wooden signs with family names and route numbers. He turned and began to climb a long dirt road.

With the APB, every uniform with the authority to arrest would be on high alert for signs of the escaped murderer—the main roads would be well covered. And he knew she wouldn't be headed for the hills. Cara Campbell wouldn't survive twenty-four hours without lip gloss, much less food and shelter.

The only question was whether she would be dumb enough to use her stolen phone to post on Instagram, as Gracia believed, or call a friend for help, before Jordan could find her. Gracia considered herself something of a social media expert since she had volunteered to run the department's Facebook page, then been drafted into handling the X account before drawing the line at Instagram and TikTok. Jordan knew Beto had already filed a request with the cell phone provider for data and tracking, but they'd be lucky to get anything for at least twenty-four hours.

His rearview flashed red as he climbed out of the trees onto an unshaded turn in the road. The fiery setting sun was losing its battle with the smoke from the valley floor and the new fire that had flared up next to the crash site. He was angling the mirror down when his cell phone rang.

The caller ID read AMBER ALERT. Sydney had programmed that into his phone as a joke.

"Hey, honey," he answered.

"I know you're not coming home for dinner," his wife said, her voice tight with worry. "Is there any update on Bree?"

He'd texted her earlier, right after he called Steve and Joanne, Bree's parents, asking her to keep the news from Sydney until they knew more.

"It's still touch and go."

"You mean she might not . . ." Her sentence ended with a sound halfway between a gasp and a sob.

Neither of them said anything for a while. Bree had been a hot mess with terrible grades, tragic taste in boys, and an unfortunate habit of spending money that wasn't hers. But she was also sweet, hilarious, and awkward—in other words, a perfectly normal teenage girl. A living, breathing, laughing best friend to their daughter. Jordan had seen enough death to know that if she didn't make it, the hole in her family's lives would be deep and dark, that for a while it would swallow everything, and even after it shrank almost out of sight, it would never, ever go away.

He steered carefully out of the red glow into deep blue shadow as the road entered a ravine.

"We can't put it off any longer," Amber finally choked out. "Sydney has to know. I'll tell her."

"You don't have to."

"I'm here, you're there. Maybe you've got enough to deal with right now. On the news, they're saying five people died in the crash and two prisoners escaped."

"You're never going to believe who—"

"Cara Campbell."

"That was fast. We haven't even announced it."

"Social media. You will not believe how quickly this thing is blowing up. People on Nextdoor in Fresno are like, 'Lock your doors!' Some idiots are out there driving around and looking for her. There's already a Facebook group called, 'Where Is Cara Campbell?'"

"That's what I aim to find out. Tonight, if possible. Hug Sydney for me."

"I will."

Jordan sighed, grateful for his amazing wife. "I love you."

"Love you, too. Stay safe."

She hung up. Jordan gunned his engine up a steep driveway and braked to a halt below a three-story alpine-style lodge with a half-dozen SUVs parked in front.

He knew it didn't make sense to blame Cara for Bree. Then again, if Cara hadn't killed her husband, she wouldn't have been transported to prison, and maybe that prison van wouldn't have left exactly when it did, and Bree—even if she had been stupid enough to use her phone behind the wheel—would have steered safely back across the center line. And five other people would be alive right now.

It seemed possible, anyway.

ELEVEN
CARA

@carasloveisgold blocked me on Insta for saying she's guilty as sin. How much more evidence do you need?
—@beckywiththebesthair

Not only did Cara feel like the grim reaper in Day-Glo orange, but her own survival was growing less likely by the hour. The mountain lion clearly preferred deer meat; what about the next carnivorous creature? Humans—furless and soft—had to be the fast food of the animal kingdom. At her next encounter, she had no idea whether she was supposed to make herself big and loud, stand completely still, or run like hell.

As dusk fell and she continued to propel herself into the unknown, Cara spotted clusters of light from houses set into hillsides and ramshackle rural neighborhoods. She would have given anything to sleep indoors. Simply having heat and running water—no matter how rusty, broken-down, or double-wide the accommodations—sounded downright luxe. Of course, she couldn't risk being spotted by a guard dog, Ring camera, or whatever people out here in the country used to deter criminals.

Criminals like *her*.

She wanted to cry, but somehow held out hope that she might stumble upon an abandoned lean-to, decrepit mining cabin, or even an unoccupied cave—anywhere she could curl up with her beach towel and catch a few hours of badly needed sleep.

As it grew dark and chilly, Cara thought about Karl's elderly Aunt

Evelyn, the woman who'd raised him and whom Cara had come to think of almost as a grandmother. She'd come to the trial every day her ailing body allowed, offering winks and supportive nods even as the supposed evidence of her guilt mounted. After the verdict was read, Evelyn had leaned over and hugged Cara, saying, "Don't worry, they'll find the person who really did this, and you'll be exonerated. I'm sure of it."

Her rose-tinted positivity, which she'd passed down to her nephew, was really all Cara had to hang onto as she was led away in handcuffs.

But when Aunt Evelyn heard about the accident, even she would be worried.

If only for her sake, Cara knew she had to shift her perspective to survive. She decided to think of her increasingly dire circumstances, not as a matter of life and death, but as if she were in a game. Back when she was dating, she'd certainly spent enough hours pretending to care about Xbox to know *Halo* was dumb and that she had no intention of settling down with any guy who had a gaming room in his Hollywood Hills pad. She did, however, remember the rush she'd felt after unlocking various "accomplishments" and clearing each stupid level. It wasn't so different from the strange elation she felt after each of the feats that had gotten her to this moment in the middle of nowhere, needy and miserable, but still very much alive.

Like she'd earned points in a real-life game of survival.

Escaped from Fatal Crash: New Level Unlocked

Stole Towel, Shoes, and Food from Angry Skinny-Dippers: Mission Achieved

Avoided Attack by Lethal Mountain Lion: Invincibility Points Awarded

She decided she was now attempting to complete an invisibility challenge, which required her to feel her way around a darkened labyrinth. She was at the mercy of anything and everything that clawed, bit, or shot bullets, but she'd figure her way through.

She couldn't worry about what awaited her there.

Not until she survived whatever came next.

TWELVE
JORDAN

Texting While Driving Is Not That Dangerous (Reddit thread)
I'm texting and driving rn and I've never had an accident.
—/u/Dull_Pickle

Charles Darwin would like a word with you.
—/u/Rationalvoice

Jesus.
—/u/Jesushimself

The extended family in the rambling alpine lodge was having some kind of a boozy reunion and had not seen Cara Campbell. True, they probably would have been too drunk to notice even if she had pressed her face against the glass and peered in their windows, but the sheer noise and size of their gathering would have likely caused her to give the place a wide berth anyway. If she had even made it this far away from the highway. After warning them to extinguish the fire burning in the pit on their back patio, Jordan moved on.

The next house was smaller, a single-story modernist box nestled into the trees, obviously very expensive. He imagined it was the kind of place Cara Campbell would have felt very at home, live-streaming her wine-and-cheese cocktail hour from the Brazilian Ipe wood deck.

No cars were outside, and when no one answered the door, he circled the place on foot, checking the windows for breakage and the dusty ground for signs of her presence in the glare of the motion-triggered security lights. He was tempted to stake the place out for a while and see if she showed—there was a more or less natural path to it from the crash site, if she was smart enough to follow the folds of the land—but he decided to keep moving.

He hated searching blind. He was covering ground as methodically as he could, but the odds of finding her while they were both on the move were getting smaller and smaller, especially while darkness was falling. The bougie cottage made him wish there was some kind of trap he could set. He could bait it with a gourmet gift basket from Whole Foods or that place down in LA with the twenty dollar smoothies that Amber was always going on about in mock horror.

Which reminded him of that term Amber had explained to him: *thirst trap.*

But wasn't that a trap someone set themselves?

As he drove downhill, the smoke thickened, rising up the slopes of the Sierra with a steady push from the prevailing west winds. The blaze at the crash site had flared up and started spreading in a matter of minutes. The fire rescue truck, ironically, didn't carry water, only fire extinguishers that had been deployed to no avail. The weather this spring had been weird: rivers were still roaring with melting snowpack from record-setting winter snows, while so little rain had fallen that fire season had arrived early. Now Cal Fire, already warring against a suburban wildfire on the valley floor, had to battle on a second front. How bad it would get tomorrow was anyone's guess.

Jordan's cell rang again. His stomach dropped when he saw it was Sydney.

He answered and heard her racking, convulsive sobs.

"Honey, I'm so sorry."

"Dad, are you sure it was her?" Sydney snuffled, her voice wet with snot and tears.

"I'm sure."

"So, you, like, *saw* her?"

"Yes, honey."

"Maybe you didn't recognize her," she insisted, her voice cutting in and out due to the spotty cell service. "Maybe she loaned some other girl her truck. It can't be her. Bree *never* texts and drives. I made her promise!"

Jordan's chest felt ripped wide open. Once again, his eyes blurred with tears as he pictured the blood on Bree's pretty, freckled face.

"It was her," he said. "But maybe she'll be OK."

Silence. The call had dropped. No bars.

Swearing, he backed up the road until a lone bar appeared on the dashboard screen. He shifted into park and called her back.

"The call dropped. I'm sorry. I'm up in the hills."

"Mom said you're looking for Cara Campbell." Sydney sounded a tiny bit more composed.

"Uh-huh."

"Can you look for Bree instead?"

Jordan took a deep breath. "Honey, Bree's in the hospital. Her folks are with her."

"But I looked at my Snap Map," Sydney sniffed, "and her phone is moving."

THIRTEEN
CARA

OMG! Cara Campbell is loose in the forest!
#NotGoingCampingThisWeekend

No matter how often she slipped and stumbled as she zigzagged down the hillside, Cara didn't turn on the phone's flashlight. The glow would give away her position, and she didn't want to run down the battery. Every so often, she peeked down into her bra and checked the screen for cell coverage, but other than one fleeting bar at the peak of the ridge and a heartbreaking text that flashed on the spiderwebbed screen—*Bree, Bree, where u be?*—the device was nothing more than a flat, hard security blanket.

Her own phone, certainly dead by now, was probably still zipped into the outer pouch of the sensible Coach bag she'd carried with her to court. Early in the trial, when Abel believed there were at least two sympathetic jurors, both female, in their twenties, with enough social media savvy to know Cara's brand as an influencer was about honesty and self-worth, not greed, she had real hope of being acquitted. She planned the moment perfectly: as soon as the verdict was read and she'd hugged her lawyer (for the photo that would hang on his Wall of Exoneration), but before he escorted her out of the courtroom to make a statement to the press, she would press *share* on the one-word post she'd written in preparation.

INNOCENT.

Hours earlier, when she'd allowed herself to indulge in pie-in-the-sky manifestation, she'd fallen on her face. But as she trudged into a grassy meadow bordered by dots of light, she couldn't help feeling hopeful when she peeked at the phone and saw not one, but two bars.

Three bars and the connection would be strong enough to get online. She'd be able to google herself and see what was and wasn't being reported about the accident, her escape, and how and where they were looking for her. She could start to figure out what to do next. Did she still have any supporters besides Aunt Evelyn now that she'd been convicted? Now that she'd escaped? She needed to see what her best friend, Stephanie van der Lind, was posting. Cara wasn't sure if she wanted to ask for a ride back to civilization or somewhere she could permanently escape it.

The smoky, moonless sky provided concealing darkness as she took cautious steps in the direction of what she hoped was a rural farm—and not, for all she knew, the outskirts of downtown Fresno. She stopped when she was close enough to make out stables, a barn, outbuildings, and the lighted windows of what was indeed a farmhouse, keeping her distance so she wouldn't spook the livestock or arouse the attention of any guard dogs.

The first thing she saw as she pulled the phone out of her cleavage was four bright bars. Then her throat tightened. She had been refreshing the phone at regular intervals to keep it from locking, but she had waited too long, and now the screen—which displayed a picture of kittens in a basket—demanded a passcode.

Shit!

Her fingers were cold and stiff as she pecked out the first combinations that came to mind: 1234, 1122, 2026. If she were a teenager, she knew she'd have used her own birthday year, but 2007, 2008, and 2009 didn't work. She moved on to high school graduation years. After 2026, the screen locked. Too many attempts.

Shit! Shit! Shit!

Now more than ever, getting online was her lifeline.

A horse whinnied from inside the barn, as though laughing at her stupidity. The animal wasn't wrong, considering she'd overlooked the most obvious issue of all: if the phone had service, even spotty service, the authorities could find her. She had been carrying around something that couldn't get her online, with a flashlight she shouldn't use, that was effectively a tracking device.

It seemed stupid to cry, and even more so to hyperventilate, but she began to do both.

Her chest was heaving. She needed air but couldn't get any, no matter how quickly she gasped for breath. *Paper bag*, she thought, which panicked her more and left her gasping.

In desperation, she reached down and grabbed the neck of her baggy jumpsuit, pulled up the fabric, and plunged her face inside, recoiling at the nauseating stench of smoke, industrial detergent, and her now overpowering BO.

"Get your shit together!" she growled into her chest.

Forcing herself to keep breathing—*in through the nose, out through the mouth*—Cara slowly sank to the ground. She could barely feel her hands and feet, and numbness crept up her arms and legs, but slowly, she brought her breathing under control. She let go of her lapels and transitioned into four-count box-breathing, then into deep and slow belly breaths. Finally, her heart stopped palpitating, and the squeezing panic loosened in her chest. She'd stopped crying.

As she lay in the dirt, feeling slowly returning to her limbs, she considered tossing the phone, or better yet, burying it. But she was going to need the flashlight at some point. And if she was too hurt or too hungry or dehydrated and had no choice but to give up, she had to be able to contact 911. Both features worked, even on a locked phone.

What she needed to do was to get rid of the SIM card.

ASAP.

Cara had no idea how to bypass a locked Android, but popping out a SIM card was standard procedure. All she needed was the conservative gold-post earrings she'd been forced to surrender after the verdict, along with her bag, phone, and all of her courtroom clothing. Believing she'd never need any of it again, she'd asked Abel to donate her outfit to Dress for Success. Better it be worn by a woman who needed a Zimmermann suit for job interviews than sold to a true-crime memorabilia collector on eBay.

Now dressed in torn prison garb that would sell for even more, she started feeling around in the dirt for a small stick, twig, or bramble, something with a tiny protuberance that might open the SIM card tray.

Headlights swept the field. A truck was bouncing up the farmhouse driveway.

Feeling a surge of adrenaline, Cara popped up and ran, gripping the phone tightly as she headed back toward the hills. She didn't stop until she was in a dark tangle of trees where there were absolutely no bars of service at all.

FOURTEEN

JORDAN

Social media influencer and convicted murderer Cara Campbell has reportedly escaped following an accident with multiple fatalities on State Highway 41 outside Coarsegold, CA. Campbell is not known to be armed but should be considered dangerous. This is a developing story.

—AP Wire

Gravel sprayed like buckshot off the bottom of his vehicle as Jordan sped down an unpaved road, checking his position against the screenshot Sydney had sent fifteen minutes ago.

Apparently, she and Bree had enabled location sharing through Snapchat, which allowed them to see each other's whereabouts at all times with caricatures of each other—bitmojis—on surprisingly accurate Snap Maps. According to the screenshots Sydney had been sending, Bree's phone had traveled some distance from the crash site, in a completely different direction from where Jordan had been searching. He had gone west while Cara Campbell turned east.

He'd wasted time chasing his gut instinct when the safer play would have been to wait for more information. Cursing himself—once again, he'd done something he would have been angry with his deputies for doing—he reversed course. But now she had a big head start.

Campbell had covered a lot more ground than he expected, climbing up into the hills before dropping down over a ridge, almost as if she were heading for Bass Lake. If she made it to the mountains beyond that, it was going to take a large-scale operation to bring her in. Was she trying to lose herself in the woods, or was she just lost? He probably shouldn't have been surprised by her endurance, though. She was the type who punished herself on a Peloton and in high-energy gym classes, so she had probably been in great physical shape when she was taken into custody following the trial. He wondered if she planned to make use of the free weights in the yard at Chowchilla.

Although most of Campbell's outdoor experience consisted of what Amber called "fake camping," the fact that she ran instead of waiting for rescue indicated that she was highly motivated to avoid recapture. And if she had killed once for money, she would likely kill again for her freedom.

He hadn't told Beto or anyone at the department about the screenshots yet—departmental policy was fuzzy on whether or not he could accept his daughter's help. But it gave Sydney something to do and kept her from worrying about Bree. He had to catch Cara Campbell before he lost her signal in the hills.

He pulled over near a house with a barn and a sign that read *Hoof and Paw Pet Boarding*, the location of Campbell's last digital footprint. Was she still there?

He picked up his phone and texted Sydney. *Anything?*

Waiting for a new signal, she answered. *I think she's going in and out of range.*

Jordan drummed his fingers on the steering wheel.

Then the radio crackled. "This is Deputy 504, I'm at the substation. Just had a couple of walk-ins report that somebody stole several items from their campsite."

Back at the station, Steve Symonds, the night dispatcher, said, "Go ahead."

Jordan considered muting his radio. He was amped up and impatient, with too much stuff already buzzing around in his head. Five-zero-four was the call sign of Germán Lopez, who was new. All Lopez had to do was fill out an incident report and create a new case file for the detectives to review in the morning. There was no need to call the station over pilfered coolers and beer.

"Somebody stole a pair of shoes," continued Lopez.

"Crime of the century," chimed in some wiseass, probably Osman.

Jordan almost laughed—but something tickled the hairs on the back of his neck.

"Yeah? Well, get this," said Lopez. "They left their own footwear behind. Want to guess what they were?"

Jordan grabbed his mic. "If it was a pair of jail-issued orange Crocs, then let's quit playing games and share the information. The clock is ticking."

"Yeah, orange Crocs," said Lopez sheepishly. "One of them has a torn strap. Looks like someone tried to run an obstacle course in them. That you, Sheriff?"

"Bag them and get them to K9," Jordan said. "We're going to want those in the morning."

"Roger that."

Jordan's phone vibrated as a new text from Sydney appeared on the dashboard screen: *Here she is! Are you close dad???*

He expanded the image. Campbell was still moving. The latest signal appeared to be less than a half mile away but was nowhere near the road.

He put his vehicle in gear and drove forward. Houses were few and far between on this road leading to state forest land. If she was a survivalist, the route would have made sense, but his panicked quarry, running blind, couldn't have realized she was heading away from civilization.

He hoped her recapture wasn't going to turn into a body recovery.

When he'd gotten as close as he could in the car, he parked and got out. He pulled on his tactical vest and tightened the Velcro straps until they were snug, then zipped a windbreaker over the top of it. He retied his bootlaces, put on a headlamp, and looped a six-cell Maglite into his gun belt. He grabbed his shotgun from the dashboard mount but didn't rack a shell into the chamber.

Standing outside the trees, he checked his phone, feeling a tug as he studied the location of Bree's smiling, purple-haired bitmoji. It felt like seeing a ghost.

Then he texted Sydney again. *Give me one more screenshot? I'm close.*

It's still in the same place, she answered after a moment.

Thanks, honey. I'm going to go look.

Be careful dad!!!

I'm not your dad right now, he didn't reply. *I'm the goddamn sheriff.*

FIFTEEN
CARA

Does everyone lose that little ejector tool they give you for the SIM card slot or is it just me?

—@macgyverjr

After several failed attempts to trip the SIM card door with blunt, flimsy twigs, Cara found a thin, hardwood stick and frantically shaved its tip with a sharp-edged rock.

In second grade, her class went on a field trip to the Los Angeles Natural History Museum. After touring the Native American dioramas, they were led into a learning room where a docent taught them how to make their own arrowheads using two shiny black pieces of obsidian. Their hands-on learning experience was short-lived, lasting only until Tommy Monroe realized he could "burn" the girls on their arms and bare shoulders with heat caused by the friction. Mrs. Johnson shut down the experiment and sent them outside to eat their brown-bag lunches.

While no one had honed a rock into anything remotely resembling an arrowhead, the memory was reassuring. If a rock could sharpen another rock, it could certainly sharpen wood into a point precise enough for her needs.

Cara honed the stick to a sharp point, small enough to fit into the tiny hole by the SIM card door.

Nothing happened on her first attempt.

Yes. You. Can.

She turned on the flashlight. While she obviously couldn't aim it at the phone itself, the beam reflected off the tree trunk she was squatting next to. She angled the light toward the base of the tree until she had enough illumination on the phone to see the SIM card door. She guided the tip of the stick into the pinpoint-sized hole and pushed harder.

The spring load clicked.

The compartment opened.

Cara pulled out the SIM card, snapped it in half, and dropped it on the ground.

And then she was gone.

SIXTEEN
JORDAN

They watch. They listen. They track. We are all under surveillance. Always.

—@notparanoidatall

Jordan zipped his cell into a pocket and locked his vehicle. Then he walked along the tree line until he found a narrow game trail. The bushes lining the road were thick, but once he got through them, the woods opened up and the trail was easy enough to follow in the glow of his headlamp's red light. The haze of smoke in the sky blocked almost all the starlight and moonlight.

He walked slowly, placing his feet carefully and listening for any unexpected sounds ahead. Blundering along at speed would have only made his own movements easier to hear. Ahead, eyes gleamed and then winked out as an animal, probably a fox, scurried away.

The trail led more or less in the direction he wanted to go. Half a mile in, the sawing of crickets started getting drowned out by the white noise of rushing water. He guessed it was China Creek. Even the smaller waterways were still swollen with spring runoff from the slowly melting snow in the higher parts of the Sierra. Banks were eroding, bridges had washed out, and at least one hundred-year-old cabin had been washed away. He began walking more quickly as the noise got louder: if he couldn't hear her, she wouldn't be able to hear him, either.

Jordan swiveled his head, searching for movement in the trees, but suspected he'd find her at the creek's edge. She would be thirsty, and if she had half a brain, she'd know rushing water was safer than stagnant pools. The rushing stream was as good as a wall at her back. Jordan knew from experience that the icy water's pull was so strong that it was difficult to stand even thigh-deep without being swept away.

Or maybe she hoped to follow China Creek to the Fresno River and down to the valley floor, where she could disappear in Fresno. *And good luck with that*, he thought. Although that route would skirt the fire, it would lead her right to downtown Oakhurst, where her orange jumpsuit would cause her problems. If she made it through, traveling the steep and thickly wooded banks of the winding river would be an extreme test of endurance.

Soon Jordan was close enough to see gaps in the trees that indicated the creek behind. He turned off his headlamp and let his eyes adjust to the darkness before creeping forward, trying to spot anything that could indicate the presence of the fugitive. The water's steady rumble swallowed all other sounds.

He stopped in the tree line. Against the frothing whitewater, he was able to make out boulders, snagged tree trunks, and a deadfall at the creek's edge.

Taking his phone out of his pocket, he hid its glowing screen inside his windbreaker as he checked the screenshot again. The Snap Map showed city streets in detail, but here it recorded only the obvious landmarks, the road and the river, showing the forest as a featureless blob of black. It was hard to tell how far off course the game trail had carried him, but he guessed her last location had been within several hundred yards of where he stood.

Upstream? Or downstream?

His mental coin toss came up heads.

So he headed downstream.

SEVENTEEN
CARA

Aquaphobia, or fear of water, is common in people who have experienced a traumatic event, such as a near drowning or a boating accident. As a certified cognitive behavioral therapist with over eighteen years of experience, I can help. Results guaranteed!

—www.TedLoebPsyD.com

Cara couldn't see very far in the darkness, but she could clearly hear the sound of water. Not the gentle trickle of a stream or the playful splash of beavers frolicking in a stagnant pond, but a full-on rushing and tumbling river. As she got closer, she felt the temperature drop. Soon, she came to a break in the trees.

It had been five years since the catamaran incident. The trip to Cabo, her first as a sponsored content creator, ended in the harrowing rescue video that established her as an influencer. It was a balmy, sunny afternoon with light southern winds, ideal for learning how to reach, tack, jib, and record the glamorous outing. Her instructor, José, was documenting the one-hour lesson via the GoPro on his safety helmet. Everything was going as planned, even the staged moment when she leaned too far and nearly capsized their two-person craft. But then, while José was teaching her how to balance on the trapeze, a rogue wave—she'd never heard of such a thing—rose up like a frothing monster, slammed into the boat, and sent them flying in different directions. José was knocked out by the boom as the catamaran sailed on without them. She swam over, looped an arm around his neck and made sure his head remained above water while Karl, who had been watching from the dock, commandeered a jet ski and rushed out to help. The unconscious instructor's video of their dramatic but ultimately happy ending topped out at nearly a million views.

Cara had assiduously avoided what she and Karl jokingly referred to as "water sports" ever since.

Now, as she stepped out of the forest and onto the banks of a churning, swollen river, its water frothy and white even in the blackness of the night, she was overcome with thirst-quenching joy.

But was it safe to drink?

Given both the dangers she'd already survived and the ones that lay ahead, she really didn't want to die from diarrhea, immortalized in an obituary headlined: *Cara Campbell, 38, Couldn't Outrun the Trots.*

The best chance for the cleanest water, she decided, was in the middle of the river, where the current was too fast and cold for parasites to thrive.

Using the phone's flashlight, Cara worked her way up the bank, scanning for a narrow chute or rocky outcropping, but there was no way to reach the middle. After painstakingly traveling a hundred yards or more, she finally came upon an inlet formed by two water-snagged logs and closely spaced rocks where, assuming she didn't slip and fall in, she could get far enough out into the water for a theoretically safe drink.

Water is good . . .

She needed the light, but it was more critical to keep her balance, so she tucked the cell phone back into her bra. The logs and rocks were too slippery to cross in bare feet, so she pulled her pant legs out of her shoes, rolled them up above her knees, as far up her thighs as they would go, then tightened and double-knotted her shoelaces.

Water is life . . .

She stepped out onto the first log, wobbled, and then steadied herself.

Yes.

The second log bobbed, but somehow, she didn't.

You.

She leaped onto a big rock half submerged in rushing water.

Can.

With each step, the air got colder and the rumble of the rushing water grew more thunderous.

She took a final hop onto a flat-topped boulder that was as near to the middle as she dared to go. Kneeling, she dipped her cupped hands into the icy current and brought them to her mouth.

The first sip was so deliciously frigid it stung her teeth.

So was the next.

Cara gulped as much as she could hold, then washed her dusty face, even though it made her shiver. She felt like she could live indefinitely on nothing but fresh, clean water.

Hydration: achieved.

She would shelter for the night in a bush away from the river's coldness but close enough that she could drink again before daybreak. From there she planned to head away from the fire, figuring out what to do next as she went along.

She made it almost back to the bank before she slipped off the log, landing calf-deep in the current. At least she hadn't fallen in.

Then a blinding light made everything go white. She squinted in confusion as a deep male voice called out.

"Put your hands up and turn around slowly!"

EIGHTEEN
JORDAN

*$50 that dumb b*tch don't make it thru the nite.*
—@gamblinman69

Jordan turned on his headlamp, racked his shotgun, and leveled it at Cara Campbell.

The tunnel of white light was so bright it hurt his eyes—outside it, the soft shadows of the forest disappeared into darkness. Moths made dizzying circles as the fugitive stood unsteadily in the rushing water.

"Put your hands up and turn around!" he bellowed. "Face away from me!"

Her whole body flinched. She turned her head toward the water, away from the glare of his headlamp.

"I said, put your hands up! Turn your whole body around and then move slowly toward the shore."

She raised her arms halfway, a sagging scarecrow. Then she lost her balance and stumbled, finding herself thigh-deep before she regained her footing. Her hands were open and empty. She appeared to be unarmed.

Jordan was about thirty yards away. Careful of his footing, he began closing the distance. He didn't know why she wasn't complying, but he needed to get her to shore before she fell and was swept away.

At twenty yards, he saw Campbell more clearly. Her orange jumpsuit was too large, making her look small and vulnerable. Her blond hair was stringy, and her face was scratched and smudged. Outwardly, she resembled a hundred other sad sacks who'd made bad choices, gotten in over their heads, and found themselves at the ends of their badly frayed ropes. By the time he arrested them, he often sensed they were grateful to be caught by someone who was going to finally take control of their disordered lives.

And yet.

Standing in the swollen stream, struggling to stay upright against the pushing current, Cara Campbell didn't look beaten. Something about her body language made him think she was still hoping to change the outcome of this encounter.

Even though he had racked his shotgun mostly to get her attention, and even though she was not holding a weapon, he continued to aim at center mass.

Ten yards away, he stopped.

"Cara Campbell, I'm Sheriff Jordan Burke of Madera County," he barked in his command voice. "I'm here to bring you back into custody. I need you to get those hands high in the air and get out of the water right now."

She raised her hands a few inches more, to shoulder level. Maybe he was wrong. Maybe the reason she had been so slow to comply was that she was in shock and confused.

But she still wouldn't look at him. Her face was angled down toward the creek. Which could have been because she was avoiding his headlamp's glare. Or . . .

"Are you hurt?"

She shook her head.

"Can you understand what I'm saying?"

Her nod was so small he almost missed it.

Why wouldn't she look at him?

Then he knew. She was watching the water and calculating her chances. Even though the current was strong enough to break her against logs and boulders, she was still thinking about trying to get away.

"Listen to me," he said, softening his voice. "I need you to get out of the water. The current is much higher than usual and it's very dangerous. If you go in, you won't survive."

Cara Campbell didn't comply.

But she did finally look at him.

NINETEEN
CARA

Looking for some class 5 whitewater rafting in Cali this summer. Suggestions for the gnarliest spots?

—@watersports4ever

Cara's mind swirled faster than the eddies circling her legs. *Don't want to die. Can't go back to prison. Hate water.*

"If you go in, you won't survive," Sheriff Burke said.

She had been so focused on not slipping and falling in the darkness, she had completely missed his approach. She couldn't tell what he looked like, not when she was blinded by his flashlight beam.

"Two people have died this year in water just like this," he warned her. "You'll be tossed around like a rag doll, bashed against rock after rock."

Any vague thoughts she'd had about feigning shock or amnesia or both were drowned out by the fearsome roaring water. "I thought people kayaked or rafted down these things."

"A long way downstream from here, and not while the water's this high. We had record-setting snowfall last winter."

Her teeth were chattering and she couldn't feel her feet. The water in Mexico had been bathtub-warm, its current like a water-park wave pool. And unlike the rescue in Mexico, there was no Karl on a jet ski to pluck her out of the roiling rapids.

"I don't want to die," she said.

"I don't want you to die, either."

It sounded like he meant it. The headlamp beam shifted, and she got a quick glimpse of a stocky man, not unhandsome, about her age. She had expected him to be wearing a sheriff's cowboy hat, like Dudley Do-Right, but apparently it didn't accessorize well with the headlamp.

"But you'll shoot me if you have to," she said.

"Not if you come peaceably into custody."

"So you can send me back to prison to die. Maybe I should get it over with. Everyone else in that accident is dead."

"Not everyone. LaDonna's doing just fine."

She must not have gotten very far. Cara felt sad, thinking she wouldn't see her kids.

"And Bree . . ." The sheriff's voice cracked. "Is clinging to life."

"If I had known that, I would have stayed with her."

He lowered the shotgun and reached out with his left hand. "Come on, Cara, let me help you."

If she went back with Sheriff Do-Right, how could he help her? By testifying to the judge that she should get natural life, instead of life plus additional years for attempted escape?

Shaking from cold, she took one step into the current, gasping in shock as the water reached her waist.

He raised his gun again and stepped toward her. "Don't do it, Cara! Out of the water, *now*!"

TWENTY
JORDAN

I will forever be searching for Karl's killer.
—@carasloveisgold

Cara Campbell would not obey Jordan's order. Bringing her under control without backup, in the dark, would be a challenge. He sure as hell wasn't going to shoot her, but he wasn't going to allow her to stand in the water until she froze to death, either.

Handling noncompliant subjects was a gray area. Law enforcement officers were supposed to keep themselves safe while preventing physical harm to prisoners, which was often easier said than done. Again and again, Jordan had reminded all of his deputies that his number one rule was to never lay hands on a suspect without complete control of the situation.

On the other hand, Cara Campbell couldn't weigh more than a buck-thirty, despite being somewhat tall for a woman.

He switched on his shotgun's safety and set it down in the rocks. Behind his back, he unsnapped the handcuff pouch on his belt. Then, with his hands open and empty, he stepped into the water and started edging toward Cara.

The water that filled his boots and soaked his socks was so frigid, he didn't know how she'd stood it as long as she had.

"Come out of the water, and I can take you back to my vehicle," he coaxed her. "I can run the heater, and I've got a warm blanket. I can get you a cup of hot chocolate ten minutes down the road."

"Tea," she whispered.

He stopped three yards away, encouraged.

"Chai with unsweetened oat milk," she clarified. "At least that's what I used to like. Before all of this."

"You got it," he lied, knowing there was no way he was getting his hands on either of those ingredients at this time of the night. "We'll make sure you get it just how you like it."

He thought he saw a hint of a smile.

When Jordan stepped forward again, Cara backed away, struggling to maintain her balance against the relentless push of a creek flowing at God-knew-how-many cubic feet per second.

She stumbled, her foot no doubt slipping on a moss-slick rock, and almost submerged.

Jordan lunged forward to catch her, but she regained her balance and stopped him with a glare.

"I'm not going back," she said.

Now he was exasperated. "Listen, Ms. Campbell. I don't want to fish out your dead body a few miles downstream. Let's go back to my vehicle, warm up, and take a selfie to let everyone who loves you know you're safe."

He wanted to get out of the water, too, damn it.

She was almost within arm's reach and could fall at any moment. It was now or never.

"Well, let's talk, then," he said, only to distract her as he forced himself forward and reached out to grab her.

His fingers closed on empty air.

Cara Campbell had thrown herself into the raging torrent. It all happened so fast, he didn't even realize what she'd said until he had watched the frothing water carry her out of sight.

"I did not kill my husband."

CALIFORNIA DEATH TRIP PODCAST

SEASON ONE, EPISODE ELEVEN

Hi, crime fam, it's me, Dylan Danvers. I'm sorry for the crappy audio but I'm recording this on my phone, in my car, because this will not wait until I can get to the studio. I just heard from a very reliable source that Cara Campbell was in a crazy, horrible van accident on her way to prison this afternoon. Miraculously, she survived. And even more improbably, she escaped. If you're just joining us for the first time, please do yourself a favor and go back and listen to the first ten episodes of Season One, "The Ojai Plastic Surgeon Hammer Murder," which tells how influencer Cara Campbell was railroaded by a system that just couldn't wait to convict a famous person for the crime of being famous.

I'll be back with a full episode first thing tomorrow morning, but in the meantime, send me all your tips and theories, and links to any news you think I might have missed. This story is moving fast and it's hard for one podcaster to stay on top of it. Cara Campbell is out there somewhere. She may be lost. She may be hurt. She definitely needs our help. So we're going to find her. I'll talk to you tomorrow. This is Dylan, signing off.

DAY TWO

TWENTY-ONE
JORDAN

VOLUNTEERS WANTED! Join the search for escaped fugitive Cara Campbell TODAY. Rendezvous at Bass Lake Recreation Area at 8:00 AM.

—Silverman for Sheriff Facebook page

Standing at the kitchen island well after midnight, Jordan used his fork to saw off a corner of the lasagna he hadn't bothered to reheat. The cheese was cold and congealed, the pasta wading in a puddle of the Italian dressing he'd poured too fast over his handful of salad. But he had to eat. The moment he turned off his car in the driveway, adrenaline had begun flooding out of his body like a wave receding on the beach.

He lifted a bite to his mouth and forced himself to chew.

Seated on the opposite side of the breakfast bar, Amber scrolled on her oversized phone with tired, red-rimmed eyes. She wore an old cardigan over her nightgown and her dark brown hair was held in place with a half-broken banana clip.

He had driven out to Valley Children's Hospital on his way home to see Steve and Joanne and get the latest update on Bree. She was finally out of surgery and doctors had placed her in a medically induced coma to give her the best chance to heal. Her physical survival seemed assured, but what lay next, no one knew. No one was celebrating her miraculous survival. Her parents' stricken faces would stay with him forever.

When Sydney met Jordan at the door, her face alive with hope, he wrapped her in a hug that might have been the longest they ever shared.

Certainly, she would not have tolerated it under any other circumstances.

"But she's alive, right, Dad?" Sydney asked when he finally let go, studying his eyes for signs of evasion.

"She's alive," he confirmed. "Beyond that, we don't know."

"What do you mean?"

"She has a brain injury and a broken back, honey. All we can do now is love her, wait, and pray."

As disbelief transformed into understanding, Sydney burst into tears. As Jordan reached out to hug her again, her arms fell limp by her sides, and she stumbled away to her room.

"I love you," he said to her back.

Amber reassured him that he'd handled it the best he could.

Jordan tried to think of a worse day in his career but couldn't. Five people dead. Two rapidly spreading wildfires. Mile-long backups on Highway 41, which was still restricted to a single lane while the wrecker crew tried to safely remove the jackknifed semi from an active firefighting scene.

And, of course, one escaped fugitive—the most notable escapee Madera County had ever seen.

After Cara Campbell had thrown herself into the water, he chased her for as long as he could, but the current carried her faster than he could follow. She disappeared almost immediately into the frothing white rapids, resurfacing for only a second before she was swept out of sight. The glimpse of her face in the cold, white light of his headlamp had been so brief he couldn't be sure he hadn't imagined it.

The morning's search would be a body recovery. With the dogs, it wouldn't take too long.

Amber glanced up. "Have you heard of Dylan Danvers?"

"No. Should I?" He forked and sawed another bite of lasagna, telling himself to finish the whole thing. He needed calories.

"He's the son of a model and some big football player."

"Nico Danvers?"

She nodded. "Dylan's a total nepo baby. He didn't inherit his dad's athletic talent, so he did some acting, but his career didn't really take off. Then there was a cooking show, which got canceled, so he tried being an influencer. Now he's a true-crime podcaster."

"Does he make a living at it?"

"I'm not sure he has to. But his season on Cara Campbell totally blew up. I guess it was the perfect combination, with a celebrity covering a celebrity murderer."

"When I was a kid, celebrities were people who actually accomplished something."

Amber chuckled, reached across the breakfast bar, and patted him on the forearm. "Don't forget to take your meds, grampaw. Other podcasts covered the trial, too, but Danvers seems convinced she's actually innocent."

"And you're telling me this because . . . ?"

"He just released a short episode, really an update. I didn't listen, but according to this summary, he wants his 'crime fam' to send clues and help find her."

"Just what I need," said Jordan, chewing. "And people listen to this guy?"

"It's a top-ten podcast on Spotify. All the true-crime yahoos are going to be glued to their couches, studying each other's TikToks and trying to decide whether you're merely a bumbling incompetent or actually a sinister villain in league with a shadowy cabal of lizard people who run the US government from the basement of a Chuck E. Cheese."

"How do we know they're not lizard people themselves?"

"That's exactly what a lizard person would say. I'm just waiting for someone to say the whole accident was staged by paid actors in order to distract the public's attention."

"From what?"

Amber shrugged. "Changes weekly."

Jordan gave up on the lasagna and shoveled the rest into the garbage disposal. He went around the breakfast bar and hugged her from behind, resting his cheek on the top of her head and inhaling deeply.

She'd been prickly about being touched lately, frustrated with her weight, but he had never cared, only loved her softness and warmth and the way she smelled.

She reached up and awkwardly squeezed back. "Is there any chance Cara Campbell survived?"

"I think the couch detectives are wasting their time. But I'm going to find her, either way."

Amber was quiet for a moment. "That's sad. I saw this Instagram story earlier from Cara's best friend, maybe her only remaining friend, Stephanie van der Lind. She's a realtor who got famous by appearing on *Selling to the Stars*—during Cara's trial."

"Let me guess: she's using the escape to market her next open house?"

"Well, that, too," Amber said with the smile that usually came so easily. Letting go of him, she called up the Instagram story and showed him her screen. A pop song blared from the phone's tinny speakers as Campbell and van der Lind posed next to a pool, wearing tiny swimsuits, enormous sunglasses, and toothy smiles.

She is NOT America's Most Wanted, read the blocky text. *She is my friend. Bring her home safe!!!*

Jordan's stomach rolled. So many people were learning their loved ones had died today. "Does anyone think she's actually guilty? Besides, you know, the judge and jury."

"I think most people know she did it. Social media is never an accurate barometer because it pushes controversial opinions to the top. Her stepdaughter, who apparently never liked her in the first place due to the whole gold-digger thing, definitely thinks she's guilty."

Amber swiped until she found what she wanted, then showed him her screen again. The tweet from Taylor Campbell made his skin prickle.

IF SHE'S DEAD, SHE DESERVES IT.

TWENTY-TWO
CARA

FYI @carasloveisgold. There's no such thing as a faux fur throw in the real wilderness.

—@helpfulhintress21

Every part of Cara's body hurt, especially her knuckles, elbows, knees, and feet. Her head throbbed like she was having a migraine, her ears were ringing, and her throat was raw from vomiting up what felt like gallons of water. But surely the pain meant she was still alive. Then again, she had never died before. Maybe this was just how it felt.

The icy water—like a million simultaneous bee stings—had to have killed her. She'd been launched like a log through one rapid after another, submarining through a gauntlet of stabbing sticks and bruising rocks. Every time she managed to surface and gasp some air, she was pulled right back under.

Over and over.

Back when she was alive, she'd once read a sign beside the ice plunge at a spa: *Give in to the pain. Surrender to the bliss.*

There had been no bliss to be found as she was tossed around in the river, only overwhelming agony and the certainty she was about to crash into a boulder headfirst.

After which, presumably, she would feel nothing at all.

She'd tried to surrender, to give up peacefully and allow the current to take her where it wanted. Instead, as she was sucked down and dragged along the bottom of the river, she fought back, flailing toward the surface, desperate to relieve the incredible pain in her lungs. Adrenaline spiking in her chest, her numb limbs began to tingle with unexpected energy as she kicked, weakly at first, then harder, scooping with her hands until her head surfaced again.

The first painful gulp of air made her cough and choke, but she didn't allow herself to be pulled back under. She put her arms out like wings and got her feet out in front of her, knees bent to take the impact. When she collided with a car-sized boulder, she pushed off, back into the stream.

Maybe the water finally got tired of playing with her. After who knew how many terrifying minutes, it dumped her into a shallow eddy. She paddled to shore and shakily stood, her throat, lungs, and stomach burning. She retched until her stomach was empty.

Somehow, she scrambled onto the bank, crawled into the brush, and collapsed beside a log. The last thing she remembered was hoping she was hidden from the glare of the sheriff's flashlight.

Then she gave herself permission to die.

Her face was warm and her closed eyelids glowed red. Had she been sent to hell?

She opened her eyes—the left one only opened halfway—and winced at a beam of sunlight that cut through the forest canopy. Raising her head, she saw she was covered in leaves, decomposed wood, and God knew what other forest-floor gunk.

The pile of detritus must have insulated her well enough to stave off hypothermia. The gods who ruled rapids—like those in charge of head-on collisions, carnivorous creatures, and even hypothermia—had rejected her as an unfit sacrifice.

Cautiously, she lifted herself to a sitting position and flicked a pill bug from her sleeve. Her cotton-poly jumpsuit was still damp but had shed the water surprisingly well. While it had new rips at the knees and elbows—the cuffs were hopelessly frayed—it was otherwise still in one piece. She listened for voices or footfalls but couldn't hear anything over the rushing water. Lifting her head, she peered cautiously over the log and saw that she was less than fifteen feet from where she'd washed up. How far had she traveled in the water? How soon would the area be swarmed with searchers?

Cara scanned the riverbank and the woods on the other side, but as far as she could tell, she was only being observed by a family of chipmunks and a bird making a *dee-do-do* sound high in a nearby tree. She hoisted herself onto the rotting tree trunk to take inventory of her injuries. She had a bump the size of a walnut on her forehead and her left eye throbbed. Her lower lip was split and bleeding. Red scrapes connected the bruises dotting her arms and legs. But everything moved properly and in the right directions. She probed her belly but couldn't feel anything unusually tender—not that she knew where anything vital was actually located. She could only hope there was no internal bleeding.

In twenty-four hours, she'd amassed enough near death experiences to start a YouTube channel: *Watch Cara Campbell Almost Expire.*

Water survival: achieved.

How many other ways were there to *not* die?

Leaning on the log for support, she stood up slowly to minimize the head rush. Even with the smoky haze filtering the sun, she could already tell it was going to be a hot day. Her clothing would dry fast—faster than her shoes, which, amazingly, were still on her feet.

After checking again to be certain she was alone, Cara undid the snaps—two of them were already broken and hung open—and allowed the jumpsuit to drop to her ankles so she could pee. Not much came out. But when she pulled down her prison-issue, high-waisted, white underpants and perched over the log, she saw blood. Lots of it.

"Shit."

The phrase *on the rag* had never made more sense as she considered ripping a sleeve off her jumpsuit to use the fabric as a makeshift pad. But it was too cold at night to sacrifice an entire sleeve. A hunk of moss might work but she didn't see any nearby. In the meantime, she had to do something, so she settled on a handful of the leaves she'd slept on all night. If they were poisonous, she'd know by now.

#FreeBleedHack, she thought as she shook them to make sure there were no bugs, then wiped and grabbed another pile to place in her underpants.

Her self-congratulatory DIY moment was interrupted by a sudden thought. Escaped prisoners were tracked by dogs, weren't they? Baying, slobbering dogs. And not just any kind of dogs.

Bloodhounds.

TWENTY-THREE
JORDAN

Pray for @carasloveisgold.

—@deathtripdylan

@deathtripdylan I pray for YOU. How damaged do you have to be to be a murderer groupie?

—@TayCamp

Scanner activity indicates search party assembling near China Creek.

—@madera_watchdawg

"Show me again," Jordan said.

Bill Pfaff, a stocky guide who ran rafting trips on big rivers—Kings, Tuolumne, American—traced a stubby finger over the hydrological map spread out on the hood of Jordan's vehicle.

"Hard to predict, given the unusual amount of water this year, but I'd say your most likely washout points are here, here, and here."

Jordan handed him a fine-tipped marker. "Mark them, please?"

Pfaff shrugged, then drew three Xs on the paper. They were lopsided and looked to Jordan like little crosses. A riverine cemetery.

"'Course, this is all guesswork, Sheriff. I mean, she could have gotten snagged anywhere in a strainer. Since she's not wearing a life vest, she could be rolling at the bottom of a hole."

"I understand, but we have to start somewhere. Just to confirm, you wouldn't send a kayak down the creek with this much flow, right?"

Pfaff stared at Jordan like he could see through the hole in his head. "I wouldn't send a paper boat down there."

"I appreciate your time."

They shook hands, and Pfaff made his way back to a dusty Chevy Suburban with *Sierra Whitewater Adventures* stenciled on the driver's-side door.

After stealing a few hours of fitful sleep, Jordan had risen before dawn to return to the area where he'd last seen Cara Campbell. At the crash site on 41, his headlights swept over the scorched earth where the fire had started before climbing into the hills. In the distance, an eerie orange glow marked the fire's progress. It almost seemed as though the fire was chasing her, too.

Circling around the fire and getting ahead of it, he'd taken a back road to the gravel turnout where the search party would assemble, Beto arriving as the first sunlight flared over the trees. They were soon joined by the RICO-repo RV that served as the department's mobile command post, or MCP, plus a dozen deputies' vehicles, and the personal cars and trucks of the Madera County Search and Rescue, seasoned outdoorsmen who usually looked for lost or hurt climbers in summer and avalanche-trapped snowmobilers in winter. Last to arrive was the K9 van, whose dogs barked eagerly while their handler waited for orders.

Now, three TV news vans parked along the shoulder of the road were shooting B-roll of the whole operation while reporters waited impatiently for a statement from Jordan, who refused to grant any interviews until he had something to say.

All this to find one woman. A woman who had admittedly married for money and then killed her husband, apparently to cash out because his money was about to run out.

Most manhunts were actually quite simple. Those who escaped custody, broke parole, or fled imminent arrest rarely had the resources to leave the country or even the state. Jordan usually managed to track them down by sending deputies to knock on doors at known hangouts or simply wait until the offender showed.

He'd never actually had to search the woods before.

Jordan waved Beto over and showed him the map. "See these three Xs? I want a team to start at each one and then work their way upstream. If she somehow got washed past the third one, someone will probably spot her body in Oakhurst."

Beto squinted at the map, calculating routes with an internal GPS that was better than Google's, at least when it came to the county's snarls of unmarked back roads.

"Got it."

While Beto strode into the center of the lot, barking commands as he assembled teams, Jordan looked again at the map. He was pretty sure he knew where he'd been standing when he watched Campbell go in, but how far she'd gone was anybody's guess. She could have gotten snagged around the first corner in what Pfaff called a "strainer"—a tree or root system crossing the stream—where she would have been pinned in place by water pressure. She could have died of hypothermia even if she was still able to breathe.

It would be a gruesome way to go, even for a murderer. But nature offered no leniency.

Hearing shouts and revving engines, he looked up. An orange Ford Bronco with a pointless snorkel was bullying its way into the crowded turnout, refusing to stop for the deputy—Lopez—trying to wave him away. Parking at center stage, Troy Silverman climbed out, ran his fingers through his hair, and turned in a slow circle, making sure the TV cameras on the road caught his whitened smile.

A handful of men Jordan didn't recognize climbed out of the Bronco and an extended-cab dually pickup that had followed it in. Amber had warned him Silverman was putting together his own search party, but he just hadn't had time to give it any thought—what with leading the official search party and all.

Not wanting to give the man any satisfaction, Jordan pretended to study the map while he waited for Silverman to come to him, only looking up when he heard, “You running a used car lot here or what, Burke?”

“You need to move your vehicles,” he said, feeling his neck getting warm. “You’re interfering with an official operation.”

Silverman raised his hands in what was supposed to look like a conciliatory gesture. “Just tell us where you need us. We’re here to help.”

“I have plenty of bodies already, thanks.”

“So you found her?”

“Not yet.”

“I’ve got some good men with me—hunters and trackers. Unless you want to risk letting Ms. Campbell slip through your fingers.”

“Go home, Silverman,” Jordan growled.

“What are you going to do, arrest me?” Silverman raised his voice, playing to his followers, no doubt hoping his words carried to the TV cameras. “Me and my fellow volunteers?”

Jordan was well within his rights to remove the men from the scene, but any action he took would only be fodder for Silverman’s next campaign ad. But if he let them help, they would only get in the way, because they weren’t trained like the Search and Rescue volunteers. And—Jordan hated himself for thinking it—what if Silverman’s team actually found Campbell first?

It was hard to think with the barking dogs disrupting his thoughts. But there was a third option: just ignore the asshole.

Leaving a puzzled Silverman behind, Jordan stalked over to Beto. “You’re in command here. I’m going to take one of the teams.”

Beto hardly reacted, but to Jordan, the veteran deputy may as well have winced. “Are you sure?”

He nodded toward Silverman. “Removing myself before I do something I regret.”

“Understood.”

Without acknowledging Silverman, Jordan returned to his vehicle, calmly folded the map, and got behind the wheel. Lighting up his flashers, he drove directly toward Silverman’s Bronco, which was now blocking his exit. He stopped a yard short of the driver's-side door and gestured impatiently at its owner.

Well?

The TV cameras were definitely rolling.

With a false show of good cheer, Silverman squeezed into his vehicle and pulled forward so Jordan could get out. As soon as Jordan's tires were on the gravel, he gunned the engine, hoping to kick a few rocks toward the Bronco's perfect paint job. Not very politic behavior.

Four cars—the deputies and volunteers on Jordan's team—followed along behind. Jordan watched in his side mirror as the orange Bronco and the big pickup pulled U-turns and followed, too.

TWENTY-FOUR
CARA

Gender neutral fashion continues to gather momentum in today's generation. We love this trend because it's so liberating!

—Fashionmomentonline.com

Cara cupped her hands and gulped water from the creek, soothing her scratchy throat. Rising, she stumbled into the smoke-hazed trees. She had no way to carry water and didn't know when she would find more, but had to assume the sheriff wouldn't be far behind. By the time she'd hiked a hundred yards, she had a more pressing problem: the dried leaves in her underwear had already turned into a soggy blob.

Even worse, the stems poked in every direction.

Given that she didn't know an oak leaf from poison ivy, grabbing a fresh fistful of leaves wasn't a great option. A few hundred yards further, she was so desperate to keep the blood from running down her leg that she replaced the leaves with a semi-pliable chunk of bark. Not only was that even more uncomfortable than the leaves, feeling like a loofah between her legs, but it didn't absorb a drop. A sun-dried piece of brown paper bag she found entangled in a bush was so filthy that it was a nonstarter. She'd given in to the reality of free bleeding and was trying to ignore how gross it felt when she spotted something in the distance.

Something teal and lime green.

Hiking along a shallow slope, she saw a small, domed tent—an actual tent! A home away from home where one of the occupants could be female. Menstruating, even! Probabilities weren't Cara's strong suit, but there seemed to be a decent chance she could find a tampon or a pad inside. If she scored food of any kind in the process, it would be like winning the lottery.

She crept closer, moving as quietly as she could while she watched the campsite for signs of life. When the tent flap rustled, she ducked behind a tree, closed her eyes, and hoped she hadn't been seen. Nothing happened. She peeked around the tree trunk and saw the tent fabric gently rippling in the breeze. She waited for agonizing minutes, but no one came or went from the campsite.

Time to move. She couldn't stop thinking about the dogs that had to be sniffing for her trail. Big, snarling, bloodthirsty dogs who were trained to attack.

Cara approached one silent step at a time until she reached the camp table with a gas stove and an aluminum teapot. She touched the side of pot. It was only slightly warm, so she gulped every last drop of its tepid contents. After drinking from a stream, boiled water felt unbelievably decadent. As she put the teapot down, she noticed a charred piece of fish clinging to the side of an unwashed frying pan.

Had it only been yesterday she'd turned up her nose at the processed, packaged food in a stale MRE? Today, she was literally salivating over a dry scrap of fish from last night's dinner. *#InadvertentFasting*—the most radical diet plan Cara had ever undertaken—was definitely going to be a challenge.

Sniffing the meat to confirm it was edible, she popped it into her mouth. As she chewed and swallowed, she ran her fingers around the inside of the pan to scoop up the last few morsels.

She unzipped the tent. The fluffy, two-person sleeping bag filling its small interior looked so cozy and comfortable that she suddenly—desperately—felt Goldilocks-level tired. Not that she could risk napping.

The neon yellow sleeping bag was far too bulky and conspicuous to lug around. But the gray sweats and black T-shirt balled up in the corner would allow her to finally get rid of the bright orange target on her back. She also found a pair of socks, a rain jacket, and a blue bandanna. A thorough search of the tent revealed no feminine hygiene products, but there was—miracle of miracles—a nearly full roll of soft, two-ply toilet paper.

Charmin, if she had to hazard a guess.

Cara carried her booty away from the campsite before she stopped to change. She unsnapped her jumpsuit and let it fall into a ripped, bloodstained pile at her feet. Ignoring as best as she could the grime and sweat stains on the black Under Armour tee, as well as a glob of something whitish and sticky she sincerely hoped was roasted marshmallow, Cara slipped it over her head. A mere two-and-a-half weeks ago, she would have been too disgusted to even touch a shirt that reeked of multiple days of wear. Now, Cara just got on with it. If the dogs were tracking her scent, wasn't someone else's body odor a helpful decoy?

The sweatpants were generic gray and not nearly as dirty. Far cleaner than her panties, which she wished she could leave behind with her jumpsuit but still needed to secure her folded toilet-paper "mini-pad." The sweatpants were thick, so she rolled the waistband down and pulled the legs above her knees to keep herself as cool as possible. When she put her hands in the pockets, she found two bills, a crumpled twenty and a ten.

The chance of ever making it back to civilization was between slim and none, but if she somehow managed to do it, she had thirty bucks to treat herself to a nice salad and a cheap glass of wine before she was picked up and sent back to the slammer. What special hell awaited lifers who attempted to escape?

As she tied the rain jacket around her waist and the bandanna around her head, hiding her hair and the big bump on her forehead, she felt a glimmer of confidence. Cara had never considered anonymity or even a quiet life to be viable life goals, but she'd read several books about women who went off to find themselves by adventuring alone—hiking, biking, even swimming—for long distances in the middle of nowhere. While her present circumstances were anything but a dream trek toward self-discovery, solo woman hikers were definitely a thing, and she 100 percent fit the part.

Wiping away a hopeful tear, she folded the jumpsuit until it was small enough to fit it into a packing cube and hid it under a rock.

Now she could hike in plain sight.

TWENTY-FIVE
JORDAN

The US Marshals Fugitive Task Force is searching for convicted murderer Cara Campbell, who has escaped and is currently at large. She was last seen on Highway 41 near Coarsegold in Madera County, CA.

—@USMarshalsHQ

Jordan had to give Silverman credit. He was persistent.

An asshole, an idiot, and a self-promoting blowhard, but persistent.

Completely ignoring Jordan's order to stop interfering with the search operation, Silverman and his men had tailed Jordan's team, parked behind them, and were now following them through the smoke-hazed woods toward the river. They were close enough behind that Jordan could make out the general outline of their jokes and laughs—which were clearly meant for him—if not any of the actual words.

Silverman was trying to provoke a confrontation. And he had probably instructed one of his followers to record the whole thing on video.

Well, if he wanted video, Jordan would give him one he couldn't use, one that showed a dedicated public servant doing a demanding job under difficult circumstances while keeping his cool.

No matter how much he was boiling inside.

What would happen to Madera County if he actually lost the election to this narcissistic clown? The possibility once seemed so remote that he hadn't given it much thought. Should he be worried? Stranger things had happened. He also had no idea what he would do with himself if he was suddenly out of a job—or how he would sleep at night knowing that self-interested Silverman was the man tasked with keeping his neighbors safe.

Better not let it get to that.

Also, was "self-interested Silverman" a phrase he could use somehow? It was both memorable and accurate.

Jordan had assigned himself the search location closest to where he'd last seen Cara Campbell, simply because he believed she wouldn't have made it far. They would probably find her white, bloated body within a few hundred feet of where he'd abandoned last night's search. If they were lucky, she would have washed up on the rocky shore. If she was hung up on a snag in the middle of the river, recovery would be tricky.

As his team—one K9 officer with two floppy-eared bloodhounds, two search and rescue guys, and two deputies—neared the creek, somehow the whitewater didn't seem quite as loud as it had the night before. Jordan waved away a bug, then realized it was a falling cinder. The morning's heat was undoubtedly fanned by the nearness of the flames.

"Right behind you!" called Silverman, unnecessarily. "Sounds like we're almost there."

"You want me to pepper-spray him, Sheriff?" asked Deputy Narvaez.

"Don't even joke," Jordan answered under his breath, dreading a hot-mic moment. "But I appreciate the offer."

One of the S&R guys was ranging ahead, zigzagging from side to side with his eyes on the ground. He had a reputation as a good tracker and seemed intent on proving it. The dogs were listless and snuffled along without much conviction. If she was here, they'd find her, but Jordan thought it was more likely they'd need the dive team. Not that he would send someone into that water. They might have to use a grappling hook.

He definitely wouldn't want *that* on video.

Suddenly, the dogs got excited. Barking and straining against their leashes, they pulled the handler, Mark somebody, into the trees. Jordan hurried up to follow and the whole party weaved single file through the underbrush.

When Jordan reached the dogs, they were sitting obediently and happily with their tongues lolling. Mark was sitting on his haunches by a decaying log whose north side was abundantly shelved with brown-and-white fan-shaped mushrooms, looking at something on the ground.

"Stand back." Jordan held out an arm to keep everyone from tromping through the scene. "What do you have?"

Mark used a long, slender twig to point out a disturbed pile of leaves. "Blood. Still fairly fresh."

When Silverman's team crashed through the brush and caught up, Jordan didn't even bother to warn him off again.

"Sure don't look like she drowned, now, do it?" chuckled Silverman, folksy accent cranked to the max.

"We have no proof it's hers. Or even human."

"The sign around it looks human," added the S&R tracker helpfully, over Jordan's shoulder. "Deer don't wear sneakers."

"Maybe you couldn't take her alive," said Silverman. "Are we going to find her with a bullet hole in her back?"

Jordan whirled. When he saw an iPhone aimed at him, he chose his words carefully.

"I suggest you avoid making any accusations you're not willing to repeat under oath, Silverman."

"Whoa, whoa, whoa!" Silverman nodded at his henchman, who put the phone away. He finger-combed his hair, then smoothed his L. L. Bean safari shirt. "Don't get ahead of yourself, Jordan. Just kidding around."

Mark lifted the leaves in his hands and gave them a sniff. "Human, I'm pretty sure. Alive, too."

"What do you smell?" asked Jordan.

"Urine. Strong ammonia smell, so I'd say she's dehydrated. That should slow her down."

"Which way did she go?" asked Silverman, crowding in eagerly.

"Easier to tell if you back the fuck up and let my dogs do their job," said Mark cheerfully.

Jordan eyeballed Silverman. "You heard the man."

Everyone backed up while the dog handler, speaking quietly to his bloodhounds, let the dogs inhale the blood-and-urine-soaked leaves. After only a few seconds, he told them, "Suke!" They bayed and began leading him back toward China Creek. But after wagging their tails at the water's edge for a few moments, they headed northeast.

"We've got 'er," said Mark, letting the dogs lead the way.

Jordan grabbed his radio and thumbed the mic, then thought better of it. He had two bars of cell service, so he called Beto on the phone.

"Sheriff?"

"We've got a trail. Probably her but not confirmed. Send those Crocs. I want the dogs to give them a sniff."

"Will do. You'd better get back here, though. We've got a situation."

Beto's voice was cutting in and out, so Jordan wasn't sure he'd heard him right. "Situation?"

"US Marshals. They're here and I think they mean to take over."

TWENTY-SIX
CARA

Follow your own path and respect everyone else's. Hike your own hike, people. #HYOH

The campsite had been right next to a hiking trail, but Cara didn't want to run into the campers. She kept moving through the trees, bushwhacking through brush, clambering around rocks, and crunching along the forest floor while moving steadily downhill. She had no way of knowing how much time had passed, but after what seemed like hours, she eventually found a different trail. At least, she assumed it was a different trail. A boulder with a camel's hump looked familiar, but then, so did a couple others. She was so turned around it was hard to say where she was. Thinking civilization might be somewhere below her, she decided to head uphill.

Walking was so much easier on an established path that even hiking up a switchback was a relief—until she heard voices. Before she could think what to do, a pair of male hikers appeared from above. Headed straight toward her.

Despite her normal-person disguise, Cara's brain fogged with panic.

It was too late to hide, and running into the bushes was something only an escaped prisoner would do, so she crouched and pretended she was looking at a spiny plant with a yellowish berry that looked plump and semi-edible.

Her hunger was no act. Everything was starting to look like food.

"Looks like a gooseberry," she pronounced as they neared, as if she had any fucking idea. As if she was just another chatty hiker. "But I can't be sure because I don't have my guidebook."

The two men stopped just uphill and looked at her with expressions she couldn't quite read.

"Nothing worse than losing something important," said the stockier one, who had a sandy beard and hair.

The other man pointed to a bush within arm's reach. "I'm not sure what your plant is, but these are wax currants." He was handsome and fortyish, like his friend, but taller, leaner, and tanner. Dark curls crept out from underneath his San Francisco 49ers baseball cap.

Both of them were grubby and unwashed, loaded down with full backpacks. They looked like they'd been in the backcountry long enough to have missed the news that an escaped convict was on the loose in the area.

Cara plucked a small red berry from the bush and popped it into her mouth. It was surprisingly tasteless. "How did I miss these?"

"Probably distracted by—"

"I'm Sanjay," the darker-haired, friendlier hiker said. "He's Devin."

Devin scrunched his face but nodded.

Cara uttered the first name that came to mind. "Karoline. With a K."

"Nice to meet you, Karoline with a K. I have some trail mix left if you'd like it." Sanjay reached into the side pocket of his cargo shorts and pulled out a cloudy, quarter-full baggie.

Cara tried not to stare at it. "I couldn't take your food."

"We're packing out after four nights up here," Devin said, confirming her assumption. "We would have stayed one more, but that smoke in the west seems like it's getting closer fast so we're going to clear out."

"Help yourself," Sanjay said. "It's not far to the trailhead."

"In that case, thank you."

She accepted the bag and its half-handful of crumbled nuts, dried fruit, and chocolate chips, willing herself not to dump the whole thing into her mouth. She could gobble it down as soon as the two men walked on.

But neither of them made any move to go.

"You might want to think about getting a move on, yourself," Devin said. "How long have you been up here?"

Cara didn't know how much to say, or not to. "Just a few hours. My friends are down by the river."

"We did some fishing in a little lake. Where is there a river?"

"That way, I think," Cara pointed in what she thought was the right direction.

Sanjay's eyebrows furrowed in concern. "Look, Karoline—is everything OK?"

"Sure," she chirped, too brightly. "Why?"

Devin looked like he wanted to comment but fiddled with the chin strap of his wide-brimmed hat instead.

"I mean, I *was* turned around for a little while there," she continued, rushing on to fill the silence. "This little saddle between hills is a bit confusing, but I know where I am now."

She really needed to get her story together, not just for these two, but anyone else she might encounter.

"Then what happened to your eye?" Sanjay asked with what seemed like genuine concern.

Cara touched her face. It was even more puffy and swollen than it had been that morning, and she could only imagine how it looked. How she looked. "Oh! I slipped while crossing a river last night and the current dragged me a little ways. I know it looks awful but really, it doesn't hurt."

It stung and throbbed.

The two men looked at each other, some kind of silent communication passing between them, before Devin said, "I'm glad you're OK, but none of this explains why you're wearing my shirt and sweatpants."

Shit! Shit! Shit!

"I was looking for them everywhere when we packed up our campsite," he added.

It had occurred to Cara that she could cross paths with the people whose clothing she'd taken—which was why she'd avoided the first trail. She also knew she needed to be on the lookout for a couple—but hadn't considered that the couple sharing a sleeping bag might be a same-sex couple.

#Clueless.

"I'm so, so embarrassed," she stammered, embellishing her story as quickly as she could, knowing it was held together by the thinnest of threads. "My clothes got wet and were basically ruined and I . . . I didn't have anything to change into or . . . I would never have done it if it wasn't absolutely necessary . . . The truth is, I got separated from my friends and the clothes I was wearing got wet and covered in cockleburs. I was so uncomfortable that when I spotted your tent, I couldn't help myself. I'm not a thief, I swear. Which reminds me . . ."

She reached into her pocket, pulled out the money she'd found, and tried to give it back.

Sanjay put his hand up, refusing. "Sounds like you need it."

"I really can't take it," she said in a small voice.

"You already did," Devin pointed out.

Sanjay gave his partner a sharp look. "Keep the money, Karoline."

It was humiliating enough to be caught wearing Devin's clothes. The fact that they were smelly, stained, and had money in the pockets somehow made it worse.

"I'll repay you as soon as I can, I promise," she told them. "If I had my cell, I'd get your contact info right now."

"Our phones are back at the car, too," Sanjay said.

"I told you we should have brought a SAT phone for emergencies," Devin said.

An agree-to-disagree moment passed between them, nonverbal communication that suddenly made her heart ache for Karl and everything she thought she knew about their relationship. What she would have given to grouse at him over gas tank levels, their different definitions of the ideal lazy Sunday, or his pet peeve, heavy appetizers for dinner in lieu of entrées because of the portion-size-to-cost ratio.

If only she could tell him she now knew that any food at all was the best deal ever.

"Your friends have to be frantic," Devin said, his tone warmer, but still without the kindness that seemed to come so easily for his partner.

"I know they are," she said.

She hated lying to them but had no choice. Did they even believe her?

"You're hiking out with us," Sanjay pronounced.

Devin was clearly not as convinced. "I'm not sure our phones even had service at the trailhead."

"If they don't work, we'll take you to the nearest town so you can get in contact with someone who can let your friends know you're safe. Plus, we can't let you hike back toward the fire."

Influencer Cara would have asked them a dozen questions to decide whether she could trust them, and still not trusted them at all. Escapee Cara fell in step between them, with Devin leading the way and Sanjay bringing up the rear.

As they hiked, a butterfly fluttered toward Cara and landed on her shoulder. *Adorkable,* she'd always said when Karl called out the name of any flying creature he found interesting or beautiful. Apparently, she'd paid enough attention to his nerdy hobby to recognize this particular insect as a Gray Hairstreak butterfly, whose orange markings—like backward peering eyes on the wings—were an adaptation against predators.

It had to be a sign.

TWENTY-SEVEN
JORDAN

#IrrigosaFire moving NE toward Yosemite Lakes. Highway 99 has been reopened. Highway 41 closures between Coarsegold and Oakhurst are imminent. Homeowners NE of River Road Estates advised to evacuate immediately.

—@CAL_FIRE

Jordan expected a US Marshal to be a rectangular chunk of man with weathered features, piercing eyes, and a no-BS Texas drawl.

This one had the piercing eyes, but that was about it. She was a fit-looking Asian woman with spiky hair and a loose-jawed surfer accent that sounded wrong coming from someone who wanted to relieve him of his command.

"US Marshal AJ Wen with the Pacific Southwest Regional Task Force," she said, squeezing his hand vigorously.

"Madera County Sheriff Jordan Burke," he said, gripping her hand just as hard.

He waited for her to let go first. Petty, maybe.

Behind Wen, three mismatched men, presumably also US Marshals, leaned against a black Ford Explorer with tinted windows. The wide-shouldered blond one looked like he had to turn sideways to get through doorways. The tall, slender Black one was sizing Jordan up, his mouth pursed like he was holding in a wiseass remark. And the fair-skinned, redheaded woman, if this were a movie, would have been the one who could hack into a criminal mastermind's Swiss bank account from an ordinary laptop.

Beto stood shoulder to shoulder with Jordan, eyeballing the Feds impassively. Jordan knew the deputy had stonewalled them while he angrily retraced his route.

"I welcome your help, even though I would have appreciated a heads-up," said Jordan, hiding his frustration. "But you might have wasted a trip. Before you called me back here, my K9 team found a blood trail and we're following it."

"No offense, Sheriff?" said Wen. "But we haven't, like, been driving since zero-dark-thirty just to turn around and go back home."

"You should have *seen* the traffic on the Five," said the Black guy.

"The only time US Marshals head home is when we have the fugitive in handcuffs," Wen added.

Jordan was starting to take offense. "The *fugitive* is injured and losing blood. It's only a matter of time before we catch up to her."

"That's a pretty big assumption."

"So what do you want here, Wen?"

Wen tilted her head to indicate the people and vehicles around them. "You've got a growing, multiagency operation. Let me coordinate."

Most of his deputies and S&R guys were in the field, but there were still plenty of onlookers. Above the paper masks some of them were now wearing as protection against the thickening smoke, eyes were watching. Ears were listening. Jordan knew he had to handle this without losing his temper. But while he stood here negotiating with the minutes slipping away, Silverman was still shadowing his search party.

"And who gets the credit? You guys?"

"Credit for what?" said the Black guy. "You guys haven't caught her."

"Am I talking to you or this guy?" Jordan asked Wen, hearing an ugly tone in his voice.

"Crosby, chill," warned Wen.

He raised his hands in mock surrender.

"Let's start over?" said Wen. "You need our help, whether you think you do or not. Every major news outlet is scrambling reporters, and if you don't make a quick catch, these guys are going to be, like, camped out inside your butt crack. You ever deal with something like that?"

Jordan couldn't believe what he was hearing. "We're getting chased by wildfire . . . and you called me off a hot trail . . . to tell me I need to hurry up."

Wen glanced around and seemed to realize the onlookers listening to their confrontation were inching closer. She nodded toward the MCP.

"Can we talk in there?"

Seething at the delay, Jordan nodded. There would be fewer witnesses when he flew off the handle.

TWENTY-EIGHT
CARA

She looked feral. Wild-eyed, you know? All she got from us was a protein bar and my favorite fashion sneakers, but I shudder to think what else she would have taken if we had been at the picnic table. Maybe our lives? I mean, she's a murderer.

—Jessica Wohrle, to MSNBC

Karoline Bell from Torrance was a divorced realtor who'd come camping with the title company VP she'd been seeing for the last eighteen months and a group of his work pals.

That story, which Cara had embellished as little as possible, seemed to fly with Sanjay and Devin, whom she'd learned were from the Bay Area, more specifically the Mission District in San Francisco, where they lived on the second floor of a subdivided Victorian house. Sanjay was a social worker, and Devin was in tech sales. They had an overweight tortoiseshell cat named Mona.

Not only did they insist she eat their last handfuls of trail mix as they hiked down the trail toward their vehicle—she picked at it as daintily as she could, chewing one raisin, cashew, or chocolate chip at a time—but they graciously shared their water, too.

"I'm so glad we found you before anything worse happened to you," Sanjay said, before taking a swig and passing the bottle to her.

Cara was careful to waterfall from the bottle, not putting her mouth on the rim. She wanted them to know that even though she'd stolen from them, she was a good person, respectful of boundaries.

"How did you get separated from your friends in the first place, again?" Devin asked.

"There are only two women in the group—me and the wife of one of my boyfriend's coworkers," she said. "We both had to go to the bathroom but went in different directions for privacy. She must have finished first and thought I was already done. When I went back to where we'd split up, she wasn't there."

"She just left you behind?" Sanjay asked, sounding genuinely concerned for her well-being.

"I'm sure she didn't mean to." Cara hated lying to these truly nice men. "But I don't know her very well, or really any of them."

"Except your boyfriend, of course," Devin said.

"Jordan is . . ." she surprised herself by using the sheriff's first name. "He hikes faster than everyone."

"Surely he came looking for you?" Sanjay asked.

"Oh, definitely. It's my fault for not staying in one place."

"If you ask me, he doesn't sound like all that great of a guy," Devin muttered.

"Well, to be honest . . ." Cara was planning to make something up about him pursuing her a lot more heavily than she'd expected, saying their relationship probably wasn't going to last, anyway, when a middle-aged couple came into sight below them.

Climbing the hill with their small backpacks and matching purple trekking poles, they had to be day hikers. They could very well have heard the latest news about the infamous Cara Campbell.

Shit. Shit. Shit.

Sanjay and Devin politely stepped off the trail as they approached. Cara crouched, pretending to tie her shoe. Had they seen her face?

"Howdy," the man said, pausing when he should have kept going past.

"How smoky is it up there?" his wife asked. "I have asthma."

Cara herself could barely breathe.

"Blue skies on the eastern side," Devin said. "But the smoke is coming in fast from the west."

Cara wondered how long she could possibly fiddle with her laces. She could feel eyes on the back of her head but didn't want to give them a better look. Surely they'd been listening to the radio and learning all about the dangerous fugitive terrorizing the hills.

"Hear that, Rob?" she said. "Maybe we should turn around."

Keep going, Cara beseeched the woman silently. *Nothing to see here. Just three friends hiking.*

"It's not that bad, Joan," said Husband Rob. "Just a little bit further."

Joan assented in silence as they finally moved on.

"Be careful," Sanjay called after them.

Cara hung back so Sanjay and Devin wouldn't see how badly her legs were shaking.

That was, until she heard the sound of barking dogs in the distance. Then she began to power walk.

TWENTY-NINE
JORDAN

This whole thing would make a great women-in-prison movie. Rated X, I hope.

—@TarantinoIsGod

Jordan led the way into the repurposed RV that served as the department's mobile command post and saw Wen take in the pictures of hot rods and gun-toting women in bikinis that covered the walls. None of his deputies had bothered to take down the decor chosen by its former owner, a local tax attorney serving a twenty-year sentence for distributing drugs, because they found it amusing. Or maybe they liked it. Jordan hadn't bothered to weigh in—a decision he now regretted.

"Give us a minute," he told the surprised-looking members of his communications team.

While they stepped out, leaving the crackling radio unmonitored, Wen opened the fridge and helped herself to a bottled water.

"Want one?" she asked.

Jordan shook his head. "I'm good."

"Suit yourself." Wen sat down and tucked her knees under the small table. "So, do you remember five years ago, when an LA County Jail bus got hijacked by inmates and there was, like, that slow-motion chase down the 405?"

"Sure."

She unscrewed the cap of her water bottle and took a small sip. "Yeah, so, the lead on that particular situation had the bright idea to just let them keep driving. You know, let them get out of rush-hour traffic and box them in in a less populated area. Obviously, no one was going to let them drive to Tijuana, right?"

Jordan, still standing, didn't answer. Even he remembered how that one had ended.

"I mean, they were trying to escape. So why would they ram a church bus that was trying to pull out of their way? Why would they crash and burn when most of them were chained to their seats?"

Wen's tone had changed from matter-of-fact to something like wonderment.

"That was horrible, but it wasn't the good guys' fault," said Jordan. "They weren't driving the bus. And I'm not sure how that relates to our situation. We have one badly injured woman, on foot in the woods."

"My point is that everyone is watching and waiting for you to blow it." She swallowed more water, then screwed the cap back on the water bottle. "But I can help stop you from, like, letting your case explode? So to speak."

"No offense, but you're a long way from LA freeways. You planning to pound the trail in those?"

Wen straightened one leg and looked at her shoe, a leather stacked loafer that would give her feet zero traction or protection on a rocky trail.

"You really think Clawhammer Karen is going to hike the Pacific Crest Trail? First chance she gets, she's making a beeline to a beauty parlor."

Jordan couldn't help but admit to himself that that had been his own initial assessment. Doubt had taken up residence inside his objections. A mistake now could cost him the election. But shouldn't the mistakes be his? It wouldn't sit right, blaming anything on the Feds.

Letting them run his operation didn't, either.

A fist hammered hard on the flimsy door of the MCP. Beto shouted through it.

"Sheriff! Marshal! Get out of there NOW!"

THIRTY
CARA

Whole thing is fuckin staged bro. She never went anywhere. Or if she did, she just laughin and sippin Cristal in the limo. Shit.

—@alleyezonme_O_O

The barking grew louder as the wind shifted toward them. After hiking twenty minutes in tense silence, Cara finally saw, through a break in the trees, a road and a half-dozen parked cars.

Thank God.

"You're like a racehorse running back to the barn," Sanjay said.

"I just really need to . . . pay a visit to the outhouse," she told him.

A horrible-smelling, fly-ridden public shitter was the only thing Cara could think of that might put the dogs off her scent.

"I guess we'll catch up to you there," Devin said.

She sped up. "See you shortly!"

At the trailhead, the cars were dusty and the outhouse was empty. Karoline from Torrance dove right in. It was a chance to catch her breath—more like hold it, given the olfactory assault. She stayed inside, breathing through her mouth, until she heard the crunch of Sanjay and Devin's boots.

And fat rubber tires kicking rocks.

She climbed onto the toilet seat and peered out the vent on the back wall. A Madera Fire District SUV pulled into the small lot and stopped beside Devin and Sanjay.

What were the chances he hadn't been briefed about missing fugitive Cara Campbell?

Cara balanced over the blue-tinted, almost overflowing cesspool as the fireman rolled down his window.

"I'm about to close this trailhead due to fire danger," he told her new friends.

"We're actually on our way out," said Devin.

"Headed back to Fresno?"

"San Francisco, actually."

"In that case, take 49 to 140 to I-5. Highway 41 is closed to non-essential travel south of Oakhurst."

"You got it," said Sanjay.

Cara closed her eyes and exhaled so deeply that she forgot to hold her nose when she breathed back in.

Someone rapped on the door.

"Karoline!" called Devin. "My turn."

The fireman had pulled into a space next to the trailhead's information board, but she couldn't stay inside.

All she could do was lean into her hiker-girl persona and hope for the best.

"Delightful, like roses in here!" she said, opening the door and waving her hand in front of her nose.

Devin shucked off his backpack. "Can't wait."

"Want me to take that back to the car for you?" she asked.

"OK, sure."

Cara hoisted the backpack, which must have weighed fifty pounds, even without food, and went looking for Sanjay.

Who, it turned out, was loading into a black Jeep right next to the fireman's truck.

Cara angled her body, doing her best to keep the bulky backpack between her and the fireman, who was stapling a warning to the plywood information board.

Nothing to see here. Just three friends finishing up a hiking trip.

Cara handed Devin's bag to Sanjay, who tossed it in the back of the Jeep. Then, as he opened the passenger side door, she kept her head down, pretending to move things around. When she risked a peek at the fireman, he was reading the visitor's log. Probably counting how many hikers were still out on the trail—those who had bothered to sign in.

Suddenly, Sanjay was beside her again, offering her a heather-gray T-shirt with a Batman logo.

"It's clean," he said.

"I'm embarrassed to have the one I'm wearing. I don't want to—"

"Trade Devin's favorite hiking shirt for a clean one? I think I speak for everyone when I say it's a good idea. That is, if you plan to get in the car with us."

"Deal."

Cara took the shirt and moved several vehicles away to change into it.

The fireman was talking on the phone as Devin returned from the outhouse. Why wouldn't he leave?

"Karoline!" called Sanjay. "Let's go!"

She hurried back, gave Devin the dirty shirt, and jumped in the back seat.

As Devin backed out of the parking space and swung the Jeep around, the barking was so loud that she expected the dogs to burst out of the trees at any moment. Cara couldn't help looking—and found herself locking eyes with the fireman, only ten feet away.

Did he recognize her?

Go! Go! Go! she shouted silently.

THIRTY-ONE
JORDAN

Thanks for all the tips, crime fam. Keep 'em coming!
—@deathtripdylan

Jordan stumbled out of the MCP into unfolding chaos. A swirling wind fanned sparks and cinders from the trees like the bellows of a blacksmith's forge. The TV crews were throwing gear into their vans and climbing inside while a straggler tried to capture it all using her phone's camera. Everyone else was running for their cars, but access to the road was blocked by an unoccupied vehicle for which nobody seemed to have the keys. A deputy's vehicle and an S&R truck were jockeying at each other, each one trying to be the first one to get through the narrow space that remained.

Jordan saw the red glow and felt the heat on his face before he heard the roar. A wall of fire was a hundred yards away and closing in fast. There was no time to wonder how it had gotten so close so quickly.

"Evacuate your team *now*," he told Wen.

"Got it," she said. "We know a little something about fire in LA, too, you know."

Fortunately, she jogged away. They'd settle the jurisdictional bullshit later.

Beto was already directing traffic. Jordan joined him, barking orders and waving his arms to make sure no one panicked and crashed a departmental vehicle. He wished his team would be more levelheaded, but who could be calm when faced with the prospect of getting cooked to death?

"Where should we regroup?" Jordan shouted.

His chief deputy thought for a moment before he answered. "Parking lot of the Seventh Day Adventist church. Should be safe, and it won't be in use."

Jordan gave the instruction over his radio, then started shouting it into open car windows for good measure.

The rising dust was almost as bad as the billowing smoke, but after only a few minutes, he had managed to direct an orderly evacuation. Jordan watched the MCP lumber safely toward the road just ahead of the fire.

Then the radio suddenly spiked in volume. Several voices went back and forth excitedly, static blending with the crackling of grass and wood. He grabbed the mic.

"Everybody, quiet if you're not the one making a report," he ordered. "Now, give me the information again."

Narvaez's voice: "We found an orange jumpsuit. Definitely Campbell's. But we think she changed her clothes."

"Unless she's really going back to nature," muttered Beto.

"OK, good work," Jordan told Narvaez. "Go get her."

"Well, about that. The K9 team followed her to a trailhead but lost the scent."

"Trailhead where?"

"Thornberry Mountain."

"Where can she go from there?"

A pause. Then: "Lots of places. We think she got in someone's car."

THIRTY-TWO
CARA

This is Troy Silverman, your future sheriff. Me and my team were just part of a boots on the ground operation in the hunt for missing convicted murderer Cara Campbell. I can tell you firsthand this whole thing is a disaster. Jordan Burke's bozos have bungled this from minute one. And they nearly got me killed in the process. Watch this space for a livestream update.

—Silverman for Sheriff Facebook page

Cara leaned back on the utilitarian bench seat as Devin and Sanjay's Jeep moved swiftly along the narrow mountain road.

Her immediate relief at leaving the search dogs and fireman behind was tempered by her lack of a master plan. Where was she going to go? What was she going to do when her rescuers' phones got service and alerts from their news apps started pinging? All she could think to do was keep the back doors unlocked so she could jump out from either side the second they figured out she wasn't Karoline Bell from the South Bay but Cara Campbell from Beverly Hills. The fall would probably kill her, and that would be that. But what else was new?

Devin reached for the dashboard stereo and pressed the radio button.

Shit.

"Driver's choice," he said, choosing the preset for the Sirius Grateful Dead channel.

Sanjay rolled his eyes as the wheezy harmonies of *Sugar Magnolia* filled the cab.

"My hus—ex-husband really likes the Dead," Cara sputtered.

"Hope it's not too bumpy back there," Sanjay said. "This road sure is twisty."

Her car sickness was definitely Dramamine-worthy, but at least the rough road and the loud music had masked her flub. "Totally fine."

Sanjay chatted amiably about Devin's new Jeep (*not very practical in the city but perfect for here!)* and the increased fire danger (*my throat is starting to bother me, how about yours?*) He also kept checking the phones to show her they didn't have service.

"Sorry the route is taking us further out of cell range," he said, seemingly trying to ease her mind about being in a car with two virtual strangers.

She couldn't express just how *not* worried about them she was, or how downright happy she felt to be sitting in a vehicle heading swiftly away to anywhere.

As Devin slowed down to navigate a tricky bend with a steep drop-off on her side of the car, Cara slid over, just in case she had to make a quick exit. After a while, the road straightened out and they rolled into a tiny town with a gas station, a crystal shop offering tarot readings, and a country store. It gave her an idea.

"I'm sure there's a place I can make a call around here," she said. A fake call to connect with her "boyfriend" enabled her to make an excuse and say goodbye. That would give her some breathing room to figure out where to go and who, if anyone, she could trust to help her. Her rescuers had moved her precious miles away from her pursuers, but she couldn't stay with them much longer. And she had thirty dollars to help her survive the day. It felt like a fortune.

Sanjay pointed to a roadside café and gift store called Grits 'n' Gifts. "Let's try that diner. I'm hungry, anyway."

Devin pulled in and parked.

One step inside the place and Cara was nearly overcome by the dizzying aroma of burgers, fries, coffee, and pancakes with maple syrup. It was all she could do to stop herself from opening the rotating dessert case and face-planting into a slice of chocolate cream, Dutch apple, or strawberry rhubarb pie.

"Do you have a pay phone?" Devin asked the hostess before she could.

"In the hallway between the restrooms, but someone's on it," said the hostess, whose youth and purple hair reminded Cara of Bree. "Table for three?"

"Yes, please," Sanjay said.

"You don't have to feed me," Cara said. That definitely wasn't part of the plan. "I'll just wait here and—"

"Drool over pie?" Devin said. "Come on. Sit down with us."

The purple-haired girl grabbed three laminated menus and led them into the crowded, wood-paneled restaurant. Cara had no choice but to lower her head, doing her best to hide her swollen eye, and follow her hiking companions. She was hoping for a table in the back, but their booth was right up front. Cara slid into a cracked brown Naugahyde bench with her back to the hostess stand.

Sanjay and Devin sat down opposite her as a waitress appeared with a black plastic carafe. "Coffee?"

Sanjay nodded and she put it down on the table. "Be back in a sec to get your order."

Cara had given up caffeine and dairy three years ago, but after the first sip of perfect diner coffee, she couldn't remember why.

"Chicken-fried steak for me," Devin said after briefly scanning the menu. "I mean, when in Rome . . ."

"Et tu, Karoline?" Sanjay asked.

"I'm thinking the all-day country breakfast." She looked up at the clock and noted it was just after two.

"I'll order for you so you can make your call. How do you like your eggs?"

"Scrambled, please."

"Sausage or bacon?"

"Bacon. Thanks."

Cara stood up and headed for the front hallway.

The OG payphone hanging from the wall was so authentic, it even had a worn phone book encased in an aluminum cover hanging from a metal cord. Sanjay and Devin couldn't see her from their table, so she spent the time it would have taken to make a call to instead go into the ladies', where she washed her hands and face—and as luck would have it, scored a tampon from a woman who was on her way out.

When she returned, only Devin was at the table.

"Where's Sanjay?" she asked.

"He's never met a gift shop he couldn't get lost in. Did you get ahold of whoever you needed to?"

"I had to call directory assistance, which amazingly still exists, to get the number for my boyfriend's company," she said, inventing details with increasing ease. "Jordan's administrative assistant will leave messages for him and a couple of the other people on the hike, telling them to meet me here."

"You must be really relieved."

"So relieved." She took a long sip of coffee and chased it with ice water. "I really do plan to pay you guys back for all your kindness as soon as I get to my phone. What's your Venmo?"

"Just pay it forward," Devin said.

She really couldn't have stolen from nicer people.

"Seriously."

"You'll never remember mine, but Sanjay's is @thejay."

"Got it."

Could she even access her Venmo? And what about her spending account? The police would be alerted immediately. Even if Fugitive Cara could open a new bank account, how was she going to make any money to deposit? She pictured herself washing dishes for cash under the counter, like a road-weary criminal in a black-and-white noir movie. Or worse.

Neither of them said anything for an uncomfortably long beat.

Finally, Devin spoke. "It could take a while. Do you think we should let the local authorities know, just in case—"

"None of the people on the hike brought their phones, either, so they can't contact anyone and won't be able to hear the messages until they make it out," she said quickly.

"Well, that could take hours."

"I'm totally fine. If I get bored, I've got the gift shop. Or I can head down the street to the crystal shop. I'm just happy to have food and a bathroom."

She wasn't lying.

"Speaking of the bathroom, I need to wash my hands," Devin said.

The waitress arrived with three overflowing plates of food a moment after he left. Devin's chicken-fried steak was smothered in gravy alongside a pile of thick-cut fries. Sanjay had apparently ordered a Cobb salad with a waffle on the side. Cara was dying to dig into her eggs, or cut into her pancakes, or eat one of the fries that had fallen off Devin's plate onto the table.

She tried to wait.

Couldn't.

Cara allowed herself one, then two bites of her home fries, which were every bit as crunchy, salty, oily, and delicious as she imagined. She took a tiny taste of her eggs before she made herself stop. She really couldn't keep eating—not without letting them know their food had arrived.

Reluctantly, she got up from the table and went looking for Sanjay in the gift shop. She saw him right away, but before she could say his name, she saw Devin with him, partially hidden by a row of mugs and decorative shot glasses.

"You assume everyone is in some sort of crisis," Devin was telling Sanjay.

"We found her alone in the woods, desperate enough to wear your filthy T-shirt."

"You hate that shirt. I would have thought you'd be happy to have it stolen."

"Be serious, Devin. We both saw how banged up she is. She tried to hide when she changed, but I saw her. It looked like someone beat the shit out of her and dragged her around."

"She seemed happy enough on the hike out."

"When people are in real trouble, they deflect. And she never made that phone call. I saw her go straight into the bathroom."

Shit.

"But she didn't want me to call the local authorities."

"Because they'll just deliver her into the hands of the monster who caused those injuries. The lady at the register told me there's a family crisis center in Merced. Let's feed her and then we'll drive her there."

She had to go. Now.

With one last, longing look at the pie case, Cara waited until the hostess glanced down at her cell phone, then slipped out the front door.

THIRTY-THREE
JORDAN

The increasing frequency and intensity of wildfires is merely one more symptom of an ailing planet.

—*@ClimateReality*

"Sheriff Burke! Sandy Rivers, ABC 30 Action News. Can you confirm that Cara Campbell is still on the run?"

Jordan had just pulled in, taking the first available space in the parking lot of Oakhurst Adventist Church. He hadn't even seen the reporter who stuck her microphone in his face the moment he opened the door of his vehicle. As he climbed out, more reporters crowded around, including some he hadn't seen at the gravel turnout they'd just evacuated. The media monitored police scanners, he knew. But how had they all gotten here so fast?

The MCP's driver was still in the process of parking on the other side of the lot, so Jordan had no choice but to make his way through the scrum.

"We were tracking her location only minutes ago," he told the reporter as he started walking. "We're right behind her. Recapture is imminent."

As the journalists moved with him, it was like trying to navigate in the middle of a football huddle. Jordan couldn't even see the ground due to the press of bodies. He was acutely aware of their microphones and phones with flashing red RECORD buttons.

"If you know where she is, why haven't you picked her up yet?"

This reporter, a pink-skinned bro type, looked fresh out of college. Jordan recognized him from KMPH, the local Fox News affiliate.

Because I thought she was dead. Because she had a head start. Because she has no idea what she's doing so we can't predict what she's going to do. Because wildfires, dumb shit.

"We're close," he said curtly.

Then a warmly resonant voice rose above the din. "Jack Schapiro, CNN."

Jordan turned his head, slowing slightly. National media. Just like Wen predicted.

"Sheriff Jordan, a source tells me you confronted Campbell last night, but she got away," said Shapiro. "Can you explain to us what happened?"

Someone in his department leaked, that's what happened. But who? Jordan had always thought of his force as a family. They didn't always get along, but they always put each other first. Clearly, someone else saw things differently.

Jordan quickened his pace. He was halfway across the parking lot.

"I'll make a full report on the operation when the time is right," he said, meeting Schapiro's steady gaze. "But right now, we're in the middle of an active search and every second counts."

"KVPR, Elias Sotelo," said a reedy voice. "Can you tell how many people have been evacuated due to the Coarsegold Fire?"

"I don't have current information on that. Try Cal Fire."

"Troy Silverman, candidate, Madera County Sheriff," boomed a voice behind him.

Jordan couldn't help himself. He stopped and turned. Silverman's Bronco was idling in the middle of the lot, and Silverman himself stood outside its open door. His hair was wild, his face was smudged with soot, and his clothes were dotted with cinder burns.

The reporters all turned, too, aiming their microphones at Silverman as he spoke.

"Can you tell me why your deputies deliberately led search and rescue volunteers into harm's way?" he asked theatrically. "We were lucky to escape with our lives."

Jordan took a deep breath as the microphones—and cameras, he now noticed—swung back toward him. "My deputies are brave men and women who put their lives on the line every day. Our S&R volunteers are just as brave. Everyone here should know, however, that you—"

"Nearly died." Silverman interrupted before Jordan could say he had inserted himself into the situation. "While the sheriff here was coolin' his heels in his RV, we were closin' in on Cara Campbell. But nobody at the top thought to warn us, let us know we were in the crosshairs of a fast-movin' wildfire."

Jordan shouldn't have stopped. Now he was facing away from the MCP, and worse, he had allowed Silverman to bait him into a public confrontation. Video of him turning his back on Silverman would be all over the ten o'clock news.

"We all truly appreciate your help, Troy," he said through gritted teeth.

Then—screw it.

"If the danger's too much for you," he couldn't help adding, "maybe you're not suited to the office of sheriff."

Never had camera lenses felt so much like eyes to Jordan. The journalists quieted and leaned forward, eager to watch the fireworks.

"Is this a campaign event to you?" shouted Silverman, impressively irate. "Because it sure isn't to me!"

A hand pulled Jordan's sleeve insistently. He turned and found himself face to face with Wen.

"Sheriff Burke will have to finish talking to you later," she announced. "I have very important information for him that can't wait."

Equal parts galled and grateful, he let her pull him through the crowd so forcefully he almost lost his footing. Moments later, they were inside the MCP again. This time they huddled in the bedroom-turned-storage room to avoid disrupting his comms team.

"What do you have to tell me?" he asked.

"That, like, facing the media is harder than it looks?"

He examined her expression carefully but found no trace of gloating or self-satisfaction.

"I think I may have come to that conclusion on my own."

She shrugged. "Your move. So what do you want to do now?"

On the wall behind her was a large, glossy poster of an oiled woman in a camo bikini, fondling an AR-15. Jordan reached out, tore it off the wall, and crumpled it.

"Let's bring her in."

THIRTY-FOUR
CARA

Another L.A. vegan repents.
—@Eatmeatitsneat

With its hickory facade and hand-carved sign, Ye Olde Country Market looked like the kind of place that would have farm-fresh produce, homemade muffins, and maybe even an actual pickle barrel.

A bell jingled as Cara pushed through the door. Inside, it was little more than a small countrified grocery store with a rusty cooler of *LIVE BAIT* near the entrance. Since abandoning her all-day country breakfast back at the diner, she was so hungry that she might actually have considered eating a worm. She grabbed a Slim Jim instead. Never had one looked so appealing.

You're eating yourself into oblivion, her mom would whisper under her breath, can of Tab in hand, whenever Cara picked out a Reese's or a pack of M&Ms at a gas station. *Successful men are attracted to shapely but slender women.* As an adult, she sometimes succumbed to the allure of a Tootsie Roll, which lasted longer and was fat-free, or made a bargain with herself: if she didn't buy anything, she could splurge at the next stop.

Cara felt a film of syrup and potato grease on her fingers as she scanned the produce and settled on a slightly bruised banana. If she were smarter, she would have taken at least one bite of everything on her plate before finding Devin and Sanjay. She grabbed a yogurt from the dairy section, three protein bars, the Reese's she always wanted, a generic water bottle she could refill at water fountains, and a small package of tampons. Plucking an area map and a bus map from a carousel near the front of the store, she headed for the register.

A shopper materialized behind her as she placed her purchases on the conveyor. Instead of pushing her cart into the line, the woman stepped in close, bent over, and grabbed a Milky Way from the bottom shelf of the checkout display.

When she stood, she eyed Cara up and down.

"OMG!" she gasped, pulling out her phone. "You're the woman they're . . . you're Cara—"

"I must have left my credit card in my car," Cara told the cashier, pretending to check her pockets as she speed-walked toward the door. "Be right back."

She was outside and behind the store, where no one from the highway could see her, before she realized the Slim Jim was still in her hand.

Being a fugitive had caused her to steal yet again—something she would have never, ever done. For the first time in her life, she really was on a crime spree.

She thought about dropping it, but then it would be wasted. Would an animal try to eat a meat stick wrapped in plastic?

She was far from out of the woods. Figuratively and literally.

Cara peeled open the plastic wrapper, broke the Slim Jim into pieces, and shoved the whole thing into her mouth. Then she started running up the hill behind the store.

THIRTY-FIVE

JORDAN

Check this video OUT! @carasloveisgold in the flesh! Badly in need of moisturizer but alive and well at the general store. #CaraOnTheLoose #Fugitive #AmericasMostWanted #Influencer #InfluencerLyfe #GlamLife #BadHairDay #Busted

—@momneedswine77

Lights flashing and siren howling, Jordan slalomed from lane to lane on a road so narrow there wasn't much shoulder for drivers to get out of his way. He knew this road well; Wen didn't. He had lost her some miles back.

The tip had been another Amber Alert, a text from his wife with siren emojis and a link to a TikTok video. When he opened it, it took him a moment to cut through the audiovisual overkill—subtitles competing with captions and a song that had been added as a soundtrack—and see what was actually happening.

It was her. Cara Campbell had a black eye and was wearing sweatpants and a T-shirt as she tried to check out at the cash register at Ye Olde Country Store. She still had a Slim Jim in her hand as she hurried away from the TikToker. According to Amber, it had been posted twelve minutes ago.

Somehow Cara had gotten eleven miles away from the Thornberry Mountain Trailhead and somehow she'd found some money. Hitchhiking? Begging?

If he couldn't catch her now, he would canvass for more witnesses.

Ten minutes later, he braked to a halt in front of the store. A dozen people were milling around out front, talking and showing each other their phones. Nothing moved faster than social media.

He killed the lights and siren and stepped out of the car. "Has anyone here seen Cara Campbell?"

"Yeah, we all did, dude," said a kid with a braided chin beard and an embroidered Mexican blouse.

"In person," Jordan clarified.

The kid looked down at his phone and shrugged. Nobody else volunteered.

He tried again, raising his voice. "Did any of you take the video of Cara Campbell in the store that was posted to TikTok?"

A woman in shorts and an *I READ BANNED BOOKS* T-shirt smiled and shook her head. "I think she left before I got here."

Jordan realized that several people in the group were now aiming their phones at him. He was about to be all over the internet. He ducked inside the store—then, as everyone started to follow him inside, opened the door to address them.

"I need you all to stay outside. This is an active investigation." Seeing looks ranging from resignation to outrage, he added, "I appreciate your cooperation."

Only one of the two checkout lanes was open. The cashier was talking to a stock boy, who backed away nervously as Jordan approached.

"She was totally just here!" the cashier told Jordan with a broad smile. "See?"

Jordan looked down at the conveyor belt. A nonfat vanilla yogurt, three granola bars, and a package of Reese's peanut butter cups, plus a Mountain Spring water and a small box of Tampax. Which made him realize something about the blood trail. She might not be injured after all, which would explain why she was covering so much ground.

"I didn't touch it in case you need to dust for fingerprints or something," said the cashier proudly.

"Smart move," Jordan said politely. "It would help even more if you can show me your security video."

"No can do."

"Look, a warrant's going to take too long. Every minute matters right now."

"I don't have the access code. You think my manager trusts me with shit like that? I'm lucky she lets me handle money, and I'm a cashier."

"Get her."

No sooner had the cashier picked up his phone than Jordan realized he was wasting his time. The TikTok was the security video. It gave a better close-up than the ceiling-mounted camera would provide.

Think.

Campbell tried to buy supplies, got recognized, and ran. Where would she run? If she was smart, she wouldn't risk going back on the road. And she had survived a good number of cross-country miles already.

In the video, it had looked like she was headed for the motion-activated front doors, where the pack of rubberneckers was now looking in.

Jordan didn't want to go out the front.

The cashier was bargaining with his manager: "Look, if you give me the code, I can show him the video, and you can change the code tonight. This is a police investigation . . . Yes, he's the sheriff. He has the hat and everything."

Jordan pushed through a swinging door at the back of the store. He made his way past an unused kitchen and food-prep area, through a crowded stockroom, to the back doors. Outside, on the other side of an asphalt pad for delivery trucks, a tree-studded hill sloped steeply upward.

A red-and-white scrap of something at its base. He moved closer.

A Slim Jim wrapper.

Jordan walked back and forth until he found disturbed earth. Her feet had slid as she climbed.

He radioed it in and started to follow.

THIRTY-SIX
CARA

Jail is NOT kind to women with fine, brittle hair. Announcing my GoFundMe for @carasloveisgold's haircare commissary account.

—@JamiesCuts4LessOKC

The shadows had lengthened, and the air held the last warm breath of afternoon heat as Cara continued moving uphill, deeper into the woods and farther from the little town. As she ran, she found herself thinking about Sanjay and Devin. Sanjay would be distraught when he learned he had aided and abetted a fugitive. While she suspected Devin would find the whole encounter amusing (and be consoled by the fact that he hadn't lost his favorite black shirt to a convicted murderer) she hated what the shock might do to sweet Sanjay's trust in humanity.

She could practically hear Devin telling him, *I told you so.*

Cara hoped she hadn't given them anything but nice things to say about her and that they were telling everyone who would listen: *Yes, she stole from us, but she was so apologetic. She really looked beaten and bruised. It never occurred to us that she was Cara Campbell.*

Devin's voice continued to echo in her ear as she continued on into the middle of nowhere. At least, that's where she thought she had arrived—until she spotted a cluster of dilapidated buildings in a nearby clearing. It was a fenced compound consisting of two or three old trailers that had been welded together, as well as a Quonset barn and just enough rusty car parts and farm equipment to convince her the rutted, weedy dirt track leading to the compound wasn't a creek bed but a road. The gates were padlocked and the whole place looked abandoned.

Creeping forward for a better look, she spotted a watering trough with a spigot inside the open-sided Quonset barn.

The need for water trumped her fear.

She hung back until she was sure there was no movement inside any of the buildings or the Frankensteined mobile-home mansion. The two trailers in the front were identical except for their colors, one a faded orange-and-white, the other flat gray. The small opaque slider windows on each side were probably bathrooms. One large window was boarded up and another had closed curtains. A rough-hewn deck wrapped around the entire front.

Cara sprinted over to a patch of tall grass bordering the back of the barn and crawled on her hands and knees to the gate. She waited, listening, hearing only the chuckling clucks of chickens somewhere on the property. Then she climbed over the rusty fence, stepped around some cow or whatever pies, and crept into the barn.

She approached the trough, turned the spigot, and gulped water as fast as she could.

Two brownish, fuzzy sheep were peering at her from the far side of the trough.

"Are you guys thirsty?" she asked, only slightly terrified. Did sheep bite?

She sensed movement behind her and turned. A large black goat with white eyebrows and a chin beard had appeared in the doorway to the open barn, blocking the exit.

She'd done goat yoga, but with adorable baby pygmy goats, not a full-sized goat with yellow teeth and knobby horns.

He gave her a nudge.

"How about a little drink for you, too?" she asked nervously, hoping that was all he wanted.

While the goat put its head into the trough, she stepped over and grabbed a coat—military green and smelling of musk and mutton—from a nearby hook. Below the jacket hung a pair of giant shears. Unlike regular scissors, they looked like two large triangular knives attached by a vinyl-coated squeeze grip. Her next thought surprised her—that she should cut a tuft of wool from one of the sheep, rinse it, and use it for a not-so-sanitary pad.

She'd had worse ideas.

The shears were spring-loaded, and the handles squeezed together like those old-timey hand strengtheners. When they heard the blades scrape together, the sheep bleated loudly and backed away.

But then she had another idea.

The grocery shopper's video of Cara, capturing her leaving the store like a bandanna'd Bigfoot, would be all over the internet. Feeling one of her hair extensions—which now had the consistency of Barbie doll hair that had been washed with dish soap—she grabbed a hunk and snipped it off.

Cara had made it halfway around her head before she realized the animals had suddenly gone completely quiet.

Then she heard the unmistakable sound of a shotgun racking.

She whirled around. Holding the shotgun was a grizzled, muscular man in a yellow tank top with a hissing cobra on the front. He had a shock of wavy gray hair, and a full, long beard to match. The glint in his blue-gray eyes seemed to say he wasn't afraid to use the weapon.

"I'm not dangerous!" she blurted.

He eyeballed her for a moment.

"Are you sure?" he said. "Because you're holding my sheep shears, and you look like a Victorian mental patient."

THIRTY-SEVEN
JORDAN

Joining the search for @Carasloveisgold. #HowHardCanItBe #InstagrammerInAHaystack #TrackingIsTheTits

—@MyNameIsBob_JAMES_Bob

Jordan kept his eyes on the ground as he worked his way through the trees. His progress was slow, but from what he could see, Campbell was slowing down, too. Her scramble up the hill had been wild, with her slips and trips clearly marked on the ground. But she would have quickly grown winded—the climb left him breathing hard, too. As the slope became more gentle, she left fewer obvious signs and her trail became more difficult to follow.

Most of his tracking experience had been earned on hunting trips with his dad as they followed the blood sign left by dying deer or elk. But he had learned a lot from observing S&R trackers, too, for whom the smallest disturbances on the forest floor told a larger story. The most important lesson? Tracking was never as fast as running. Patience was the key.

As he covered the mile or so since leaving the market, about thirty minutes of hiking, he'd been on the radio the whole time, directing the search operation. His deputies had arrived to interview potential witnesses while the team back at the MCP pored over maps to triangulate all the routes Campbell might take based on Jordan's updates. He had ordered vehicles to patrol the surrounding roads and managed to finally call a helicopter off fire duty to search from above. And the dogs were coming up behind. He could already hear them barking.

Fortunately, Marshal Wen wasn't on Jordan's radio frequency. He'd gotten two missed calls and several texts from an unknown number—*SHERIFF CALL ME NOW THIS IS WEN*—before his cell coverage evaporated again.

He was typically not afraid to ask for or accept help, even from outside agencies. But what could these Angelenos do for him in the trees? He was so agonizingly close. And with the story going national, spreading even faster than the wildfires, he desperately wanted the win.

Beto called him on the radio. "Sheriff? Wen wants me to put her through."

"Tell her you can't raise me," he answered.

"Um . . . pretty sure she just heard that. She's standing right here."

Jordan swore, then thumbed the mic. "Put her on."

"Were you *trying* to lose us?" demanded Wen.

"I'm trying to catch Campbell. I found a sign and followed it."

"Leaving four reinforcements behind."

"No offense, but you would have slowed me down. I'm on her trail and she's unarmed. I don't need backup."

"You had her one-on-one last night, and we're all still out here."

Jordan dropped the transceiver and kneeled. Had the slim green branch been recently broken? It was hard to tell. But there—in the fine, dry dust, about the size of a playing card, was her tread pattern. She had spotted an easier route and was taking it. Jordan knew it would lead her into a gentle bowl between two ridges. Broader than a ravine, not quite a canyon.

He also knew what she would find there.

"Did I, like, hurt your feelings, Sheriff?" Wen's staticky voice sounded more amused than sarcastic.

"This time she won't have a river to jump into."

"Maybe she'll jump off a cliff."

"She's headed toward Black Bear Road. That's four-wheel drive only.

Assuming Beto is still listening in, he'll direct you, as well as other members of our team. The Sheriff's Department of Madera County is happy to cooperate with the US Marshals Service. Just don't show up like a bunch of cowboys because I don't want to scare her off."

"No offense, but you're the cowboy," said Wen. "We're the city slickers, remember?"

THIRTY-EIGHT
CARA

Is there a seven-word sentence scarier than, "It places the lotion in the basket?" #ClassicHorror

—@FilmFanForty

Cara couldn't decide if she was more afraid of the wild-haired, gun-toting mountain man or the ominous *thwap* of the approaching helicopter.

"You don't have to worry too much about those whirlybirds," the man said. "They look for heat signatures, and you happen to be standing ass-deep in domesticated ruminants."

"What makes you think I'm worried about helicopters?" she asked, not looking up.

The man chuckled, which only made her feel dumb for playing dumb—and that much more worried.

"They only come around here when something's on fire." He pointed toward the horizon, where the red sun was lowering toward a dense wall of smoke. "If they can spare one, it must mean they're looking for something important. *Someone* important."

"Not all that important," she mumbled.

"And here you are, in my barn, chopping off your hair with my sheep shears."

"It's not as bad as it looks," she said, knowing it was. "It's a case of mistaken identity and it's really complicated, not because I'm guilty of anything, but because—"

"We're all running from something."

There was no denying that.

"There was a big car accident. Everyone but me and this other woman I was traveling with were . . . it was really bad." It was hard to get the next few lines out, even though she was determined not to stumble like she had with Sanjay and Devin. "I was in shock when I took off into the forest. I should have stayed put but there were things . . . totally out of my control . . . that I needed to—"

"Put an end to?" he asked, watching her down the barrel.

Cara was sure she'd run out of second chances. "Please, I don't want to die. I've come so close, so many times in the last twenty-four hours."

He chuckled. "I was talking about your hair."

She felt around her head until she reached a tangled mass of someone else's hair she had paid *#Ridiculous* money to have attached to her head to give herself fuller, more luscious locks. Snipping quickly, she grabbed another extension and did the same. With no mirror, and a man who lived in a trailer mansion watching with amusement, she did her best to give herself an even trim.

"If I had to guess, I'd say you need a safe spot to ride things out," he said.

"That would really help," she admitted.

The man lowered his gun, gave her an almost imperceptible wave, and walked past her, which she took as an invitation to follow.

She couldn't allow herself to think about how it had all come to this—trailing a middle-aged, rifle-toting hermit through his barn, out the other side, and past a series of buildings with overhanging roofs. The route allowed them to remain sheltered from above, she noted.

He stopped abruptly in front of a wooden door set into the hillside.

"What is this?" she asked.

Instead of answering, he turned the dial of a combination lock. With a click and a pull, he opened the door. Inside was a U-Haul-sized earthen room stabilized with the same rough-hewn wood he'd used for his front deck. It was filled with feed bags, farm tools, and well-maintained equipment of various kinds.

A storage shed, she thought with relief.

Cara hung back in the doorway as the man moved multiple sacks of grain. He used a broom to sweep the dirt floor underneath until a heavy metal trap door appeared.

"What do you keep down there?" she asked.

He bent down and pulled it open. "For the moment, you."

A ladder disappeared into darkness.

Fuck. Fuck. Holy fuck. "I r-really appreciate your of-offer." Her voice had never trembled so badly. "B-but I'm not sure this is a good idea."

Somewhere behind them, a bell jangled.

"What is that?" she asked.

"My warning system. It means someone's on my property."

Was he just saying that so he could get her to climb down in the hole without pointing his gun at her head?

"Is that how you discovered me?" she asked, stalling for time. "Did I set off one of your alarms?"

"I spotted you trying to hide behind a tree and watched you slink through the grass like a starving fox coming for my henhouse. That was before Joanie, Lucretia, and Ruth began bleating away about you being in their barn."

The bell jangled again.

"Lady, we can keep talking, but you've got about three minutes to make yourself invisible. Otherwise, I'm going to point my gun at you again and hand you over. Honestly, that would make my life a whole lot less complicated."

She felt paralyzed by her two choices. Go to prison or . . . the man was twice her size and looked capable of things too horrible to consider.

"When you get to the bottom, turn away from the ladder, take three steps, and feel around on your right side at shoulder height," he said.

Cara chose to take a tentative step into the dugout.

"What am I looking for?"

"The flashlight," he answered.

When he didn't push her in, she peered hesitantly down the open hatch before forcing a foot onto the ladder.

"Don't turn on the generator and don't make a sound," the man instructed.

As her legs and then her torso became enveloped by darkness, Cara thought of something she'd read in a book about hostages humanizing themselves. Making friends with their captors.

"What's your name?" she asked.

"Fisk," he said, as her head went underground.

He didn't ask hers before he sealed her in, the trap door closing with a resonant thud.

In gamer-speak, boxed in.

THIRTY-NINE
JORDAN

The @USMarshalsHQ are on the case! They're gonna do a hard-target search of every gas station, residence, warehouse, farmhouse, henhouse, outhouse, and doghouse. Bimbo don't stand a chance!

—*@BackTheBlue911*

Jordan felt a tug on his shin and looked down. A thin strand of wire creased the leg of his olive-green duty pants. He clenched and froze, instinctively expecting the flat *crump* of an explosion. If it was a booby trap, he was already dead.

Nothing blew up. Somewhere in the middle of Fisk's ramshackle compound, a brass bell clanged.

He should have guessed the antisocial man would have secured the perimeter of his "property" with a DIY alarm system. In the past, Jordan had always driven right up the overgrown track.

Would Cara Campbell know what the bell meant—if she was in there?

Jordan reached down and grabbed the wire before he pulled his leg back, then released the tension slowly. He couldn't keep it from clanging a second time. It was possible, if unlikely, that the sounds had been masked by the heavy chop of the helicopter's grid search above.

He stepped over the wire, jogged twenty yards, and took cover behind a washing machine so rusted it would probably dissolve if he sneezed on it.

Taking a small spotting scope out of a pouch on his belt, he raised his head and scanned the ragged cluster of outbuildings. Fisk had added on another trailer, but it was so old and battered it looked like it had been there since the beginning.

Jordan had never had any problems with the guy and thought there was nothing wrong with wanting to live off the grid. Not everyone agreed. Madera County dispatchers had received complaints about the unsightliness of Fisk's property and even his livestock's living conditions. Jordan suspected the callers were from the Bay Area. When he followed up, he found the animals well fed and healthy—if not recently shampooed.

Fisk's right to be on the land was a gray area. He was almost certainly squatting, but no one could find the man whose name was on the deed, and a trust administered by a law firm in San Jose kept up the tax payments. Unless someone made a legal request, Jordan had no reason to evict the guy. Sometimes he wondered how many people in the Golden State were living in a similarly precarious state of grace.

Jordan worked the scope carefully from side to side. If Fisk was on his property, he probably knew Jordan was, too. The question was whether Cara Campbell had stopped or kept right on going.

He couldn't imagine a pampered Los Angeleno—or anyone—banging on that dented trailer door and asking for help. Then again, when someone's whole world changed, who knew how they would react?

Nothing moved at the windows of the trailers as Jordan stared for a long minute. The sheep and the goat milled aimlessly outside the Quonset barn. A red chicken hopped down from its coop, which appeared to have been made from a repurposed baby crib.

Jordan decided he might as well just ask Fisk if she'd been there.

Before he went in, he radioed Beto. "Campbell's trail leads to Fisk's place. I'm going to go up and say hello."

FORTY
CARA

People always ask me how they can become successful social media influencers, too. For me, the answer was to find a niche and then commit.

—Cara Campbell, interviewed for LifestyleInfluencer.com

Not counting the souls of the others Fisk had coaxed down here before her, Cara was utterly alone in the loamy darkness.

Cara's feet touched ground, and she took three steps forward. As she turned and reached at shoulder height as instructed, she prayed she wouldn't grasp the tail of something scurrying past. Things were bad as they could be. Worse—and much like becoming an influencer in the first place, a decision that led her to where she was now—she'd put herself directly into harm's way.

#Consequences.

Her knuckle hit something metal. She fumbled around a shelf until she touched the familiar plastic cylinder of a flashlight. Locating the switch on its side, she pushed it upward with her thumb.

Thank God, the beam of light illuminated no bodies and no row of shallow graves. Instead, it showed a kitchenette, complete with a mini-fridge, a two-burner hot plate, and a sink with a water spigot on the far wall.

Shining the light around, Cara saw she was standing in the middle of a low-ceilinged, concrete-walled, fully stocked survival bunker. Next to the kitchen area was a fully made cot with an extra blanket folded neatly at its foot. Behind the ladder was a toilet with an unopened roll of toilet paper. Floor-to-ceiling shelves covered all usable wall space, and every shelf held clearly marked and itemized plastic crates: *FIRST AID*, *TOOLS*, *CLOTHING*, *DISINFECTANTS*, and more.

Fisk had warned her not to turn on the generator, but there was no need to conserve the flashlight battery, not given the crate filled with batteries in seemingly every size. There was also a container labeled *LIGHT SOURCES* with a list of its contents:

Flashlights (8)
Candles (124)
Gas lanterns (4)

On the opposite wall was food. So much food: gallon buckets of rice, beans, sugar, and even powdered cheese. There were plastic-wrapped cases of cans, bottles, and other packages of consumables: freeze-dried meals, tins of Spam, canned veggies, spices, and even cooking oil and margarine. Cara had been hidden away in a doomsday prepper's pantry, which, while comforting—nutritionally speaking, anyway—was equally terrifying. There was enough food down here to feed her for the rest of her natural life.

Was she doomed to serve her life sentence here?

She saw a locked metal door set into the far wall. Was another victim locked up deeper in the hillside? Did that door have a door that led into yet another cell? Who knew how many women Fisk had lured down here.

From a bin marked *TOOLS*, Cara removed the hammer, wrench, saw, and pliers. She placed them strategically: the hammer under the cot, the wrench beneath the small pillow, the saw between two bins, and the pliers on top of a bucket. Knowing she had weapons eased her panic, if only temporarily.

Scanning the shelves, she helped herself to a box of crackers, a jar of peanut butter, and a can of chicken-noodle soup with a metal pull tab. She needed energy for whatever came next. God help her. With no time to lose, she began to suck the cold, congealed salty broth into her mouth, chewing and swallowing carrot bits, chicken cubes, and soft noodles, trying not to gag.

She prayed, too.

But mostly ate until her belly was full.

FORTY-ONE
JORDAN

Coyotes provide many ecosystem benefits, such as controlling rodent and other small mammal populations. They will consume nearly anything, including rodents, rabbits, birds and eggs, reptiles, fruits, and plants, as well as pet food, human food, and trash.
—California Department of Fish and Wildlife

The dim red sun was dropping toward the treetops as Jordan crossed the packed dirt in front of the trailer complex, heading toward the open door of the barn.

"It's Sheriff Jordan Burke!" he shouted. "We need to talk!"

Fisk came around a corner carrying a shotgun in the crook of his arm.

Jordan showed his open hands. "You can put that down. Just here to ask you a few questions."

Fisk pressed the safety with his finger and leaned the shotgun against the side of the porch, taking his time.

"Thought I heard a critter out there," he said matter-of-factly.

"See anything?"

Fisk shook his head. "A few days ago, I found coyote scat with wool in it."

"You need a license, even to shoot coyotes."

"Not if they're threatening my livestock."

Jordan didn't want to get into it with him. The fact that he had heard an animal and not found one was more urgent.

"Have you seen any people up here?" he asked. "Anyone you don't know?"

"Well, I recognize you, but I wouldn't say we *know* one another." Fisk appeared to think about it, then shook his head. "Couple of kids on dirt bikes last week, but that's about it."

Jordan nodded at the shotgun. "You scare them off with that?"

"What do you think?"

"I think an escaped convict came through here. A blond woman in civilian clothes. She's originally from LA, but now she's been on the run for twenty-four hours and could be getting desperate."

Fisk's mouth curled in a smirk. "What, desperate for a latte?"

"Desperate enough to throw herself into the rapids to get away from me. Her name's Cara Campbell. She's an Instagram influencer convicted of murdering her husband, so we consider her dangerous, although we don't believe she is armed. I'm asking you point-blank: have you seen her on your property?"

Fisk kicked the dirt, spat in it, and laughed. "I do believe she was on the arm of Brad Pitt."

Jordan had had a half-dozen encounters with Fisk over the previous dozen years and had always known him to be brusque and taciturn. Never in all that time had the man made a joke, let alone two.

"Answer the question."

Fisk seemed to sense something before he did, looking up and over Jordan's shoulder. A second later, Jordan heard the high whine of a big engine in low gear, rocks rattling off an undercarriage, and wide tires sliding in the dust.

Jordan turned to see Wen and her team climbing out of the black Ford Explorer with tinted windows. Unholstering their guns.

He turned again and saw Fisk pick up the shotgun.

Caught in the middle.

"Who the fuck are they, Sheriff?" yelled Fisk.

"Feds. US Marshals. Here with the search party," said Jordan, keeping his voice as even as he could. "Nobody's here for you."

Wen and her team were fanning out, taking cover.

"Drop the shotgun, *now*!" she shouted.

Fisk aimed the shotgun at Jordan's stomach and moved closer, careful to keep Jordan between him and the Marshals. "This all some kind of trick? Let them use you as a decoy?"

"Not helping, Wen!" Jordan called over his shoulder. "Everything is fine here."

"Then tell Jethro there to drop the gun, get on his knees, and put his hands behind his back!" yelled Crosby.

"Not gonna happen," muttered Fisk.

"You saw her, didn't you?" pressed Jordan. "How long ago was it? Are you protecting her?"

"Get down, Sheriff!" barked the big Marshal. "I have a shot!"

Jordan stayed between them as Fisk moved backward with careful steps until he was partially hidden behind the barn, only the shotgun barrel showing.

"Get to safety now, Burke!" screamed Wen.

He turned around and faced them, exasperated. "Goddamn it, I'm just talking to the man. This is not how we're going to do this! Back off and let me do my job!"

Nobody moved for a full minute. Then Jordan heard Wen say something to her team. Still with guns trained on Fisk's location, they retreated to the Explorer. The doors closed and Wen backed it down the road.

"I suppose you want my gratitude for that," Fisk said, showing a sliver of his face.

"I want to find Cara Campbell. Let me search and then I'll go."

"You'll go now."

"I'll come back with a warrant."

"That's what it's going to take."

"Don't do this. It's not worth it."

Fisk's visible eye stared at him implacably. "For you, or for me?"

Jordan knew they were done. As he turned to go, he glanced inside the open door of the Quonset barn and saw a pair of sheep shears and what looked like wool.

Not wool.

Ratty blond hair extensions.

FORTY-TWO
CARA

It's shocking and upsetting to think we unknowingly helped a fugitive and that she's still on the loose. She did seem like a fundamentally good person, though.

—Sanjay Jain, speaking to ABC News

She stole my favorite shirt.

—Devin Mayer, speaking to ABC News

But gave it back.

—Sanjay Jain

Cara stood at the base of the wooden ladder, listening. She had no idea how much time had passed. Thirty minutes? An hour? Two?

Was Fisk still in the shed-cave above her? Or had he returned to his Frankentrailer to start a vision board of all the diabolical things he planned to do to her? If he was telling the truth and the warning bell did signal that someone was coming to find her, wouldn't he have shown more concern about being apprehended himself?

The longer she was down here, the more certain she became that Fisk was a madman whose tweak was luring desperate, gullible women into his hidey-hole, where he lulled them into complacency with food, shelter, and warmth. Then doing as he pleased until . . .

The food she'd stuffed so quickly into her mouth now rumbled ominously in her lower belly.

At least there was a toilet down here.

She shined the flashlight on the handwritten instructions taped to the lid.

> *COMPOSTING TOILET INSTRUCTIONS:*
>
> *Do your business as normal and wipe with TP. For Number One, you're all done. For Number Two, add a handful of bulking agent to break down the waste. DO NOT put feminine hygiene products of any kind into the bowl.*

The open box of wood shavings next to the toilet was labeled *Bulking Agent* and sat on top of a clear plastic storage crate filled with sanitary supplies. Courteously prepared for a menstruating female captive.

Or multiple captives.

"Stop it!" Cara told herself.

She'd seen curtains in one of the windows of the mobile home. Had they been hung by a wife who was free to come and go? Cara tried to imagine the female who relished living with him in the rugged compound he'd built, all but cut off from the world, preparing to live underground with him possibly for years.

What if she was his accomplice? Weren't women like that typically colder and even more vicious than their male counterparts?

No! She couldn't let panic run away with her. Besides, she had to pee and needed to change the tampon she'd gotten at the diner. Setting the flashlight on the ladder with the beam of light facing toward her, Cara lifted the cover of the toilet. Inside it had two sections, with a siphon that directed the urine into one container and solids into another.

As she hesitated, she thought of something else: if Fisk opened the hatch, she'd be directly below him, with her pants around her ankles.

"No can do," she said, clenching everywhere.

Maybe lying down on the cot would relax her enough to do what would eventually have to be done.

And eating a chocolate bar. With graham crackers. And a dab of marshmallow fluff from the jar she'd spotted on an upper shelf.

Was this how Stockholm Syndrome started?

FORTY-THREE
JORDAN

Turn yourself in and accept justice.
—@TayCamp

The smoke was back. It poured into the shallow valley on a wind warmed by the fire itself. The hillside to the west seethed with red and orange, the glow sometimes briefly illuminating silhouettes of the firefighters working desperately to halt its advance. But the blaze had the upper hand for now: the planes and helicopters dumping retardant and water had been grounded at nightfall and wouldn't be back until morning.

Jordan hated wearing masks but had one on now, just to give his lungs and his raw itching throat a break. Looking at the growing assembly of men and vehicles a few hundred yards down the road, just out of sight of Fisk's place, he wished they could wait for daylight, too.

A Madera Sheriff's cruiser parked down the road and Beto got out. He made his way up the line with a large paper bag, offering coffee and sandwiches to his fellow deputies. Not looking at the Feds.

"Narvaez got the last sandwich," he said apologetically when he finally reached Jordan. "Coffee?"

"Appreciate it."

Jordan took the paper cup, lowered his mask, and sipped. It was lukewarm and bitter, only marginally better than swallowing smoke.

"Can't believe this shit," said Beto, taking in the scene. "You OK? Heard you got a gun stuck in your belly."

"I was honestly more worried the Feds would shoot me. Fisk's finger wasn't on the trigger. He's pretty cool, even when he gets hotheaded."

He had been so certain the man would have given up what he knew with a little more time. That changed after he saw the hair cuttings. But why was Fisk protecting Campbell? What did a grizzled off-the-gridder care about a lost-in-the-woods creature of the internet?

Jordan's argument with Wen afterward had been as intense as it was futile.

He knows something! He was about to talk.

What was I supposed to do, let him blow your guts out?

He wasn't even holding the shotgun until you showed up.

You're fooling yourself if you think old meth mouth up there is going to help us, said Crosby, despite never having been close enough to get a look at Fisk's teeth.

The man's mouth looked normal enough. Jordan found himself wondering where Fisk got his dental work done, or if he did, a sure sign of mental fatigue.

In the end, he could find no reason not to tell Wen what he'd seen in the barn.

That's our girl, she said. *Time to call in the cavalry.*

While they waited for the warrant to be issued by an off-duty judge in Sacramento, Wen ordered her team of three to "seal the perimeter." Jordan wished them luck. A full platoon would find it a challenge to seal off all escape routes in the rocky, heavily wooded hillsides, especially with the smoke offering cover.

But reinforcements were coming soon. Wen had commandeered Fresno PD's SWAT team with their armored personnel carrier. A new vehicle carrying more men from a different agency seemed to arrive every ten minutes or so. The search helicopter had refueled and returned, its pilot flying high above the fire with a spotter using infrared technology.

As the minutes ticked past, the two teams—Jordan's and Wen's—eyeballed each other from opposite sides of the poorly maintained road.

Jordan's phone vibrated with a text. Amber Alert.

Coming home anytime soon?

Wouldn't count on it.

Your dinner's in the fridge. Should I put it in the freezer?

Jordan's stomach growled. *Or give it to the dog.*

Rough day here, too. I took Sydney to see Bree. The machines are the only thing keeping that girl alive.

How to answer that?

Love you both, he wrote. *Miss you.*

Miss you, too. Stay safe?

I'll do my best.

Across the road, there was a flurry of activity as men and women began to stand and check their equipment.

"Guess the search warrant came through," said Beto. "Things sure move faster when the almighty Feds get involved. Looks like they're about to go Full Metal Jagoff."

When he heard the groaning engine of the APC coming up the road, Jordan poured the rest of his coffee into the dirt and went looking for Wen.

When he found her, she was huddled with a half-dozen Feds he didn't recognize. He was pretty sure a couple of them were officers from CDCR's Fugitive Apprehension Team. One man's jacket said BATF on the back. What next, Homeland Security? It was madness.

Jordan touched Wen's elbow, pulling her away from the group. "Let's talk him out. We don't know what he has up there. The guy's a vet. He could have land mines and mortars, for crying out loud."

"You're right, Sheriff. We don't know. That's why we have armor, men, and superior weaponry."

"So it's one guy against an army. Ever heard of Ruby Ridge?"

"I've seen the PowerPoint."

"We don't even know if she's in there. Maybe she just used his shears and kept running."

Doubt flickered across her face, quickly replaced by certainty. "He caught you on his property. How would he miss her?"

"I'm just saying we don't know. Let me go up there again, alone, to try talking to him."

"I'm not letting this hick disappear into the woods."

A man with a pockmarked face and a gray stubbled head glared at Jordan. "Need you, Wen."

"We go in ten," Wen told Jordan. "Your men follow our lead."

"I'm going to tell them to hang back, take it slow, and not do anything stupid," he retorted. "I don't want anyone getting shot by a gung-ho clerk from the BLM."

"Black Lives Matter?" she asked, clearly confused.

"Bureau of Land Management."

Jordan recrossed the road with a sinking feeling.

"Will sanity prevail?" asked Beto.

"We'll find out. They're going in ten minutes, and I want our guys in the rear. First, I'm taking a leak."

Stepping into the trees, Jordan took a wide loop around the compound, aiming to drop in from the thickly forested hillside. He moved from tree to tree, watching for trip wires, pausing periodically to make sure he didn't surprise one of Wen's nervous men. Eerily, the helicopter's searchlight when it passed made the smoke almost white and the shadows blacker than black.

Five agonizing minutes later, he was at the edge of the trees, a stone's throw from Fisk's barn.

"Fisk!" he hissed, not willing to risk full volume. "Fisk!"

No reply. He had to move fast.

Zigzagging to the safety of the barn, he turned his headlamp on red and scanned from side to side. It was empty.

As he army-crawled past the chicken coop to the trailers, he heard excited voices over revving engines. Then the chopper dropped lower, lighting the compound brighter than day. Jordan had never been to war, but imagined soldiers' hearts must pound like his was now. That their pupils would dilate and their throats would dry out, too. Everything felt hyperrealistic—or maybe it was surreal. He wasn't sure he knew the difference.

What the hell was he doing?

The front porch was in full view of the approaching troops. Jordan ran to a side door and banged on it with the flat of his hand.

"Fisk!" he yelled. "Fisk, goddammit! Let's keep everyone alive here!"

No response. He tried the handle. Locked. Not wanting to bring the Feds in with guns blazing by shooting the lock, he put his shoulder to the flimsy door and barged it open.

His headlamp now on bright white, he swung inside, both hands gripping his pistol, sweeping the room.

The place was worn and dated but surprisingly tidy, despite the canning supplies and giant spools of twine piled against one wall.

Jordan raced from room to room until he found himself in the front trailer. On the table was a note.

Dear Feds,

Took off because I knew how this was going to go. Don't let my chickens die.

Fisk

Jordan turned to leave. At least no one was getting shot today.

Blinding light filled the windows as a bullhorn crackled. Wen's garbled voice gave Fisk ten seconds to surrender. Jordan lifted a corner of curtain and peered out. Impossible to see against the glare. The ten seconds was probably a bluff, but he couldn't take that chance.

He threw open the front door and kept his body pressed against the wall. Was this what a heart attack felt like? He grabbed a light-colored jacket off a peg and waved it in surrender. Before he could yell, he heard a gun crack.

Feeling a tug on the jacket as a bullet hit it where the heart would be, he dropped to the floor and curled into a ball, expecting a hail of bullets to riddle his body through the thin trailer wall.

Instead, there was a momentary silence, as though everyone outside was as surprised as he was.

"It's me, you assholes!" he bellowed. "Sheriff Burke! Don't shoot!"

"Everyone, stand down!" screamed Wen. "Like, stand down!"

When nobody fired again, Jordan stood up and left the trailer with his hands over his head.

Still half expecting to die.

CALIFORNIA DEATH TRIP PODCAST

SEASON ONE, EPISODE TWELVE

DYLAN DANVERS: *Hi, crime fam, it's Dylan. Today I was able to speak to someone with a unique inside view of law enforcement's hunt for Cara. Troy Silverman is a real estate entrepreneur who also happens to be the only one challenging Jordan Burke in this fall's sheriff's election in Madera County, north of Fresno, where all of this is going down. Welcome, Sheriff.*

TROY SILVERMAN: (laughs) *Not sheriff yet.*

DANVERS: (laughs) *That just sort of slipped out.*

SILVERMAN: *It's like you can see into the future.*

DANVERS: *Let's get right into it, because I know our listeners want to know. What's going on on the ground?*

SILVERMAN: *Dylan, it doesn't look good. Me and some of my men assisted the Madera sheriff and his deputies in the tracking of Cara Campbell. And I wish I didn't have to say this, but what I saw was basically disorganization and incompetence. We were lucky we weren't killed. No one warned us that we were smack dab in the path of the Coarsegold Fire.*

DANVERS: *That must have been scary.*

SILVERMAN: *When you're runnin' for your life, you don't have time to be scared. But it was a close one.*

DANVERS: *Is Sheriff Burke any closer to catching Campbell?*

SILVERMAN: *Let me tell you somethin' about Sheriff Jordan Burke. His daddy was sheriff before him, and his granddaddy was sheriff before that. We're talkin' three-quarters of a century of Burkes runnin' Madera county, in what we like to think is a democracy—*

DANVERS: *I understand where you're going, but the focus of this interview is the hunt for Cara Campbell.*

SILVERMAN: *Of course.*

DANVERS: *Do you have any idea where she is?*

SILVERMAN: (laughs) *What's happenin' now is that the US Marshals have taken over the operation. Burke isn't runnin' shit, if you'll pardon my French. And I don't think voters are going to be all that thrilled to learn the federal government has taken over law enforcement operations in Madera County. That's not how I plan to run things, take my word.*

DANVERS: *So in your expert opinion, Cara is no closer to being apprehended today than she was yesterday?*

SILVERMAN: *She's in the wind.*

DANVERS: *With the wildfire, wild animals, and incompetent law enforcement, I'm worried she can't survive out there much longer.*

SILVERMAN: *I guess that could be a silver lining. Maybe the taxpayers are off the hook for her lifetime room and board.*

DANVERS: *To be clear, I believe Cara Campbell is innocent.*

SILVERMAN: *I've met my fair share of gold diggers, and believe you me, innocent ain't a word I'd ever use.*

DANVERS: *If Cara is going to come through this safe, we have to find her first. Crime Fam, if you see something, say something—to me!*

DAY THREE

FORTY-FOUR
CARA

Hey y'all, check out my new dance. I call it rich lady dancing with bears.

—*@tiktokBOOM*

As Cara inhaled the aromas of nutty coffee and crisp pine with subtle notes of musty loam, she felt safe, warm, and protected. She was in Ojai, glamping with Karl.

Or were they in the Sahara?

Cozy beneath the fluffy duvet of a king-sized, four-poster bed in a tent appointed with colorful rugs and priceless Moroccan antiques, they snuggled together, drinking spiced tea he'd brewed for them and gazing out the window at the dunes they planned to zip-line over at sunset. Setting aside his mug, Karl leaned over and kissed her passionately.

"Your love is worth all my gold," he said, looking deeply into her eyes with his baby blues. "What's left of it."

Then her lawyer, Roy Abel, entered through the tent's open flap holding a hammer wrapped in an evidence bag.

"Did you forget something?" he asked.

Laughing, he rushed toward them and began hitting Karl in the head.

Cara reached out to stop the attack but couldn't. The bed was gone. She was sinking into the sand.

Why was Abel wearing a black ski mask? She hooked her thumbs into the mask's eyeholes and pulled it off. It wasn't Abel—it was the grandmotherly jury foreman, her purple hair glowing menacingly.

Then she morphed into Cara's stepdaughter, Taylor.

"Guilty as charged!" Taylor said, aiming her hammer at Cara.

"Over my dead body," Karl said. He laughed, like he always did, at his own joke.

The bright red blood spewing from the top of his head was anything but funny.

Cara screamed and opened her eyes.

She definitely wasn't glamping. She wasn't even in a tent. She was lying on hard, rocky ground, looking up at a pine tree and sweating in a mildewed sleeping bag. Her mouth was so dusty she must have been inhaling dirt while she slept.

Fisk was crouched next to a small gas stove, watching her as he stirred instant coffee in a banged-up metal camping cup.

"Bad dream?" he asked.

"A nightmare. And I'm still not sure I'm awake."

He stood up and brought her the cup.

Backlit by the hazy dawn, his curly hair formed a wispy aura around his head. Cara couldn't help but notice the coarse gray tufts sprouting from his ears and nose, and couldn't help hoping no strays had fallen into her coffee.

"Drink up," he said matter-of-factly. "We need to rock and roll."

He'd used exactly the same words the previous night when he'd opened the trap door and dropped into the bunker with a shotgun tucked under his arm.

All she could think to do at that moment was try to make things as personal as she could in the hope of delaying whatever lay ahead.

"How long have I been down here, Fisk?" she'd asked.

"Too long," he'd grunted.

"I hope it's OK that I ate a little bit of your food."

Fisk had eyed the cracker crumbs, open peanut butter jar, and Hershey bar wrappers. "More than a bit by the looks of it."

"My name's Cara, by the way." Thinking she might as well be honest this time.

"Oh, I know."

He'd stepped past her, matter-of-factly noting the tools missing from the open bin. She had flinched as he stuck a key into the deadbolt lock. That door led to another one—large and metal with a built-in combination lock. He had twisted the tumbler until it clicked, the heavy door swinging open ominously on well-oiled hinges.

Inside was a stockpile of firearms so extensive that the hammer and wrench she'd hidden suddenly seemed about as useful as water pistols. Fisk had quickly traded his shotgun for a black assault rifle and wordlessly pointed her up the ladder.

They'd hiked into the night, leading a heavily laden mule with white-ringed eyes, the goat, and two sheep, while carrying heavy backpacks themselves. Cara stumbled over rocks and tree roots, trying to keep up. Her feet were sore, her knee throbbed, and the backpack straps dug into her shoulder, but she didn't dare complain. Finally she grew so lightheaded that she tottered with every step. Fisk must have taken pity on her because he eventually let her lie down. She passed out immediately.

Now it was morning and her captor or savior was serving her coffee. She had no idea how long she'd been out or if Fisk slept at all.

He handed her a thick hunk of homemade-looking jerky. "Eat up. You'll need the energy for today."

Beef, she reassured herself. *Turkey at worst.*

After breakfast, Cara stuffed her sleeping bag and put it into her backpack while Fisk reloaded the mule with the white-ringed eyes, whose name she now knew was Maybelline. He had a warm heart for his animals, given the affectionate way he baby-talked to them and patted them sweetly after they negotiated tight turns. She still wasn't sure how he felt about humans.

"What else do you know about me?" she asked, hobbling stiffly as the little party started moving.

Fisk didn't even look over his shoulder. "Cara Campbell, convicted of first-degree murder. You escaped after your prison van was in an accident, and now you're on the run."

Either he'd fired up his dial-up internet or adjusted the rabbit ears on his black-and-white TV, or he'd been filled in by whoever tripped the bells on his homespun Ring system. "Did the sheriff tell you that? Was he the one who showed up looking for me?"

Fisk spat the blade of grass he'd been chewing into the dirt. "Him and a few friends with armor and automatic weapons."

The hunt for her had ballooned even faster than she'd imagined. "Did they see the bunker?"

"They didn't see shit."

"I'm innocent," she pleaded.

"Doesn't much matter to me either way," he responded, leading them straight uphill.

FORTY-FIVE
JORDAN

A warm welcome to our many new followers! Our aim is to serve our community with honor and transparency.
—@MaderaCASheriff

@MaderaCASheriff Whole thing was staged with paid actors. Jordan Burke accepted bribes to let Cara escape. Campbell is selling the rights to Netflix and moving to a country with no extradition. #Facts
—@t1ghs_lfh563

Jordan gripped both sides of the podium and looked out at the thirty-odd members of his department who had gathered somberly for morning roll call. Usually, there was chitchat and horseplay before things got started—but usually, they weren't hunting a fugitive with the eyes of the world on them.

Jordan's mind was still on the phone call he'd taken a few minutes ago. Steve and Joanne, Bree's parents, had called to demand justice for their daughter, who was still in a coma. Their sobs and wails on the microphone—they were on speaker—made it even more difficult for Jordan to communicate that, to the best of his investigators' understanding, and although he wasn't ruling anything out, Bree had caused the crash. He had hoped to shield them from that information for as long as possible.

Unbelievably, Bree's phone had been found by searchers on the banks of China Creek, its screen shattered and its circuits water-damaged. The techs still hadn't been able to get anything off it.

Our baby girl is lying in the hospital, Steve said desolately. *While that woman is still running around free.*

Not for long, Jordan promised them.

Snapping back to the present, he cleared his throat and began. "A quick update and then I'll let Deputy Soto make assignments so you can all start your day. Despite the best efforts of both our department and the combined federal task force now led by the US Marshals, Cara Campbell remains at large. We tracked her to the compound of William Fisk but now both of them are missing. It's possible they're together, although we don't know what motive Fisk would have for assisting Campbell. It's also possible they died in the fire."

Jordan saw that the raid on the compound was obviously news to some people in the room. A couple of newer deputies seemed to be masking nerves with over-serious expressions, probably because of their sudden proximity to such a high-profile case. And everyone, from the investigators to the dispatchers, looked as tired as Jordan felt.

Witten, a veteran deputy, raised his hand. "Sheriff, I was off duty last night, but I heard shots were fired at the compound."

"Someone got excited and squeezed the trigger, but thankfully no one was hurt."

Jordan couldn't blame Witten for fishing. And while he couldn't stop his department from gossiping, he wasn't about to confirm that a fed—a BLM guy after all, it turned out, who didn't usually carry a weapon—fired on their boss. Not unless he wanted them to rebel outright against Wen's command.

And one of them was already talking to CNN.

Maybe a pep talk was in order. Jordan uncapped his water bottle, took a swig, then rubbed a stray drop off the lectern's laminate top with his thumb.

"Look," he said, screwing the cap back on the bottle. "Yesterday was a rough day. It can be weird working with the Feds, and none of us are used to having the media breathing down our necks. But those are just distractions. We're all good at our jobs. If we keep our heads down and do the work, the results will come. When we find Cara Campbell, things will get back to normal."

He hoped.

"Do you have any other questions for me?" he asked, thinking it was best to wrap up quickly.

In the back, Gracia raised her hand. "Sheriff, our X account has a hundred thousand new followers, and we have forty thousand new likes on our Facebook page."

That brought a few chuckles and ironic cheers. Lopez tried to start a slow clap but gave up when nobody joined in.

"Some of the stuff people are saying about—us—is horrible," Gracia continued. "They're sending me direct messages with links I'm afraid to even open. I volunteered to post departmental updates, not fight with trolls."

Jordan smiled at her. "I'm very sorry you're being subjected to that. Don't open links, don't respond, and please don't take it personally. Please continue to post official updates as usual—let's hold off on any silly dances for now—and I'll see if we can hire a temp who's trained in crisis management to help us out."

Thinking that Sydney and her teenage friends would probably do a good job slapping down the assholes. Then picturing Bree's broken phone with a twinge that almost made his eyes water.

In the front row, Beto touched his watch, reminding Jordan he needed time to discuss logistics and make assignments.

"Anybody else?" Jordan asked.

Nobody else. Jordan wondered if he should try to flush out the leaker, but after scanning the stressed and weary expressions in the room, decided on a gentler approach. He nodded at Beto to signal he was wrapping up.

"Our department is in unfamiliar territory and we need to support each other. I know some of you will be contacted by reporters asking for inside information. Don't talk to them. Your friends will be asking you, too, because they're curious. And while it's tempting to share stories, remember even your friends will also want to share what they know. Leaks not only make the department look bad, but they can even get in the way of what we're trying to do. So save the war stories until after this is all over."

Jordan wasn't sure when he would be ready to tell anyone his version of last night's events. He looked at the men and women under his command and felt a sudden swell of concern for them.

To disguise it, he picked up his water bottle and headed for the door. "Have a good shift," he told them. "And stay safe out there."

FORTY-SIX
CARA

Same shit. Different day.
—@TayCamp

The ever-present wood smoke had to be tickling Fisk's throat, too, because he grumbled intermittently about *the damn fires* and *man-made disasters sure to end us all.* He was otherwise silent as they hiked higher and further into the backcountry. Cara thought he might not speak to her at all until they stopped briefly at a stream. As he knelt by the edge and filtered water into a plastic bladder, she reached for a pretty sprig of Queen Anne's lace growing beside the water.

"Don't touch that!" he said so brusquely that she jumped and Maybelline brayed loudly.

Cara instinctively dropped her hand to her side. "It's Queen—"

"It's water hemlock, the most lethal plant growing in the United States."

"Are you sure? I learned about it back in Girl Scouts when I earned my nature badge."

"Hemlock has small purple spots and a smooth stem. Queen Anne's lace doesn't have purple spots and it's hairy."

She deflated. "I could have—"

"Yup." Fisk motioned for her water bottle. "It's dangerous out here."

And yet she'd somehow survived.

"I stayed alive my first night outside by burrowing into a pile of leaves," she said, glad to be having any kind of conversation.

"You're lucky the temperature didn't drop too much that night."

She watched Fisk pumping filtered water into their bottles, wondering why she felt the need to prove she wasn't totally helpless in the wilderness.

"I also figured out that water is safer to drink in the middle of a rushing stream."

"Unless it isn't."

"I survived rapids the sheriff said would kill me!"

"When he told me that part, I knew you wouldn't last another day on your own."

Was that the moment he decided to up the stakes and take her along with him?

"What else did they say to you?" she asked.

Fisk screwed the tops back on the water bottles and put his filtration kit away. When he handed her bottle back, he was smiling. "They told me you weren't armed but to consider you dangerous."

He obviously didn't. But he might well consider her valuable, worthy of a reward if he turned her in. If Fisk was smart—and he increasingly seemed to be—could he be taking her somewhere, not to maim and torture her, but to wait it out and watch the pot grow?

As he whistled at the animals to get them moving again, she asked, "Are you going to tell me where we're headed?"

"Not until we get there."

"What are your plans for me?"

"Good question," he answered.

FORTY-SEVEN

JORDAN

Still waiting for an update from @MaderaCASheriff.
—@JackSchapiroCNN

On the screen of his computer, Jordan studied the PDF of Cara Campbell's arrest record he'd requested from the Ventura County sheriff. First, he looked at the photos of 6' 2", 210-pound Karl Campbell, his face beaten beyond recognition. Jordan had seen plenty of murdered people before, but this attack seemed particularly vicious: the hammer blows had destroyed the man's facial structure and removed half of his teeth.

There were a couple of defensive wounds to his hands and arms—Jordan noted pale skin on the left wrist, indicating the dead man usually wore a watch—but most of his killer's fury had been concentrated on the face.

He looked at the crime scene photos, which were poor quality and showed too many footprints to be much help.

He read Cara Campbell's sworn statement.

> Glamping International, LLC reached out to me and offered a three-day, two-night stay, all expenses paid, to promote their resort on my Instagram. I was excited because I thought the trip would be great for all of us: Glamping International, my brand, and Karl, who always works too hard. He wanted to come, even though he knew it wasn't just a romantic

getaway—I had to work. He didn't like being on camera but he knew what to expect.

After we were shown our lovely tent, we did a photo shoot with a team I've used before. I took a swim and a few pictures in the saltwater pool while Karl checked his emails. That's what he said he was doing, anyway, but I suspected he just wanted a nap because we were going to be up late. We enjoyed a cocktail at our tent before heading to Johnson's Point for the moonlight picnic dinner that had been arranged for us.

The path was lighted by luminaria. Halfway there, I heard a crunching noise, like a footstep on a dry leaf. Karl scanned the area with his headlight beam but couldn't see anything. We both assumed it was a staff member who forgot something important for the picnic and was trying to drop it off before we arrived.

At Johnson's Point, there was a wicker basket waiting on a plaid blanket with matching camping table and chairs. We just looked at the view for a while—the stars were bright, and the view of the valley below was amazing. I had just pulled out my phone to take a short video on night mode when suddenly someone was there. I think they were hiding behind a rock outcropping. They were wearing all black, including a black mask like a balaclava.

Honestly? I froze. It was just so surreal. But Karl shouted and rushed toward the intruder to protect me. But he was farther away.

I remember seeing long, straight blond hair spilling out the back of the mask. I saw a flash of metal and felt an unbelievable pain in my skull.

I grabbed my head and fell to my knees. I heard Karl fighting back. My hands were sticky with my own blood.

"No!" I heard Karl say. "No!"

And then everything went black.

I will never, ever recover from what I saw when I finally came to: Karl was dead.

I did not kill my husband. I loved him more than life itself.

There was a rat-a-tat knock on his office door. Before he could answer, it opened and Beto stuck his head inside. "Ready, Boss?"

Jordan closed the file and looked at his old-fashioned wall clock. It was nearly 2 p.m. "Fifteen more minutes."

Beto frowned, unconvinced. "Going to have anything new to say by then?"

"If I don't eat something, I might pass out. Not a good look in front of the cameras."

"I'll tell them ten."

Jordan nodded and Beto withdrew.

He knew he had tested everyone's patience and failed, having promised updates every hour for the past three hours and postponing each time. But he *was* feeling lightheaded. He hadn't eaten anything since the breakfast sandwich Amber put in his hand as he headed out the door just after dawn. His stomach was a bubbling acid pool filled by too many cups of coffee.

Cara Campbell did a convincing job of pleading her innocence, but so did a lot of killers. And wasn't her whole career about making things look better than they were in reality?

Guilty or innocent, she was still out there, and he didn't have any answers for the people who wanted them. A thorough search of Fisk's property had revealed him to be either a man with no interests other than survival or a man so paranoid he had eradicated all traces of a social life.

Almost all. One of his deputies had found two frames from a photo-booth strip showing a younger, less grizzled Fisk grinning alongside a cute woman with long, black hair. Marshal Wen had promptly confiscated it.

The bloodhounds confirmed Cara had been there and had departed via a trail at the rear of the property. Signs on the trail indicated Fisk and

Cara were moving together, along with some livestock. Then fire had moved in, sealing off their escape route from behind. Marshal Wen had ordered the search parties to regroup at a new location, and in a role reversal he was sure was intentional, now she wasn't returning Jordan's calls.

Jordan opened a desk drawer, fished out a power bar, and took a bite. It tasted like sawdust. The foil wrapper showed it was six months expired. He ate it anyway. Somehow, it helped.

He stood up and brushed off his pants, then checked his face for crumbs in the small mirror he kept on his office shelf. For some reason, he had put it between the pictures of his dad and granddad, which looked like stock photos of every old sheriff on the walls of every sheriff's station: slicked-back hair, clean-shaven cheeks, and placid expressions that betrayed no trace of doubt.

Jerry Burke had been born to do the job, just like Chester Burke before him. Of course, Jordan had been born to do it, too. Did either of them ever wonder if they were up to the task? They may have had fewer reasons for self-doubt: most of the times they ran for re-election, they ran unopposed.

Jordan's phone vibrated. Beto telling him to get a move on.

He smoothed his hair, straightened his collar, and re-tucked his uniform shirt so the white T-shirt underneath wouldn't show on camera.

Hopefully, his face would be every bit as convincing as his forebears.

FORTY-EIGHT
CARA

It may be tempting to try and help wildlife displaced by fires but keep your distance. They are desperate and dangerous.

—@maderaanimalservices

Cara remained as quiet as Fisk all morning, afraid to say anything both because of the assault rifle strapped to his chest and the way he intently scanned for threats every time they neared an exposed rise or open ground.

But when they paused in a protected, shady area so Fisk could examine Maybelline's hoof, she decided to speak up. If his plans were anything like she'd been imagining, she had to at least try to plead her case.

"Fisk," she said, as he crouched by the donkey. "I know you said you don't really care, but I need you to know that I didn't do what they say I did."

The goat—Lucretia—tugged a bramble off a bush and chewed it, looking at Cara skeptically.

"I was on a glamping trip with my husband—"

Fisk's laugh cut her off. "*Glamping?*"

"Luxury camping," she said, wincing at the defensiveness in her voice, but glad she had piqued his interest.

"Ruth and Joanie, did you hear that?" Fisk asked the two sheep. To Cara, he said, "These ladies are show-quality California Reds and they're used to luxury treatment: fresh hay, a mucked stall, and only the best dewormer. Glamping would be right up their alley."

"Ha."

Fisk had finished with Maybelline and they set off. "So your husband liked glamping, too?"

"Karl was a plastic surgeon."

"Naturally," Fisk said with a chuckle.

"He worked hard, way too hard, and was always antsy to get outdoors. Because I was an influencer"—which had to sound as ridiculous to him as glamping, but she couldn't hold back anything now—"I was able to arrange an all-expenses-paid weekend getaway for us by agreeing to promote the resort and the activities they offered. He was more than game."

"What kinds of activities are we talking about?"

"Knife throwing, wood splitting, horseback riding, zip-lining. That sort of thing."

"Sounds fun enough," he said, nodding.

"Honestly, I was much more interested in the fancy tent, gourmet meals, and chilled champagne. Plus quality alone time with my husband."

"A little practice at outdoor activities might have come in handy in your current situation."

"If only the weekend had gotten that far." She almost couldn't finish the sentence.

They hiked in silence, broken by the occasional grunt of an animal and crunching footsteps.

Cara had relived and recounted the story so many times and it never got easier. She told him anyway.

"Jesus," Fisk said.

He said nothing else for what felt like a mile.

Then, finally: "The spouse is always the most likely suspect."

"Yes," Cara admitted. "And I am . . . was . . . infamous for my social media platform, so the authorities never really considered anyone else."

"What the heck do you mean, infamous?"

"I gave lifestyle advice to women looking for wealthy men."

"Whoa," Fisk said, inadvertently causing the animals to halt. "Hell of a career choice."

"I had tons of brand ambassadorships, and I was making money," she said defensively, as soon as Fisk clicked his tongue to get Maybelline and the others moving again. "No one really believes it, but Karl supported my brand. I mean, he didn't have any social accounts, and he didn't like appearing on camera, but he was all in when he saw what it did for his practice. People who liked me tracked him down."

Why hadn't the forensic accountant mentioned the 20 percent increase in patients when he testified at the trial? Or the extra investors who'd come on board to help Karl build his surgical center? Karl had always kept his business dealings to himself, and she had never bothered to ask.

"Karl and I were opposites in so many ways—age, interests, career paths, you name it—but he was my partner in all things. I married him for love. And yes, security. I grew up with a lot less than I needed, so I've always believed in being honest about the need to feel safe, whether emotionally, financially, or both."

"I suppose I know a thing about unlikely relationships," Fisk said, not unkindly.

As they continued on over rocks, through stands of trees, and up and around a ridge, seemingly a million miles from where they'd started, Cara couldn't help but wonder when they were going to reach wherever it was they were going.

"I've shared my story and I haven't tried to get away," she said.

"Nope," he agreed.

"Then why won't you at least tell me where you're taking me?"

"Because if you can't make it all the way, I don't want you telling the authorities where I am."

"The middle of nowhere?" she said. "Trust me, if I can't find my way out on my own, I won't be able to lead anyone back here."

FORTY-NINE
JORDAN

Now @MaderaCASheriff is finally at the podium. Live feed in my pinned tweet.

—@JackSchapiroCNN

Jordan peered through the glass front doors at the crowd that covered the narrow strip of lawn outside the station and spilled into the parking lot. There were easily sixty or seventy reporters, cameramen, and looky-loos, a record level of interest in the Madera County Sheriff's Department. He took a quick breath and pushed through.

They started shouting questions the moment they saw him, their overlapping voices making it impossible to hear what any one person was saying. He made his way over to the portable podium, where the department's microphone was wired to a one-speaker PA and a half-dozen network microphones had been clamped onto the front.

Beto, standing guard, nodded and stepped aside.

Jordan gripped both sides of the podium, noting the reporters' phones and digital recorders littering its surface. His mouth was dry, and he wished Wen was giving this briefing, not him. But she was up in the hills of his county, directing the search for Cara Campbell and William Fisk.

He held up his hands for quiet.

"I've got fifteen minutes, folks," he said, the PA speaker squealing until someone lowered the volume. "I'll make a brief statement, and then I'll take questions."

"Is Cara Campbell still alive?" yelled someone.

That question set off another—"Do you have any response to Troy Silverman's latest tweets?"—and another, and another, until he had to raise his hands again.

"I understand this is a case of massive interest, due to both the notoriety of Cara Campbell and the brutal nature of her crime. Like the victim's family and all of you, we are disappointed that we do not have Campbell in custody. But the situation is complex and very fluid."

"Stop stalling and answer the questions!" yelled a scruffy reporter for a conservative local news site, who was standing near the back.

Jordan spotted a grinning Silverman behind him, standing between one of his goons and a handsome young man with an expensive-looking microphone.

How on earth did the asshole find the time?

Jordan almost snapped at the reporter and then stopped, remembering how he'd told his team to keep their cool. Reminding himself to act like the goddamn sheriff.

"Yesterday, we tracked Cara Campbell to a civilian residence," he said flatly. "The landowner did not allow us permission to search, so after obtaining a warrant, a multiagency task force breached the compound. By that time, both the landowner and Campbell were no longer at the location."

A pretty, brown-haired TV reporter stood up on tiptoes. "Are they together? Does this mean she has help?"

Jordan was irritated at the unprompted question but decided to roll with it. "We believe they left together, but until we find both of them, we simply won't know. It's possible they left separately or are separated now. One or both of them could have died in the fire. The landowner is an experienced outdoorsman but Campbell is not."

Not saying, *And I have zero idea why he would be helping her, if he actually is.*

"If you had them surrounded, how did they get away?" The voice of the CNN guy, Jack Schapiro, was impressive. He wasn't shouting—it was more like orating.

"As I said, the situation is highly unstable," Jordan answered. "It was night, the area is heavily wooded, and the trail was cut off by a fast-moving fire."

"It's my understanding that you had a helicopter with infrared spotting technology," Schapiro prodded, taking a second question and obviously irritating the other reporters. "How did that fail?"

And who is your source, Jack?

Asking would be a bad look. Jordan regulated his breathing and tried not to react.

"The hot spots of the advancing fire create their own heat signatures, as do wild game fleeing the blaze. The homeowner's livestock also appear to have escaped. Our aerial spotter identified so many heat signatures he was unable to make a conclusive judgment."

Beto leaned over the mic. "Five more minutes, folks."

"What do you say to the growing numbers of people who doubt Cara Campbell is even guilty? That she was wrongfully convicted?"

This question came from the handsome young guy next to Silverman. Jordan thought his mild, slightly high voice sounded familiar.

At least this answer was easy. "It's not my job to determine guilt or innocence. That's up to the judicial system."

"So your job is catching them?" interrupted Silverman, obviously teeing himself up for something.

They were both drowned out by bass and drums pumping through overtaxed speakers as a billboard truck with a huge LED screen rolled slowly past on the street. The driver slowed, looking like he wanted to turn into the parking lot, but there were too many bodies in the way.

As Jordan saw a black-and-white Photoshopped image of himself behind bars, quickly covered up by the text of Silverman's greatest-hit tweets, a voice boomed out: "*Silverman for Madera—the Burke Stops Here!*"

Reporters turned to watch and found themselves facing Silverman in the flesh. He almost seemed to grow in size, inflated by their attention.

"I'm just here as a civilian, folks," he said, as the truck rolled away.

"Your questions should all be for Jordan here, about what he is and isn't doing."

But when no one filled the stunned silence immediately, Silverman took it upon himself.

"If your job is simply catchin' criminals, and you couldn't catch this one, wouldn't you say you been failin' at your job?"

"Look, sometimes they get away," Jordan began angrily, then paused, forced to wait through another blast of amplified nonsense from the truck, which had pulled a U-turn. One of his deputies waved the driver on. By the time he could finally be heard again, Jordan had collected himself, concluding, "But the Madera County Sheriff's Department doesn't quit, ever. We will find Cara Campbell and bring her to justice."

Beto stepped in front of the mic. "Thank you all for your time. Please direct any inquiries to Sergeant Mark Stevens. We will continue to issue updates through official channels as new developments arise."

Jordan had already turned his back on the throng and was trying not to hurry too obviously as he headed inside. He hoped his true feelings didn't show on his face: he was furious at Silverman, at the situation, and above all, Jordan Burke. Once again, he'd allowed himself to be baited into losing his cool.

Maybe the biggest mystery was why Silverman was so damned intent on taking his job. Did a professional heckler really want to sit in the hot seat, with an army of anonymous trolls watching his every move and second-guessing every decision?

Or maybe that was the attraction. The man obviously craved attention. It was possible he didn't care what kind.

Jordan wondered why he was still intent on keeping the job. Would he still want it if the hunt for Cara Campbell ended in failure and things in his quiet county never went back to the way they were before?

FIFTY
CARA

Wildfires! Forest fires! The world is one big dumpster fire!
—@conservationnowand4ever

Cara's stomach was rumbling, but she hesitated to ask Fisk if he'd brought anything else to eat.

"Edible plants are a lot harder to identify than I thought," she said, going at it sideways.

Fisk halted Maybelline and let the sheep and goat wander ahead as he leaned down and foraged beside a log. "There are always bugs."

"You have to be kidding."

He showed her his palm, offering a wiggling beetle for her inspection. "Insects are the most abundant protein source on the planet."

"Snail slime for wrinkles, sure, but snails are edible to begin with."

"So are many bugs. Don't knock 'em 'til you've tried 'em."

He dropped the wiggling insect without popping it into his mouth, she noted.

Fisk reached into Maybelline's saddle bag, pulled out two flattened PB&Js, and handed one of them to Cara. It was touching to think that, while she cowered in his hidey-hole, he had been making her a sandwich. And even smashed and jelly-soaked white bread was a delightful treat, considering the alternative.

Fisk was probably the first survivalist Cara had ever met. Definitely the first one she'd ever spent any time with. And maybe it really was the Stockholm Syndrome talking, but she did appreciate being accompanied through the wilderness by someone so capable. Under slightly different circumstances, she might really believe she wasn't a hostage.

Fisk saw her glance at his holstered handgun. "Believe me, if I was the kind of guy to do half the things you've been thinking all day, I'd have found a gal with a lot less to say and more meat on her bones."

Cara laughed for the first time in . . . she had no idea how long. "Why didn't you just leave me in the bunker?"

"I had to get the animals out of harm's way, so I figured I might as well do the same for you. You had about as much chance of escaping the fire without help as they did."

"Isn't your bunker fireproof?" she asked as they continued to hike, sandwiches in hand.

"Theoretically, but I built it for more long-term, man-made disasters."

"The last few years have been crazy—politically, environmentally, really every way," she said, continuing to look for common ground.

"No crazier than it's ever been." Fisk took a bite of his sandwich, chewed, and talked with his mouth full. "Can't trust the government to have anything but its own best interests in mind. But you learned that the hard way."

"So you believe me?"

"I believe you got yourself into a hell of a pickle and you won't be free for long. Not if Sheriff Burke has anything to say about it."

"I don't understand why you've gone to so much trouble to help me."

"Maybe I don't like helping the government."

"Hiding me away from the authorities, then dragging me countless miles into the middle of nowhere is a lot more than just not helping the government."

Fisk stopped to watch as his sheep go around a muddy hole in the trail. "Do you know what burn pits are?"

She knew they were a military thing, and judging by the pain in his faded blue eyes, they were bad. "I've heard of them."

"During the Gulf War, we got rid of trash by burning it with jet fuel. Everything—medical supplies, paint, plastic water bottles, batteries, even entire Humvees. I was in charge of a unit whose job it was to manage a burn pit over an acre in size. Our barracks were next to that spewing fireball of billowing black smoke."

"Given what you were breathing down by your compou—"

Fisk grimaced.

"I mean your farm," she said, correcting herself. "I can see why you wanted to get away ASAP."

"So many of my buddies got sick. COPD, autoimmune diseases, cancer. So much cancer. When my friend Ron was diagnosed with colon cancer, he went to the Department of Veterans Affairs right away. He waited for two years. A week after they denied coverage, he died, and his wife lost their house trying to pay for it all."

"That's terrible."

Fisk spit into the dirt. "I went in green, but true red, white, and blue. Now, I'm as gray as my hair."

In the past, Cara had written off people like Fisk as ignorant crazies and kooks without a second thought. But if it weren't for his righteous civil disobedience, she would be in custody right now.

"Thank you. For your service. For everything."

"Might want to hold off on your gushing and eat your sandwich," he said, pointing to a steep scree field ahead. "You may not like me nearly as much by the time we get to the top."

FIFTY-ONE
JORDAN

Hope @MaderaCASheriff is watching social media. I know I am! Vote Silverman for Sheriff!
—@Troy4MadSheriff

Jordan carried his fistful of signed paperwork to the front desk, dropped it in the out-box, and made sure the duty sergeant saw it was ready to go. An UberEats driver was lining up Burger King sacks, dinner for the second shift. Jordan's stomach gurgled. He'd ordered a double Whopper meal and planned to inhale it as soon as the CDCR van arrived and LaDonna Williams had been loaded on board.

The pickup was scheduled for 4:45 p.m. and the transfer was routine—but then, Molly Bailey's had been, too, two days ago, and now the habitual drug user was lying in the county morgue waiting for a family member to claim the body.

Jordan wanted to check in on the prisoner for his own peace of mind. He also wanted to ask her one last question.

At the back of the station, Deputies Lopez and Cameron already had Williams cuffed and shackled and were watching the video monitor as the prison van entered the outer gate of the sally port. The inner door would not open until the outer gate was securely closed. Jordan had instructed them to actually bring the van inside to avoid providing a photo op.

"You again!" said Williams when she saw him.

"You cleared the medical exam?" Jordan asked. "No injuries?"

"I tried to tell the doctor I sprained my ovaries so they couldn't transfer me, but he wouldn't listen. Guess I'm healthy enough to incarcerate."

Jordan had to admire her sense of humor. Not many people cracked jokes on their way to Chowchilla. Even though she had been thoroughly questioned by his team, a CDCR investigator, and one of Wen's Marshals while she waited for the next van to arrive, maybe she'd remembered something new.

The outer gate was closed. The security door shielding the garage bay began rolling up with a loud clatter.

"Listen, did Cara Campbell tell you anything about what she had planned or where she was going?"

Williams rolled her eyes. "Like I told you and everyone else, we weren't all huddled around plotting our *escape*. Opportunity knocked that van wide open, so we just took off, and I wasn't about to star in some movie about a sassy Black thief and a famous White murder lady on the run."

Lopez had been pretending not to listen, but he couldn't help laughing at that.

"But if you're still looking for her," Williams added, seeming to reconsider, "maybe I should have followed that fancy bitch."

The CDCR van backed inside, loud beeps echoing around the spotless garage bay. One of the guards climbed out and came around to open the rear doors of the van. As Cameron started helping Williams into the inner cage-like compartment, Jordan headed for the door.

Williams stopped him by calling out. "Seriously, I can't believe you haven't caught her yet. You still looking out in that nasty-ass forest? Hunt that lady down in the nearest mall. She needs to get her hair and nails done. And she wants some clothes. She won't be happy until she trades out those Crocs for Louboutins. If I were you, I'd be searching every store from here to San Francisco."

Jordan turned and nodded. LaDonna Williams may have been a career criminal likely to spend most of her life behind bars, but he liked her.

His pocket buzzed. He took his phone out.

Amber Alert.

I know you're busy. But our daughter's kind of falling apart. Can you come home?

FIFTY-TWO
CARA

"Sometimes they get away." Is that the kind of sheriff you want, Madera County?

—@Troy4MadSheriff

"If you really didn't kill your husband, then who did?"

They had climbed over the scree-covered ridge and down the other side before Fisk finally said it was safe to eat a meal "like civilized people." This, apparently, meant stopping to sit on flat rocks for a meal of salami and cheddar cheese which Fisk sliced and handed to her while he ate his portion off the blade of his pocketknife.

Maybe it was sheer exhaustion, or maybe it was the fact that a hermit survivalist who looked like an extra from *Game of Thrones* was the only person besides her lawyer who'd bothered to ask the one question that mattered. Whatever the reason, the tears she'd managed to hold back all afternoon began pouring down her cheeks.

"Sorry," she said, sniffling, as she wiped her eyes and nose with the back of her hand.

He pulled a tattered blue bandanna from his back pocket and gave it to her. It didn't look exactly clean, but she didn't care. His kindness only made her cry harder.

Fisk stood, raised his arms above his head, and stretched. "Let's talk while we walk. We aren't all that far from where we need to be."

Cara nodded and forced herself upright. Her legs felt like concrete and her back was so sore it was nearly numb. But somehow she put on her backpack, helped Fisk collect the animals, and fell in step beside him. There was no smoke on this side, and the fresh air felt good in her lungs.

It did feel easier talking to his back as they trudged along the rugged game trail.

"All I know for sure is the person who attacked me and killed my husband had a slim build, was dressed in black, and had straight, shoulder-length blond hair. According to the police, the killer was approximately five-nine."

Fisk raised an eyebrow.

"I fit the description, I know, but I didn't do it. And I didn't steal the watch off Karl's wrist. The prosecution claims I tossed it into the bushes to make it look like a robbery."

"Hmm."

"If I was trying to make it look like a robbery, I'd have gotten rid of my own jewelry too. It was even more valuable."

"Who else could be a suspect?"

She was glad he didn't make fun of her for wearing expensive jewelry to glamp. "He had a patient, Sherri Babbitt, who sued him and then stalked him after her case was dismissed as frivolous." The procedure had been a nose job she insisted wasn't upturned enough. "There was also Ezra Threlkeld, who checked us in at the resort and testified against me. He seemed to be everywhere that night and was the first person I found when I finally made my way down the trail. He had blond dreadlocks."

"I guess Sherri at least had a motive. What about this Ezra?"

"That's why they ruled him out—no motive. And Sherri had an alibi."

"The suspect could have been wearing a wig," Fisk observed, scanning the route ahead.

"Which certainly deepens the pool of possible suspects, but the authorities were only focused on me. I held my dead husband in my arms, so I was covered in his blood. And in my panic, I apparently trampled the real killer's footprints. The emergency responders corrupted the entire crime scene, ruining any evidence that I hadn't already. And because the coroner got pulled out of a charity gala and was wearing dress shoes, he didn't want to make the one-mile hike."

Fisk stopped and looked back, surprised. "The coroner didn't look at the scene of the crime?"

"Not until the next day."

"I wish I could say I was shocked," Fisk said.

"I was the only viable suspect, so the media—and social media—went crazy. Especially with my stepdaughter Taylor and Karl's ex-wife Barbara saying things like I killed him because he wouldn't reverse his vasectomy, and I wasn't influencing enough people and was looking to rebrand. At the trial, I found myself in front of a jury who had already heard more opinions about the case from the media than they ever would in the courtroom. And that was before a forensic accountant testified that Karl was having money problems. Which I knew nothing about."

"You got fucked all right," Fisk said.

They trudged onward in a silence broken only by their own footfalls, clomping hooves, the occasional hoot or snort, and as Karl would have said, the divine chirp and hum of the outdoors.

Weirdly, despite her fatigue, Cara was starting to feel stronger. Maybe she was delirious or near death, but she felt like she could keep hiking indefinitely if she had to.

But as dusk fell, Fisk stopped and pointed. Through a break in the trees, she saw a small domed roof. They walked closer and Cara was relieved to discover a rustic yurt with an outhouse and a lean-to barn.

"It ain't Aspen or the Alps, like you're probably used to," Fisk said. "But given the circumstances, I think you'll find the accommodations to your liking."

FIFTY-THREE
JORDAN

What an ugly photo. Of my evil stepmother.
—@TayCamp

Amber met Jordan on the porch. Her eyes were tired, her hair was disheveled, and she was already wearing her pajamas. When she wrapped him in a hug, he squeezed her back gratefully. The coconut smell of her shampoo was a respite from the campfire smell that still lingered over their cul-de-sac.

"How are you doing?" he murmured.

She kissed him and then leaned back. "A little embarrassed to have called you home. But Sydney . . . she's had a rough day. I think I just needed a change of parent."

Ever since their teenager was a toddler, Amber and Jordan had played tag team during difficult emotional episodes. Jordan always wished they'd been able to have more kids but didn't know how this strategy would work if they were outnumbered.

"How are *you*?" Amber asked.

"Still standing."

"That goddamn Silverman."

The way she said it raised the fine hairs on the back of his neck. They broke off their embrace.

"What about him?" he asked.

"You haven't seen the meme from the press conference?"

"No, and I don't want to."

"You need to. But come inside first."

She took Jordan's hand and led him into the house. In the kitchen, he declined her offer of leftover pizza—he had wolfed the burgers while driving home—but accepted a beer since she already had one open for herself. They stood together at a corner of the breakfast bar while she called up the meme on X.

There were two pictures, side by side. On the left, Jordan had been captured looking like a doofus, with his mouth open and eyes half closed. On the right, a luminous Cara Campbell, wearing an off-the-shoulder dress, playfully waved bye-bye.

The caption: *SOMETIMES THEY GET AWAY.*

"You have got to be kidding," he said, giving her phone back.

"I thought everyone would see Silverman for the joke he is, but here we are. He's making this his one and only campaign issue."

"Out of my hands at the moment," Jordan said, tipping back the bottle for a swallow. "I figure maybe it's not such a bad idea to let the Feds chase her, while I keep as many of my people as possible out of danger."

"She's not actually dangerous, is she?"

"There's danger any time you have a bunch of armed, excited people running around in the woods."

He still hadn't told her about his own close call.

Amber squeezed his arm. "Sydney's really upset about the meme. And Bree, obviously. She stayed super optimistic, even after seeing her in the hospital, but I think reality's starting to set in."

Leaving his half-finished beer in the kitchen, Jordan went to Sydney's room, where she was sitting cross-legged on her bed and staring at her phone like it was a Magic 8 Ball. When she looked up, her red eyes and flushed cheeks made his heart ache.

"Hey, honey."

"Hey, Dad."

He sat on the foot of her bed and wiggled her big toe. It was an old joke: when she'd told him she was too big for hugs, he'd insisted she would never be too big for him to hug her big toe. Her eyes brimmed with tears, then overflowed, but she wasn't crying, not exactly.

"It's hard, huh?" he said.

"At first I was just, like, well, if anyone's going to snap out of a coma and be normal again, it's totally going to be Bree. Even after we went to the hospital. But she's probably always going to be messed up. Her life is going to be so *hard*. Assuming she, you know . . ."

"She's at one of the best hospitals in the country."

Sydney suddenly changed the subject: "People are assholes."

"Some of them are." He played along, waiting to see where she was going.

"I can't believe they *memed* you."

"It goes with the job."

"Yeah, but it's already on a top-ten cops-are-a-joke list on Reddit. Such bullshit."

He let go of her toe and poked her foot with his finger. "Maybe I don't need *all* the stats."

"You have to find her and shut them all up, Dad," she said earnestly. "You probably shouldn't have come home."

His phone vibrated in his pocket. He checked it reluctantly. A 310 area code.

"I was getting tired of looking at Beto and I wanted to see you and your mom," he said, rising from the bed. "Sorry, honey, I have to take this."

He answered in the hall.

"You wanted, like, an update? How about this: the fire is hot but the trail is cold," said AJ Wen. "We've chased a butt load of false sightings by area civilians, some of them mischievous. But we think they're still in what you so poetically call the backcountry. Absent any bodies or signs of life, our working theory is that they're hiking together for some reason yet unknown. We're continuing to search with planes and helicopters, but the odds of finding them are getting less and less likely."

"You going to tell that to the media?"

"Too busy."

"Look, Wen, if you're in charge, then you're in charge. I can't tell people what I don't know."

She sighed. "OK, tomorrow. I'll make a statement."

"What are the next steps?"

"Your people continue to support my people. We're going to wallpaper all surrounding towns with wanted posters and blanket the media with her picture."

"And me?"

"This is a federal task force. Last time I checked, sheriffs are paid at the county level. I'll call you if I need anything."

When she ended the call, Jordan put the phone in his pocket so he wouldn't throw it down the hall.

CALIFORNIA DEATH TRIP PODCAST

SEASON ONE, EPISODE THIRTEEN

Hi, Crime Fam, it's Dylan. If you've been following the events of today, you already know that Cara Campbell is in the smoky wind. This afternoon, I was at the so-called press conference given by Madera County Sheriff Jordan Burke, who admitted that Cara was tracked to what sounds like some sort of compound, but by the time a search warrant came through, both she and the landowner had slipped through the dragnet.

I, like the other journalists on the scene, am left with more questions than answers.

Why would this unnamed person help her? Are they together?

Maybe, maybe not.

Are they even alive?

Maybe. But maybe not.

Because of both the absence of information and the bad acoustics in this cheap hotel room, I'm going to keep it short and sweet. Spotify informs me I have a lot *of new listeners—welcome, all—and I want to direct all of you to something that just appeared on Reddit. It's the full text of something Cara posted from two years ago, months before Karl was murdered.*

The link is in my show notes. I think you'll agree it gives context to who she truly is, which is so important to remember.

If Cara is still alive—and I know we're all praying she is—girlfriend's in grave danger. Crime fam, until we find her, I will be signing off exactly like I did yesterday: if you see something, say something—to me.

R/TRUECRIME

CARA CAMPBELL, INSTAMURDERER

Knowledgeable_Owl • 7 hr ago

Always knew these screengrabs would come in handy. Read it and weep. Or laugh. Or puke.

My name is Cara Campbell.

I grew up right next to Hollywood, a sticky stone's throw from the La Brea Tar Pits. My mom, an actress without many credits, had me at twenty. She spent her short life trading on her looks in an attempt to "marry well." It never panned out for her.

I was at Santa Monica College when Mom was diagnosed with cancer. School seemed suddenly much less important than trying to help her get through chemo. I'm glad I prioritized my time with her because she passed away six months later. She was only forty.

Before she died, I promised her I would find a way to live the comfortable life she'd been unable to provide for both of us.

I found that life with my awesome, smart, and yes, wealthy, husband Karl.

Am I a gold digger?

If that is the name given to someone seeking emotional and financial security, then yes, the Jimmy Choo fits.

I became an influencer—with Karl's blessing—because so many women (and a few men) were constantly asking me how I did it.

Here are some tips that worked for me:

Attend high-end events. I met Karl at an auction.

Location matters. I certainly didn't live in Beverly Hills, or Century City or anywhere cool, but I made sure I made my way to the clubs, restaurants, and watering holes where successful people eat and socialize.

Network. Who do you know that knows someone you should know? You can't meet your friend's wealthy second cousin unless you ask. Karl was my friend's mom's plastic surgeon. While he would never discuss a patient, we knew people in common.

Take up high-end hobbies. Like golf, sailing, and wine tasting. Don't think of it as a dating ruse but as an opportunity to educate yourself about the finer things in life.

Dress well, carry yourself with confidence, and be yourself. Really. Authenticity is the most important trait of all.

DAY FOUR

FIFTY-FOUR

CARA

My new Topanga Sunset Eco Yurt is everything the brochure promised! I'm buying another one so I can put them together and live the dream. ★★★★★

—*Suzanne S*

Perched on a rocky outcropping, Cara held pigeon pose and gazed out at the dewy, forested hillsides. Last night, she had slept on a mattress—however thin and worn—inside the tidy, rustic yurt. This morning, she'd used a clean outhouse, washed with soap and a bucket of fresh water, eaten a full breakfast, and done a series of asanas to relieve her epically sore muscles. Thanks to Fisk, she felt almost safe. Nearly peaceful.

In the before times, Cara used to practice yoga in the hope of finding inner harmony, but really to tone her abs and arms. *Namaste to that*, she thought as she got up and headed back to the yurt.

Fisk was out front examining Lucretia's front hooves.

"Had to remove a couple of pebbles, but she's none the worse for yesterday's wear," he said.

"I have aches and pains in places I didn't know I had," Cara said.

"A few hard days in the high country will do that to a body."

"How far did we go yesterday?"

"Probably eight miles as the crow flies but at least double that on the ground."

Fisk slid a rope halter over Ruth's muzzle. Lucretia and Joanie already had their leads on, and Maybelline was tied to a post, wearing saddlebags.

"What's the plan for today?" Cara asked, expecting an answer along the lines of, *Give a woman a fish and she eats. Teach her to fish in a crystal clear mountain lake, however . . .* If they were going to be up here for a while, she needed to get outdoor savvy. ASAP.

"What's your long-term plan?" he asked instead.

It was a good question. In fact, it was *the* question. "I've been so distracted by trying to stay alive that I haven't been able to really focus on the future until . . . well, now."

"Here we are. It's now."

What *did* she want to do? Right after the verdict was read, with the courtroom spinning around her, Roy Abel had whispered, "This isn't over. Not by a long shot."

He could have said anything—*an asteroid just hit the earth, the judge is a cyborg, I have two Dodgers tickets, but I guess I'm not taking you*—she knew it was just lip service. But now, maybe it wasn't. The only thing Cara wanted more than to have Karl back was to prove she was innocent of his murder. Ironically, the best chance she had of making that happen was probably from prison, where, if she was extraordinarily lucky, she might live long enough for Abel to come up with a technicality or uncover new evidence and have the case reopened.

Going back to prison was a nonstarter.

In fact, she'd survived so many almost-endings in the last three days that she was definitely starting to believe in miraculous second chances. LaDonna was right: the Lord had truly giveth. With Fisk showing her how to live off the grid, it seemed possible to stay out of sight until she figured out her next best move.

"I guess I thought we'd stay here for a while until I can figure out how best to proceed," she said.

"I figured you might say that."

He headed toward the yurt, motioning for her to follow.

As Cara stepped through the squeaky aluminum front door, she saw that his sleeping bag had been stuffed in its sack. On the worn wooden stump that served as both countertop and dining table there was a PB&J, a log of sausage, some cheese, and other snacks similar to the ones they'd eaten along the trail.

"Are we leaving again?" she asked.

"I am. You're welcome to stay here for as long as you want."

He might as well have punched her in the stomach.

"*By myself?*"

"I need to make myself scarce until things blow over. I'm not sure when I'll be able to go back to my place—assuming it hasn't burned down by now. But they have to know we're together, so I'm aiding and abetting a convicted murderer."

"I really am sorry to have dragged you into all of this."

He shrugged. "Shit happens."

"Not this much shit."

"War was worse," he said. "To that end, the camo on top of the yurt is looking good, but with drones and satellites, you're going to want to lie low during daylight. Best case scenario, they won't find you until winter."

She'd assumed he'd be with her, teaching her things until . . . she really hadn't thought things through. By now, shouldn't she have gotten used to the feeling of having her world upended every day?

"Have you ever spent a winter up here?"

"Tried it. Got snowed in for a whole month."

Breathe. Breathe. Breathe.

"I'm going to leave you with a gun. Do you know how to use one?"

Karl kept a Glock for protection, which she'd seen only once on the day he brought it home. The whole idea of having a weapon in the house freaked her out so much she'd told him she never wanted to see it again.

If he'd only ignored her and brought it on the glamping trip. . .

Fisk stepped over to his cot, grabbed a book from a small pile of yellowed paperbacks, and handed it to her. The title was stamped on the tattered forest-green cover in caution-orange block letters: *How to Stay Alive in the Woods.*

"Here's the instruction manual. Read it cover to cover. But if you keep your firewood stocked, boil your drinking water, and don't eat anything with white, milky sap that tastes bitter or soapy, or smells like almonds, you'll be off to a good start."

Why did it feel like another end?

"There are a few basic medications around, but if you get sick or hurt, or get any kind of significant infection—"

"I'm a definite goner."

He nodded.

#LauraIngallsWilder

She wasn't cut out for prison. But she wasn't cut out for this life, either. "I don't think I can make it out here alone, Fisk."

"Well, people do tend to do better in the environments they know best."

She could figure out how to cross the border into Mexico . . . but what did she know of the country besides Cancun, Cabo, and how to order a skinny margarita in Spanish? She couldn't stow away on a ship . . . all that water. Without a passport or any money to get a fake one she wasn't getting near an airport. The only place Cara really knew was Los Angeles. And even then, only the Westside. "I can't go back to Beverly Hills as the fugitive du jour. I'll be recognized immediately."

"That city goes on forever. It can be easier to get lost there than here. Most places, really."

And what would she do when she got there?

Outside, Maybelline brayed in what sounded like sheer panic. Then Joanie, Ruth, and Lucretia joined in.

Without a word, Fisk rushed out the door.

Cara stood frozen, trying to decide whether to dive under a cot or run outside into the bushes.

"Got him!" Fisk shouted.

Cautiously, Cara peeked out of the yurt. Fisk had planted the blade of a shovel into a patch of grass near the donkey, severing the diamond-shaped head of a thick, tan snake whose body still wriggled enough to weakly rattle its tail.

"Is she . . . are you . . . ?"

"Everything's OK."

Cara stepped outside as Fisk dropped the shovel and petted Maybelline until she settled down enough to let him check out her legs, from hooves to haunches.

"You're OK," he murmured. "You're OK."

Cara's heart was still racing. "What would you have done if—?"

"Can't even think about it," Fisk said, wiping away what might have been a tear. "Scoop up what's left of that thing so Maybelline doesn't start freaking out again."

Horrified by the request, Cara stepped over to a pile of kindling and grabbed the longest stick she could find. She resisted the urge to close her eyes as she used both hands to lift the snake with trembling arms—it was surprisingly heavy—keeping it as far away from her body as she possibly could.

"Where do you want me to put it?"

"Edge of the firepit. I'll show you how to skin and cook him before I take off."

"The other white meat," she managed, trying not to pass out.

Fisk laughed and shook his head. "Deep down, you really aren't one of them, what do they call them—"

"Gold diggers?"

"I was going to say Karens."

No Karen she'd ever known had a bingo card of grievances like hers: *Husband Murdered. False Arrest. Life Sentence. Horrifying Van Accident. Harrowing Escape. Near Death Experience. Handling Bloody Rattlesnake Carcass* was practically the free space.

"I can't believe you know the term Karen."

Fisk seemed to smile beneath his bushy mustache. "I've been watching you and thinking about starting my own YouTube channel to show people how to live off the land."

"Very funny." Cara dropped the snake by the firepit. "All I ever wanted or needed in life was security, and look at me now. How could I possibly be any more insecure?"

"It's just my two cents, but it seems to me you've looked to everyone but yourself for that security."

It was true that she'd been completely dependent on Karl. After his death, she'd briefly trusted the police to find his killer. Then she'd relied wholly on her lawyer. When the system failed her, she'd accepted that her conviction was the final word. Her only chance of clearing her name was solving the crime herself. And there was no possibility of that happening—not here in the backwoods. But if she returned to LA, maybe she could find out what she didn't know about Karl and his business dealings. The spouse was always the primary suspect, but wasn't she also always the last to know?

"Are you heading back to civilization?" she asked.

"I suspect our definitions of that are a bit different. But I think I'll be safer on the streets for the time being than out here."

As soon as he answered the question, she knew the answer to her own.

"Fisk, take me with you."

"Are you sure?"

"I'm sure that if I'm going to get caught, or even die, I have to do it finding my husband's killer."

FIFTY-FIVE
JORDAN

U mad, bro?
—#10 on "The 100 Greatest Memes Ever, Ranked," Thrillist

"Maybe you can find her by going online, Dad," said Sydney at breakfast. "I mean, a TikToker spotted her last time."

Jordan pushed back his empty plate and wiped his mouth with a napkin. "If that happens again, I guarantee my phone will blow up."

Sydney put her elbows on the table and tilted her head. "And everyone else's will, too. Maybe we can find a clue or something before that happens."

"It's a little late for me to learn social media," he countered. "Plus, I think Steve Jobs should have been buried upside down with a stake through his heart."

"It certainly couldn't hurt to try," said his wife, giving him a look as she stood up to refill her coffee.

Her expression told him he should let Sydney help to keep her mind off Bree. Amber was so good at nonverbal communication he sometimes wondered why she used words at all.

"You're both aware I don't have any social media accounts," he said.

Sydney rolled her eyes. "Don't worry, Dad. We do. And we can do the hard parts for you."

Which was how he came to spend the next couple of hours looking over his wife's and daughter's shoulders at their phones as they burrowed down rabbit holes on the internet. Sydney was in no shape to go back to school yet, so Jordan put off work and gave in, deciding it probably qualified as family time.

It seemed like a million people had joined the hunt for Cara Campbell and the volume of commentary was deafening, even though it was clear hardly anyone had bothered to read past the headlines before telling everyone in law enforcement how to do their jobs. Both Amber and Sydney were quick to swipe or scroll away from his memed picture, doing their best to spare his feelings, but he couldn't help seeing the unflattering image over and over again. It was like being the winner of a twisted popularity contest.

But not all of the information they uncovered was useless. They listened to the latest update from the *California Death Trip* podcaster Dylan Danvers—who had been at yesterday's press conference with Troy Silverman, which couldn't be good—then followed his link to Cara Campbell's defense of chasing rich husbands.

"Who knows, maybe she *is* innocent," mused Amber.

To which an offended Sydney replied, "*Mom!*"

"She was honest about what she wanted, and her husband was cool with it. They had a prenup, so even if she did it and got away with it, she wouldn't have gotten very much money."

"A multimillion-dollar life insurance policy isn't very much money? And she was totally covered in his blood."

"Both fair points."

"And at trial they said she was worried he might go bankrupt, so she would lose her lifestyle."

Amber shrugged. "She's certainly lost it now. All I'm saying is that, from what I can tell, it seems like she really did love him."

"And his money." Sydney looked at Jordan for help.

"From what I've seen, some people love their partners until they don't," he offered. "And then they kill them."

Most people clearly believed Cara was guilty and were rallying around Karl's adult daughter, Taylor. But a vocal minority seemed to think she was innocent, citing her own injury and the sheer unlikeliness of it all: they couldn't believe she was the type to do it. There were alternative theories of the killer, from a robber (Cara claimed Karl's watch had gone missing), to a disgruntled plastic surgery patient, to a wannabe gold digger who decided that if she couldn't have Karl, Cara couldn't, either. Jordan couldn't help wondering if any of these sleuths knew anything about the case they hadn't learned on social media.

"Let's focus on finding clues to her whereabouts," he continued. "Remember, my job is not to relitigate the trial but to catch her. Is anybody out there talking about Fisk?"

Amber shook her head as she attacked her phone with both thumbs. "The guy has no online presence and there are no photos of him. People are really leaning into the Sasquatch theory."

"Wait, the *Washington Post* found his military ID," said Sydney. "Here it is. Sergeant First Class William Fairfax Fisk, California National Guard."

Jordan was surprised by Fisk's aristocratic middle name, which suggested a family background he wouldn't have guessed. Like so much about the man, it was a mystery. He had been hiding from the world for such a long time that it probably wasn't surprising they couldn't find him now. If he *was* with Campbell—still a big *if,* but one that seemed more and more likely—what the hell were the two of them talking about?

When the Burke Family Task Force's social media investigation started leading them in circles, Jordan finally begged off and headed into work. Even though he'd steered them away from the subject, he puzzled over the question of Campbell's guilt while he drove.

There was no question that many people were wrongfully convicted in the US. But most of them were Black and Brown, urban or rural poor folks railroaded by corrupt or incompetent cops because they couldn't afford decent representation. Meanwhile, Campbell's attorney, Roy Abel, charged five hundred dollars per hour—it was right there on his website—and got most of his clients off. That he had failed with her seemed particularly damning.

Opinions were like assholes, Jordan concluded. Everybody had one. And when every asshole in the world was on the internet, it looked more and more like a toilet. One he wished he could flush away forever.

FIFTY-SIX
CARA

I encourage Cara Campbell to turn herself in. Her best chance of exoneration is through legal means, and I plan to help her every step of the way.

—Roy Abel, Esq., speaking to Fox News

They had been hiking in the dark for hours, aiming for a distant cluster of lights, when Fisk abruptly led Cara and their animal companions out of a wooded area onto a paved street. The homes were mostly one-story with big yards, some with barns and others with garages larger than the houses themselves. One had a semi cab parked in front. Dotted among the older, modest properties were a few incongruously large, modern structures with late-model SUVs crowding the driveway.

Cara thought they looked like Airbnbs. Had Fisk brought her to the outskirts of Yosemite?

Maybelline began to trot, and the other livestock followed suit. Cara and Fisk jogged along with them until the donkey stopped abruptly at a one-story cinderblock house with dark green shutters and brayed loudly.

Cara tried to shush her, but Fisk seemed unconcerned as he swung open a weatherworn, waist-high gate.

"No one pays much attention to domesticated animals around here."

Before they reached the painted wooden front door, it creaked open and a woman with long, purplish-black hair appeared in the doorway. She wore red pajamas that clashed with her zebra-print slippers.

"Well, look what the cat dragged in," she said affectionately.

"There she is, my number one cutie-wootie." Fisk wrapped her in his arms and they shared a lingering smooch that ended only when Maybelline snorted and stamped a hoof.

"Come here, you big, jealous jenny!" The woman kissed the donkey on the nose and then hugged Lucretia, Ruth, and Joannie.

"Rae, this is Cara," Fisk said. "She needs to crash here tonight."

"Cara," Rae repeated with a nod.

Was Cara more surprised that Fisk really did have a woman in his life, or that he'd brought Cara home to meet her?

"Hi," she said, meekly, wondering if Rae recognized her. Either way, Fisk's boo seemed surprisingly unconcerned that he had appeared in the dead of the night with another woman in tow. Maybe Cara wasn't the first stray he'd brought home.

"Well, come on in," said Rae. "But you both smell worse than Maybel. Billy, take the girls to the barn and use the outdoor shower while I show Cara to the bathroom."

Cara followed *Billy* Fisk's partner into her cramped living room. The small house was filled with gems, crystals, and decorative rocks hanging in windows, displayed on shelves, and in the case of several expensive-looking geodes, resting on decorative stands. Rocks were even arranged around the computer desk wedged into a corner.

"I used to own a rock shop," Rae explained, patting the brown microfiber sectional that took up most of the living room floor. "There's no guest bedroom, but the couch is comfy."

"I appreciate it," Cara said.

She tagged along as Rae went into a bedroom with a king-sized bed and matching oak nightstands. On the dresser, next to a bowl of multicolored polished stones, was a framed photo of Rae and Fisk holding hands. She looked radiant, with long, coal black hair, a beaming smile, and a multicolored sundress. Fisk's hair was blond, and he was clean-shaven, revealing charming dimples.

"That was from when we were young, pretty, and thin," said Rae, opening a drawer and looking through her clothes. "Billy's still pretty slim. I've been saving these, thinking I might actually get on a diet and squeeze back into 'em at some point."

The clothes she put in Cara's hands were a *Florida Is for Lovers* tank top, a sports bra, and lavender leggings.

"Thank you."

Rae pointed to a bathroom across the hall. "There are towels in the linen closet, and I'm sure there's a new toothbrush in one of the drawers."

In the brown-and-tan tiled bathroom, Cara dropped her filthy clothes on the curled linoleum floor and stepped into the shower stall. Hot water needled every cut, scrape, and bruise, and the Irish Spring bar soap added a sharp secondary sting. As a kid, Cara's mother always kept the same brand on hand for Martin, the man who was going to be her stepdad but never quite left his actual wife. Cara had to shampoo and rinse three times to clean her hair and get the soap's scent off her skin. When she looked down at her body, she was amazed to see that, despite her injuries, her muscles were more defined than they'd ever been. Scarily, being on the run was the best fitness plan she'd ever had.

Thank God, she was out of the wilderness.

When she emerged from the bathroom, she found a folded blanket and a pillow on the couch. Fisk—scrubbed clean and wearing a fresh T-shirt and shorts—was seated next to Rae at the dining-room table, attacking a plate of hot dogs and tater tots. A similar plate was waiting at an empty chair.

"Sit. Eat," Fisk said, through a mouthful of hot dog.

"You must be hungry," Rae added flatly.

Judging by her cooler expression and body language, Fisk had filled her in. If she hadn't known Cara's last name was Campbell, she did now.

Cara sat down. "Rae, I swear on my life—although I realize it's not worth much right now—I'm innocent."

"Billy says there's at least a fifty-fifty chance."

"More like sixty-forty," he corrected, popping his last two tater tots into his mouth.

"I need to go back to LA. I haven't figured out how, or exactly what

I'll do when I get there, but I have to find out who killed my husband and why."

"Any idea how you'll accomplish that?"

"At the end of the trial, a forensic accountant testified that Karl was having money problems."

"Shouldn't you have known? You're the gold-digger lady."

"Honestly? Money just showed up in my account on the first of every month, and I never questioned it."

Fisk flashed Rae a look that said, *I told you so.*

"Yes, I was a fool, which is why I have to figure out was going on. It was a bombshell, at least to me, and that's the only lead that wasn't looked into." Cara met Rae's gaze. "So, I'm going to follow it."

"Too bad it took all this for you to pay attention to your personal finances."

"The irony is not lost on me, believe me."

"I've never had enough money to lose track of," Rae said, but with a conciliatory tone.

Relieved, Cara started eating. She hadn't had tater tots since she was a kid, and they tasted exactly the same now: crispy and slightly frost-bitten.

"Do you have anyone who can help you?" Rae asked.

"Karl's aunt still stands by me, but she lives in a nursing home. My best friend, Stephanie, will probably help. I'm thinking I'll contact my lawyer first."

"We don't trust lawyers as far as we can throw them," Rae said. "Do we, Fisk?"

Fisk shook his head.

"And yours failed you," Rae pointed out.

"He did, but he also promised me it wasn't over. I can't imagine me escaping was what he meant by that. He at least owes me more information from the forensic accountant—he clearly wasn't ready for what the guy said in court."

"Isn't your lawyer obligated to tell the police you contacted him?" Rae asked.

"I'm just going to talk to him, not tell him where I am."

"You should run my wig theory by him," Fisk said.

"What's that?" Rae asked.

Cara sighed. "My husband's killer had long, blond hair. Fisk thinks it might not have been real."

Fisk yawned and pushed back from the table. "You ladies can keep working through this, but it's time for me to brush my teeth and hit the hay."

"Nose trimmers are in the top drawer," Rae told him, giving him a tender pat on the behind.

"Yes, dear."

Rae stood up as he went into the other room. "I better go with him. He needs his ears done, too."

Cara was left alone at the table, her heart aching for Karl and their own everyday moments, forever extinguished. As she leaned forward to pluck a worn cloth napkin out of an agate napkin holder, the glowing power light from the computer in the front room caught her eye.

Beckoning her.

During the trial, she'd avoided social media and press coverage. But now she wanted to know everything.

While electric toothbrushes whirred behind the closed bathroom door, she crossed the room to the computer and jiggled the mouse. The screen illuminated the room, revealing a piece of paper with all of Rae's passwords taped to the desk by the mouse pad.

Fisk playfully protested in the next room—it sounded as though Rae had begun grooming him in earnest—as Cara logged in and googled her name.

The search results went on for innumerable pages, but the accident, her escape, and the intensifying search were top stories. So, too, were the fires hampering efforts to find her. According to the *Modesto Bee*, a tip line was already inundated with calls. There was video of a press conference given by Sheriff Jordan Burke she couldn't watch without turning up the sound and a link to Dylan Danvers's latest episode on Spotify she definitely did want to hear.

"Jesus, Rae!" Fisk hooted. "Are you trying to kill me?"

It had been six months since Cara logged into Instagram and there were now thousands of unread DMs. She was about to open one from a user called @TotesTeamCara when the commotion in the bathroom stopped.

She logged out, rushed back to the table, and popped a tater tot into her mouth.

The computer screen went dark just as the door opened. Fisk walked across the hall into the bedroom. Rae appeared in the doorway holding a box of Nice'n Easy hair color.

"That talk of wigs gave me an idea," she said.

CALIFORNIA DEATH TRIP PODCAST

SEASON ONE, EPISODE FOURTEEN

DYLAN DANVERS: *Hi, crime fam, it's Dylan. I'm still in my favorite motel room in Madera, California, as you can probably tell from the totally jacked audio. It sounds kind of like a prison cell, ironically. All this place is missing is the flashing neon sign outside the window. Anyway, an hour ago, I concluded a very interesting interview with Taylor Campbell, the daughter of Karl Campbell and the stepdaughter of Cara Campbell. Taylor has always refused to talk to me, so I'd pretty much given up hope—which is why I was so surprised when she contacted me out of the blue. What follows is the audio of our Zoom discussion, lightly edited for pacing and clarity.*

[Theme music.]

DYLAN: *Thank you for joining me, Taylor.*

TAYLOR: *I can't believe I still have to talk about Cara Horowitz but here we are.*

DYLAN: *By Cara Horowitz, you're referring to Cara Campbell, correct?*

TAYLOR: *I will never accept Campbell as her last name. She brainwashed my father into marrying her and then killed him when he had a blip in his finances. That woman is a world-class narcissist. I wouldn't be at all surprised if she plotted this whole escape business and is living it up on some tropical island with another wealthy man who has no idea what's coming.*

DYLAN: *I'm going to push back on that. I saw the crash scene and what was left of the transport van. It's hard to imagine anyone could have engineered such a horrific accident and expected to survive.*

TAYLOR: *You have to understand what kind of person she is in real life. She learned all the tricks of the trade from her mother, who spent a dozen years trying to convince a big real estate investor—whose name I won't drag into this—to leave his family.*

DYLAN: *But when Cara's mother died of cancer, she was single and penniless, right?*

TAYLOR: *Which was sad, of course. But Cara definitely played up the whole, I'm just a poor, pretty, orphan girl from the wrong side of Fairfax thing. I still can't believe my dad fell for it and then let himself get dragged into her hustle. She would have worked him to death with her insatiable quest for fame if she hadn't murdered him.*

DYLAN: *Does some of your resentment come from the fact that it's hard to accept a stepmom who's only five years older than you?*

TAYLOR: *Look, I grew up in Beverly Hills. That happened to half my friends. Why are you focusing on me instead of Cara Whore-owitz? Cara, if you're still alive, turn yourself in, you murderous gold digger. You're lucky you didn't get the death penalty!*

DYLAN: *Even if we have different motives, I want to find her just as much as you do. The world needs to know she's innocent.*

TAYLOR: *Ha! She's not.*

DAY FIVE

FIFTY-SEVEN
JORDAN

I told my husband I wanted a new car. Next thing you know, ads for cars start popping up everywhere. They are watching. They are listening.

—@JJM1234

His overheads flashing and siren wailing, Jordan put the pedal down, pushing his vehicle well over the fifty-mile-an-hour speed limit as he raced north on Highway 41. Vehicles were slow to move out of his way, forcing him to slalom in and out of oncoming traffic. At the crash site where Bree had broadsided Campbell's transport van, he used the piercer siren to get the attention of rubberneckers who had slowed to gawk.

The debris littering the shoulder and the scorched earth were good reminders to slow down.

Instead, he sped up.

AJ Wen had called forty-five minutes ago to tell him, "We've got her."

"In custody?" It was so sudden, he couldn't quite believe it.

"We have a location and warrant. This morning, one of the techs monitoring her online accounts noticed that someone logged into her Instagram last night. We traced the IP address to Sugar Pine, which Google Maps tells me is—"

"Down the road from Yosemite."

"It totally has to be her."

"That's in my county."

"Which is why you get to come."

Wen's sigh pissed him off, but he ended the call without letting her know how much.

Before leaving the station, he had told only Beto where he was going, worried the mole might tip off Silverman, who would beat him to the scene. Jordan hated thinking or acting like a politician, but that's what he was, and if this was Silverman's number one campaign issue, Jordan had to win it.

And make sure there was a picture.

Fifteen minutes later, as the midmorning sun finally topped the mountain peaks, Jordan pulled up a block away from the address Wen had given him. A half-dozen vehicles were already on the scene, a few blacked-out SUVs along with a CHP cruiser and a marked CDCR car.

As he parked and opened his door, Wen climbed out of an Explorer that had seen hard miles since their last encounter.

"No APC this time?" Jordan asked.

"My men will, like, back you up, but I want you to knock on the door. Just the local sheriff, not an army."

"So you realize you fucked up with Fisk. Is this how a fed apologizes?"

Despite the fact she had to look up at him, her fuck-you stare was impressive. "Just do it."

There was nothing to gain from needling her. He didn't fear Campbell, and he believed Fisk was too smart to shoot him. And being first through the door was exactly what he wanted.

"And you don't have any BLM guys with you this time," he said.

"You're safe. The one who shot at you is on desk duty."

Jordan tightened the Velcro on his ballistic vest and pulled on a windbreaker with *MADERA SHERIFF* printed on the back in yellow letters. As the federal agents fanned out behind him—some of them already in position with sniper rifles—he walked around the corner toward the house.

The dusty cul-de-sac was a classic rural California mix of new construction and third-generation shacks. A brand-new house with a BMW in the driveway sat next to a shingled shack with an owner-operated semi-truck in need of a wash.

The address was a squat cinderblock box with green shutters and a weedy front yard decorated with folk-art sculptures and large, unusual rocks that didn't look local. Its sagging fence appeared to have been climbed by every kid in the neighborhood. The shutters were closed, but the place looked lived-in. He heard a soft *baa* and a snort from the backyard.

Jordan swung open the front gate and went up the front walk. He stepped onto the concrete-slab porch and rapped on a splintery front door.

There was no answer.

He knocked again, louder. "Madera County Sheriff!"

Sometimes he just had a gut feeling no one was home. But gut feelings could be wrong. Drawing his gun, he shielded himself behind the doorjamb and tried the doorknob. It turned easily.

He swung the door open and stepped inside.

FIFTY-EIGHT
CARA

Librarians are my heroes!
—@shawondacakes

Cara pulled down the passenger visor and checked the mirror. The woman who stared back had blackish-purple hair with short wispy ends and looked nothing like Cara Campbell of internet fame. She looked janky, but that was a good thing.

Rae had woken her up twenty minutes ago and hustled her into the garage and the passenger seat of an old, yellow Toyota truck. Fisk had left before dawn, Rae informed her, leaving instructions to get Cara out of there.

Where he went, she didn't say, only that the authorities couldn't be far behind either of them.

Cara put the visor back up as Rae checked her rearview mirror and then scanned the empty highway ahead. "I wish I'd had a chance to thank him. I can't believe he took off without at least saying goodbye."

"That's my Billy for you."

"I'm sorry I messed up your time together."

Rae grinned. "We had a nice night. We've never been able to live with or without each other, so we just do both."

"You've been together a long time."

"Thirty years, minus two when we called it quits—twice."

Cara noted from the highway signs that they were heading away from Yosemite. As the traffic became steadier, and the houses closer together, the relative comfort of being with Rae dissolved and her old fear returned. Even though Rae had given her a broad outline of where they were headed, Cara was still flying blind. But what else was new? Sweat broke out on her forehead and the base of her neck when they reached the town limits.

Welcome to Oakhurst, California. Population 5,945.

Driving with one hand, Rae reached into the glove compartment, pulled out a white #10 envelope, and gave it to her. Cara opened it. Inside were two Visa gift cards for $200 each, $250 in cash, and a slip of paper with a handwritten Tarzana address.

"What is this?"

"Travel insurance. From Billy and me."

"I can't accept—"

"You're gonna need every dime and a safe place to crash. When you get there, look for a peace sign in the window. If it's there, then there's room."

"And if there isn't?"

"Let's assume the best. A woman named Willow will answer. Tell her you're from Blue Skies Window Washers."

Assuming the best felt risky, but what else could she do?

"You seem like you've done this before," Cara said, thinking Fisk had clearly been several steps ahead of her as he nudged her toward this inevitable conclusion.

"There are plenty of good people around who won't or can't play by the usual rules," Rae confirmed.

"How do you know Willow?"

"I've never actually met her. But I do know she helps people who don't want to be found."

Cara slouched down in her seat as Rae signaled a right turn and pulled up to the entrance of the Oakhurst Public Library. "What are we doing here?"

"You can use one of the library computers to buy your tickets. Head north on Greyhound to throw them off the trail—Sacramento would be good—and then buy an Amtrak ticket to LA."

"But I don't have a library card or any kind of ID."

"Don't need either one. Walk in, get online, and create an email under a made-up name. Use that email to buy your tickets, then buy a burner phone at the mini-mart so you can download them and have them on hand."

"Where do I get on the Greyhound?"

"In Madera. The local bus leaves at 10:48 a.m. from the Best Western on Highway 41. You can pay the driver in cash."

Cara checked her reflection in the makeup mirror one more time. The concealer she had borrowed from Rae didn't exactly match her skin tone. She would have to trust that, if she didn't recognize herself, no one else was likely to, either.

Rae reached across her and opened the passenger door. "Better get going. It's about a ten-minute walk from the library to the bus stop if you hustle. But don't skulk. Walk right up like you belong."

Cara wanted to give her a hug but received no indication the gesture would be welcome, so she simply climbed out of the truck.

"I can't thank you enough for all of your help. Please tell Fisk I'll pay you guys back as soon as I can."

"You know where we live," says Rae. "But the best way to thank us is by getting as far away as you can, as fast as you can."

FIFTY-NINE
JORDAN

Fuck the police.
—@stingrae2

The home was registered to Rae Ann Salter, a licensed massage therapist, holistic healer, and avid rock collector. She clearly preferred crystals, but minerals of all kinds littered the surfaces of her home, from countertops to coffee table, bookshelves to windowsills. Judging by the clutter, she had lived there for years. Judging by the damp coffee grounds at the top of her full compost container, she had been there that morning.

Fisk had been there, too, at some point. In the pens behind the house were two brown sheep, a black goat, and a ring-eyed mule—the same animals Jordan had seen at the compound four days ago.

But Rae Ann Salter and William Fisk were gone.

Assuming Cara Campbell had actually been there—and there was no reason to believe either Salter or Fisk knew her Instagram login—she was gone, too.

CHP had issued an APB for Salter's vehicle, a canary yellow 2003 Toyota pickup that Jordan imagined wouldn't be hard to find. In the meantime, Wen's men were pulling the place apart for clues. The redhead, Ellett, had pulled on nitrile gloves and was scrutinizing the browser history of the ancient PC balanced precariously on the narrow writing surface of an old rolltop desk. When she was done, the whole machine would be bagged and taken to a state lab for forensic analysis.

Jordan felt antsy and useless, like a sprinter watching someone put together a jigsaw puzzle. Wen obviously believed his talents were limited, and even he had to admit he wasn't a crime scene investigator. What he really wanted was someone to chase.

He was sitting on the couch, leafing through a ten-year-old copy of the *Utne Reader* when the big, blond marshal—his name was Hart, Jordan had finally learned—came inside.

"We got her."

Wen leaned out of the bedroom, holding a baggie of dried mushrooms. "Campbell?"

"Salter. The homeowner. She just drove up."

Jordan stood up and turned to face the door. "It's her house. Why don't you let her in?"

Rae Ann Salter was a short, middle-aged woman with a pretty face, a plump figure, and long purple-black hair that appeared to be a match for the bottle of Clairol Nice'n Easy they'd found in the bathroom trash. She looked more upset than surprised about seeing her home filled with law enforcement officers.

Jordan looked at Wen and raised his eyebrows, wondering if she would let him handle it. She nodded back.

"Good morning, ma'am," he began. "I'm Sheriff Jordan Burke, and these people tracking dirt all over your floors are from various federal agencies, including the US Marshals Fugitive Task Force."

Jordan could see in her eyes that she knew exactly why everyone was there. She was caught but calculating her chances. He guessed she was smart.

"Did you have any visitors last night?" he asked.

"My husband was here, along with some hitchhiker he picked up," she answered matter-of-factly.

"William Fisk is your husband?"

She nodded. "We don't have a marriage license. But we've been together some thirty-odd years."

"What was the hitchhiker's name?"

"I didn't ask."

Which was a neat feint, Jordan had to admit. "And what was he driving when he picked up this hitchhiker?"

"He was hiking out of the backcountry. He spends a lot of time in the woods. She wouldn't be the first hiker he's helped out of a jam. She seemed pretty clueless."

"Where is your husband now?"

"He left this morning. I assume he went back into the woods. He only came here to get our animals away from the fire."

"And the woman?"

Salter glanced at the clock. "I dropped her off in downtown Oakhurst."

Wen moved closer and showed Salter a photo on her phone. "Is this her?"

"Uh-huh."

"You really had no idea who she was?" prodded Wen. "She's famous. She's been all over the news."

Salter crossed her arms. "I got a flip phone and a computer I use to play solitaire, moderate a holistic health message board, and read my spam."

"You don't have any social media accounts at all?"

She grinned, nodding down at her perfectly normal middle-aged body. "Do I look like selfie material?"

"You said you dropped her downtown," Jordan cut in, hoping to get back on track. "Anywhere near the bus stop?"

Salter looked down and started tidying the mess on her coffee table. "Sure, it's possible. But I have no idea where she's headed. I didn't ask. I personally think people have a right to privacy. If she's the big deal you say she is, she's probably calling an Uber. Bet she's never ridden the dog in her life."

Wen looked at Jordan, and for the first time, he felt they were in sync.

"We'll get there faster if I drive," he told her.

She followed Jordan as he ran to his car.

SIXTY
CARA

8.5 tsp sugar in a 12 oz serving? Sweet tea may look innocent, but some doctors say it's diabetes in a bottle!
—Chyron, HLN Morning Express

The Oakhurst library computers were directly across from the reference desk, but the librarian couldn't have been less interested in the woman with savagely chopped, purple-black hair who was using them. Cara hoped her look was so off-putting that everyone else would avoid eye contact, too.

She logged in to one of the terminals and created a new Gmail account using the name Carly Cooper. Using the Visa gift card and her new email, she purchased a Greyhound ticket to Sacramento and researched the Amtrak to LA.

Noting the location of the Best Western, she headed first to a nearby gas station with a convenience store, walking like she belonged, just as Rae had instructed. The day wasn't particularly warm yet, and the cold blast of air-conditioning as the doors whooshed open made her shiver. She grabbed a basket and headed straight for the teriyaki beef jerky. She added three single-serve boxes of breakfast cereal, along with crackers, cheese, and a bag of M&Ms. As she opened the cooler door to grab a coconut water and a Dasani so she could reuse the bottle, a muted TV on the back wall caught her eye. Over the news anchor's shoulder was Cara's glammed and Photoshopped Facebook profile picture.

"Can you believe this shit?" The woman standing beside her yanked open the cooler door and shook her head in disgust.

," he told her. "I'd like to get a second opinion but we're short ."

n moved her finger across columns of type. "If it left on schedule, venty minutes late. But it makes four more stops before even leavn, so that helps. It gets to something called the Chukchansi Gold and Casino at 11:12. After that, the next stop is Madera at 11:51."

dan looked at his watch. "If we're lucky, we can catch her at the "

oments later, Jordan was behind the wheel again, heading south , using all the siren tools at his disposal to hurry a minivan that oxing them in. He floored it as soon as he got past, then called on his cell. He needed to keep this off the radio.

Beto, I want you to send two cars to Madera Intermodal. Campay be en route via an MCC bus. I'm going to try to intercept her, ust in case."

Got it," Beto told him.

Keep it subtle."

Understood."

You want my team, too?" Wen asked from the passenger seat.

'Did you hear me say, 'Keep it subtle'?"

She glared at him. "Let's wrap this up."

He wanted nothing more. Once again, they were agonizingly close. the good news was that Silverman was nowhere in sight.

Driving all out, retracing his path from that morning, Jordan caught with the stubby white MCC shuttle bus just before the turnoff to Indian casino. When he lit the overheads, the bus slowed to a stop wide spot on the shoulder. Jordan rolled past it and pulled over.

As they got out, Wen spoke to him over the hood. "How are you ng to handle this?"

"I'm going to get on the bus."

"She could be armed."

"So could half the passengers. We have a lot of concealed carry linses in this county."

In the narrow aisle, Cara was pinned between the heavyset woman and an ice cream freezer wedged into what probably should have been a fire exit.

"Crazy," she agreed, willing herself not to panic.

"You can't tell me they aren't tracking everything we say and do. You even just think about something, and next thing you know, it's right there on the TV!"

Cara wondered what was coming next. She also wondered whether she could push past the woman without breaking the hinges on the glass door.

"I saw online that this iced tea is supposed to be organic, but what does that matter if it spikes my blood sugar? Might as well have a goddamn Coke Classic. That's what I really want, anyway."

Cara's water bottle crinkled as she unclenched her fist. The angry woman wasn't looking at Cara's Facebook photo, but the scrolling chyron below it—a warning about the sugar content of so-called health beverages.

"Buyer beware," Cara said, trying to smile as the woman made her selection and closed the door. She scooted past and hurried to the front of the store, where she grabbed a disposable smartphone and paid the cashier.

In front of the store, she powered on the phone and keyed in one of the few numbers she'd committed to memory. He answered after only one ring.

"Roy."

He'd given her a special line to call, apparently for clients who hadn't fared as well as those on his vaunted *Wall of Exoneration*.

"It's Cara," she said, feeling short of breath.

There was a stunned pause. "Oh my God. I'm so relieved! Are you OK? You do realize the entire world is looking for you. Just tell me where you—?"

"I need help."

"Anything. I'll come get you. I'll—"

"I need to know everything you've found out about the forensic accountant's testimony."

"All I know is his testimony was a surprise to everyone."

"But you didn't contact him directly to follow up?"

"Not . . . yet."

Why hadn't he already jumped on this for an appeal?

Cara had suggested he look into the general contractor Karl hired to build the surgical center. Karl, who rarely badmouthed anyone, had twice told her the general contractor was a pain in the ass.

Roy dismissed her concerns, saying, "Everyone's general contractor is a pain in the ass."

"I need to go through your files," she told him now. "Everything you have about the surgical center Karl was building."

"OK . . ."

"Also," she added, "The killer could have been wearing a blond wig and that idiot coroner would never have figured that out."

"Are you in town? Let's meet right now."

"Not—" She stopped herself before saying *yet.* "I couldn't exactly come to your office even if I was."

"I definitely get that. Can you give me an email or somewhere I can send you information. Or wire you money?"

Cara heard the rattle of a diesel engine. Her bus was turning off the highway and headed toward the stop.

"I have to go. I'll get back in touch soon."

She ended the call.

SIXTY-ONE
JORDAN

Traffic slowdown on 41 South due to
Expect delays.

—@mad

"Have you seen this woman?"

After striding into the lobby of the Best Weste
way Inn in Oakhurst, Jordan showed his phone to
a man with gray hair and a red face who was perc
walker. *Rodkey Reunion* was printed on his sweatsh
atrium with faux rock and plenty of wood, was cr

The man glanced at it and shook his head. "Ni

"Check again," Jordan urged him. "Her hair has
this photo. Her appearance is likely to be a lot roug

The man looked at Jordan's badge, then examin
"Wait, is that Cara What's-Her-Face? The one who's

Jordan nodded. "We believe she may be in the a

"Well, I did see a short-haired blond who went
bus arrived. Reason I noticed was she was the only or
like a seasonal worker. You know, all the rest of ther
and water bottles and such, and she just had all her stu
But she did look like eight miles of bad road."

Jordan thanked him and crossed the lobby to the f
Wen was consulting a paper bus schedule.

"Possible ID by a man who saw a slim blond with s

"I'm not taking any chances. We let the passengers off one by one and cover the door."

"Fine."

Jordan walked back to the bus. Its passengers were invisible behind tinted glass. The operator had the door open and waiting.

"I wasn't speeding!" she said testily.

"No, you weren't. I need you to ask the passengers to get off in an orderly fashion and line up on the shoulder. Tell them to leave their belongings."

As the driver picked up her handset, looking more alarmed than relieved, Jordan stepped back to a safe distance. He kept his gun holstered as the puzzled passengers began to disembark. Wen drew hers, covering the doorway from an oblique angle that wouldn't alarm anyone.

Jordan counted a half-dozen blonds, male and female, none of whom looked particularly like Cara Campbell. The one who probably looked most like her was a slender, androgynous male with spiky hair.

The bus driver came off last. "That's everyone. Find who you're looking for?"

"Are you absolutely sure that's everyone?" asked Wen, visibly frustrated.

"It is unless someone's hiding behind a seat in the back," said the driver.

Jordan looked at Wen. "I'm going in."

She lowered her weapon while he drew his own. Then he stepped up into the bus.

SIXTY-TWO
CARA

Self-made men are successful, driven, and sexy!
Broke men? I can't be bothered.
—@carasloveisgold

"Is Cammie short for Camille?" asked the driver, Jeffrey, as they headed south on Highway 41.

"Yup," Cara said.

"It's a beautiful name," Jeffrey said. "It suits you."

"Thanks," she said warily.

Never in a million years could Cara have imagined herself approaching a man at a gas station, claiming to have missed her bus to Sacramento, and then asking for a ride. Even from a man who looked suburban and safe in his cargo shorts, On Cloud sneakers, and neatly trimmed beard.

Now she calculated risk differently. After seeing herself on cable news, she knew she couldn't board a bus where all the riders would be on their phones. And wasn't the bus exactly the place authorities would look for a fugitive with bad hair and a box dye job?

"I'm divorced," Jeffrey told her.

Cara considered inventing a partner named Jasmine or Heather but instead decided to keep it simple. "I'm sorry."

"I just keep moving forward," he said, obviously fishing for more sympathy.

"That makes two of us."

"Honestly, I don't mind being single again. It's given me the opportunity to try new things and to meet new people."

Jeffrey's BMW was at least ten years old and had worn leather seats but seemed well maintained. He was a normal person driving a normal person's car. And she had asked him for a ride, not the other way around. Still, just in case, Cara kept her bag of snacks on the floor between her feet and her hand on the phone she'd tucked into the waistband of her leggings.

"I really thought Susan and I were forever," continued Jeffrey. "When we met, I was in the clothing business, and she was in marketing—or so she said. Honestly, the only thing she really marketed was herself. And I was stupid enough to buy what she was selling."

While he continued chatting as if they'd agreed to meet for coffee after matching on Hinge, Cara concluded that Jeffrey was desperately lonely. She could certainly relate.

"I really loved her until I realized she was just after me for the money," he went on. "The money I used to have, that is, before Covid forced me to shutter my business . . ."

Fifteen increasingly excruciating minutes passed, during which Jeffrey reassured her he'd learned his life lessons and was evolving. There would be no more blonds or bimbos, or any relationships that weren't based on mutual respect. It was the kind of conversation that might have ended with her giving him a list of red flags to watch out for, if only he were a little less needy and she wasn't pretending to be the opposite of who she was.

But who was she now?

Up ahead on the highway, Cara spotted a white shuttle bus with tinted windows idling on the gravel shoulder. *MCC* was written on the side in big blue letters.

Jeffrey tapped his brakes as Cara sank in her seat. "Is that your bus?"

"It must have gotten a flat tire or something."

"I can drop you off if you want," he said, sounding a little sad about it.

As they passed, she saw a Madera County Sheriff's cruiser parked in front with its lights flashing. Passengers were filing off, watched by an Asian woman with a drawn gun and—*was that Sheriff Burke?*

Jeffrey laughed. "Whoops! *Someone* is sweating it out right now. It looks like that bus might not be going anywhere for a while."

"That's the problem with public transportation," Cara said, aware of her dampening armpits. "You never really know who's riding with you, what's going to happen, or how long it's going to take to get there."

"I'm headed to Oakland," he said. "I'm happy to give you a ride to the bus station if you want."

Cara couldn't believe her luck. The Coast Sunrise train, which originated in Seattle, stopped in Oakland after Sacramento on its way to Los Angeles. "Are you sure you don't mind?"

"No problem." He smiled and stepped on the gas. "Do you like jazz?"

"Love it," Cara said, a little more warmly than she'd intended, since she didn't want to lead Jeffrey on.

But for the moment, her relief at her narrow escape was intoxicating.

SIXTY-THREE
JORDAN

Q: How many lawyers does it take to change a lightbulb?
A: None. They'd rather keep their clients in the dark.
#LawyerJokes

Jordan slid behind the wheel as he watched the MCC bus lumber off the shoulder and signal its turn into the Chukchansi Gold Resort and Casino. Wen climbed into the passenger seat, already working her phone. It sounded like she was talking to Ellett, her redheaded keyboard jockey, as she ordered someone to round up security camera video from downtown Oakhurst and use some ominous-sounding database to capture bus ticket purchases in Madera County over the last twelve hours.

Jordan called Beto, who answered with, "Just a sec," and put him on hold.

He couldn't decide what to think about the bus. Had he and Wen simply made two bad assumptions? Despite her earth-mother appearance, Rae Ann Salter was a cool customer. She hadn't confirmed his question about where she'd dropped Campbell off, but she hadn't denied it, either. Either she was simply trying not to perjure herself while protecting the fugitive—or she had craftily sent them in the wrong direction.

And either the lobby ID of Campbell was bad to begin with, or she had been there but was smart enough not to get on the bus.

Where *was* she?

"Sorry," said Beto, coming back on the line. "Little busy here."

"You can pull our guys off Madera Intermodal," Jordan told him. "We just swept the bus and she wasn't on it."

"Did you look underneath? Maybe she tied herself on with a belt."

Jordan almost snorted. "Your jokes are so rare, I never see them coming."

"Laughter is the best medicine."

"Maybe I'll have Amber immortalize that one in needlepoint."

Beto chuckled.

"I *know* libraries don't release patron search records," Wen was saying beside him. "But you can find the library's IP addresses, right?"

In his ear, Beto asked, "So what's next, boss?"

"You never call me boss unless you don't have any ideas."

"Well, I'm fresh out."

"Me, too."

Jordan and Wen ended their calls at the same time. Out of the corner of his eye, he saw her poke the red button on her screen almost hard enough to crack the glass.

She turned, scowling. "Are you going to drive?"

"Tell me where."

His voice sounded a little more hopeless than he intended, but he was starting to wonder if they'd truly lost Campbell. The Ford rocked and settled as a semi rolled past. Then silence filled the cab.

Jordan's phone vibrated. Amber Alert.

"Kind of busy at the moment," he told her, even though it wasn't true. He just felt weird talking to her with Wen around.

"Turn on your radio. KMJ. That's 105.9 FM."

She hung up before he could ask why. He so rarely listened to over-the-air radio that it took him a few precious seconds to remember how to work the tuner. When he located the station, he heard a man's polished voice, milking the moment.

"—betray my client's confidence. I can't say anything about her whereabouts or what she intends to do. I believe she is safe. Her voice was strong, and her spirit is unbroken. I hope to work with both her and the authorities to negotiate a safe surrender. As at trial, Cara Campbell maintains that she did not kill her husband."

"We have to learn this from the *news*?" Wen said angrily as an anchor cut in.

Jordan's scalp prickled. Suddenly, he knew. He fucking *knew*. He pounded the steering wheel with the heels of his hands.

Wen shot him a look. "Is that how you treat government property in Madera County?"

"She's going to LA."

"That's not what lawyer man said. How do you know?"

Jordan closed his eyes and pictured Cara Campbell's face in the bright white light of his headlamp on the bank of China Creek. She was cold, tired, and afraid—but she didn't look suicidal. Just before she'd thrown herself into the raging water, he saw a hint of a smile, then a hard glint of determination. He'd dealt with a few murderers in his time. None of them were like her.

"She wants to clear her name. Her home turf is the only place she can do it."

"So she's, like, crazy."

Jordan shifted into drive, checked his mirrors, and pulled into traffic.

"You're going the wrong way, Sheriff," said Wen. "My ride's back up there in the hills."

"Do you want to get to LA before Campbell or not?"

"Leaving right now. With you driving me there."

"That's the idea."

Wen huffed out a sigh and shook her head but seemed to be considering it. "It's a little out of your jurisdiction."

"You lead a multiagency task force. I'm just one more funny-shaped badge."

"And why do I need a county sheriff pounding the pavement in my city?"

It was a good question. This would be nothing like chasing Campbell through the woods. He'd visited LA a number of times over the years, but it wasn't like he knew his way around without GPS, and he had no idea how to navigate the maze of law enforcement that was Wen's specialty.

"Because I can't let it go, I guess."

As Jordan lit the overheads and pushed down on the accelerator to move around a slow-moving car, Wen glanced down at his feet and smirked.

"OK, you can come. But I'm warning you, you're wearing the wrong kind of shoes."

SIXTY-FOUR
CARA

If she was Black, they would have just left her in the woods for the bears to eat.

—Althea P., commenting on "Influencer's Flight Just Our Latest Bronco Chase," an op-ed in the Los Angeles Times

As Cara reached for the BMW's door handle, she felt a soft touch on her elbow.

"So this is it?" Jeffrey asked.

She paused, turned, and flashed him a smile she was sure looked genuine. "I can't imagine what I would have done without you. Thank you so much for driving me all the way."

It was the first truly honest thing she'd said since he insisted, "Tell me all about yourself," forcing her to launch into an embellished version of her mother's life, making it her own. This included a childhood in St. Louis, a move at eighteen to the Sacramento area, the mismatched marriage that quickly ended, a series of brief, bad relationships, and the toxic situation she was escaping in Oakhurst, where she'd gone for a mental reset. Cara claimed she was headed to live with her half sister and that because she was a massage therapist she could easily find work anywhere.

Jeffrey looked at her soulfully. "I feel like we're just getting to know each other. We still haven't talked about how long you're planning to stay in Sacramento. I get up there sometimes and I'm always looking for a good masseuse."

What a dummy she was for inventing that particular profession.

The single friends she once had all swore by a safe word—*Holmes*—a play on the desire to get home and a veiled reference to the 1970s porn star. A text including the name Holmes in any context was a plea to disrupt the date with an urgent message. If Cara had any friends, she'd have sent it in all caps. But she wasn't on a date and had only chatted so relentlessly with Jeffrey to keep him from checking his phone or turning on the radio. He'd badly misinterpreted why.

"I'd love to talk more, but—"

Jeffrey pointed through the windshield to a bar with a neon Bud Light sign, now apparent as the reason he stopped a block short of the train station. "The least you can do is buy me a drink before you head off."

"I don't drink," she said, reaching for the handle again.

"Cammie." He leaned toward her. "Camille."

Cara's back was pressed against the door.

"You can't deny our vibe," he wheedled. "I mean, there were two other people getting gas back in Oakhurst, but you asked *me*."

"You had a friendly face."

"I'm not a one-night stand kind of guy, if that's what you're worried about."

"Not at all," she said, with complete sincerity.

"Well, it seemed like you might be. I mean, considering what you said about the string of toxic relationships you've had." He smiled. "Not that I'm judging."

"I really do have a bus to catch."

"I'm sure they go to Sacramento every hour—I'll look."

As he picked up his phone to do just that, she reached for her bag of snacks. "Thank you, but I'm really just going to—"

Dropping his phone, he gripped her forearm hard and pulled her toward him. She smelled his stale breath and the cloying tang of overworked Speed Stick.

"I'll settle for a kiss goodbye," he said.

She pushed him away with both hands, then pulled the door open and half-fell out onto the sidewalk.

"Tight-ass bitch!"

He reached across to slam the door closed, then peeled out of the parking lot, taking her snacks with him.

The Cara she used to be would never have taken a ride from a stranger and would have been horrified by the whole encounter. But as she walked to the station, her only real regret was that she hadn't eaten her M&Ms along the way.

SIXTY-FIVE
JORDAN

Only an innocent person would fight this hard to evade capture. #TeamCara

—@lizlemonade

Only a guilty person would fight this hard to evade capture. #BringBackTheDeathPenalty

—@judge_jody

They stopped in Bakersfield for lunch. According to Google Maps, they were about two hours from LA, but with traffic it could easily be four. Or five. From Jordan's limited experience, it took fifteen minutes or two hours to get anywhere in LA, depending on freeway congestion.

A man who looked like an off-duty cop slowed his roll as Jordan parked in the lot at In-N-Out Burger, looking quizzically at the Madera County Sheriff's logos on the Ford Interceptor.

Wen climbed out and stretched. "Hope nobody I know sees me. I'll never live it down."

Grandpa Chester had been a fan of some show—or was it a made-for-TV movie?—about a New Mexico lawman improbably reassigned to New York City, where he faced big-city condescension wearing a cowboy hat, a sheepskin coat, and a disarming smile. His grandpa loved it, believing it proved the moral superiority of small-town people—and Madera was indeed a small town back then. It was still relatively small, with a county population of 160,000.

LA Metro was nearly twenty million. Wen would be back in her element, where her skills and resources would be at their most useful. If Jordan wanted to help find Campbell and be there at her arrest, he needed to play up the big-eyed country sheriff routine.

"I can let you drive, if it makes you feel better," he said as they crossed the parking lot.

Wen rolled her eyes. "Maybe you should just cuff me and throw me in back, so everyone knows I'm traveling against my will."

"Happy to help in any way I can."

Inside, they carried their trays to a table in the corner. Jordan sipped his strawberry shake as Wen took a big bite of her Double-Double.

"So what's our plan once we get to LA?" he asked.

"We'll cover likely points of entry and known associates. But the dirty secret is we usually catch them off a tip. That woman's face is, like, *everywhere*. The APB covers the whole state now, and we're posting a reward of $25K. That's a lot of cash to people like Rae and Fisk."

Jordan didn't think either of them were motivated by money but kept that to himself as he worked on his own burger.

"I gotta say," Wen added, dunking a trio of fries in ketchup and shoving them in her mouth. "I'm not sure I understand why you're so into this ride-along. Is it because she got away from you? Or are you worried about re-election?"

Jordan shifted uncomfortably on the molded bench seat, wondering if Bree's involvement in the crash had made him take it more personally. Not that he'd bring that up.

"Probably a little bit of both," he admitted. "It might be because I've never had anything like this happen and I just need to see it through to the end. Campbell's certainly not the typical murderer. You know, my wife thinks she's innocent."

Wen snorted. "Jury said guilty, she's guilty. And anyway, I don't care."

"So you're just doing your job."

Wen took a long drink of her Dr Pepper, then set the cup down and looked at him. "You remember when I was talking about that incident with the county jail bus hijack?"

Jordan nodded. "Someone decided to let them keep driving until they crashed into a church bus."

"Seventeen people, eight of them civilians, burned to death. Six survived with life-altering injuries. That someone was me—I was lead on that action. Which is why they now send me to shitholes like Madera County. No offense."

"Only now it's bringing you back to LA. Which is apparently not a shithole?"

Her eyes locked onto his with smoldering intensity. "My superiors thought this was going to be an easy pickup but now that it has gotten more complicated, there are people who want to take it away from me. I'm going to catch Cara Campbell and haul her ass back to jail."

Her phone chimed. While she answered, Jordan used the opportunity to eat faster. Somehow, despite doing most of the talking, Wen had cleared her tray while he was only half finished.

She listened, barely speaking, then swore and ended the call.

"What is it?" he asked.

She waited until a customer with an overflowing tray lumbered out of earshot. "Someone used a brand-new Gmail address and a Visa gift card to buy a Greyhound ticket this morning. The IP address is a 99 percent match for the Oakhurst County Public Library."

"Where's she going?"

"From Madera to Sacramento. You were wrong. She's headed north."

SIXTY-SIX
CARA

The name says it all: Quiet Car. Why is there always someone who can't understand I have no interest in talking to them?

—@introverted414

Cara settled back in her seat, feeling almost relaxed as moonlit fields rolled past outside her window.

At the opposite end of the Amtrak quiet car, two women were defying the posted no-talking policy by maintaining a murmured conversation, but everyone else was minding their own business in silence and no one had given her a second look. Cara had an untraceable smart phone and a strong internet signal. She slipped in the cheap, wired earbuds that had come with the phone and got ready for a deep dive.

The first thing she found when she googled her name was that the search for her was centering on Oakhurst—*Oakhurst.* Yet another too close call. From a video of Sheriff Burke's afternoon press conference, she learned just how unnervingly close they'd been to catching her. The proceedings were briefly interrupted by a loud billboard truck, after which some douche in a black felt Stetson and rhinestone-studded western shirt pressed the sheriff into admitting that "sometimes they get away." The line had already become a meme, and it was showing up in headlines, too.

She almost felt sorry for him.

The US Marshals Fugitive Task Force had announced a $25,000

reward only an hour ago. More evidence Sheriff Burke had no plans to quit searching for her.

Cara plugged in her phone to save the battery and began clicking and scrolling in earnest. She found a Pinterest board where someone had compiled a list of likely places *for Cara C. to hide out, refuel, and rest* around Fresno. She saw that Trey and Jessica Worhle of Newport Beach had described their lakeside encounter with *the dangerous fugitive* as *truly chilling.* There was video of Sanjay and Devin talking about her, too, but for some reason the sound didn't work. Although she couldn't quite read their lips, their expressions were incredulous but kind. Thankfully, Cara found no mentions of Fisk or Rae. She hated to think she'd drawn a bull's-eye on their backs.

After craning her neck and confirming the woman seated behind her was snoozing, Cara clicked on an *LA Times* op-ed by Althea Plemons, professor of media and communications at a university she'd never heard of. The essay decried the attention and resources devoted to recapturing *the white lady so bored with her wealth, privilege, and free fillers that she bashed in her plastic surgeon husband's head. One can only wonder, weren't her glamping accommodations quite posh enough?*

Cara's fingers froze when she saw a familiar name a couple of paragraphs down.

It comes as no surprise that LaDonna Williams, a woman of color with a history of drug convictions, was recaptured almost immediately following the van accident. She remains barely a footnote. Meanwhile, Ms. Campbell somehow slipped through authorities' fingers and her celebrity grows exponentially with each passing day—as do the resources being squandered to locate the quintessentially attractive, blond, White fugitive.

One Lawrence Bonner, Esq., who claimed to have law enforcement experience, responded with a chilling comment: *Black or White, they're both going to have the book thrown at them for leaving the scene.*

Cara knew she was doomed if she didn't figure out who killed Karl—and maybe even if she did—but the accident had been so bloody and traumatic, surely the authorities had to have mercy on LaDonna.

Didn't they?

Users on both X and Threads had an endless stream of hot takes. Cara had already proven wrong a wilderness expert named Sebastian Sala who gave her *three days outside and she's dead* due to her *profound lack of skills*. Meatless12309 dissed her for being a fake vegan even though she'd never professed to be even vegetarian. Someone named searchguruOK claimed to have it on good authority that Cara joined a Sierra-based cult. (And maybe she had, she thought with a smile: *Fiskism*.) *I Found Cara Campbell* was trending on Instagram with her face Photoshopped into people's vacation pics: on a yacht in the South of France, peering out from behind the Sphinx, and waterskiing on Loch Ness, pulled by Nessie herself.

She definitely found herself in monster-infested waters when she discovered a clip of Roy Abel—a man incapable of crying—pretending to fight back tears while talking to Anderson Cooper.

Her voice was strong, and her spirit is unbroken, he proclaimed as though he actually knew. *I plan to work with both Cara and the authorities to negotiate her safe surrender.*

Cara should have known Roy's reaction to her call—asking repeatedly where she was and how to get a hold of her—had less to do with surprise or relief she was alive, and a lot more with making himself the center of the media blitz. Since she retained him, he'd spent more time giving TV interviews than meeting with her to strategize the case for her innocence. She wanted badly to call Aunt Evelyn, but didn't dare put her plans, or Evelyn, at risk. Nauseated, Cara put down her phone and took deep, silent breaths, inhaling through her nose and blowing out of her mouth, until the feeling passed.

Feeling overwhelmed and unsure where to look next, Cara logged onto Instagram. Without bothering to check her own feed or DMs, she typed in myfriendisinnocent, the account her oldest—and now only—friend, Stephanie van der Lind, had set up to support Cara's doomed bid for justice.

The pinned post was a photo of Cara looking like Bigfoot on the grocery store security camera. Stephanie's caption read: *I'm beyond relieved you're alive. Stay safe my misunderstood, falsely convicted bestie!*

Fat tears rolled down Cara's face, and she smiled when she saw the arrows pointing to the Golden Goose shoes and the Under Armor shirt with links for purchase. That Stephanie had negotiated a brand ambassadorship was comfortingly true to form. Swiping the picture revealed an ad for Winsome Natural Weaves. *The Go-to Choice for Women on the Go!*

Her next post was a repost from *California Death Trip*, urging people to listen.

The host, Dylan Danvers, was originally known for being the child of Los Angeles Rams quarterback Nico Danvers and French supermodel Daphne Boulet, although Cara seemed to remember he'd dabbled in acting and was often in the tabloids during his high-profile romance with model Finola Moore, now his wife.

He'd hit his stride as a true-crime podcaster, one of the very few who'd maintained his belief in Cara's innocence. She felt a warm flush of gratitude as she remembered listening to his season about her, the case, and the initial days of the trial during her house arrest, wishing Roy had allowed her to do an interview on the show. Was he still on her side?

As the woman behind her began to snore, Cara downloaded the most recent episode.

Hey crime fam, it's Dylan, and things just get crazier and crazier in the search for Cara Campbell. Authorities aren't telling me much, but with help from a couple of sources, I learned that this morning they surrounded a house on the outskirts of Yosemite, expecting to find her inside. But she . . . wasn't there. The search moved to Oakhurst but she . . . got away. The APB has been broadened to include the entire Golden State, which tells you something right there. And there's now a big reward for information leading to her recapture. But Cara Campbell is nowhere to be found.

And I say, YOU GO GIRL!

Cara was now buzzing with hope. She had completely given up on the possibility that anyone beside Stephanie and Evelyn could possibly be pulling for her. But Dylan Danvers was fully Team Cara, even after the verdict and her escape.

Carried away by good feelings, she paused the current episode. Skipping his conversations with Taylor and some guy running to be the next Madera sheriff, she cued up "Episode Four: The Trial," just to hear it again. She basked in warm fuzzies as Dylan leaned into the showboating of the Ventura County Coroner, mocking his incompetence. When he made fun of the man's Prada loafers she almost cheered.

She was only halfway through when the back door of the quiet car whooshed open and the conductor entered—apparently, to conduct a random ticket check. As the first passenger reached into his wallet to show the photo ID that matched his confirmed fare, Cara rose and headed for the snack bar as quickly as she could without running.

From the snack bar, she moved to another quiet car, and then into a restroom. Locked inside, Cara quickly found Dylan on Insta and slid into his DMs with a simple message.

It's me, Cara Campbell. I need to talk to you. ASAP.

DAY SIX

SIXTY-SEVEN
CARA

A beautiful and historic train station with lots to see and do inside and out. Make sure you know where you're headed when you get there because it's easy to get lost in Downtown LA. ★★★★★ *(5 stars!)*

—Kim L., Atlanta, GA, TripAdvisor

As the train made its way east toward Santa Barbara, hugging the coast, Cara studied the public transit options between Union Station in Downtown LA and the safe house in the San Fernando Valley. Metrolink was the quickest option and would get her directly to Reseda in forty-five minutes. The bus would take at least twice as long and would require her to make transfers, but the White Oak stop was very close to the address she'd been given. She wouldn't take a cab unless she absolutely had to.

Cara checked her DMs for the millionth time.

Still nothing from Dylan Danvers.

She dodged the conductor all night, until he finally stopped walking from car to car. Her eyelids were so heavy that she finally allowed them to close, sleeping in a window seat for the last thirty minutes of the train ride.

The squeal of metal on metal woke her abruptly. She opened her eyes to see downtown high-rises, old warehouses, and graffitied stucco. The train slowed steadily as it approached the raised platforms above the sprawling, Spanish-style Union Station.

Cara had attended a Children's Hospital gala in the gold-and-brown-tiled art deco ticketing concourse and a wine festival on the tree-lined north patio but had never actually arrived at the station on board a train. At those events, she'd been a VIP. She was today, too, although anyone waiting to greet her would be in uniform and offering not to take her jacket but handcuff her. And instead of looking distinctive in Carolina Herrera, or edgy in Rachel Comey or another hot local designer, she was dressed to fit in. If only she had luggage. Its absence was a dead giveaway.

Spotting a frail-looking elderly woman trying to wrestle her luggage out of the overhead storage bins, she hurried to help.

"Can I help you with that?"

"Thank you, dear," the old gal said gratefully.

Cara was relieved to note the woman's hair color also came out of a bottle and was strikingly similar to hers. As she lugged the bag off the train and onto the platform, the two of them probably looked enough like mother and daughter that no one gave them a second glance.

They emerged into a cavernous passageway that smelled of urine and hot pretzels. Cara lingered, chatting with the woman, until she met up with a potbellied, middle-aged man who appeared to be her actual offspring.

Cara headed for the Metro Rail tunnel toward the front of the station but stopped when she got there. An LAPD cop was standing at the entrance, watching faces with what looked like professional interest. Plan B, then.

The bus left in ten minutes, but to reach it, Cara had to pass a gauntlet of tunnels, some of them also guarded by policemen. Her throat went dry. Were they here for her? The station was busy, but not so crowded they couldn't see everyone passing by.

Whenever she was passed over for a part, her mom always quoted Marilyn Monroe: "Dreaming about being an actress is more exciting than being one." And before she went to her next audition, she always looked in the mirror and gave herself another inspirational boost: "If you're going to do something, do it with style."

Cara took a deep breath and decided to follow the latter advice, with a codicil: *You're dressed different. You look different. You are different.*

She forced herself to approach a man wearing a *Beer Me* T-shirt and a telltale red baseball cap.

"Do you know your way around this place?" she asked, for the first time in her life hoping for directional mansplaining.

He stepped closer just as a strolling cop glanced over. They must have looked like a couple, because his gaze didn't linger.

Red ball cap flashed a yellow-toothed smile. "What are you looking for?"

"A bathroom, actually."

"I think there's one right by the fish tank outside of the bus depot. I'm headed that way, too."

"Awesome!" she said, with as much sincerity as she could muster.

None of the cops seemed to notice her as they passed, probably because they were on the lookout for an unaccompanied blond female. But as they neared the women's restroom, she saw a female officer questioning everyone who entered.

"I *thought* I smelled Wetzel's," Cara said, rerouting toward a pretzel kiosk at the far end of the main terminal.

"Mind if I come with?" asked her companion.

"I've got it from here," she told him. "But thanks for showing me where the bathrooms are."

Escaped convict Cara Campbell certainly wouldn't stand in line buying cinnamon pretzel bites, right?

"What is going *on* around here?" the woman in front of her asked. "There are cops *everywhere*."

Cara shrugged. "No idea."

And then she saw a man wearing a cowboy hat. In his khaki shirt, and army-green Madera County Sheriff's jacket and pants, Sheriff Burke stood out from the all-black LAPD. Stationed in the center of the concourse, he looked methodically from face to face.

Cara didn't dare to move as he trained his gaze on the Wetzel's Pretzels line, scanning from front to back. When he reached her, his eyes widened.

She pretended to check the time on her phone. “Oh, shoot, my bus is about to leave.”

As she fast-walked outside and up the stairs, she heard her Instagram ping.

SIXTY-EIGHT
JORDAN

"It's all about the attention. That's really all she's ever cared about anyway." #TeamTaylor #CatchCara

—@desireek

Was that her?

Jordan hardly had time to register a flickering feeling of recognition before his view of the pretzel stand was blocked by a group of laughing, jostling sailors in dress whites. He started moving closer.

After wasting the previous day driving north and then south again, and a restless night in a cheap downtown hotel, he was overstimulated, sleep-deprived, and dead on his feet. Watching faces in the crowded train concourse he'd had a hard time shaking the feeling he was in a zombie film. He just didn't know if he was surrounded by zombies or if he was a zombie himself.

But that face . . .

Her features matched, although so had a dozen other women who'd gotten some work done. And her rough-cut hair was purplish-black, the same color as Rae Ann Salter's. She'd shared her home with Cara Campbell, and most likely, the bottle of Clairol Nice'n Easy he'd seen in the bathroom trash.

Most damning was the fact that she seemed to recognize Jordan, too.

He moved faster, shoving his way through the crowd. When he reached the pretzel stand, she wasn't there.

"Did you see a black-haired woman just now?" he asked the last woman in line, realizing as he did that she had black hair, too.

The woman pursed her lips and looked him up and down, her eyes lingering on his sheriff's badge. "They say it's the most common hair color."

"Did you see where she went?"

"I didn't see. *So* sorry."

Her tone was confrontational, as if she was ready for a fight. He definitely wasn't in Madera County anymore. Giving up, Jordan turned in a circle, scanning the crowd. When he saw a sign for Metro buses, he started running.

"Coming through!" he shouted, shoulder-barging a man who didn't get out of the way quickly enough.

A worker was buffing the floor to a slippery sheen, but his waffle-soled tactical boots kept their grip.

He ran outside, pounded up an escalator, and emerged on the sidewalk of a bus plaza. The black-haired woman was waiting to board a bus.

"CARA CAMPBELL!" he yelled.

She turned and looked, a victim of instinct. It was her.

Oh, shit, she mouthed.

Other people had heard him. Confusion was coalescing into recognition. As she turned and fled into the crowd of early morning commuters, Jordan chased after her. He finally had the presence of mind to use his radio.

"Target sighted on the east side of the station, at the bus plaza," he said as he broke into a run. "I'm in pursuit."

SIXTY-NINE
CARA

We canceled all endorsement contracts with Cara Campbell immediately after she was charged with murder.
—@readysetgofashion

Leaving behind the bus to Reseda, Cara ran forward to the next one, cut through the line of boarding passengers, and slipped through the gap between it and the one ahead. Shielded from view, she crossed the roadway and hopped the low iron fence to the north.

She didn't dare slow down to look back as she skirted a county transportation building and took stairs three at a time down to East Cesar Chavez. She ran west, into the concealing darkness of the railroad overpass, her own breathing ragged in her ears.

Even with the US Marshals and LAPD on her trail, it was somehow scarier that Sheriff Jordan Burke had followed her to LA himself.

The underpass seemed to go on forever, but when she finally emerged into sunshine, she felt painfully exposed, trapped between traffic and an endless wall. Risking a look behind her, she couldn't see any pursuers, so she slowed to a gasping walk. As soon as she had the chance, Cara ducked into the parking area of a sprawling apartment complex, then jaywalked across Alameda to Placita De Dolores. From there, she worked her way toward the crowd of people at El Pueblo de Los Angeles Historical Monument.

Even though it was still morning, Latin music was already thumping from the bandstand in the center of La Placita and hundreds of tourists were gathered around. Panting and sweating, Cara paused under a trellis covered in brilliant red bougainvillea to catch her breath and cool down. She pretended to admire the dancers while stealing looks over her shoulder for Sheriff Burke. She had to figure out a Plan C. Or was it D? She also needed whatever help she could get.

When she checked her phone, Dylan's message was short and to the point: *You can reach me at 310-777-5479.*

She started to write back immediately: *Thank you! I will definitely call first thing—*

"Care to dance?" asked a small, sturdy man in an aqua western shirt and cowboy boots with matching piping. Above his toothy smile, bored eyes suggested it was his job to dance with tourists.

What she really needed was a long, comforting hug and a ride.

She added the word *possible* and sent her reply to Dylan Danvers.

"I'm afraid I don't know the steps," she said to the man.

"I'll show you," he said, gently taking her elbow to lead her toward the bandstand.

"I just stopped here for a minute to figure out the bus schedules. I really need to get to the . . . Valley."

"Give me one dance and I'll show you. I know how to get from here to anywhere."

As a half-dozen LA cops emerged from Union Station across the street, she gave in and grasped the man's outstretched, fleshy hand.

"One dance," she told him as he placed his hand on her waist.

"I'm Federico."

"Carla."

With the first beat of the salsa tune, he started, and she followed by shifting her right foot behind the left, taking a small step in place, and moving her right foot back. Then she repeated the sequence starting with her left foot, pretending she was just as carefree as all the other people spending a sunny day taking in the sights and sounds of historic Los Angeles.

"Where do you need to go?" Federico asked, honestly sounding more interested in giving her directions than a dance lesson.

"Sherman Oaks," she told him, because it was close to where she was actually headed.

Federico considered this for a moment before making his recommendation. "I would catch the B-Line toward North Hollywood from the Pershing Square station. I'm not sure exactly which bus you'll need to transfer onto, but you can ask the driver if you can't figure it out on your way."

"Thank you."

As the song ended, she gave him a little hug, then took off around the corner at a fast walk.

SEVENTY
JORDAN

Expect delays at Union Station due to police activity.
—@metrolosangeles

Jordan raced into the Patsaouras Bus Plaza. The transit hub was big and crowded, nothing like the rinky-dink bus station back home. The huge oval was laid with red-brick pavers, shaded by evenly spaced palm trees, and jammed with airport shuttles and double-length orange Metro buses.

Fifty yards ahead, Campbell crossed the roadway and slipped between two idling buses. Jordan, cut off by a lumbering bus, ran behind it and sped toward her. But by the time he reached the center of the oval, he had lost her among the passengers waiting to board for destinations all over LA County.

Breathing hard—Campbell was a fast runner, he grudgingly admitted to himself—he ran to the east side, where a bus was easing toward the exit. When he waved the driver to a halt, she was apparently so startled she didn't realize he wasn't with the LA Sheriff's Department.

He boarded and stalked down the aisle, checking every face. She wasn't there.

"Black Lives Matter!" shouted someone as he climbed off.

"Back the blue!" someone else retorted.

By now, reinforcements were arriving: Wen with Crosby, Hart, and Ellett in tow.

"Search every bus before it leaves!" Jordan screamed at them. "Purplish-black hair and a tank top!"

For once, Crosby didn't give him any guff. The Marshals just fanned out and did their jobs with remarkable precision. As uniformed cops arrived, Wen ordered them to seal the perimeter.

Jordan fought sensory overload at the center of the swirling crowd, many of whom were aiming their phones and narrating what they thought they saw.

"Is this a movie?" a teenage girl asked him, looking around for cameras.

Within five minutes, Jordan knew they'd lost her again—how, he had no idea. He was furious at Campbell for this waste of time and money. He was furious at himself, too. He took a final lap, his back drenched in sweat, and found Wen climbing off a bus.

"You had her and you lost her. Again."

"I was the one who told you she was coming to LA." It was weak, but he wanted to say something in his defense.

Wen put on her sunglasses. "And what have you done for me lately?"

Jordan looked around at the milling crowd. "In the woods, she was just lost. She had no idea what to do. Here, she's getting lost on purpose. Hiding in crowds. Maybe she went back into the station."

"I don't think so. We had at least a dozen people right behind you."

"She's from here. You're from here, too. Where would you go?"

"To lose myself in a crowd? Olvera Street."

SEVENTY-ONE
CARA

Olvera Street feels like an authentic mercado in Old Mexico. It's a great place to get lost and forget you're in the heart of Downtown Los Angeles except for all the homeless encampments nearby. Why don't they do something about that?

—Dave L., Las Vegas, NV, Yelp Review

Cara had visited historic Olvera Street, a cobbled pedestrian passageway filled with traditional Mexican shops, clothing stalls, and restaurants, many times before. She'd brought out-of-town guests and even spent an afternoon there as part of an LA staycation weekend as a brand ambassador for Millenium hotels. She and Karl had spent two nights at the Biltmore, taken a ride on the Angels Flight funicular, then made their way to Olvera Street for shopping. They'd eaten lunch at the El Paseo Inn, where the waiter prepared its famous Caesar salads at their table.

The throngs of tourists had added to the all-around charm on that happy weekend. Now, the density allowed her to hide in plain sight.

She ducked into a small shop and bought a pair of sunglasses big enough to conceal her bruise, a bucket hat, and a black unisex T-shirt with Frida Kahlo splashed across the front. She pulled the T-shirt over her *Florida Is for Lovers* tank top before leaving the shop.

Sheriff Burke was walking toward her, this time with the short Asian woman Cara had glimpsed alongside the pulled-over bus on Highway 41 outside Oakhurst.

Hoping to hide the shock on her face, Cara turned and kept walking, careful not to run. How had they known she was here? Two very big men in matching blue windbreakers, one Black and one White, were coming from the opposite direction. They obviously weren't tourists—they were looking at people, not merchandise.

She cut between two vendor carts and ducked into a storefront on the west side of the street. Inside, she squeezed past shelves filled with brightly colored sombreros, blankets, maracas, leather goods, and assorted knickknacks—ignoring a friendly, "Can I help you, miss?"—until she found a door at the rear of the store.

Thank God, it wasn't alarmed.

Cara heard the shop owner say, "What's going on?" as she opened it and pushed through. On the sidewalk of North Main Street, a beverage-delivery truck idled at the curb while its driver wheeled a hand truck into a nearby restaurant.

After quickly checking to make sure no one was watching, Cara used both hands to lift the rolling door on one of the truck's back bays. Other than two cases of Mountain Dew Baja Blast, it was empty. She climbed inside and pulled the door down all the way.

Escape achieved.

SEVENTY-TWO
JORDAN

WHERE IS CARA CAMPBELL?
—Headline, People.com

Jordan was the first one to see her. She had changed clothes already—a new shirt, hat, and sunglasses—but by now he recognized her gait.

She saw him, too, reversing direction, then ducking between two stalls and hurrying toward a store on the first floor of a brick building.

Jordan pointed the way, and he, Wen, Crosby, and Hart all converged on the door at the same time. He barged in first and scanned the room. Low ceilings and narrow aisles, a couple of sunburned tourists gaping at him over a cheap embroidered sombrero.

"What's going on?" asked the owner as the rest of the US Marshals crowded in.

"The woman who just came in—where is she?" he demanded.

"I-I-I think she went out the back."

Crosby and Hart flanked him, but Jordan had the center aisle and reached the back first. The metal fire door was still ajar. He charged through.

Outside, the sidewalk was empty. A delivery driver returning to his truck with an empty hand truck looked at him curiously, then got in and drove away.

Wen ordered her men to spread out and search the neighboring businesses, but most of them were closed. In stark contrast with bustling

Olvera Street—which was little more than an alley—there were few pedestrians here.

"I'm actually starting to respect this girl's skills," Hart chuckled as they regrouped.

Jordan had to reluctantly admit that he was, too. Was her ferocious drive to escape driven by guilt?

Or innocence?

SEVENTY-THREE
CARA

"Hello Sunshine, Hello Mountain Dew"
—Official campaign slogan, 1974

As she sat in the refrigerator-sized truck bay, Cara figured she'd simply hop out when the driver stopped to make his next delivery a few blocks away. But the truck kept moving, jolting her with every turn, until it merged onto what she assumed was the 110 Freeway. She braced herself as best she could, anchoring her body by pressing her feet against the far wall. With each mile, her breathing normalized further. Wherever they were headed, it was safer than where she'd been.

Then the truck came to a sudden stop.

When the door rolled open, Cara was briefly blinded by a flash of sunlight.

The driver jumped back in surprise. "Whoa! The fuck?"

"I'm so sorry!" She held up her hands to show him she wasn't armed. "I didn't mean to startle you."

Which was a joke, because he was definitely not the type to startle easily. The hefty man had a thick, tattooed neck and muscular arms. "What the hell are you doing in the back of my truck?"

"Joy riding?" she improvised.

"Um . . . no."

Cara didn't mean to smile but she couldn't help it. The sheer, surreal ridiculousness of the whole situation—of her new reality—just caught up with her.

"You really shouldn't leave your doors unlocked when you're making deliveries," she told him.

Shaking his head, he took a few steps back and pulled a phone out of a belt holster. She scooted out of the truck, hands still up and open.

"Please don't call anyone," she pleaded. "I didn't take anything. Or drink anything, I swear."

"Good for you."

"Look, I'll be honest with you. I just needed a ride away from Olvera Street as quickly as possible. My date was super scary." Cara had lied more in the last week than she had her entire life and hated that she was getting so good at it. "We matched on Bumble and met for lunch, and it went really, really badly. When he started talking about his fascination with BDSM and suggested we go back to his dungeon, I told him I had to go to the bathroom and just ran out the back of the restaurant."

The delivery driver lowered his phone, seeming to soften. "You know, you're lucky I don't carry a gun."

"I really am so sorry I scared you."

"Surprised me," he clarified. "Don't you have Uber or Lyft?"

"I just didn't feel safe waiting for a rideshare. He could have come out and seen me."

"Dating sucks."

He appeared to be in his early thirties and wasn't wearing a wedding ring, so he probably understood the minefield of online dating a lot better than she did. She had come up with the cover story about a bad date without thinking because it seemed plausible. After meeting Karl, she had been certain she would never date again.

The truck had stopped in front of a mom-and-pop tortilleria on a street that could have been anywhere in the city.

"Where are we, by the way?" she asked.

"South part of Boyle Heights. I'm headed back to the distribution center. Do you need me to call someone for you?"

"You've already been so helpful. I can't thank you enough."

Before he could respond—or follow—she ducked around the corner and disappeared.

SEVENTY-FOUR
JORDAN

She was a quick study when it came to learning the Cumbia, but the LA bus schedule is a whole different dance.

—Federico Santos, Latin dance instructor, speaking to KTLA News

"So what's the fallout online?" Jordan asked.

"Not as bad as it could be," Amber answered.

Phone pressed to his ear, Jordan sat on his heels and leaned against a wall in a hallway outside the Union Station security office.

"Let's hear it."

"Honestly, now that Cara Campbell is in LA, people are super excited and they're seeing her—well, people who look like her—*everywhere.* Which means a lot less of the coverage is about you."

"What about back home?"

"That's where things are more amusing—to me, anyway. Silverman, along with a small army of internet sleuths and murderinos, camped out at the Sacramento Greyhound bus depot overnight. When she didn't show, they fanned out, chasing all kinds of wild rumors. Sydney's watching TikTok and says the party there seems to be breaking up."

Jordan was more convinced than ever that someone inside the station was passing information to Silverman. And Silverman couldn't help blabbing what he knew, the minute he knew it. What even Jordan's deputies hadn't known was his last-minute U-turn after a call to

Roy Abel convinced Wen he'd been right all along: Campbell had been headed to LA.

"Well, our team came pretty close to joining them."

"Silverman's trying to spin it, of course," continued Amber. "His latest Facebook post is an all-caps rant about how you're running around LA instead of taking care of business back home. He even said—get this—you really want to be a movie star. In one of the comments, someone said they had inside information that you have a pitch meeting at CNN for one of those in-depth specials."

Jordan stared at the blank, utilitarian wall and tried to picture himself taking a meeting with Hollywood executives while he was supposed to be tracking a fugitive. He couldn't.

"Silverman was the one who made Cara Campbell a campaign issue, not me."

"All the more reason for him to try to pin it on you."

The certainty that someone was leaking Jordan's movements bothered him. Who was doing it, and why? Did they have a reason to resent Jordan? Did they, God forbid, actually admire Silverman? Had Silverman promised them a promotion if he won the election?

The most likely leaker Jordan could think of was Symonds, the perpetually disgruntled night dispatcher. The man was a walking complaint. But that seemed far-fetched because Symonds didn't trust *anybody*. And Jordan's Achilles' heel as a lawman was that, in his heart, he was basically a trusting person.

Wait until Silverman caught wind of *that*.

"I should get back. Have you talked to Steve and Joanne?"

"We took them breakfast this morning. No change with Bree. They're doing better than yesterday, but that's not saying a lot. I keep looking at Sydney and thinking I never want to let her drive a car again."

"After this, she'll be the most cautious teen driver on the road."

"I'm sure you're right. Love you."

"Love you more."

Jordan ended the call, stood, and knocked for admittance. The

Union Station security center was a dimly lit room with a desk ringed by video monitors. Wen hovered over Ellett's shoulder as she played back recordings from different cameras.

"There," she said, stopping her. "Freeze it. Which one do we like best?"

Ellett worked the joysticks deftly, bringing up four different images of Campbell passing through the station. In the first one, she was getting off the train while carrying the bag of an older woman. Obviously posing as her daughter—smart. In the second, she strode confidently down a concourse, head held high. In the third, she waited in line at the pretzel stand, looking like she really did plan to order. In the fourth, she emerged at the top of the stairs leading to the bus plaza with her wary face plainly visible. Either her bruised eye was healing fast, or she had covered it with makeup.

"That one," Jordan said, tapping the screen.

"I'm kind of fond of the picture with granny," said Ellett.

"Burke's right," said Wen. "Use the fourth one. Clean it up and get it out as soon as possible. I want an updated press release to go out, like, ASAP. Location details, our girl's new hair color, and remind them about the reward."

"Where do we go now?" asked Crosby from across the room.

"It looked like she wanted to get on the bus to Reseda," offered Jordan.

"I'm starving," said Wen. "Anyone know a good restaurant in Reseda?"

SEVENTY-FIVE

CARA

Our state-of-the-art surgical center is situated in a beautifully landscaped private campus featuring hotel-style recovery suites with access to gourmet meals, on-site specialists, and a broad array of wellness-focused holistic treatments.

—www.campbellcosmetic.com

City of Industry was probably fifteen miles away, but Cara was already in East LA, and Sheriff Burke had spotted her as she tried to board a bus to Reseda—two good reasons to hop on the 194 bus line, take an empty seat near the back, and head further inland.

The third reason was the most crucial, she reflected as she pulled her hat down low and leaned against the window as if she were sleeping.

Although Karl's offices were located in Beverly Hills, he had purchased land in City of Industry precisely because it was the last place anyone expected to find a celebrity plastic surgery facility.

The detailed architectural model, which predated their relationship, sat in a position of honor in the living room on a custom-built table. Cara could still hear his enthusiastic pitch for the place, which he shared with all visitors to their home.

"The surgical suite will of course be state-of-the-art, and the recovery suite will be five-star all the way—Frette linens, automated voice control for nursing care, a full-time chef, you name it. Combine that with a full array of spa services and a guarantee of total privacy . . . it's going to be booked two years in advance!"

During the groundbreaking, a giddy Karl had gripped his brand-new shovel and whispered to Cara, "Once this thing takes off, I'm not sure I'll even need my Beverly Hills office."

Cara found it hard to imagine his clients would want to schlep to City of Industry just for consultations but kept her opinion to herself. It was so far away, she herself hadn't returned since the groundbreaking. A year and a half later, Karl was still practicing out of his Beverly Hills office but had told her he was moving some of his operations, including his four-person financial department, to City of Industry.

After Karl's death, she moved the model to his office along with myriad other painful reminders of her loss. She assumed Karl's longtime business manager, Ravi Davis, would settle the finances with his investors and recover any assets, if possible, while winding down the business. He still had other clients, and as far as she knew, was still working out of the new campus.

Maybe she could catch Ravi coming back from lunch to ask him how Karl could possibly have been running out of money.

As the bus reached City of Industry and neared Hanover Road, still two blocks away, she pulled the cord and the driver stopped the bus. As she got off, she looked ahead, half expecting to catch a real-life glimpse of the familiar cardboard model. Maybe she was still too far away.

She trudged up the littered roadway toward the intersection where a giddy Karl had gripped his shovel and grinned, saying, "It's taken ten long years but here we are."

And stopped in shock.

The center wasn't finished. Construction hadn't even begun.

A chain-link fence still surrounded the property, and the pennants she'd helped to hang were torn and flapping in the wind. A banner reading, FUTURE HOME OF CAMPBELL COSMETIC sagged from the locked gate that blocked the cracked driveway.

Cara walked up to the fence, steadied herself, and stared.

The weedy expanse of dirt was strewn with random trash and broken bottles. Someone had tagged the parking lot with the word SORAK in large white script. The only sign of any improvements on the property were the pathetic little holes they'd dug during the groundbreaking photo op.

Cara cried, great gulping sobs that sounded to her own ears like bitter laughter.

Karl was an excellent surgeon, and she had thought he was a competent businessman. Maybe the location couldn't support such a lavish and expensive surgical center. Or maybe the impressive returns he forecasted were too ambitious, given his plan to recruit a cohort of highly trained but young and inexperienced surgeons. But either way, he'd never had a chance to find out. Why had he acted as though everything was proceeding as planned?

Wouldn't it be better to spread out the risk by recruiting a couple of more senior doctors to be your partners? she remembered asking.

The best business partners are silent, he'd told her.

Exactly who had he gone into business with?

SEVENTY-SIX

JORDAN

Now that is good labneh.
—Bart Simpson

"What's the worst thing you ever ate?" Crosby challenged Hart as they all waited for dinner to arrive.

"Hákarl," Hart said promptly. "My girlfriend and I went to Iceland and it's their native dish. Rotten shark, if you can believe that shit."

Crosby seemed intrigued. "What did it taste like?"

"Like . . . cheese soaked in ammonia. I'm gonna get the dry heaves if I try to describe the texture. What about you?"

"I was at this diner in the Midwest, and they served something called a 'loose meat sandwich.' Kind of like a sloppy joe. Which would have been fine except the meat was turning . . . and I found a fingernail in it."

"Jesus, guys, grow up!" said Wen, grimacing. "And shut up. Here comes the food."

Ellett, a Reseda native, had directed them to her favorite Middle Eastern restaurant, a clean, no-frills place still quiet in the dead zone between lunch and dinner. She had been deputized to order for all of them and was now returning from the counter bearing two trays laden with baba ghanouj, labneh, falafel, chicken and lamb shish kebabs, and even salads. No sooner had the food hit the table than the hungry Marshals fell on it like they were starving.

Jordan dug in, too, glad to fill his stomach and take a break from the banter of his companions. Crosby and Hart had been talking nonstop, pointedly excluding him from their jokes—unless he was the butt of them. Ellett didn't seem to know what to do with him. Wen seemed to want to get rid of him but didn't know how to do it. She had been happy enough to work with him one on one, but now that her team had regrouped, he was the fifth wheel on their well-oiled machine.

"So, what now?" Jordan asked, after the gorging lost momentum.

"Ellett's in touch with LAPD, monitoring CCTV," said Wen, swallowing and wiping her mouth with a napkin.

Ellett nodded. "She'd be caught in sixty seconds if she was driving a car."

"And her photo and last knowns have been shared on every channel we have."

"So we're back to waiting for a tip?" Jordan asked.

"That's what she said," said Crosby, fist-bumping Hart.

"You are," said Wen, eyeing the remaining food like she was thinking about going back in. "I'm taking Ellett to HQ so she can use some fancy electronic toys while I brief the chief deputy. And Crosby and Hart are going to spend a couple hours rolling past bus stops before they turn in for bed."

This was clearly news to the two big men.

"Seriously?" said Hart.

Crosby just groaned.

"I'm happy to join in," Jordan told her.

"We're cool," Wen said. "Take a break and call your wife. Call in to your department. I'm sure they've got their hands full up there."

Which was true enough, but Beto had that covered. Jordan was here and couldn't stand the thought of killing time. A few hours ago, he'd thought the chase had come to an end. He wasn't leaving LA without Campbell.

Wen pointed across the table. "Pass the labneh, will you?"

Crosby chuckled as he passed it over. "Cheese. Soaked in ammonia."

"I can't believe how lucky I am to work with a hella amazing team like you guys," she said sarcastically.

Jordan couldn't believe he wanted to be part of it, too.

SEVENTY-EIGHT

JORDAN

A lot of people thought OJ didn't do it, either.
—@Z003Y

HER PRINTS WERE ON THE HAMMER.
—@StocktonStoic

Ignoring Wen's order to go straight to his room and wait for her call, Jordan spent the late afternoon and early evening hours driving the streets of Reseda, slowing at bus stops and crosswalks to scan faces for Campbell's. Once, he had to take evasive action to avoid a familiar black Ford Explorer that pulled over ahead of him to question a group of teens idling on a corner. The last thing he wanted was for Crosby and Hart to tell Wen he was on the street.

But after emptying a tank of gas over five or so hours, he finally called it quits and went back to the motel, where he had nothing to do but stew, exiled to a room that smelled faintly of weed and air conditioner mold.

Wen was probably right that a tip would come in. But the new picture of Cara Campbell had blanketed the media, and they hadn't had any credible sightings yet. Trying to remember if he'd ever seen an image of Karl Campbell alive, Jordan picked up his phone and searched.

A moment later, he was staring at a sixty-ish, affluent-looking man with a practiced smile and white teeth. He had been handsome, but somewhat generically so. His full head of salt-and-pepper hair was probably

SEVENTY-SEVEN

CARA

It's a long day, livin' in Reseda.
—Tom Petty, "Free Fallin'"

The sun had set by the time Cara made her weary way up Tampa Avenue to the address Rae had given her. She pushed open the creaky metal gate and saw a beige stucco house with a rainbow peace flag hanging in the front bay window.

After the day she'd had, she wasn't quite sure she agreed with Fisk that it was easier to get lost in LA than the woods while she searched for Karl's killer. But this place—a random house she never would have looked at twice—was as good a place as any to start.

Because the most direct routes from City of Industry to Reseda would have taken her back to Union Station, Cara had had no choice but to take the long way around on different buses that allowed her to avoid stations. After first heading east, back toward Boyle Heights, she transferred to the 106 south toward Long Beach. From there, she transferred west at Manchester, went north again at Crenshaw, got off at Wilshire, and caught another bus north at Fairfax that took her all the way to Sunset Boulevard. Another bus went over Laurel Canyon into the Valley, where she transferred one last time to reach Reseda. Along the way, she had ducked into a Goodwill to buy a clean T-shirt, well-worn skinny jeans, and a Billabong surfer hoodie.

Cara had once expressed her dismay about LA's stop-and-go traffic to the mayor over a gin and tonic at a cocktail party. Now that she'd spent a sweaty afternoon and evening transferring from bus to bus, Cara was mortified she'd ever dared to complain about anything from the comfort of a Range Rover.

Breathing in the warm evening air, she stepped through the gate and crossed a small front yard with mismatched pavers and weedy clay pots. As she neared the front door, she couldn't help but notice the scrolled-metal security door clashed with the plain vertical bars on the windows.

Cara rang the doorbell next to a mailbox covered by a spiderweb.

No one answered.

She knocked, then finally heard a female voice from behind the closed front door.

"Yes?"

"My name is Claire."

"What do you want?"

"I'm from Blue Skies Window Washers," Cara said, wishing Rae had given her a coded phrase that would sound more believable after hours.

After a pause, two locks clicked open, and a woman appeared behind the security door. She had the deep wrinkles and frazzled, sun-damaged hair of someone who had either spent too many hours at the beach or lived too hard—or both. Her loose floral sundress suggested she was trying to hide a thick middle, but her lean, deeply tanned arms and calves indicated otherwise.

"I have one bed for tonight," she informed Cara briskly. "Tomorrow night is a maybe. It's twenty bucks for a bed and shower, ten more if you want breakfast. The shower is mandatory and happens first thing."

Cara pulled a ten and twenty from her pocket.

The woman pushed the door open. "I'm Willow."

Inside, the living room looked like the set of a very low-budget San Fernando Valley porn shoot. The original dark wood paneling was almost retro, but the mint-green paint and coordinating curtains would never come back in style. Two men and a woman were sprawled on a

dilapidated tan sectional watching *House Hunters I*
huge HD TV.

"No illegal drugs," Willow added, as a twentyis
through a sliding glass door from the back yard, the n
blue glass bong. "Weed and cigs outside."

"No problem." Cara was just relieved she wasn't stayi
house, a fact that wasn't entirely obvious.

She followed Willow down a hallway to a small, lemon-y
room where two metal bunk beds had been wedged togethe
an L shape. The lower bunks were occupied by women who a
to be sound asleep and one of the upper bunks had been claim
a backpack.

"Unaccompanied female sleeping quarters," said her host. "T
bed is yours after your shower."

Back in the hallway, they stopped at a linen closet, where Wi
gave Cara a thin, scratchy towel. "Keep this as long as you're stay
here, but don't leave it in the bathroom. Shower's in there."

She nodded at an open door and then left Cara alone.

Cara went inside the bathroom and locked the door. The floor was tacky, the grout was moldy, and the stained toilet—given the number of people sharing it—definitely warranted paper on the seat. When she was done, she ran the shower full blast but didn't get in. The noise would cover the call she had to make.

Her fingers trembled as she dialed the number Dylan Danvers had given her. She was still struggling to process what she had learned today and had no real idea how to start her search for Karl's financial partners. But Dylan had thrown her a lifeline she would grab with both hands.

The call went to voicemail.

"It's Cara Campbell," she said quietly, cupping her hands around the phone. "I need your help."

enhanced with Rogaine or even hair implants, and his face showed no obvious signs of plastic surgery but seemed suspiciously smooth.

Jordan tried to picture Cara Campbell swinging a hammer at that head and couldn't quite do it.

Finding the obituary, he learned *the handsome plastic surgeon was a standout offensive tackle at UC-Davis.* He remembered from the arrest report that Karl had not been a small man. So how had Cara taken him in hand-to-hand combat? A well-placed hit from a hammer could take down anyone if it came from behind. But Karl had defensive wounds, and most of the hits he'd taken had come from the front—as he rushed to help, according to her.

Jordan fluffed the thin pillows and leaned back against the headboard, bumping it into the wall. He had been moving so constantly that it felt weird sitting still, like getting off a merry-go-round to stand on hard, unyielding ground. He knew he needed more sleep, but the mattress was lumpy and the idea of rest felt like a waste of time. It was more worthwhile to learn about the woman he'd been chasing—specifically, the crime that had sent her to prison.

Unfortunately, he didn't have his laptop and couldn't access the arrest report on his phone. But there was still plenty of reading material.

Sensational social media and web "content" dominated the search results, including the Danvers podcast, which had chronicled the ins and outs of the trial, but he zeroed in on the traditional media. There were long articles in the *New York Times* and the *Los Angeles Times*, and *Rolling Stone*, of all places. The last one was the most useful, because it paired an in-depth story with dates and time stamps.

> 3:01 PM: Cara and Karl Campbell are captured on video at the Mira Monte Shell station. Despite the lack of audio, their body language and facial expressions clearly suggest they are having the kind of argument only deeply unhappy couples can have.
>
> 4:36 PM: Cara posts a reel on @carasloveisgold, gushing about the accommodations at Glamp Ojai. Karl is nowhere

to be seen as she breathlessly catalogs the amenities—luxurious tents, locally sourced gourmet food, and outdoor activities from horseback riding to a zip line—that promise "the most romantic getaway ever!"

5:15 PM: Ezra Threlkeld at Glamp Ojai sees Cara near the unlocked toolshed that contained the hammer used in the crime. At trial, Cara confirmed she was in the area creating video content but had no reason to enter the structure. Because there was no security camera in this area of the glampground, neither assertion could be confirmed.

6:00 PM: Cara swims in the saltwater pool, again sans Karl. Thorsten Markus, a self-described "venture capitalist and adventurer," testifies at trial that "she showed an unhealthy amount of interest in my marital status and what I did for a living." Cara denies speaking with him other than to politely ask him to get out of her shot. Her subsequent post about the pool includes no record of their encounter.

7:28 PM: Cara posts a picture of a bottle of champagne and a tray of light hors d'oeuvres, writing about the imminent moonlight hike to Johnson's Point. In what appears to be a lighthearted tone, she adds that Karl is reluctant to hike because the path is lighted by luminaria—*not exactly roughing it.*

11:24 PM: Ventura County Sheriff's Department receives a panicked 911 call from the lodge at Glamp Ojai from Cara Campbell: "My husband—oh my God, my husband!"

11:51 PM: A sheriff's deputy arrives at Glamp Ojai. After fire department EMTs arrive, they hike to Johnson's Point, led by Ezra Threlkeld.

12:30 AM: At Johnson's Point, the deputies and EMTs discover the lifeless body of Karl Campbell. Savagely beaten, he is covered in coagulated blood, as is Cara, who is treated for a scalp contusion and possible concussion at the main lodge.

1:48 AM: The forensics team arrives and discovers a

hammer nearby. Cara Campbell's bloody fingerprints are later identified on the handle. Ezra Threlkeld identifies the hammer as having been taken from the resort's equipment shed.

Despite the preponderance of circumstantial evidence, and the fact that spouses were always the most likely killers, it still seemed strange to Jordan how quickly Cara Campbell had been charged. The hammer was the only physical evidence linking her to the murder—wasn't it possible she had picked it up to defend herself? Or grabbed it in horror? At trial, she had guessed the latter while admitting she couldn't remember.

Moreover, the killing blows had been delivered to Karl's face. Had Cara Campbell, 5'7" and 126 pounds, really faced off with her big, burly husband and bashed his face in?

The place was isolated enough, but if she really had wanted to kill him, why would she do it while she was working and had told the whole world they were going to spend a romantic night together?

Online, speculators called it an attempt to stage the perfect crime. Many claimed the romantic evening and the public posts were well-planned misdirects, and that the gas-station argument, unwittingly caught on video, showed the true nature of their relationship. Everyone knew #InfluencersSoFake.

Jordan did know from experience that women sometimes killed their partners, but he also knew they rarely did so with blunt instruments when a physical mismatch created a much smaller chance of success. Too, Cara herself had been hit on the head with the hammer—even though the defense couldn't prove the single blow had, as she claimed, knocked her unconscious.

The Ventura County Coroner had become an internet figure of fun because he'd refused to hike to the crime scene in his designer dress shoes. In the court transcripts Jordan found, he came across as a pompous, self-regarding blowhard. But Cara's fingerprints on the murder weapon, the existence of a three-million-dollar life insurance policy naming her as beneficiary, and the lack of an alternate suspect—along with questions about Karl's financial health and Cara's self-incriminating online persona—had convinced the state's attorney to charge Cara Campbell with the murder of her husband.

Given that approximately ten hours had passed between the murder and the coroner's arrival at the clearly contaminated crime scene, Jordan couldn't see how any of the circumstantial evidence found there was admissible in court.

Campbell had never once strayed from her story: Her husband had been killed by a masked, black-clad figure with blond hair spilling out from under a baseball cap. But she had offered no plausible theories as to who that person might have been, other than to claim her husband's missing watch could be a motive. He remembered from the arrest report that it was valuable, but not exceptionally so, and had not turned up in any local pawn shops or online marketplaces.

The trial transcript had been requested by a citizen journalist and reposted online.

PROSECUTOR CAMERON: Ms. Campbell, who would have lain in wait for your husband, choosing such an unlikely time and place? Was it a disgruntled patient, angry at a botched plastic surgery job?

ABEL: Objection, Your Honor. My client is not responsible for trying the case against her.

JUDGE PRUITT: Sustained.

PROSECUTOR CAMERON: Your Honor, surely the defendant would be willing to share any theories about the actual perpetrator, if indeed it is not her.

ABEL: Objection! Speculation!

CAMPBELL: Karl was an excellent plastic surgeon with almost all five-star reviews. Everybody loved my husband. Even his ex-wife. They got along very well. He always saw the best in everybody. He didn't have an enemy in this world that I knew of.

Jordan was seeing spots from staring at the bright screen of his phone. Putting it down, he got up to wash his face. He couldn't do much more than splash it—the cold water trickled from the faucet. He hoped Wen was planning to check on Campbell's remaining friends and family in the morning.

Because if Campbell had come to LA to clear her name, she clearly had a theory she hadn't shared in court.

CALIFORNIA DEATH TRIP PODCAST
PROGRAMMING NOTE

DYLAN DANVERS: *Hi, crime fam, it's Dylan. Sorry, no podcast today. But keep your notifications on and be ready to download my next episode the moment it appears. The next time you hear from me, I promise I'll have something for you that will absolutely blow. Your. Mind.*

DAY SEVEN

SEVENTY-NINE
CARA

WANTED: Cara Irene Campbell. $25,000 reward for information leading to her capture. Please contact US Marshal Justice Prisoner and Alien Transportation System.
—@USMarshalsHQ

Cara opened her eyes, confused, daylight beating on the window shades. The woman in the bunk across from her was snoring. The phone under her pillow was vibrating.

Snapping awake, she lifted the covers and climbed down from the top bunk as gingerly as she could. As she crept across the airless room to the door, the woman who'd slept below her snorted and rolled over.

She answered in a whisper while she padded down the carpeted hallway. "Hello?"

"This is Dylan Danvers." His voice sounded higher and slightly more nasal than on his podcast. Did he use digital effects to deepen it?

"Please hold on." She opened the sliding door to the backyard and tiptoed barefoot over wet grass and cigarette butts to a lopsided picnic table. "Thank you for calling me back. And thank you for continuing to believe in me."

"I do have to ask you a question," he said.

Her heart felt heavy, like a piece of lead in her chest. "But I thought—"

"I'm one hundred percent Team Cara, but give me a little something no one else would know. I need to confirm it's really you. You're the third person who's contacted me claiming to be her."

Of course they had. In a way, it was surprising there were only two before her.

Seeing movement through the partially open window of the men's bedroom, Cara turned toward the dirty white fence. "You said on your podcast that I was on probation at Santa Monica College my first year, but it was actually the first semester of my second year, and I wasn't dating my instructor for a good grade. I'm guessing my old roommates fed you that lie."

"Interesting. And what are the names of those roommates?"

"Pia Valenzuela and Justyn Mallo."

"Either you've done as much research as I have or you're really Cara Campbell," Dylan said, sounding genuinely relieved.

"Too many people have tried to take ownership of my story. I contacted you because it's time for me to take it back."

"Preach," he said. "How can I help you?"

Cara swallowed hard and pressed the back of her hand against her eyes. "Well, my initial plan was to contact Roy Abel and have him help me review my case but—"

"You didn't actually tell him where you are, did you?"

"No," she said, wondering if Dylan was about to ask her to tell him instead.

Thankfully, he didn't. "Listen, I'm completely convinced you were railroaded. And Roy Abel was clearly more interested in fame, fortune, and airtime than helping you find justice. Otherwise he wouldn't have been blindsided by that forensic accountant."

Hearing what she already knew, from the only other person who'd questioned the truth of her case as much as she had, was the closest Cara had come to exoneration since the trial had ended.

A tall, skinny man with an unlit cigarette in his mouth stepped through the sliders and disappeared around the side of the house.

"I can't tell you how much I appreciate this," Cara told Dylan, lowering her voice even further.

"Look, like everyone else, I'm working an angle. I'll help you by telling you everything I know, but in return, I want you to come on my podcast. To tell me absolutely everything that happened from the night Karl was murdered until—"

"I'm captured and sent back to prison?"

"I'm doing whatever I can to keep that from happening."

Cara heard voices and clattering pans in the kitchen. The smell of frying bacon drifted across the yard, making her stomach gurgle.

"Deal."

"OK, here's what I know: first of all, every patient of your husband's who ever complained about anything, from scratchy examination gowns to a surgical outcome, was investigated and cleared. So were all the employees at Glamp Ojai, even dread-headed Mr. Threlkeld."

"I went out to City of Industry to see Karl's surgical center and it—"

"Was never completed," he said. "I know. Kind of surprised you, didn't it?"

There was no point in defending herself. "Karl told me he had some arguments with the general contractor, Michael—"

"Yeah, Michael Donner. The guy is known in the business for his big mouth and his tendency to threaten people with all sorts of stuff. But he never follows through. Plus, he has an alibi and no known criminal associates. But the bigger point is that he never even started the job. He pulled out because he wanted money up front and your husband wouldn't give it to him."

"Oh," Cara managed, deflating. "He was the only actual person Karl told me about. I was kind of banking on whatever happened being connected to him."

"Funny you should say banking. The one thing no one looked into, at least as far as I know, was the financing. I was at a party where people were gossiping about the case, and a very prominent banker told me Karl had been turned down all over town."

"So that's why construction didn't start? But he told me he had the money. He said they were silent partners."

"I can't prove it yet, but I believe your husband may have agreed to a nontraditional financial arrangement with a company that appears to be a front for the Albanian mafia."

Cara had seen a Netflix documentary about the way organized criminals lend respectable businesses money, then load the businesses with debt, force them into bankruptcy, and disappear. Had Karl been desperate enough to make his dream come true that he would have risked it all by taking dirty money?

"How do you know this?" she asked Dylan. "About the Albanians?"

Willow popped her head out of the open door. Cara hid her phone against her body, muffling Dylan's reply.

"Brunch time!" Willow chirped, sounding much more friendly than the night before. Maybe she was just a morning person.

"I'll be right there," Cara said. Then, after Willow went back inside, she told Dylan, "I have to go."

"Next time we speak, it's on the record," he said.

"I promise. But before we do, I'm going to do some more checking myself."

Cara ended the call and went inside. In the kitchen, a platter of crispy bacon waited on the round oak table. The young couple was cutting fresh fruit, and one of the men had just finished pouring water into the coffee maker.

Willow shoveled a stack of pancakes onto a plate and smiled. "Ready for the most important meal of the day?"

All the boarders crowded around the table and introduced themselves. The snoring woman was Deb, the young couple were Anna and Anthony, and Cara's two other roommates were Vida and Ines. A bald guy was Lucas, and a bearded, stout, and heavily tattooed man told her his name was Zeke.

"Nice to meet you all. I'm Claire," said Cara.

She found it ironic that brunch, which she'd always thought of as a Millennial phenomenon she just couldn't get into, had provided her most important moments of on-the-lam camaraderie—first with Sanjay and Devin, then with Fisk, and now at this safehouse deep in the San

Fernando Valley where she was about to sit down with transients, hippies, and ex-cons.

In other words, her peeps.

"I can finish setting the table," Cara offered, having spotted placemats and napkins on the beige Formica counter.

When Deb opened a cabinet and reached for a stack of paper plates, Willow reached over and pushed it shut. "No paper today. We're using the real stuff."

"Gotcha," the unnamed woman said, opening a different cabinet with mismatched plates inside and handing them to Cara.

Willow counted out the silverware and handed it to her.

The whole thing felt downright civilized, like a bed and breakfast for the downtrodden.

When everyone was seated, Willow reached out to Cara and Lucas. Everyone joined hands as she lowered her head and intoned, "For the meal we are about to eat, for those that made it possible, and for those with whom we are about to share it, we are thankful."

"That's beautiful," Cara said.

"It's a humanist benediction. Don't want to offend anyone's beliefs or lack thereof."

"Fruit?" Lucas asked, offering a large bowl filled with berries and melon slices.

As he spooned a portion for her, Cara speared two pancakes and put them on her plate. A bottle of syrup suddenly appeared over her right shoulder.

"Get your hands off that!" Willow grabbed it from the tall, skinny man who'd just appeared in the kitchen and carried the syrup with him to the table. "You know the rules, Joey. You don't pay in advance, you don't eat."

"Aw, c'mon, Willow. Can't I just—?"

"Chill out in the living room? Go ahead. You can pay to eat the leftovers, if there are any."

"Gotta use the can," said Joey, who definitely looked like he needed a meal or three, as he shuffled disconsolately toward the bathroom.

Willow looked embarrassed. "Joey thinks he can pretend he paid me when there's someone new around here and I won't say anything. But rules are rules."

Around the table, people nodded somewhat sheepishly and began to eat.

"These pancakes are delicious," said Cara, hoping to change the subject.

"Willow used my secret recipe for doctoring up the old Krusteaz," Anthony said. "I also do mean slice-and-bake cookies. Maybe I'll make some tonight. You'll be here, right?"

"I don't know yet." After the information Dylan had provided, Cara knew she had a very long and risky day ahead of her. But it was comforting to know she had a place to rest her head if the plan she was making fell apart.

"You really have to try them," Anna said.

"Somewhere you have to be?" Zeke asked from beside the toaster, where he awaited a slice of browning bread. "Because before you came in, some of us were talking about doing a beach day."

Cara tried not to giggle at the thought of a safe house field trip. "Really?"

"I have a van," Willow said. "If you need a ride anywhere, I'd be happy to drop you off, assuming it's not too far out of the way."

"It's tough out there, so we all stick together," Deb said with a dimpled smile.

They were all so friendly and convivial—with the notable exception of Joey—it was disconcerting. Was this a cult? And if so, did Fisk and Rae know? Rae's comment about Southern California could have been a hint.

The answer revealed itself a moment later, when Deb jumped up to grab something from the fridge and her cell phone fell out of her pajama pocket. Cara reached down to pick it up, but Willow got there first, quickly grabbing it and passing it back to Deb.

The whole thing happened fast, but not so fast that Cara didn't see what was on the unlocked screen: a surveillance photo showing her with purplish-black hair over the words *$30,000 REWARD.*

Cara felt like her body was glued to her chair. It took all of her strength to maintain her cheerful expression. The amount had risen overnight.

"Thanks," Deb told Willow casually, slipping the phone back into her pocket. "Anyone need coffee while I'm up?"

Hands went up as, down the hall, the bathroom door opened, and Joey emerged.

They'd made breakfast to stall her. Had they already called the police? Was Deb going to bring back zip ties along with the coffee pot? No matter how leaden her legs, Cara had to get out of the house immediately.

"I'll take some, too, but I need to use the restroom, now that it's available," Cara said, trying to keep her voice as bright and cheerful as everyone else's. "Back in a minute."

She pushed her chair back, deposited her mug by the coffee maker, and headed down the hallway.

Inside the bathroom, she locked the door and quietly tested the handle to make sure. She really did have to pee, even though now she was so nervous she could barely get it out. After she flushed, she pushed open the squeaky vinyl window. No one would question her desire to air out the room out after Joey's visit.

She peered outside. A narrow sidewalk linked the front and back yards. It was a short drop, and she could get a foothold on the stucco.

Before she went through, she picked up the damp, slightly grimy bar of soap and drew a single star on the mirror along with a very brief review of her stay.

EIGHTY
JORDAN

It's a real-life Lost Angeles but starring a dumb blond influencer convict.

—@filmfanaticfred

Jordan felt like he was in a lame TV show about cops as he crouched in a backyard littered with plastic toys, staring at a cinderblock wall. On the other side of that wall lived someone who had called in a tip to the reward hotline saying Cara Campbell was there right now.

He might have missed out entirely if he hadn't been returning to the motel from an early morning shopping trip for clean clothes—the only place he'd found to buy them was a Ralph's grocery store, where he'd picked up socks, underwear, and an LA Rams golf shirt. He was pulling into the lot as Wen and her team came out of their rooms, armed and serious. He rode to the address in Wen's back seat, sandwiched between Ellett and Hart while Crosby rode up front.

Upon arrival, they gave him a US Marshals windbreaker ("Wouldn't want to shoot you by accident," joked Crosby. "I'm a Niners fan.") and told him to cover the back. When he'd asked the neighboring homeowner for access to her yard, she hardly looked at his six-pointed badge with the bear in its middle.

Maybe she felt like she was in a lame cop show, too.

Jordan stared at the wall, waiting for Cara Campbell to pop her head over the top like a gopher. Hoping she wouldn't see him crouched behind a peeling chaise longue. Wishing he had a radio so he could follow the movements of Wen's team.

When he heard shouts of "Clear!" "Clear!" "Clear!" he thought, *Screw it.*

Pulling a blue-and-yellow kids' picnic table over to the wall, he stood on it and looked over. Through open sliders, he saw Wen and Crosby and a crowd of bodies inside.

Jordan pulled himself up and over, landing on gravel and cigarette butts. As he headed toward the house, Hart began herding the occupants outside, presumably because the yard offered better crowd control. Jordan counted at least eight scraggly men and women and thought the place looked like a halfway house.

"We totally had her cornered, dude," insisted a stocky guy with biker tattoos. "Can't believe she went out that window."

"I should've thought of that," said a skinny possible junkie with a shake of his head.

"She's only been gone ten minutes, maybe fifteen," said a woman in a tie-dye tank top anxiously.

"Everyone shut up!" barked Wen. "Like, one at a fucking time, OK?"

A hard-looking woman who probably needed to get some moles checked stepped forward. "I'll talk. This is my house."

Completely ignored and with no role to play in the interrogation, Jordan slipped inside to look around.

Ellett nodded at him from the couch but quickly returned her attention to whatever she was doing on her laptop. Living, dining, and cooking areas all flowed together. Jordan passed a large, round table covered with plates of half-eaten food. As he walked through the kitchen, his boots made ripping sounds on the sticky floor.

Down a short hall, Jordan found sour-smelling rooms jammed with cheap metal bunk beds and particle-board furniture. He guessed they'd find enough misdemeanor violations and outstanding warrants to impound the property and send everyone to jail—if they weren't chasing America's most wanted internet personality.

He opened drawers, rifled through duffle bags, and peeked in closets but couldn't find any trace of Cara. She had changed clothes and discarded belongings often enough by now that he didn't even really know what to look for.

In the bathroom she'd escaped, the first thing he noticed was the open window. Its opening would have been too small for most people to fit through. He certainly couldn't make it.

The second thing he noticed was what had been written in soap on the mirror above the sink. A single star, followed by:

Dirty and unsafe. Definitely not worth the $30,000 tip!

EIGHTY-ONE
CARA

Cara couldn't have killed Karl. He was her soulmate. My friend is innocent.

—Sworn testimony of Stephanie van der Lind

If the not-so-safe house had taught Cara anything, it was that she needed to hide in a place where $30,000 was only enough to buy a low-end Birkin bag. While she still had to be wary of everyone's hunger for fifteen minutes of fame, she would be safer in Beverly Hills.

At least, that's what she told herself as the bus dropped her off at the corner of Sunset and Canon Drive.

Her oldest friend lunched on sunny Tuesdays and Thursdays in the Cabana café at the Beverly Hills Hotel, where she always ordered the McCarthy salad and an iced tea with two Stevia. Being seen by the local *ladies who lunch* had led to multiple listings. Even if Stephanie didn't speak to anyone but the server during a given meal, she firmly believed the (maximally tweaked) face time would lead to her star turn in *The Real Realtor of Beverly Hills,* a reality show she pitched to anyone who'd listen.

Both their husbands had viewed their careers as useful tax deductions, but Karl seemed to take a genuine interest in what Cara was doing—she hated to think it was because he actually needed the money—while Noel van der Lind didn't seem to care that Stephanie rarely sold a house. He was more than willing to foot the bill to keep her occupied. Cara believed this was not only because Stephanie was a lot to deal with but because Noel preferred to spend his free time with his "best friend" Timothy.

It was true that Stephanie was dramatic, pandering, and the ultimate opportunist, but Cara loved her anyway. She'd always been loyal to the best of her transactionally oriented ability.

Could she be discreet? It wasn't her forte. Not in sixth grade, when she bragged to the class they'd smoked one of Cara's mom's cigarettes. Not in high school, when Cara mentioned that Richard Margolin was kind of hot and Stephanie invited him to the Sadie Hawkins dance on her behalf, without asking her first. And certainly not when Cara met Karl and Stephanie found out he was a plastic surgeon. *Well done! Free work for both of us!*

Stephanie was, however, utterly predictable, and there was no one more capable of helping Cara do what she had to do next.

Cara entered the hotel from the back and made her way down the winding pathways, past the iconic pool. The Beverly Hills Hotel staff were no strangers to the unconventional sartorial choices of their clientele, and had for decades provided unflinching, first-class service to the filthy rich, whether they slummed it in punk leather, heroin chic rags, or I-don't-care tracksuits. Even so, Cara's weather-beaten Golden Goose sneakers were the only part of her wardrobe that didn't look like they had come straight off the racks at Goodwill. To reduce her risk of being noticed, she stopped behind a pillar to scan the peach-and-green cushioned chairs.

Even if Stephanie's hair hadn't been the same honey-blond shade as half the female diners, and she hadn't been at her usual table in the center of the patio, wearing a multicolored, striped Pucci statement dress, there was no way anyone could miss her.

Cara guessed the plain-looking young brunette sitting across from her was merely her latest assistant, whose duties included having lunch with the boss so she didn't look desperate enough to eat alone.

Feeling a light tap on her shoulder, Cara turned around. She knew the server's name was Rolf without glancing at his nametag because he'd waited on her before.

"May I help you, ma'am?"

Avoiding eye contact, she attempted a Southern drawl. "I have an important message for my boss. She's having lunch here and she's not answering her phone."

"If you can point her out, I'll be happy to relay the message."

"It's . . . secret. I can't tell anyone but her. But it's the lady in the striped dress."

Rolf narrowed his eyes, clearly wondering if this was a drug deal. "I will let her know you are here, behind this post, waiting for her."

Cara's heart thumped as he walked elegantly over to Stephanie and whispered in her ear. Stephanie looked Cara's way first with confusion and then disapproval before she stood up.

She arrived in a cloud of Black Opium perfume.

"The server said you have a message for me?"

"Steffi, it's me," Cara whispered.

Stephanie's blue eyes (enhanced by colored contact lenses) widened. Cara was the only one who ever dared to use her high school nickname.

"Oh! My!" Stephanie gave her a once-over, stopping at the shoes. "God!"

EIGHTY-TWO
JORDAN

You can take the girl out of Beverly Hills, but you can't take the Beverly Hills out of the girl.

—Kim Richards

"She's on the bus," said Jordan. "Has to be."

Jordan, Wen, and the rest of the marshals stood around a paper map that had been spread out on the hot hood of the black Ford Explorer outside the house in Reseda. Ellett had used Uber Eats to order Winchell's donuts and coffee, but all that was left was a greasy box and empty cups. After a two-hour search of the surrounding blocks, going house to house and yard to yard with the help of LAPD, they had once again come up empty.

"He may dress like a tourist, but Burke's right," said Hart. "She's paying cash and taking public transit. No idea how she learned the system so fast. I *still* don't know how to ride the bus."

Wen rubbed her face tiredly. "ETA on surveillance video?"

"I ask every fifteen minutes, but you know LA Metro," said Ellett. "They probably haven't gotten into work yet."

"Probably still stuck in traffic," said Crosby, making Hart laugh.

"We need to think about where she's going and her most likely landing points," insisted Jordan.

"What are those?" asked Wen. "Her house went to her stepdaughter, who hates her for obvious reasons. And her friends all unfriended her after the verdict, except for one die-hard with an Instagram account."

"We need to put somebody on her."

Wen looked at Hart, who said, "On it, boss."

Jordan made a mental note to call home as soon as he could, then asked, "Who called in the tip?"

"Willow Kania, the woman who owns the house. But that was after the tweaker heard her talking on the phone."

"Any idea who to?"

"Somebody named Dylan."

Dylan Danvers? Jordan's skin prickled. He started to say something and thought better of it. Every time Wen and her team came in hot, they came up empty-handed. He needed to think things through.

Wen's phone chirped and she took the call. She listened for thirty seconds and hung up.

"A waiter named Rolf says he's pretty sure Cara Campbell just turned up at the Beverly Hills Hotel."

EIGHTY-THREE
CARA

One thing's for sure, that woman definitely didn't look like she came from Beverly Hills.
—Willow Kania, speaking to CBS Los Angeles

Behind the wheel of her convertible Porsche Carerra, Stephanie removed a pair of Fendi sunglasses from the console, handed them to Cara, and smiled. "I don't know what's worse: your situation, your hair, or your clothes."

Cara put them on and slouched low in her seat, praying Stephanie didn't drive too fast or too slow.

"What did you tell your assistant when you left?"

"I told her a certain tech billionaire wanted to see a house right now, so I had to go. I told her the whole thing is NDA'd, so I couldn't give her any details."

Which was actually pretty crafty.

"So how, exactly, do you plan to prove your innocence?" asked Stephanie.

"Dylan Danvers said something that confirmed a suspicion I had and gave me an idea."

"You talked to him?"

"I have you to thank for reminding me about his show."

Stephanie entered an intersection as the yellow light turned red.

"What did Dylan tell you?"

"Believe me, the less you know, the safer you are. But I do need you to help me get back into my house so I can open Karl's safe."

"Done. I already texted my salon and told them it was an emergency, but they can't take you for two hours. Which gives us time to get you some decent clothes. I'd take you to the house and give you some of mine, but Gavin only has a half day at school—besides, we really don't wear the same size."

Stephanie had always been two sizes smaller and never failed to mention it. Cara found it comforting that she was more worried about being seen with someone badly dressed than aiding and abetting a fugitive.

They pulled up in front of Neiman Marcus, where Stephanie told Cara to get out and start shopping while she parked. They would meet at the dressing room in the contemporary department. She peeled out and turned the corner before Cara could say she didn't have enough money to pay for anything.

Cara did her best to look like she belonged—after all, she once had—as she grabbed a couple of pairs of cargo pants, some T-shirts, a blazer, and a reasonably priced Varley sweatshirt before locking herself into the dressing room. While she waited, she checked Stephanie's Instagram, just to be sure she wasn't vaguebooking about *a special visitor I can't reveal* or *a top-secret shopping trip at Neiman Marcus*. Thankfully, she hadn't posted a thing.

A few minutes later, Cara heard her on the sales floor, loudly asking for items "in a size four, obviously not for me," before she thundered into the dressing room. "Car . . . are you in here?"

"At the back, on the right," Cara answered quietly, hoping Stephanie would follow suit.

Stephanie's arms were overflowing as she handed Cara a powder-blue double-breasted jacket with a matching short skirt and a canary yellow jumper.

When Cara stripped down to her underwear, Stephanie gasped.

"They're really comfortable," Cara said, feeling defensive, but not willing to admit her bra and panties were from Goodwill.

Stephanie exhaled dramatically and left, returning with a Natori bra and a three-pack of high-cut briefs. "Please leave those things in a trash can before we leave the store."

There was no point arguing that they could be washed.

Stephanie had also grabbed a pair of Jimmy Choo booties, a white sleeveless Cinq a Sept top, and a pair of black jeans. "We need to get you a pair of Vejas. They're kind of last year, but you can't keep wearing that pair of Golden Goose."

"This is all perfect," Cara told her, "but I can't afford the underwear, much less everything else."

"It's on me. This is mostly for my benefit, anyway. I really can't take you into the salon in what you were wearing. Which reminds me, we have to get your makeup that matches your face. I'll grab the essentials, and we'll make sure you don't look like you were in a fight before we go."

Cara was starting to suspect Stephanie had wanted to give her a complete makeover all these years and was now delighted she had her chance.

She gave her a big hug anyway.

EIGHTY-FOUR

JORDAN

Sigalert on the 405 at Sunset.
Traffic backed up to the 101.
—KNX 1070 AM

Wen drove like a native Angeleno, arguing with Crosby about the fastest route to Beverly Hills.

"Let's just take the 405," he said.

"Ventura Boulevard to Coldwater Canyon," she insisted. "I do it, like, all the time."

"Exactly how often do you go to Beverly Hills?"

"Sepulveda, not like anyone cares what I think," muttered Hart.

But Wen didn't drive like a cop. Even with her flashers on, she ceded the right-of-way when she didn't have to and crept through intersections like an elderly driver. Clearly, she had never driven patrol as she rode through the ranks. Her career must have taken a more academic path.

Jordan wished he could take the wheel but knew he was lucky to be in the car. If he went back for his own vehicle, he might never catch up. And really, all that mattered now was being there when they put the cuffs on Cara Campbell.

But that didn't mean he couldn't use this time productively. As the car rolled onto the 101, heading east, he unlocked his phone and located the purple button he'd never once pressed before. To his left, Hart was watching the road. To his right, Ellett was typing furiously on her laptop. Neither so much as glanced over.

Jordan opened Podcasts and searched *Dylan Danvers. California Death Trip* came up right away, apparently the #1 true-crime podcast in the country. Or were the rankings international? Jordan had no idea what the ranking had been last week, but with Campbell's case generating endless publicity, it was no surprise the show was so popular.

He skimmed the show notes for several of the most recent episodes and then pressed the plus sign to subscribe. He'd listen as soon as he had a few spare hours—and after he bought some earbuds.

His phone chimed with an incoming call before he could put it back in his pocket. Beto.

"Hey, we need to talk," said his chief deputy.

"Kind of busy at the moment," Jordan told him quietly.

"Not too busy for this. I found our leaker."

Jordan lowered the phone and asked Wen, "How far away are we?"

"Twenty minutes," said Wen.

"If you're lucky," said Crosby.

"I'll call you back in half an hour," Jordan told Beto.

EIGHTY-FIVE
CARA

That chick and her crazy-ass hair didn't fool me. I knew who she was the second I saw her.

—Joey Lund, Freelance Entrepreneur, speaking to TMZ.com

The hair salon was on the lowest level of a three-story, 1980s strip mall two blocks off Rodeo Drive. Neither Alejandro, who tended to Stephanie's tresses, nor his first assistant, Nestor, could possibly take a walk-in, so Cara had been assigned to the assistant's assistant, Dorit, a young woman with a black cat tattoo nestled in her cleavage.

Cara hoped her ink wasn't a bad omen.

"My friend got a hold of hair color, scissors, and a bottle of Grey Goose during a bad break-up," Stephanie explained as Dorit disbelievingly ran her fingers through Cara's sheep-sheared, purple-black disaster.

"Sure there weren't hard drugs involved?" asked the hairstylist. "You really did a number on yourself."

"Maybe some weed," Cara said.

Stephanie waved her hand at Cara's new clothes, then at her hair. "I took her shopping, but she obviously can't truly start to heal until we fix . . . this."

Dorit motioned for them to follow, then led the way to her station at the very back of the long, mirrored room. As Cara sat in the black-leather swivel chair, half-moons of sweat dampened her new blouse. Despite the heavy eyeshadow and liner Stephanie had applied in the dark parking garage, she still looked too much like her wanted poster. One call from a client and the Beverly Hills police would storm the salon. Hopefully, Stephanie wouldn't slip and use her real name.

"We had someone in here the other day who decided to shave her head—like Britney back in the day—and then changed her mind after two swipes of the razor," Dorit said amiably as she put a cape around Cara's neck. "Alejandro worked his magic and she left looking incredible. A week later, people were coming in to ask for the same style."

"I keep thinking Car . . . oline kind of gave herself a wolf cut, right?" Stephanie asked hopefully.

As the two of them circled the chair, examining her from above and below, a neighboring stylist suggested, "Maybe add some choppy extensions and bangs. You know who you'll kind of look like then?"

"Billie Eilish?" Cara said, wondering how many seconds it would take to reach the fire exit.

Dorit squeezed Cara's neck. "Holy shit! *Don't* look."

"What is it?" Stephanie stage-whispered.

"Numero Uno just walked in."

The air in the salon somehow grew colder, as if a spirit had made its presence known. Cara watched in the mirror—Stephanie blatantly turned her body to watch—as Alejandro appeared from a secret office door, made his way to the front, and kissed Christina Aguilera on both cheeks.

It turned out that Christina had gray roots and needed new extensions. She had in tow her personal manicurist and eyebrow artist, who would also be working on her.

Cara knew it was gauche to even acknowledge big celebrities, never mind touch them. But she could have kissed her all the same. She knew everyone in the salon, including Dorit, would be completely fixated on its most famous patron, not Cara.

She hoped Christina was extra high-maintenance.

"Honey-hued, like your friend's?" Dorit asked Cara.

"No!" Cara and Stephanie said in unison.

"Mahogany," Stephanie decided. "And a wolf cut. Definitely."

Dorit stepped away to mix the color and gather the extensions Cara needed to rock the wolf cut. Cara tried to quiet her mind and think like a forest creature. If she was going to slink around LA unnoticed, being a wolf wasn't a bad way to go.

EIGHTY-SIX
JORDAN

Well I never did see so many TV stars
And I never did see so many rented cars
—Loudon Wainright III, "Hollywood Hopeful"

Cara Campbell was no longer at the Beverly Hills Hotel—if indeed she ever had been. Jordan tried not to let the disappointment get to him, indeed tried not to feel anything at all as he made his way through the lobby, past a comically oversized floral arrangement, toward the front doors.

Wen was interviewing the restaurant server who claimed to have seen Campbell, which gave him a few minutes to call Beto back. He walked outside, down the long red carpet under the portico, and found a few feet of privacy shaded by the hotel's lush green foliage.

"That was forty minutes," Beto said when he answered.

"You honestly wouldn't believe LA traffic."

"Unless they had a bus crash and a brush fire, I really don't want to hear about it. Look, the leak was . . . Gracia."

"You have got to be joking."

"She's in the next room. Wait a second and I'll put you on."

Jordan watched a powder-blue Bentley convertible roll past Wen's double-parked Explorer. A valet opened the door for its driver, a young woman dressed entirely in pale pink leather. She climbed out, then lifted two leashed pets from the passenger seat. Jordan thought at first glance the two furry animals were dogs. A second look, however, convinced him the bushy, wrinkly-faced creatures were in fact some breed of exotic cat. She carried them into the hotel while one blank-faced bellhop took her suitcases out of the trunk and a valet climbed behind the wheel.

"You're on speaker, Sheriff," said Beto, coming back. "I'm in the room with Gracia."

Jordan could hear her crying and her distress wounded him. She was a beloved member of the staff, almost the last person he would have suspected of wrongdoing. He waited until her sobs became sniffles before he started.

"Beto says you have something to tell me, Gracia."

"I didn't mean it," she said, almost too quietly to hear. "I didn't think this would happen. I'm just so sorry, Sheriff."

"Tell me what you said and who you said it to."

She honked her nose into a tissue and then her voice grew louder. "I know you told us not to talk about the case to anybody. But, I mean, I'm nobody, so I didn't think anyone would care what I said. My knitting circle meets twice a week, and you know, everybody has been pestering me with questions. They just wouldn't stop. So I gave them little updates, you know. After a while, it was like we were all playing this guessing game. We all just wanted to figure out where she was."

The valet pulled away in the Bentley, driving it a little roughly, as a Mercedes SUV with blacked-out windows pulled in behind it.

"Who's in your knitting circle, Gracia?" Jordan asked.

She paused, then blew out a breath. "I didn't even know it, but my friend Katie cleans houses for Troy Silverman, his rentals, and I guess she thought it would be good for her if she got on his good side. So she told him everything I said."

Jordan hardly listened as she kept talking, trying to minimize her mistake. He felt guilty about all the deputies he'd mentally accused of disloyalty. He was angry at Gracia, too, an anger mitigated by her simple human need to be the center of attention at her knitting group. He knew that if she had perceived her loose talk as being actually dangerous to him, she wouldn't have done it.

"Gracia, I'm going to have to write you up for this," he said, interrupting her. "Don't violate any other rules for a year, and I'll take it out of your file. But if you talk to anybody at all about any of our investigations going forward, there will be serious consequences. Do you understand?"

"I understand," she sniffled.

"Good. You're a valued member of our staff and I want to keep it that way."

"Sheriff?"

"What is it?"

"There's one more thing you should know. My friend—my ex-friend—told me something about Mr. Silverman you may want to know. She said he's going to LA to find Cara Campbell himself."

EIGHTY-SEVEN
CARA

> *Smudging is a powerful way to energetically cleanse negative energy and invite in new, positive energy. Our Smudge sticks contain a custom bundle of sage, juniper, mugwort, and more. Use the link in our bio to get 30% off. #TikTokShop #FlashSale*
>
> *—@LiveLoveCleanse*

"I think I should go with you," Stephanie said, parking her bright red convertible on the shoulder of Deep Canyon Drive. "It looks less suspicious if there are two of us. Plus, I have a perfect family for the house."

"Steffi!"

"Well, I do." Pouting, she accepted defeat by pulling on a black-and-silver Fendi cap and slumping in her cognac brown leather seat.

Cara climbed out and headed toward her house wishing she was wearing the broken-in Golden Goose sneakers instead of new Stuart Weitzman booties. She didn't have all that far to walk, but she'd directed Stephanie to pull over just past Denbigh Drive, out of the sight lines of her longtime neighbors.

She was watching their houses so intently, she didn't see the Golden Key SUV parked just inside the entrance to her cul-de sac until it was too late.

The private security guard spotted her immediately. Nodding, he rolled down his window.

There was no turning around.

Cara smiled and waved, trying to remind herself that, with her new mahogany extensions and Stephanie-esque wardrobe, she looked nothing like Cara Campbell of internet infamy. Channeling Stephanie, she marched right up to the car, feigning the glib ease of a seasoned realtor.

"Celia Campanozza with Canyon-to-Coast Properties," she said, her voice pitched an octave higher than normal. "I was showing a house around the corner to some clients and thought I'd pop over. Do you happen to know if the Campbell home has been listed yet? I mean, now that she's convicted and all."

"Couldn't tell ya," said the moon-faced officer, who didn't look older than twenty-five. "I'm just here to keep the lookie-loos away."

"I can only imagine."

Cara steadied herself by putting a hand on the car. As she did, she saw a white Ford F350 parked in front of the house. Her house.

What would Stephanie do?

"It looks like someone's doing work inside. I'll just knock on the door and say hello."

The guard looked dubious. "I'm not sure that's—"

"Can't win if you don't play, right?" she said, patting the guard's forearm and marching away before he could make his disapproval more explicit.

She walked past the Cohens, the Seguras, and the Olsens, then climbed the steps toward her custom tempered glass front door.

In his will, Karl left their home to his daughter, Taylor, with the provision that Cara could live there rent free until she remarried. It was theoretically technically legal for Cara to enter—that was, if the hide-a-key still worked in the lock.

Seeing no one in the big, open central hallway, she crouched behind the large planter running the length of the living room windows and scurried across the terraced garden below. On the south side of the house, she kneeled on a paver and located the fake gray rock, almost identical to the real ones, that held their spare key.

Returning to the front door, she slid the key into the lock. It turned easily and the door opened with a satisfyingly familiar swoosh.

"Hello?" she called.

Her voice echoed across the open-concept first floor of her home, a beautiful, modern space with pale wood flooring, custom furniture, and abundant original art. Had it only been three and a half weeks since she'd been here?

She stepped over to the white-stone-planked, glass-enclosed, central staircase. "It's Celia Campanozza with Canyon-to-Coast Properties. Taylor Campbell asked me to come by and take a look."

A male voice came from the lower level, which had the plush home theater that convinced Karl to write an offer on the spot. "Mike from Handy Dandy down here. I'm about to pack it in for the day."

"Doing some big renovations?" she asked, trying to sound like a friendly realtor, looking to price the place right.

"Just updating a glitch in the sound system," he said.

It was more than a glitch. She'd had three different people try to fix it and the audio sounded like it was being amplified through water. Cara wondered if this guy had had any more luck than the others.

"I'll be sure to lock up when I go," she answered, already walking toward the family room, which opened up onto the kitchen and the outside living space.

Cara knew he would hear the click of her heels as she moved through the house, so she made a show of assessing the space, just like a realtor would. She stopped briefly in the kitchen and ran her hands along the black marble countertop, just to feel something familiar. She decided not to open the refrigerator to check on the oat milk and coconut rice pudding she'd picked up from Erewhon two days before the trial ended.

As soon as she heard the garage door open and close, she hurried upstairs.

She hadn't entered Karl's study since his death. She'd asked her cleaning crew to dust and vacuum, leaving everything else just as he'd left it—until one of his diplomas showed up on eBay. After that, she closed the door and cleaned the rest of the house herself.

Now, the door swung open silently. The room still smelled vaguely of Tom Ford cologne. The cracked, old-fashioned leather desk chair Karl loved seemed to be waiting for him, alongside the dusty architectural model of his surgical center—his unrealized dream.

Cara couldn't let herself stop to feel his absence. Walking straight over to the Damien Hirst print behind his desk, she removed it from the wall and keyed in the combination to the wall safe hidden behind.

Inside was a large envelope with $10,000 in emergency cash, a set of keys on a ring with a lucky rabbit's foot, and a sterling silver ID bracelet with *Karl* engraved on it—a tenth birthday gift from Aunt Evelyn. Cara placed all three items in the Marc Jacobs tote bag (cleverly emblazoned *THE TOTE BAG*) she'd brought from Stephanie's car.

Also in the safe was the black plastic case that contained the gun Karl insisted they keep *just in case*.

Cara certainly had room in *THE TOTE BAG*, but the gun still scared her almost as much as it had the day Karl brought it home. She may have been a fugitive, but she had no plans to go all #BonnieAnd Clyde, no matter what happened. Lifting the case, she removed the folder below it and left the gun alone.

Inside the folder were copies of the deed to the house, the title to a boat Karl had part-owned in Marina del Rey, their birth certificates and Social Security cards, and a handwritten promissory note for twelve million dollars. The lender was listed as Gioni Enterprises, LLC.

The borrower? Karl Campbell, MD, d/b/a Campbell Cosmetic.

Just as Dylan said.

Cara pulled her phone from the pocket of her L'Agence jacket and snapped a picture of the contract.

What happened, Karl?

She heard footsteps downstairs.

Stuffing the paperwork back into the folder and then into the safe, she quickly popped the art back onto the wall hook.

Cara started down the hallway, thinking she'd pop into the master bedroom. But when she looked over the railing, she stopped abruptly at the top of the stairs.

Taylor was looking up at her.

"What the actual fuck?" The first words her stepdaughter had spoken to her in nearly two years.

The last time they'd had an actual conversation, Taylor—who looked like a feminine, almost pretty version of her father, complete with the same strong chin and dark brown hair—had told Cara she had a serious boyfriend. Now she wore a large sparkler on her left hand.

"You got engaged," was the only thing Cara could think to say.

"Seriously? You kill my father, escape from prison, and show up in my house . . . and that's all you have to say to me?"

"I didn't kill your father. And I didn't escape from prison. I was in an accident and managed to stay alive long enough to realize that I had to come back here and find out who did."

Taylor rolled her eyes theatrically. "You really don't quit, do you? Ever since you hypnotized my dad, or whatever you did to make him fall in love with you, I've had to deal with your bullshit. I thought maybe getting convicted would finally stop you from lying about what you did, too."

"I have a very good idea about who actually did do it," Cara said, starting slowly down the stairs.

"Then tell me."

"The killer is somehow connected to your dad's surgical center. I think he may have agreed to a bad financial deal. I went out there and the lot is empty. Nothing was ever built there. I just needed the paperwork to prove that—"

"You're fucking crazy?"

Taylor took a step toward the wall separating the kitchen from the dining area. Where the panic button was hidden.

"Don't do it—I have Karl's gun." Cara patted *THE TOTE BAG*, hoping that would be enough to fool her.

Taylor hesitated, like she was trying to decide. "Then I guess you're going to have to pretend you didn't commit another murder."

She lunged for the panic button.

EIGHTY-EIGHT
JORDAN

> *As a valet parking attendant, you will be responsible for greeting guests and transporting luxury automobiles in our hotel's ongoing effort to deliver best in class guest service. Must be able to drive manual transmission. $18.25/hour plus tips.*
>
> *—Indeed.com*

"Sir? Can you please move your vehicle? It's impeding the efforts of our associates to welcome our guests."

Jordan turned and saw a man with slicked-back hair wearing a black suit and a yellow tie. His silver name tag identified him as Jean-Christophe, Assistant Manager. Jordan didn't understand how he'd been linked to Wen's car until he realized he was still wearing the blue US Marshals windbreaker.

He felt sympathetic to Jean-Christophe, who was clearly just trying to do his job. But he also didn't have the keys.

"We're hunting a fugitive," Jordan explained. "If she was still here, you'd be looking at about a hundred more vehicles, including TV trucks. So I think you came out pretty well."

Jean-Christophe looked simultaneously relieved and disappointed. "Are you saying Cara Campbell is no longer on the premises?"

"I'm saying the car needs to stay where it is for the moment."

Wen arrived, ending the awkward exchange. When it became clear she was ignoring the hotel's assistant manager, he scuttled off. Another blacked-out Explorer pulled up, and Crosby and Hart climbed in. It pulled out and Jordan was left standing with Wen.

"What did the waiter say?" he asked.

"The visual ID was shaky, but it has to be our girl. He said she hid behind a pillar and asked him to deliver a message to Stephanie van der Lind, who he knows because she's, like, a regular."

"So they all left separately?"

"As far as we know. Ellett's reviewing video with the hotel's security team now. I sent Crosby and Hart to van der Lind's house—man, I'm already tired of saying her name. Hope you had a nice phone call home."

"I oversee a department with a hundred and four employees," he told her, not wanting to admit one of them, the grandmother who ran his department's Facebook and X accounts, had been leaking information. "One of them told me Troy Silverman is apparently en route."

"Remind me. Is he chasing the reward?"

"He's chasing Campbell, anyway. He wants to be the next sheriff of Madera County."

Wen grimaced. "Glad I don't have to campaign for my job every four years."

"Four years might be more than enough."

Wen, who had been staring at her phone, looked up. "Ellett texted. We got a relay from a private security firm. Someone hit the panic button at Cara Campbell's house. She was there five minutes ago."

EIGHTY-NINE
CARA

If you haven't got a past yet, get a Mach 1. Now.
—1969 Mustang Ad

Cara scrambled over the passenger-side door and practically fell into the Porsche. "Floor it!"

Stephanie gunned the engine and Cara struggled to fasten her seat belt as the car surged up the hill fast enough to pin her into her seat.

"I've wanted to do this ever since Noel sent me to the Porsche Track Experience in Carson," Stephanie said as she navigated a turn at what had to be eighty miles per hour. "What happened back there?"

"Taylor happened."

"Holy shit!" Stephanie glanced over. "From the way you look, I'm guessing you pulverized that spoiled little brat."

Cara couldn't yet feel any of the new scrapes crisscrossing her already bruised and battered arms and legs. "Thankfully, I didn't have to."

"You didn't even rough her up?"

"When I told her I had Karl's gun, Taylor pushed the panic button and took off out the front door. I took off out the back. I climbed the chain-link fence and came through the Oddens' rose bushes."

"Do you? Have the gun?"

"I left it in the safe. It was too tempting to use it on her."

Cara knew that was what Stephanie wanted to hear, but she didn't blame Taylor for being scared. She didn't even really blame her for believing

Cara killed her father. She had established her brand without thinking about its effect on Taylor. She had loved him just as much as Cara did.

"Right or left on Mulholland?" Stephanie asked, as they neared the crest of the hill.

"Left, and then south on the 405."

Stephanie tossed her phone into Cara's lap. "Key it into my GPS."

"It's better if you don't know where I'm going. You're going to need plausible deniability."

"Too late for that. My phone started blowing up ten minutes before you jumped in the car. Unknown number, so I assume it's law enforcement. I let it ring through to voicemail."

"Give me your passcode."

As Stephanie slowed down just enough to merge onto the 405, Cara unlocked the phone and saw one voicemail followed by five missed calls, all from the same number. She pressed play and held the phone hard against her ear so she could hear over the wind and traffic.

"*This is US Marshal AJ Wen calling for Stephanie van der Lind. We've received a report that you may have made contact with the fugitive Cara Campbell. It is imperative that you return this call immediately.*"

Cara lowered the phone and leaned back against the headrest, staring up at the smoggy blue LA sky. "I never should have dragged you into this."

"I'm not concerned in the least. Nothing's going to happen to me because you're innocent."

If only that were true.

Stephanie checked her rearview mirror and changed lanes as the traffic slowed. Moments later, the 405 was at a standstill. They hadn't even reached Santa Monica Boulevard.

Cara kicked the floorboards in frustration. "Shit! Shit! Shit!"

"Just tell me where you're trying to go," Stephanie said soothingly.

"Centinela and Washington Boulevard."

"We'll take Sawtelle part of the way. I'll put up the sunroof while we're in traffic. It does ruin our whole Thelma and Louise vibe, though."

"Stephanie!"

"Kidding!" She patted Cara on the leg as the sunroof went up and they crawled toward the exit. "But once I drop you off at this unnamed place, how are you going to get around without a car?"

"I have it figured out," Cara said, more confidently than she felt.

◆◆◆

Finally, they reached the STOR-MORE storage facility.

"Over there," Cara said, pointing.

Stephanie made a sharp turn into the driveway. "You're not planning to hide in a storage locker, are you?"

"I'm just getting a few things. But that's actually not the worst idea."

"That's ridiculous," Stephanie said. "I have a much better idea."

Of course she did.

"It's a listing in Malibu. The owners relocated to Paris and are selling the house as is—lock, stock, barrel, sheets, towels, and all. It fell out of contract because there's a foundation crack. There's nothing else scheduled because they want twenty million, and it has to be fixed before anyone else puts an offer on it. It's still listed but only to placate the seller."

The place sounded better than Cara wanted to admit. "Is it your listing, though?"

"I'm co-listing with Dana Cameron in the Malibu office, but she's on a cruise until the end of the month. Work doesn't begin until she gets back. You get whatever it is you need, and I'll drive you out there."

Cara shook her head. "I don't need a ride. And I can't put you in any more danger than I already have. The US Marshals are going to be looking for you, too."

Stephanie huffed.

"Honestly, it's too huge a risk."

"The authorities will never get anything out of me," she said testily, but pulled a pen and pad out of her glove compartment. "I'll write down the address and the alarm code. There's half a bottle of wine, an apple, and some cheese that needs to be eaten in the fridge."

Cara got out at the unmanned security gate. Stephanie blew her a kiss as she peeled out of the parking lot.

The gate opened easily with the passcode written below the storage facility's address. She pushed through and quickly found herself lost in the endless rows of lockers. Karl had never brought her here before. Finally, she located row C and locker 1144.

As she unlocked the big red padlock and rolled up the shutter, she remembered how, in the woods, she'd encouraged herself by treating each new accomplishment as another level achieved in a game. Unlocking her home, Karl's safe, and now this large door felt the same way. But would she ever complete the final level and win?

She rolled back the soft gray tarp to uncover the sleek, black 1969 Mustang.

The untitled car had been given to Karl in trade by a patient. Cara hadn't wanted him to keep it, but after his death, she kept paying the storage fees, not wanting to deal with whatever issues had kept him from getting it properly licensed in the first place.

While this sketchy trade for services had nothing to do with his potentially sketchier real estate deal, it certainly seemed to reveal a willingness on his part to engage in nontraditional business transactions.

The more urgent question was whether the classic car would still start. If it didn't, she might well be spending the night in its back seat, in the storage locker.

Cara climbed behind the wheel and put the key in the ignition.

The engine coughed weakly but didn't start. The battery had to be weak. Tapping the gas pedal, she tried again. This time the engine chugged several times and turned over. She revved it a few times just to be sure.

Then she put the car in gear.

NINETY
JORDAN

> *Enjoy our narrated tours of the glamorous world that is Hollywood. Your ticket includes a scenic drive past the breathtaking celebrity mansions of yesterday and the homes of today's biggest stars.*
>
> —*LuxelineToursLA.com*

When Sydney was twelve, Jordan and Amber had given in to her begging and brought her to LA. Over the course of an endless three-day weekend, they dutifully marched through Disneyland, Universal Studios, and the Hollywood Walk of Fame. Desperate for some time off their feet, they bought tickets for a bus tour of Beverly Hills. While Amber and Sydney oohed and aahed over the lifestyles of the rich and famous, Jordan couldn't get past the sheer amount of lawn care each mansion required.

Now that he was actually inside one of them, he couldn't get over how many hard, shiny surfaces there were to clean, either. Some were probably smudged with Cara Campbell's fingerprints, but there was no need to lift them: they had video.

"See?" Taylor Campbell stood in the huge entryway, showing Wen, Ellett, and Jordan the security playback on her iPad screen. "The bitch is a redhead now. She's too old for that haircut, though."

As Ellett took a picture of the screen with her phone, Wen asked, "Any idea how she got in?"

"I think the fucking handyman let her in. Or maybe he just didn't lock the door behind him. Either way, I'm not using that company anymore."

Jordan wondered when the fugitive would finally run out of hairstyles and colors as Ellett started hammering her phone with her thumbs, no doubt blasting Campbell's picture to the far corners of cyberspace.

"What was your relationship like with your stepmother?" he asked.

He regretted the question as soon as it came out of his mouth. Taylor, Wen, and Ellett all stared at him like he was an idiot.

"What do you think?" spat Taylor.

Jordan held up his hands in apology. "Tell us again what happened. What do you think she was doing here?"

"She was getting my dad's gun. She threatened me with it, which is why I hit the panic button and ran. You guys better be careful and shoot first."

"Take it easy, OK?" said Wen. "Let us do our jobs."

"Where was the gun?" asked Jordan.

"In my dad's office upstairs, I think. I've never actually seen it. I just knew he had one."

"I'll take a look."

As he headed for the stairs, Wen asked, "Can you think of another reason she might have come here? To hide out, maybe?"

"Hell if I know," said Taylor. "It's not her house anymore. My lawyer said I can execute the moral turpitude clause in the agreement I signed to let her live here."

Jordan climbed a glass-enclosed staircase that had to cost more than his pickup truck. The second floor was just as impressive. It was hard to place the dirty, desperate woman he'd chased through the Sierra in this luxurious, modern home.

The study was easy enough to find. The decor looked like it came out of a showroom, just like the rest of the house, but with vintage flourishes like an old leather chair and a hat rack with a seemingly unworn fedora. On a low table, an architectural model of a medical campus was labeled *Campbell Cosmetic*. Unlike the rest of the house, this room was coated in a fine layer of dust.

Jordan searched the drawers and shelves but couldn't find anything obviously out of place. He was about to go back downstairs when he noticed a framed, signed print behind the desk—red and black, it looked like a computer-generated tie-dye pattern—hanging off-kilter. He lifted a corner and then took it off the wall completely. Behind it, the wall safe's door was slightly ajar.

He wasn't sure it was legally permissible, but Taylor Campbell had implied consent to search the house, so he opened the safe. The first thing he saw was a black plastic Glock pistol case. He lifted it and felt the weight of the gun inside. He undid the catches and opened it, just to be sure. It looked like it had never been fired.

Several file folders had been resting on top of the gun. The first showed investment accounts that appeared to have been drawn down repeatedly over the past several years. Another included a promissory note for a significant sum of money: twelve million dollars. A third held a thick contract for the Magellan, which appeared to be an assisted living home. A memorandum clarified an agreement to provide care until the end of the natural life of one Evelyn Marsh.

Evelyn Marsh's benefactor was Karl Campbell.

Who was Evelyn Marsh, and what was her relationship to Karl?

Her care didn't come cheap, and it looked like Karl had funded it at the same time he was draining his other accounts and going into debt to Gioni Enterprises, LLC, to build a new home for his practice.

Jordan rapped the papers softly against his thigh. The correct move was obviously to bring it all downstairs to Wen. She'd probably find it eventually, anyway. But he was getting sick and tired of being one step behind, tagging along with the US Marshal service only to have Campbell flit away again.

And now Silverman was following along, too.

Jordan didn't necessarily want to go rogue. He just wanted a few hours to think about what it all meant. Maybe see if he could be the first to figure out what Campbell was up to.

He took pictures of the documents' top pages and put all the folders back in the safe. Then he carried the gun case back downstairs. Wen and Taylor stopped talking when he held it up.

"The gun's still there, unless your father had more than one."

Taylor shook her head, apparently disgusted that she hadn't actually been threatened at gunpoint. "Of *course* she lied."

"If she's not armed, that's a good thing," said Wen.

Jordan put it on the counter, realizing he wasn't surprised Campbell had left the gun behind. He would have been more surprised if she had taken it.

Did that mean he believed she wasn't capable of killing?

NINETY-ONE
CARA

3 BR 3 1/2 BA. Incredible Malibu beachfront property. Family fun or romantic hideaway? You decide! Pricing upon request.

—@StephanieVDLProperties

From the road, the Malibu beach house was deceptively unassuming—just a weathered gray garage with white trim and an eight-foot privacy fence. Cara climbed out of the idling Mustang and keyed in the garage door code—*2, 4, 6, 8*—thinking it seemed far too simple for a twenty-million-dollar property, even if it was overpriced and had a foundation crack. As the door rolled open and she parked the Mustang in one of three empty bays, she definitely felt like she'd completed one of the upper levels in her real, life-and-death game.

Deinfluenced: Escape from a Hell of Your Own Creation.

She came up with the name on the twenty-two-mile drive down Pacific Coast Highway to Broad Beach Road. If only she knew what the final level looked like—and whether she'd find herself at home or in prison after she finished the game.

Cara exited the garage and found herself in a courtyard with a pool and hot tub bordered by smooth, black river stones and a small outbuilding with an outdoor shower and surfboard storage. At the back of the house, she keyed in the second, more secure code—5, 2, 7, 1—and stepped inside.

Painted in light grays with navy blue nautical touches, and huge sliders opening onto an oceanfront deck, the home was warm, beachy, and cozier than she'd expected. Its vibe was East Coast cottage meets California sun.

When Karl was alive, when they had friends with beach houses, Cara would have roamed around with phone in hand, snapping Insta-worthy photos in every room. Now, she had to painstakingly inspect every inch of the fully furnished place to make absolutely sure it was vacant, and the absent owners hadn't hidden any cameras in a plant or a sconce.

When she was finally satisfied, she dropped her tote bag on the bed in the small nanny's room off the kitchen—chosen because it had its own exit outside—and padded down the hall to the office, where a desktop computer had been left behind.

Internet included.

Cara jiggled the mouse, and the screen lit up. Stephanie must have used it recently, because the guest-user icon appeared with a passcode keyed in. All Cara had to do was press the return key.

This time, she had no desire to doom scroll until she panicked. There was no need to confirm that Taylor had released her Ring doorbell video to every media outlet that came calling. And Cara didn't want to see Roy Abel's smug face ever again. For the first time, all the comments and conjecture meant nothing to her. She felt light and free as she focused on the tasks at hand.

First, she looked up the addresses for Sanjay Jain and Devin Mayer in San Francisco and Rae Salter near Oakhurst. She searched drawers in the office until she found envelopes and stamps, then addressed the envelopes, adding Fisk's name to Rae's because she somehow doubted he got much correspondence at his compound, assuming it had survived the fire. She dropped $150 in Sanjay and Devin's envelope and $1,000 in Fisk and Rae's to repay their kindnesses, then stamped and sealed them.

Then she typed *Gioni Enterprises* into the search bar.

Google returned five pages of relevant entries.

Clicking and reading every link on the first few pages, Cara learned that the Gioni family was large, lived mostly in LA, and invested heavily in real estate, as well as various import/export and retail businesses. Driton Gioni, 58, had producer credits on three B movies she'd never heard of. Identical twins Esad and Fatmir were younger and steroid-buff, appearing together in photos at ribbon-cuttings for a strip mall, a condo complex, and a large liquor store.

Driton had been accused of smuggling in 2004 but not convicted. Esad was married to a former Playboy Playmate named Ashlee, and they had four children. Fatmir was divorced and had a profile on Millionaire Match that looked vaguely familiar from her dating days. Gioni Enterprises' corporate headquarters were at 205 S. Beverly Drive in Beverly Hills, slightly more affordable than anything north of Wilshire, but the company appeared to be successful, profitable, and diversified.

If they had also invested in Campbell Cosmetic, then why did Karl have a handwritten promissory note and not a formal, notarized contract?

Cara took out her phone and pulled up the photo she'd taken of the note. She touched the screen and pinched it open to enlarge. Ajila Gioni, CFO, had signed for Gioni Enterprises. The signature appeared to match the handwriting on the rest of the page.

Cara searched for *Ajila Gioni*.

The top result was a business called Olive and Sal.

Cara clicked through to a page touting *premium organic olive oil and sea salt, and clean, enlightened southern European food and beauty products.* These were apparently sold retail from a high-end boutique on fashionable Abbot Kinney Way in Venice, along with an impressive array of tea, organic honey, nuts, dried fruits, chocolates, and olive oil-based skincare.

On the About Us page was a short biographical statement: *In the Mediterranean, the olive once symbolized wealth, and salt was a valuable trading commodity. As a young girl growing up in Albania, these two food staples symbolized so much more to me: daily life, family, income, and the bounty of the harvest. I am always looking for ways to reap, share, and grow. Please contact me for more information or to join my team.*

When Cara's eyes found the photo of Ajila Gioni under the text, she suddenly found it difficult to breathe.

The owner of Olive and Sal sat at a sunlit table with her face turned mostly away from the camera.

Her hair was long and blond.

Cara's head throbbed so hard she had to close her eyes. She saw herself at Johnson's Point. Saw Karl. Saw the long, blond hair. Saw the swinging hammer.

She opened her eyes and forced herself to breathe. Had she finally found Karl's killer?

Was the marketing copy over the photo code for *we lend money at usurious rates on penalty of death*?

After creating another fake email under the name Cora Conrad, Cara used the store's contact form to request an appointment.

Dear Ms. Gioni,

I would like to speak to you about an opportunity worth its weight in salt. 10 AM tomorrow?

Best,
Cora Conrad

Cara felt hopeful as she logged off the computer.

And hungry.

In the kitchen, she opened the beadboard-fronted Sub-Zero refrigerator and pulled out the half-full bottle of white wine, single green apple, and wedge of brie Stephanie had left behind after her last showing. In the pantry, she found an unopened box of rice crackers only a month past their best-by date.

A feast.

Grabbing a wine glass from the living room's wet bar, she carried everything out to the expansive wooden deck. While other homes were crowded in on either side, Malibu was all about laid-back privacy, and every lot had strategically placed walls. Neighbors couldn't see into each other's spaces unless they walked along the beach or swam out into the vast expanse of ocean.

As she uncorked the wine and poured herself a glass, Cara felt small, unremarkable, and reassuringly anonymous. She sipped the slightly sweet wine, then cut a slice of apple and dipped it into the brie. Before she took her first bite, she dialed Dylan.

She owed him a thank you.

NINETY-TWO
JORDAN

FACT: Sheriff Jordan Burke let Cara Campbell escape from Madera County. Do you want a sheriff who says, "Not my job?"

—Silverman for Sheriff Facebook page

Stretched out on the bed at the Starlight Inn, Jordan swiped through pictures on his phone of the documents he'd found at the Campbell house. Why had Cara left them behind? What had she taken with her?

He took a long pull on the half-empty bottle of beer sweating on his nightstand. After Wen dropped him off, he had walked to a nearby 7-Eleven to pick up a six-pack and a couple of sandwiches. The other five bottles were cooling in the sink under a mound of ice.

It had been a long, fruitless day. After their latest close call with Campbell, Jordan and Wen had pounded the sidewalks and knocked on doors until they found an eyewitness who said "two chicks in a red Porsche Carrera took off like they were in Formula One." The car was right, and the time was right.

Cara Campbell was with Stephanie van der Lind.

While Ellett, ensconced at some mysterious site, searched traffic-camera video and frustratingly sporadic hits from license-plate readers, Wen and Jordan drove to van der Lind's home off Sunset Boulevard. Crosby and Hart had already checked out her Wilshire Boulevard office and reported there was no indication she had visited it in days.

She wasn't at home, either. Jordan and Wen discovered a perplexed husband, a handsome male assistant, and an excited twelve-year-old son who right away made the connection that his mom might be aiding and abetting her most famous friend.

But none of them had any idea where she was.

"If you were neighbors and not cops, I'd be guessing she's at Pilates, therapy, or book club," Noel van der Lind told them privately on a patio that looked like an outdoor lounge at a four-star hotel. "Maybe even a showing. But I'll be honest: we don't have that kind of marriage where we check in with each other all that often."

Jordan didn't trust his gaydar much but thought the body language between Noel and his young assistant seemed less like boss and employee and more like boyfriends. Which could have meant he was telling the truth.

Crosby and Hart had shown up, and Wen told Crosby to watch the house and sent Hart back to the office. When Jordan asked what she wanted him to do, she said, "Get some rest," and dropped him off at the motel.

Jordan adjusted the pillow under his aching lower back. A quick web search revealed that Evelyn Marsh was Karl's 89-year-old aunt. A longer search told him she had more or less raised Karl after his mother died and that the two of them were very close. It made perfect sense he would have wanted to provide for her long-term care—and from all outward appearances, he had been able to afford it at the time the arrangements were made.

The promissory note was more intriguing. Jordan had never taken so much as a payday loan, but he guessed most contracts for twelve million dollars weren't usually handwritten.

He got up and opened another beer, then started looking at the Gionis, who right away looked shady as hell. He knew a similar family in Madera, American born, that used a hodgepodge of legitimate businesses to hide the fact they were trafficking prostitutes and fentanyl throughout the Central Valley. Even though the Gionis had apparently been in the country for a long time, he had to wonder if they had connections to the Albanian mafia.

If Karl Campbell had taken mob money and failed or refused to pay it back . . . Some rich people really thought consequences would never come to them. Or maybe there was another angle. They could have simply gotten their hooks into his business and drained it for all it was worth.

Jordan knew he was already on dangerous ground for withholding information from Wen. And she would probably be pissed when he told her. But if he was right, and Cara Campbell was headed where he thought she was, he had to bring Wen in. Only in a Hollywood movie would an out-of-jurisdiction sheriff tackle the mob in the big city alone.

A notification appeared at the top of his screen.

California Death Trip had just released a new episode.

CALIFORNIA DEATH TRIP PODCAST

SPECIAL EPISODE

DYLAN DANVERS: *Hi, crime fam, it's Dylan, I'm back at my home studio in LA, and I'll be releasing this about fifteen minutes after I stop recording this intro. I've been promising something big, and here it is. But today's episode is only the first of two parts—you'll find out why in a minute. Now let's fucking GO.*

[Theme music.]

DYLAN*: We're recording. Are you ready?*

CARA*: I'm ready.*

DYLAN: *Please tell my listeners who you are.*

CARA: *My name is Cara Campbell.*

DYLAN: *Can you tell us where you are?*

CARA: *Somewhere safe. For now.*

DYLAN: *Why did you agree to talk to me?*

CARA: *For a couple of reasons. Number one, because you've always believed I'm innocent. I can't tell you how grateful I am for that.*

DYLAN: *In this case, truth is stranger than fiction.*

CARA: *So much stranger.* [Sigh] *The second reason is that before and during the trial, my lawyer told me to stop posting on social media and to refuse all interviews. I followed his advice, and because I did, I lost my voice. I lost control of my story.*

DYLAN: *What do you want to tell us, Cara?*

CARA: *The next time we talk, I'll tell you everything that has happened in my journey. I'll answer every question and talk for as long as you want. But first, I have to find Karl's killer.*

DYLAN: You *know it wasn't you.* I *know it wasn't you. But who killed your husband?*

CARA: *Thanks to you, I found a suspect the authorities completely missed. Today, I found paperwork that confirmed that theory.*

DYLAN: *Is that why you broke into your stepdaughter's house?*

CARA: *My husband and stepdaughter granted me indefinite use of the house. I entered using a key.*

DYLAN: *So noted.*

CARA: *And tomorrow morning, I'm going to get the proof I need. As soon as I have it, I'll let you know. And you will help me tell the world.*

DAY EIGHT

NINETY-THREE
JORDAN

Caught up with an old friend yesterday. Old friends are the best friends. #TeamCara
—@StephanieVDLProperties

Jordan found the Beverly Hills parking lot already full of government vehicles. He stopped next to Crosby and Hart, who were leaning against a black Ford Explorer.

"Morning, Sheriff Andy," said Crosby as he climbed out. "You bring Opie today?"

Hart shook his head. "Nah, he's McCloud. Ever see that old show? My dad used to watch the reruns. Small-town sheriff in the great big city."

Tired of looking like a tourist, Jordan was wearing his uniform again. He took his sunglasses out of his shirt pocket, slipped them on, and grinned. "Come hiking with me sometime. I'll find good nicknames for you."

"Hard pass," said Hart.

Wen joined them. "You kids done? It's, like, go time."

Everyone climbed back into their cars. Jordan found himself near the tail end of a procession that included the Marshals' SUVs, several cars and vans full of FBI agents, and four LAPD cruisers for traffic control.

Wen gave commands over the radio, and on her signal, everyone hit the gas, racing around a corner and down three blocks to a two-story brick office building on South Beverly Drive. The LAPD cars blocked the intersections while the rest of the vehicles split up, half going behind the building and half in front.

Jordan followed as everyone scrambled out of their cars, leaving the doors hanging open, and beelined for a glass door sandwiched between a clothing boutique and a vegan Jewish deli. They climbed stairs single file to a hallway covered in stained carpeting. Jordan was last in line when they reached a door across from the fire exit.

The lead agent banged the door with the heel of his hand. "FBI! We have a warrant! Open the door!"

There was no answer.

Jordan had barely counted to five before two other agents with a metal ram stepped up and cleanly hit the door between the deadbolt and the handle. The splintered door jumped out of its frame and sagged inward.

"Go! Go! Go!"

Guns drawn, the Feds charged inside, moving with noise and aggression intended to stun the occupants into compliance.

The yelling stopped.

"Shit!"

Wen went in. Jordan followed and poked his head around the corner. The door had a cheaply printed label for Gioni Enterprises, LLC. But the one-room office was completely empty except for a broken office chair and a stack of letters that had fallen through the mail slot and been pushed up against the wall.

Crouching on her haunches, Wen was rifling through the envelopes, which appeared to be junk mail.

"It's a goddamn mail drop," said an FBI agent, kicking the chair in disgust.

Jordan pushed through the fire door and pounded down the metal stairs. Wen came down a moment later. They squared off in the shadow of the building next to a dumpster whose smell was surprisingly foul for a vegan restaurant.

"*This* is your big lead?" demanded Wen.

"You liked it enough to call in the cavalry."

"It's the last time I'm listening to you."

"There's no point arguing. We all want the same thing."

"You're not going to lose your job if we don't find her."

"I might," he reminded her.

Wen folded her arms and walked away from the dumpster into the harsh sunlight. "Maybe we'll both be better off, you know? I haven't surfed in weeks."

Last night, certain he knew where Cara was going, Jordan had given everything he had to Wen. He knew she'd been up late, interviewing Danvers. Van der Lind still hadn't been found.

"You're sure the podcaster gave you everything?"

"He's cooperating. He showed me their DMs and gave us the number she called him from. He played the full interview back for me, and he insists she didn't tell him anything that wasn't on the recording."

"When is the second interview?"

"According to Danvers, she said she'd call him back when she was ready to talk."

As soon as she had the proof she needed.

The dumpster smell was too much for Jordan, too, so he joined Wen in the sun. "She's innocent."

Her look of surprise mirrored his own astonishment at hearing himself say the words out loud. "Bullshit."

"Don't you see? She's investigating. If she had done it, she'd be looking for a way out of the country, not leading us in circles around Beverly Hills."

"I don't care if she did it or not, Burke. Our only job is to catch her—that's *my* job, anyway. I don't know why I let you come along in the first place."

"If you don't want me here, say the word. You're running this operation."

Wen opened her mouth, closed it, then opened it again.

"Then go home."

Hearing it stung more than Jordan expected. "Can't have a hick sheriff running around LA with you anymore?"

"I know you need this, too. But I have to do it my way. You're on your own."

NINETY-FOUR
CARA

The process of laundering money typically involves three steps: placement, layering, and integration.

—Investopedia.com

Olive and Sal occupied a blond brick building on busy, trendy Abbot Kinney Way in Venice. Three storefronts down from Vuori, it was the last place Cara would have expected to find a loan shark with a penchant for murder.

Inside, the boutique smelled of lavender, soap, and spicy teas. A large, extremely realistic fake olive tree was rooted in the center of the store, its branches dotted with green olives and shading imported, organic offerings on farmhouse-style wooden tables and shelves. Old Cara would never have given a moment's thought to the profitability of such a charming small business or wondered whether it could possibly be anything other than advertised. Were all the candle stores, sock boutiques, and perfumeries she'd ever wandered into also fronts for criminal activity?

Cara pretended to examine a bottle of black truffle olive oil while she steeled herself for what came next.

"May I help you?" The salesgirl was pretty, twenty-something, with dark curly hair and a to-die-for jumpsuit.

"Cora Conrad for Ms. Gioni," she said, hoping she sounded all business.

"She mentioned your appointment. Please come with me. My name is Leyla."

Cara felt strangely at peace as she followed. Now she would know. What would happen next, she couldn't say.

Leyla led her to the same sunlit corner she'd seen on the store's website. A laptop computer was open on the desk next to a white ceramic pail filled with fragrant, blush-colored roses. The delicate floral arrangement felt incongruous. Wouldn't red or black roses, or even carnations dyed an unnatural color, be more fitting for a murderous mafiosa?

The door to the back room opened and Ajila Gioni appeared.

"This is Cora Conrad," said Leyla.

Ajila Gioni slowly looked Cara up and down, then nodded. "Bring us some tea."

To Cara, she added, "Sit."

Cara sat down in an uncomfortable cane chair, unable to take her eyes off the other woman, unable to even blink. Like the roses, the CFO of Gioni Enterprises, LLC, wasn't at all what she expected.

Ajila Gioni moved toward her desk with an arthritic shuffle. While her hair was shoulder-length, straight, and blond—and quite possibly a wig—she had to be in her seventies, with frail arms and a dowager's hump.

"You can take off that floppy hat," Ajila said, as she lowered herself into a high-backed wood and leather task chair. "I know who you are. Even with whatever it is you've done to your hair today."

Images of Cara with long, red hair were all over the internet, so she'd cut off the new extensions using utility scissors she'd found at the Malibu house.

Still, she waited until Leyla had returned with the tea before she removed the sun hat she'd borrowed from the pool house. She rested it on the edge of the desk as Ajila raised her teacup with trembling hands.

"You're very lucky I didn't call the police."

"I know you won't do that," said Cara, with more confidence than she felt. "I also know Karl owed you money."

Ajila's smile was chilling. "*Everybody* owes us money, darling . . . until we own their buildings. And if someone needs killing, we certainly don't do it ourselves."

"I didn't think that you—"

"You haven't touched your tea."

Cara took an obligatory sip that barely dampened her lips as she tried to recalibrate. There was no way this woman could have hiked up to Johnson's Point, much less swung a hammer with deadly force. But she was certainly capable of hiring someone to kill Karl. Had he failed to make the payments on his loan? Had they planned to push him out all along, so they could take over his business?

"I found a handwritten promissory note in his safe. It didn't seem like much of a contract for such a big loan. It wasn't even notarized."

"Don't overthink. We do business the way we do business and A More Beautiful You was part of a larger plan to franchise plastic surgery centers across the country."

"A More Beautiful You?" Cara asked. "His surgical center was called Campbell Cosmetic."

Ajila shrugged. "We scrapped that plan. We were going to go bigger, and in locations much more amenable than City of Industry."

Cara hated to admit they agreed on that point. "Is that why the lot was empty?"

"One of the reasons," she said. "We needed your husband to complete our plans. His death was almost as bad for us as it's been for you."

Ajila put down her teacup with a rattle and stood up. She handed Cara the floppy straw hat.

"Well, maybe not quite that bad."

NINETY-FIVE
JORDAN

> *Thank you for the many inquiries about Sheriff Jordan Burke! He is currently assisting the @USMarshalsHQ interagency task force as they hunt for fugitive Cara Campbell.*
>
> —*@MaderaCASheriff*

> *I call bullsh*t on Hollywood Burke.*
>
> —*@madera_watchdawg*

Jordan sat behind the wheel in the parking lot as the task force disbanded, the vehicles' departure documented by a dozen onlookers with raised phones. He could somehow believe that even the might of so many federal agencies had failed to bring in Cara Campbell. After all, she was proving more intelligent, determined, and resourceful than he had imagined.

But he couldn't believe they hadn't managed to find her realtor friend.

On his phone, he searched *stephanie van der lind realtor.* She came right up and had a few active listings. There was a one-bedroom condo on South Canon Drive listed for $912,000, which seemed high, even for LA; a five-million-dollar mini-château on Coldwater Canyon; a Wilshire Boulevard penthouse for over seven million that had three whole bedrooms; and a beach house in Malibu going for a mind-boggling twenty million. The first three looked sterile and staged, but the fourth one looked lived in. *Includes ALL furnishings,* went the listing. *Meet the asking price and move in TODAY!*

Using Google Maps, he saw the closest property, the Coldwater Canyon home, was only three miles away. It was worth a shot.

As he locked in the coordinates, he saw a flash of orange and looked up. Troy Silverman was leaning against his tricked-out Ford Bronco with arms folded, watching him. Was there someone else in the department feeding him information? Someone in someone else's department? Silverman could have been connecting the dots from publicly available information—or he could have just gotten stupid lucky.

When Silverman opened his door to get behind the wheel, Jordan stomped on the gas and pulled out, cutting off an irate fed as he jumped the curb. He drove too fast and made random turns, ignoring his electronic copilot's pleas to return to the route until he was sure his rival wasn't following.

Then Jordan dialed Stephanie van der Lind's publicly listed number. She was obviously hiding from law enforcement. Somehow he doubted she would hide from a six-figure commission.

"Stephanie, my name is John Brown," he said, wishing he'd come up with a more convincing alias. "I just saw your name and number on the yard sign outside a house I know my wife would love—we're moving to LA soon from the East Coast. I'm basically on my way back to the airport, but I was hoping you might be free to meet me at the house in the next half hour."

If similar ruses worked with meth dealers back in Madera, Jordan saw no reason it wouldn't work with a Beverly Hills realtor.

He was halfway to the house when a text came in.

Hi John! I'm actually really close. Can I bring you a Starbucks?

That'd be great, he texted back at the next stoplight. *Tall latte with an extra shot.*

He was fully caffeinated but wanted to make sure he got there first.

Five minutes later, he reached the address. The house had a circular driveway screened by closely spaced Italian cypress trees, so he pulled in, hoping he wouldn't have to explain his presence to a puzzled homeowner. But no one came out.

Ten minutes after that, a red Porsche convertible rolled to a stop across the street. Jordan waited until the driver started to get out, then gunned his engine, pulled out, and boxed her in.

Two Starbucks cups slipped from Stephanie van der Lind's hand and exploded on the driveway, staining her white pants in an eruption of mocha-colored foam.

Her eyes went wide.

"Cara Campbell escaped in my jurisdiction, and I've been searching for her with the US Marshals task force," he told her, careful wording that wasn't a lie.

She glanced nervously over her shoulder. "Well, she's not *here*."

Jordan waited. The best way to interrogate a suspect was often to let them guess at the questions. But as he watched her face go from startled to scared to indignant, he suddenly knew.

"You're hiding her."

Her nervous laugh was as fake as they come. "No way!"

"Well, I guess I have to bring you in for questioning. There are a lot of people who want to talk to you. We know you gave her a ride, Ms. van der Lind."

"Should I call my lawyer?"

"You certainly can. Or you can just tell me where she is."

"Don't know," she said, unconvincingly. "Maybe she's at a hotel or hiding at another friend's house."

"We both know she's short on friends."

"True," Stephanie admitted.

"What about that beach house you have listed in Malibu?"

Again the fake laugh. "That? God, no. Cara hates water. Totally terrified of it. Even running for her life, she'd never hide at the *beach*."

That was when he knew.

Jordan got back in his vehicle and rolled down the window. "Unless you really want to complicate things, turn yourself in."

As he drove, he played the podcast again. The background noise he thought had been the static of a cell phone call was more regular than he remembered. Like waves.

He called Wen. "I just thought you might like to know Cara spent the night at a beach house that's being sold by Stephanie van der Lind. The address is easy to find."

NINETY-SIX
CARA

You just know she's going to kill herself on TikTok live.
—@socialmedpsychic414

If Ajila and company were innocent of Karl's murder, then Cara was going back to jail. Exhausted and out of ideas, she drove toward the one remaining beacon of light in her life.

When she arrived at Magellan Independent Senior Living, she parked in the lot outside, located the code on the front gate directory, and was quickly buzzed in. Too impatient to wait for the elevator, she headed for the stairwell, taking the steps two at a time until she reached the third floor and knocked on B-307.

Aunt Evelyn didn't look the least bit surprised when she opened the door. She just pulled Cara into her apartment and enveloped her in the warm, bosomy hug she so desperately needed.

"Oh, my darling girl!"

"I'm so sorry I didn't contact you sooner. I just couldn't."

"I don't imagine so. I've been watching all the coverage on television."

Cara hugged her back tightly, her eyes filling with tears as she inhaled the comforting smells—vanilla, baby powder, and old-timey hair spray—of the woman she'd grown to love like a grandmother.

Evelyn released her from the hug but continued to hold her hands as she examined her carefully. "Bruised, bedraggled, and even thinner than I expected. I can't even imagine what you've gone through."

"I shouldn't have survived it. But thinking of you helped get me through some of worst moments. The fact that you believed me when almost no one else did gave me strength."

"No one else knows the things I know about who Karl was. And who you are." Still holding one hand, Evelyn led her to the small but nicely appointed kitchen. "Let me make you a sandwich."

"I can't stay. It's not safe—especially for you."

"Nonsense." Evelyn opened the refrigerator and pulled out deli-wrapped turkey, roast beef, and provolone. "The authorities already contacted me, and since I hadn't seen or heard from you yet, I didn't have to lie at all. I would have, of course."

"The last thing I want to do is drag you into this mess."

Evelyn's wrinkles had wrinkles, but her bright blue eyes sparkled. "I can take care of myself. I'm also not above faking a bit of light dementia if I need to."

"Who contacted you?"

"That sheriff from up north in Madera."

"Jordan Burke?"

Evelyn nodded. "He told me he came down here to help out with the search."

"Another reason for me to get out of here ASAP."

"Where are you going next?"

"Definitely not the house. I went there yesterday and ran into Taylor. It went as well as I expected."

Now tears filled Evelyn's eyes as she put down the sandwich makings. "That poor girl. First her father, and now her mother has cancer and won't live to walk her down the aisle."

"Oh, no," Cara said.

Her cool relationship with Karl's first wife notwithstanding, no one deserved to suffer like that. And poor Taylor. Cara hadn't had her parents at her wedding, either. It was yet another tragedy that they couldn't support each other—Cara was uniquely qualified to help her stepdaughter cope.

"What were you doing back at the house?" Evelyn asked.

"Looking for clues. I have to find Karl's killer."

"I was afraid you would say that." Consternation clouded Evelyn's face. "If only the police had done their job in the first place."

"Did Karl ever tell you he was having financial problems?"

"He told me there had been some setbacks with the surgical center, but he didn't want to worry you. Although he didn't go into detail, he said things had gotten complicated with his new investors. But you know Karl, he was sure things would work out for the best in the end."

Cara glanced at a framed photo of Karl, smiling widely, standing between her and Evelyn at Taylor's college graduation.

"I miss him so much," Cara said.

"I know you do, sweetie."

"I really don't know what I'm going to do."

"I'm old. Which supposedly means I'm wise. Or at least that you have to listen to me when I tell you something."

"And what's that?"

"You can't think on an empty stomach. I'll make you a sandwich to go."

NINETY-SEVEN

JORDAN

Hey @socialmedpsychic414 I work for a suicide prevention hotline and have reported you for that post. Encouraging someone to kill themselves is unconscionable.

—@AnnieLCSW

Unless Wen had decided she no longer trusted any information that came from him, Jordan knew she would head to Malibu. But Cara wouldn't go back there until she found what she needed. And she had probably already discovered that the headquarters of Gioni Enterprises, LLC, was an empty shell.

A second web search led Jordan to realize that the Gionis had a lot of business dealings, mostly as financers and developers—although Campbell Cosmetic had never been built. There was only one business that appeared to be owned and operated by someone who also had a role in the corporate structure. And it happened to be a retail business with regular hours.

Owned and operated by Ajila Gioni.

He headed west on Santa Monica Boulevard, checking his rearview every few blocks for Silverman's orange Bronco.

Traffic was light and the trip to Venice Beach only took twenty-five minutes.

The door chimed softly when he walked into Olive and Sal. Jordan took off his sunglasses and let his eyes adjust, trying to determine whether the tree in front of him was real or not.

At the front window, an elegant older woman was tidying a display of little bags of salt in burlap sacks.

"You missed her," she said.

Jordan's uniform had given him away.

"You're also out of your jurisdiction," she added, beginning to make infinitesimal adjustments to a row of olive oil bottles.

The sun shining through the window lit her hair, and he understood why Cara had followed this particular lead. Not just the company that had loaned money to her husband but the killer with the long, blond hair.

But he also noted the old-woman arms with jiggling flesh hanging loose from the bone. This was no hammer murderer. He didn't know much about the Albanian mafia, but surely a highly organized criminal operation would choose a more efficient way to dispose of a business partner who was no longer needed.

"When did she leave?"

"Approximately an hour ago. I happened to look out the window and saw she was driving a black Mustang convertible, a very old one. Oh, and she cut her hair again."

"Why are you telling me this?"

"Because I run a legitimate business. I can't have criminals coming and going."

Jordan regarded her carefully. She may have been old, but her dark eyes were still keen with intelligence. "Legitimate? You lent her husband twelve million dollars and the only record of it is a piece of paper."

That surprised her but she recovered quickly. "I don't like to pay lawyers."

"Karl would have had to pay a lawyer, though, once you loaded up his business with debt and forced him into bankruptcy."

Ajila Gioni shrugged. "It's hard to say what would have happened next, now that he is no longer with us."

Gioni Enterprises was an FBI problem. Certainly not his. He would relay this conversation to Wen and let her deal with it.

Jordan left her to her window display and stepped out onto the sidewalk. If Campbell had just ruled out her best, most important avenue of investigation, where would she go next? Did she have more leads to chase? Would she ever give herself up?

Before he packed it in himself, he decided he might as well go to Malibu and take a look at the house.

NINETY-EIGHT

CARA

Free speech much @AnnieLCSW? @socialmedpsychic414 didn't encourage @carasloveisgold to kill herself. It was a simple observation that she'd record it. Which sounds about right to me.

—@trueleo405

Cara was about to enter the left turn lane leading to Broad Beach Road when she saw the flashing red and blue lights. A police car was blocking traffic. The driveway and the street by the house were crowded with official-looking vehicles.

Veering back into traffic, and ignoring the horn of the Mercedes she'd just cut off, she merged into the right lane, turned quickly into the Trancas Country Market, and parked.

It had actually taken Stephanie longer to squawk than Cara expected. Still, she had been counting on a little time to regroup before she decided how and where to turn herself in . . . or if there were any other options. She supposed she could just drive over to the house and surrender now, but she didn't want her last act of freedom to be so humiliatingly public.

She wasn't ready.

How could she ever be?

A man who looked a lot like Robert Downey, Jr. stared directly at her. Actually, it was Robert Downey, Jr.

There was a time when she would have been thrilled to be recognized by an A-list movie star. As he stepped closer, she started the car and shifted into reverse, ready to peel out of the parking lot.

"Nice wheels," he said, before continuing on into the grocery store.

She killed the engine.

When she was absolutely certain that neither Robert Downey, Jr. nor anyone else was paying any particular attention to her, she got out of the car and threw away the baggie, napkin, and empty bag of chips from the lunch Aunt Evelyn had given her.

Then she eased out of the lot and headed back down the Pacific Coast Highway toward Kanan Road, just like that was what she'd planned all along.

But nothing she'd planned had panned out at all.

NINETY-NINE

JORDAN

Both lanes of Broad Beach Road currently closed due to significant, unspecified police activity.

—@malibupoliceblotter

Jordan pulled over on the shoulder of the Pacific Coast Highway. Past the treetops and the rooftops of the beachfront homes below, he could see breakers rolling in a salty haze. He could also see, through a gap in the trees, the twenty-million-dollar house listed by Stephanie van der Lind. It was so clearly marked by police flashers and government vehicles he knew Cara Campbell would never return.

Sighing, he pulled back into traffic and drove into a shopping center, where he bought an eighteen-dollar sandwich and an eight-dollar iced tea from a boutique grocery store deli. He carried them back to his vehicle and watched the traffic while he ate.

When he was done, he called home. A mistake, because the sound of Amber's voice made him want to hit the road and drive straight there. He reckoned he could be home by midnight.

"How are you holding up?" she asked.

"By my fingernails, and I think I'm about to chew off the last one."

She chuckled. "You've never chewed your nails."

"I'm off the task force, and I'm completely out of ideas. She's still out there, and I have no idea where she's headed or what she's going to do when she gets there."

"Then come home."

"I want to."

"Silverman, right?"

There sure were a lot of sports cars on this stretch of road, he thought idly. New and old, convertible and hardtop. Even a black Mustang—but a brand-new convertible, driven by a hefty bald man with a beard.

"The job is a pain, but I want to keep it, even if it's only so he doesn't get it. I know I'm not the perfect sheriff, but at least I'm not a walking conflict of interest with millions of dollars of property investments."

"Don't assume you'll lose just because you haven't brought her in."

"He might win if he does."

"Maybe it's fine if she gets away. Sydney has listened to every episode of California Death Trip twice. I think she's starting to wonder if Campbell might be innocent, but she won't say it."

"If she's innocent, the system will clear her eventually. But she's not safe out there."

"Then go get her."

He wanted to ask her how. Instead, he asked if there was any news about Bree.

"I should have told you. The doctor is easing her out of the coma. She still can't talk, but she opened her eyes. She squeezed Joanne's hand."

Jordan's eyes watered with relief. "That's good news."

"It sure is. Where there's life, there's hope."

"I love you."

"Love you more." Amber's voice still had a way of making him feel like her fingertips were walking slowly up his spine.

"I'll be home soon."

She made a loud kissing sound before she got off the phone, which made him chuckle and raised his spirits. He dabbed his eyes and watched the passing cars. There was no point in driving around, looking for her. He could swing by the nursing home, but he'd already talked to Karl Campbell's aunt, and she sounded like she couldn't remember her own name or what she'd had for breakfast.

He thought about his daughter listening to the podcast, wrestling with a stranger's guilt or innocence.

Then he had another, better thought and called Beto.

ONE HUNDRED
CARA

F this and F you. Do it, @Carasloveisgold!
—@socialmedpsychic414

If Ajila had been telling the truth—and weirdly, it seemed like she was—then Cara had exhausted every possible lead. Forest Lawn Cemetery was the only place left to go.

She would be easy to find here, and maybe the authorities had already been alerted by the guard at the gate and were on their way with lights flashing and sirens screaming. Maybe Sheriff Burke was still with them, determined to track her to the gates of hell if needed.

It didn't matter. Nothing mattered. She was where she was meant to be. All she needed was a moment to sit in the grass beside Karl. That was reason enough for her running, for all she had endured over the previous seven days.

She could keep running. She now knew how to forage for food and stay warm in the woods, but who was she kidding? And while she could probably keep moving from place to place around LA—for a while, anyway—her money would run out. Even if she managed to make her way across the border, she would always be on the run. Forever known as the Influencer Murderer, the Gold-Digger Killer, or some other stupid nickname, reviled for a crime she could never have committed.

Maybe Mexico was the answer—at least the true-crime shows about her would be in Spanish, so she wouldn't know what people were saying about her.

Cara parked the car and got out, squinting into the red setting sun as she walked across the vast expanse of grass toward Karl's final resting place. Nearby, a group of tourists was daring each other to hop the rope guarding the marble crypt where Clark Gable and Carole Lombard were interred. She waited for them to chicken out, then kneeled, running her fingers lightly over the flat grave marker. The letters of her husband's name. The numbers that recorded the dates of his birth and death.

She took out her phone—a new one. Dylan had told her to get rid of the old one immediately after their call. She logged in to Instagram, no longer caring who was tracking her activity.

Roy Abel had tagged her in several public posts, pleading with her to get in touch. Stephanie had sent her a DM.

I PROMISE I didn't tell them where you were. I told them you wouldn't be caught dead anywhere near the beach, but somehow they still figured it out.

Ignoring them both, she messaged Taylor: *I'm so sorry we both lost the man we loved. My only regret is that I won't be there to support you.*

It was time to make her final post.

She took a picture of Karl's grave marker, then inserted a heart emoji, followed by a broken-heart emoji.

I loved this man so much, she wrote. *But there's nothing else I can say or do to make you believe me.*

The moment she pressed post, comments began to flood in.

Do it, Murderer.

They say nothing is bad enough to end it all over, although I admit this is a close call . . .

Cara, DM me or call me and I'll come get you. As your lawyer and friend, I promise there are still legal avenues we haven't exhausted.

Please get in touch IMMEDIATELY we have a KILLER sponsorship opp for you

Cara was just so tired. She stretched out in the grass, laying her head on the cool granite slab. She closed her eyes, wishing she could sleep forever and never wake up.

Then her phone rang.

ONE HUNDRED AND ONE

JORDAN

To 8201 Chelan Drive, Los Angeles, CA. 1 hr. 52 min. 34.9 miles. Expected arrival time 8:15 p.m.

—Google Maps

Jordan's luck with traffic had finally run out.

He should never have gotten on the 10, despite Google's recommendation, a mistake he realized as soon as the yellow traffic-flow indicator turned bright red. He had no idea how the system worked, just as he had no idea how the city's traffic could stop on a dime for no apparent reason.

Wen would undoubtedly have suggested a better route, but it didn't matter now. He was stuck in five lanes of traffic going nowhere fast, a river of red brake lights under a darkening sky lit by LA's otherworldly glow.

Before he'd started, Google Maps said the thirty-five-mile journey to the address Beto had given him would take just over fifty minutes by taking the 10 to the 101 north.

Now its prediction was almost two hours.

Desperate for distraction, he turned on the AM radio. A talk-show host was discussing Cara Campbell's precarious mental state.

"*The internet is awash in speculation that Cara Campbell may be considering self-harm,*" he said in a cheerful baritone. "*Her last post, from beside the grave of her husband, sounded hopeless. Well-wishers and chaos tourists alike have descended in droves on Forest Lawn Cemetery, while LAPD assures us Cara Campbell is no longer on the premises.*"

The Western Avenue exit was a mile ahead. Surface streets had to be faster.

Jordan had not yet used his flashers or siren in LA, wanting to avoid any interdepartmental awkwardness. And he had no legal jurisdiction in Los Angeles County.

But screw it.

He hit the overheads and triggered the piercer, scaring the driver of the compact car ahead of him so badly he nearly caused a rear-end collision. A little bit of room opened up, then a little more. He made a lane change so tight he almost scraped the decal off his door.

The drivers around him got the picture and made room.

ONE HUNDRED AND TWO

CARA

Choose a job you love and you'll never have to work a day in your life.

—Anonymous

Dusk fell as Cara left Glendale, wound her way through Loz Feliz, and climbed up into the Hollywood Hills. Dylan's call had been a lifeline.

Come to my house, he insisted. *You shouldn't be alone. I'll help you figure out what to do. And if you feel up to it, you can tell the rest of your story.*

Dylan had to know *figuring out what to do* was an exercise in futility. She certainly knew his invitation would only forestall the inevitable for a few more hours. So what if he was angling for the second interview she'd promised? She definitely owed him that.

And at least her story would be out there, all of it, whether she was rotting in prison or . . . gone.

Cara's headlights found Dylan, who stood waiting at the top of a driveway that dropped steeply down to a white midcentury modern home. The place had to have been created by someone famous—much like Dylan himself. Slim and wiry with high cheekbones and chestnut colored hair, he took after his willowy French supermodel mother, Daphne Boulet, much more than his football player dad.

She pulled through the gate and parked in front of the semi-attached garage. When she got out, he smiled and wrapped her in a hug that was stronger than Aunt Evelyn's but just as comforting.

"Cara Campbell. We finally meet in the flesh. Doesn't it kind of feel like we've known each other forever? I sometimes wonder if we were siblings in another life or something."

She couldn't say the same, though she'd seen enough paparazzi photos of Dylan and his family that his presence did feel strangely familiar.

"I feel like I've lived an entire lifetime in a week."

"Save that thought," he said, leading her to the front door. "I was thinking about it as you were driving up here. We need to get absolutely everything you can think of recorded ASAP while your memory's still fresh. I plan to shop this around to Netflix, Hulu, everywhere! You might be even bigger than OJ was, back in the day. The more info we can get out there, the better our chance of getting your conviction overturned."

Dylan's manic enthusiasm, while overwhelming to Cara in her exhaustion, did light a tiny ember of hope in the ashes of her heart.

"Let's do it," she said, trying to sound more energetic than she felt.

Inside, the house was warm and airy, with an open floor plan, accent walls made out of restored wood, and Eames, Florence Knoll, and Paul Evans furniture.

"What a house," she said, glancing into a living room cantilevered over the canyon with a wall of plate glass windows facing downtown LA. "It looks like a Richard Neutra."

"Good eye. Would you believe my parents were ready to buy the place just to tear it down?"

"Why?"

"Because they live at the top of the hill and it's partially visible from their infinity pool. But only if you lean out over one edge." He laughed. "My wife told them it was worth a fortune as is, and to buy it for us instead. They weren't convinced until *Architectural Digest* came out to do one of those Open Door videos."

"Finola is the one with the eye," Cara said. "Is she here?"

"She's in Milan for Fashion Week."

"And you didn't go?"

"What, and leave you running for your life? Besides, been there, done that." He led her into the kitchen, which, although remodeled with shiny white cabinets, gray stone floors, and quartz countertops, maintained the integrity of the original design. "The thing is, doors have always just opened to me, and believe me, I peeked behind all of them. I did the modeling thing. I tried my hand at acting, too. I had that cooking show on Bravo for one season. For a while, Finola and I had a lifestyle brand called Finedy."

He paused, waiting to see if it registered with her.

"Oh—of course. I didn't make the connection at the time. But of course that was you."

"It was short-lived. Shorter than we'd hoped."

He grabbed two water bottles from the refrigerator and a bag of Tate's gluten-free chocolate chip cookies from a cabinet and led them back into the living room. "Everyone just thinks of me as the son of Daphne Boulet and Nico Danvers. I had to find my own thing."

"So podcasting?"

"Ready to get after it?"

"I am if you are," she said.

She followed as he headed for a staircase in the corner that led to the lower level of the house. "You know I was inspired by you, right?"

"I didn't realize."

"I was watching a story about your arrest. I could just tell by the look on your face that you were innocent. Then I did my own research to confirm it. I started thinking about innocence and how I could use my name recognition to help bring about justice."

You never knew about people, thought Cara. No one would have looked at someone like Dylan Danvers and expected him to have this kind of awakening. Nobody would look at her and think she had changed as much as she had.

"This is only the start of what I now know is my calling—fighting for the falsely convicted. I've been looking into getting my law degree."

"Law school? Wow. That's impressive."

Dylan shrugged. "In California, you don't have to go to law school; you just have to pass the bar. Kim Kardashian is going to hook me up with her tutor."

"So cool," Cara said, even though she thought Kim K. hadn't passed.

The downstairs hallway was a floor-to-ceiling photo gallery that included candids with countless celebs, as well as professional photo portraits of Dylan's famous parents, his beautiful wife, and Dylan himself.

She stopped to look at one of them in particular. In it, Dylan's hair was shoulder length.

And blond.

Realizing she wasn't behind him, Dylan turned around and came back. When he saw what she was looking at, he shook his head. "Finola hates that picture of me. I should totally get rid of it."

"Why does your wife hate this picture?" she asked.

"Probably because my hair is nicer than hers."

Cara's heartbeat pounded in her ears as she followed him into a studio that looked completely professional, from the oversized mics with pop filters to the racks of electronic equipment to the acoustic baffles on the walls.

Dylan sat down without offering her a seat. He glanced over at an open laptop that appeared to be wired into the system.

"Oh, shoot, I forgot to reboot. I'd better do it, or the sound gets glitchy. It takes about ten minutes. Want to see my parents' house while we wait?"

She didn't.

"Come on," he said. "The view is beyond incredible."

When he abruptly stood and breezed out of the room, she followed.

ONE HUNDRED AND THREE

JORDAN

ding dong the bitch is dead that post was her suicide note
—@imag0reh0und

Jordan killed the overheads as soon as he got off the freeway and onto local streets. He didn't want to arrive at his destination leading a parade of local cops.

But he was still driving fast enough to piss them off if they saw him. He gunned the Interceptor's engine, slalomed between lanes, and entered intersections on stale yellows and fresh reds.

Driving a marked vehicle helped. Angelenos gave him a wide berth.

When his phone buzzed with an incoming text, he punched the dashboard screen to bring it up.

Ready to retire, Sheriff? I'm way ahead of you and I know where she is.

Fucking Silverman. What was he doing?

Jordan answered by voice.

Tell me where and stop messing around. She is at risk of self-harm.

No answer. No surprise.

Crawling behind two distracted drivers, Jordan hit the overheads again. When one of them moved out of his way, he gunned it again.

ONE HUNDRED AND FOUR

CARA

It's great to be a blond. With low expectations, it's very easy to surprise people.

—Pamela Anderson

Cara's mind felt fuzzy, but her body was on high alert as she followed Dylan out of the house, onto the porch, and into the shadowed side yard. He unlocked a security gate and led her outside the wall to a steep path that led up the hill.

"Is that why you cut your hair? So she wouldn't feel bad?"

"I buzzed it so I could go back to my natural color."

Taking her hand, he quickened his pace up the hill. Off balance, Cara struggled to keep up.

"You're going a little fast for me," she told him, but he didn't seem to notice as they scrambled up a path that ended at the top of a gated driveway.

"You're gonna love this reveal," he said.

Cara was both sweating and shivering as Dylan punched in a security code. The huge teak gates swung open, revealing a brightly lit Tuscan villa too enormous to be considered tasteful.

"Lovely," she said anyway. "But we should probably get back down. I have no idea how much time I—"

"How about we skip the house tour and just go around back for a peek at the view? It'll just take a minute."

"I guess so."

She tried to let go of his hand, but he continued to hold hers tightly. Leaving the gates open, he led her across the expansive front yard toward the privacy hedges on the west side of the massive house.

"Have you ever tried ayahuasca?"

"No." Where had that come from?

"The last time I did it was almost two years ago now. I trekked five miles through the Peruvian rainforest to a super-intense retreat run by one of the most renowned shamans in the world."

Cara wiggled her fingers to get him to loosen his grip. "You can let go. I can still see well enough."

"I was in a weird headspace when I went down there," he continued, ignoring her. "Everything had kind of fizzled out career-wise, even the lifestyle platform. Our managers were both positive it would work: Finola and Dylan, chronicling their budding romance, promoting their favorite places, and endorsing highly curated products."

Cara felt sick as she began to understand.

"But without all the brand ambassadorships you had. I mean, we almost had Alo Yoga, until they decided to invest in you. That didn't make any sense—our demographics were much younger and hipper than yours."

They walked around the house into the backyard. It featured two patios with all the requisite built-ins, a rectangular lawn as perfect as a putting green, and a glowing infinity pool that seemed to jut out into space.

"Brand ambassadorships are tricky," Cara said. "Much trickier than they were even a couple of years ago, when influencing was at its peak. Now it takes time and consistency."

Dylan paused by a row of partially submerged lounge chairs facing an infinity fire table along the edge of the pool, something she'd never seen before. He looked like he was considering what she was saying.

"Anyway, the thing about an ayahuasca experience is that it's magical, but also unpredictable. For six hours, I lost all concept of myself. First, I was a bobcat, then a snake, then finally a hawk. I flew all over the world and saw brightly colored cities and mountains of geometric cubes. I met ancient warriors made out of candy. Near the end, my ancestors circled around me and asked me to state my purpose. When I couldn't do it, they all laughed. All except an old woman with crazy silver hair. She snapped her fingers, and then suddenly I was with you. We were together on that catamaran when you were hit by the wave that made you famous as an influencer."

Cara wanted to vomit. "You're making this up."

He closed his eyes, reliving the memory. "You were bleeding from your wrist, and you poured it into a cup and handed it to me. You told me: 'You'll need this for your journey.'"

"But what I really needed was this." Letting go of her momentarily, he pushed up the sleeve of his shirt to reveal a watch.

Karl's watch.

Cara almost vomited. "Take that off."

"Oh, I will, when I tell the police I took it off your wrist."

Dylan gripped her with both hands and strong-armed her over to the edge of the infinity pool.

"Why did you kill Karl?"

"I honestly didn't expect him to defend a trophy wife so hard. I mean, he wasn't exactly young. But he played football like my dad, so I guess I should have known he'd try to tackle me. I honestly thought you were dead, too. But then you weren't, and everything just fell into place. After you were arrested, I had the idea for the podcast. It seemed like the perfect way to make sure no one suspected me. But also for you to nourish me with your fame. Just like the dream foretold. There's no other way to interpret that message. Things happened the way they were meant to, spiritually and karmically speaking."

ONE HUNDRED AND FIVE
JORDAN

Anybody else see a cruiser from Madera County Sheriff's heading east on Sunset Boulevard with its flashers on?
—LAPD radio transmission

It was fully dark in the hills and the map directions ended at a closed gate. Behind it, the driveway swooped downhill to a garage with an empty vintage black Mustang parked in front. From the corner of the house, Jordan could see, it looked like a 1950s Hollywood party pad.

The gate had spikes on top and was set in a white brick wall tall enough that Jordan wasn't getting over it without a ladder. Even if he could take a running jump and get his hands on top, he didn't want to risk grabbing an anti-theft deterrent like broken glass. It had happened to one of his deputies.

And he also didn't have a warrant.

He could have buzzed for entry, but he didn't want to alert the occupants. And anyway, if Cara Campbell was indeed meeting Dylan Danvers to record part two of the interview he had promised his listeners, she was safe for the moment.

Looking uphill, he saw that if he followed the perimeter, the high ground on the shoulder of the hill would give him a view inside the compound. He was just about to start picking his way through the tinder-dry grass and scrubby cedar trees when he saw movement high above.

At the edge of some kind of platform, two figures were silhouetted by an aquamarine glow. One of them he recognized right away as Campbell. The other one—taller, also slender—was probably Danvers.

What were they doing up there?

Jordan got back in his vehicle and drove uphill.

ONE HUNDRED AND SIX
CARA

Can't believe we have to say this, but fugitive rewards are NOT "dead or alive." That practice ended in the 1950s. Don't believe everything you read on the internet, folks.
—@USMarshalsHQ

Cara's arms were pinned behind her back. Dylan pulled up on her wrists, hurting her and pushing her toward the edge of the infinity pool's deck. Below her feet, the hillside fell away into darkness.

"Isn't this the most beautiful view you've ever seen?" he asked. "I think it's truly important to take in the beauty of the earth before we leave it."

"I don't want to die."

"The proper way to say it on social media is to *unalive* yourself. And everyone seems to think you're planning to do just that. If you don't want to jump, I can give you a push. Your choice."

"How many people do you plan to kill?"

"This wasn't what I had planned tonight. But when you looked at my photo, I had think to fast and change things up."

At Karl's gravesite, when she thought she was out of options and that she would never know who killed Karl, Cara had wondered whether she still wanted to live. Now, she raged to stay alive. She just had to figure out how.

"We can still record the podcast, just like you wanted. I won't talk about any of this. It'll be huge and—"

"I'm already number one on Apple. But having you unalive yourself by jumping off my parents' cliff? I'll be the one who gets to tell your story. Of course, I'll have to admit that I was wrong about you all along."

"That kind of fame only lasts a hot second."

She couldn't see his face, but she could hear the smile in his voice. "My audience loves me. Imagine what will happen when I discover another wrongly accused murderer in season two."

Dylan was gradually pressing her forward. She had no way to push back. Her stomach felt as empty as the void below.

People had loved her. Karl unreservedly. Aunt Evelyn still did. Even Stephanie, in her own way. Once she'd had more friends than she could count—real friends, not social media followers—who abandoned her only because they believed the government's claim she was a killer.

"You don't know the first thing about love," she told him, balanced on the edge, with nothing left to lose. "I loved, and was loved, and at least I don't need to swallow psychedelics to think I'm feeling something real."

"My vision was real." Almost whining, a child insisting he was right.

Below, not all that far from where her body would land, she saw a police vehicle driving up the hill. Its flashers weren't lit, but it was moving fast.

"The cops are here," she told him.

As Dylan craned his neck to see, momentarily slackening his grip, Cara hammered her head back into his. She hit something softer than his skull.

"My nose!" Wobbling, he let go and grabbed his face.

"Fuck you, motherfucker!"

She shouldered him hard, and he tumbled into the pool. Dark blood clouded the water as he flailed toward the side.

Cara stared for only a second. Then she ran, faster than she had ever run, through the yard, through the front gate, and out onto the street.

Silhouetted at the top of the path was a lanky man in a Stetson hat.

"Sheriff Burke!" she said, actually relieved to see him. "Help me!"

A security light revealed his face as he raised his gun.

It wasn't Burke.

"Stop where you are," said the man. "I'm placing you under citizen's arrest."

ONE HUNDRED AND SEVEN
JORDAN

11-99. All available units to 8201 Chelan Drive. Repeat 11-99. All available units to 8201 Chelan Drive.

—LAPD radio transmission

Jordan arrived in time to see Campbell streak through large wooden gates and freeze in the middle of the road. His eyes searched the darkness until he saw what she saw.

Silverman. Drawing down on her, holding the gun in one hand like a wannabe gunslinger.

Jordan was so stunned he could hardly think. Then instinct kicked in.

Not a man. The goddamn sheriff.

He threw the car into park and kicked open the door, unstrapping his Glock and slipping off the safety.

Dylan Danvers came through the gates, dripping wet, one hand holding his face.

"You're Cara Campbell, and as a citizen of California, I have the authority to—" Silverman was saying.

"Get that bitch!" yelled Danvers.

"PUT THE GUN DOWN!" bellowed Jordan, drawing a bead on Silverman.

All three heads swung toward him in surprise.

Silverman's arm moved, too. There was a report as his pistol fired.

Danvers staggered and screamed in pain. "Troy, you fucking idiot!"

Campbell bolted into the trees while Silverman stared at the gun in his hand.

Letting her go for the moment, Jordan closed the space and clubbed Silverman's hand with his Glock. Silverman's gun—a chrome-plated Colt revolver—clattered on the pavement. Jordan kicked it away, then grabbed Silverman's vest and kicked his feet out from under him.

Silverman flailed his arms, fighting back, giving Jordan an excuse to put a knee in his back.

It felt good.

Ten yards away, Danvers sat down in his street. He was holding his thigh and looking down at the blood oozing through his fingers.

"Face down, with your hands behind you!" Jordan ordered. "Lace your fingers together!"

"My leg . . ."

"Do it. And what the hell are you doing here, Silverman?"

"Catching your . . . fugitive."

"Yeah, great job on that," spat Danvers. "You fucking shot me."

"It was an accident," Silverman insisted indignantly.

"That can be your new campaign slogan," Jordan told him.

Campbell was gone.

Jordan put away his weapon. Then he sat Silverman and Danvers back-to-back, like captured outlaws in an old Western, and zip-tied their hands together. He made a tourniquet out of Silverman's belt and cinched it tight above Danvers's thigh wound.

"You keep turning up at the wrong time," Jordan told Silverman as he hobbled his ankles, just in case.

"You left your cruiser sitting in that motel parking lot, so I put an Air Tag on it," he said, with what sounded like petulant pride. "I was following you around until Dylan called me and told me he was going to record Campbell and then let me arrest her. So I came here. I was waiting outside his house when I saw them leave."

"She was suicidal," said Danvers. "I was trying to talk her out of it."

"I guess that's why she was running away from you," said Silverman sarcastically.

"What really went on up there?" asked Jordan.

"I won't say another word without my lawyer present."

Jordan walked away from them and took out his phone. Dropping a location pin on Google Maps, he texted it to Wen, then called her as he started off on foot.

"Jordan? I heard on the police scanner that you're still in LA."

"Send everyone to the location I just texted. You'll need EMTs. Silverman shot Danvers and Campbell got away."

"Wait. Like, seriously? What are—"

"I'm in pursuit."

He ended the call and started running down the path Campbell had taken.

ONE HUNDRED AND EIGHT
CARA

Cara Campbell as the next Bachelorette! (r/bachelorette Reddit thread)

Let's make it happen.

—/u/AmyB90210

I know someone who knows someone.

—/u/srslysir

I can't f'in believe she's innocent!

—/u/rhbblahblah

Runyon Canyon Park closed at dusk, but Cara knew there were no cameras or park personnel to worry about as she climbed a fence on the remote east side, far from the Mulholland entrance. She'd hiked there often enough, always respectfully staying on the trails to avoid trampling vegetation. And she'd commemorated every visit with a selfie, whether from the rock mandala, the yoga field after a group class, or from somewhere in the "wilderness."

Given where she'd been and what she'd survived, she found it ironic to be running for her life a Lime scooter ride away from multimillion-dollar rooftops and the Hollywood sign.

She bushwhacked in the dark until she found a trail, then followed it until she found the ruins of a 1940s resort. Hiding in the shadow of a crumbling stone pile that had once been a chimney, she stopped until she finally caught her breath.

So much hinged upon the slightest of chances. If she and Karl had stood further apart at Johnson's Point, she would be dead, and he would be alive.

Tonight, if she hadn't spotted the photo of Dylan with blond hair, she would have recorded the interview, telling him her entire story before he betrayed her and turned her over to Silverman. Dylan's backup plan—to *unalive* her—would have worked for him, too, she had to admit. He seemed untroubled by the horrible cost of his shortcut to fame. The spirits guiding him were not his better angels. They were demons, telling him to kill again.

As Cara peered out at the shadowed landscape, a coyote howled.

But she wasn't afraid of wild animals.

She heard footsteps. As they crunched closer, she moved away from the ruin until she found a tree whose lower branches were low enough to reach. She grabbed one and swung up, then climbed until she was concealed by leaves.

Was it Silverman? Dylan? Or just a nighttime trail runner? She couldn't be caught by any of them.

"Cara! Cara Campbell!"

The male voice was familiar. Definitely not Dylan.

A twig snapped and grass rustled as he drew closer.

"Cara, it's Sheriff Jordan Burke from Madera County."

Quietly moving a branch aside with her hand, she saw him standing below her, playing a flashlight over the ruins. Unlike the time they'd met by the raging water, he didn't have a gun in his hands.

And his voice was calm. "Cara, if you can hear me, I know you didn't kill your husband."

Was it a trick? Did it even matter?

She'd been running from this particular sheriff, and law enforcement in general, ever since the van crash. She could imagine Roy Abel's televised smirk when he learned Cara's justice would come from within the system. But suddenly she knew revealing herself to Jordan Burke was her safest option.

"I told you," she said.

Sheriff Burke turned, looking for the source of her voice, then stepped over to the tree. He looked up like he was looking for a missing housecat.

"Come on down, now. You're safe. Danvers and Silverman aren't coming after you."

"Did Dylan admit to killing Karl? And that he originally meant to kill me?"

"He wouldn't say anything without a lawyer, of course. But why would he have done that?"

She climbed down carefully. "To get famous."

"Wasn't he already famous?"

"Famous for being a nepo baby. He was desperate to create something authentically his. And I guess he felt I'd stolen his chance."

Unfortunately, she understood too much about that particular hunger.

Sheriff Burke shook his head in disgust. "Why don't you explain everything to me while we walk back?"

As they hiked together in the dark, equally comfortable on the trail, Jordan listened, occasionally interrupting with a clarifying question, to the story she hadn't had a chance to tell. The whole story, in order. She included everything she had learned in her LA investigations and tonight's awful encounter with Dylan Danvers.

As they neared his sheriff's cruiser, Jordan looked off into the distance at the streets of the city below them, going on to infinity.

"I was confident I'd track you down in the hills—I just didn't figure it would be the Hollywood Hills."

"Looks like you learned to find your way around."

He looked at her, his eyes glinting in the light pollution. "So this guy took psychedelics, had a vision, tried to kill you but killed your husband, and pressed the hammer into your hand? And when you took the rap and even escaped, he hid his guilt by pretending to be your biggest champion?"

She laughed so she wouldn't cry. "Some people will do anything for likes."

He shook his head, a decent man who could hardly believe it.

Cara looked past him at his vehicle, thinking the back seat could almost be comfortable. "So you're taking me in now?"

Sheriff Burke tossed his keys from one hand to another, then closed his fist and shook his head.

"Come in when you're ready. I'll be there when you need me. Seems like the story is yours to tell."

Cara was exhausted. Her legs were so tired she could hardly stand upright. But her journey did not end here. When he reached out a hand, she took it. His grip was warm and strong. She let go first.

Then, putting one foot in front of another, she began slowly walking downhill into the night.

ONE HUNDRED AND NINE
JORDAN

And baby, you go good with me.
—Walker Hayes

Bubbly blue water fanned out behind the fourteen-foot aluminum fishing boat as Jordan steered toward the shaded side of Bass Lake. On the seat ahead of him, Amber zipped up her jacket against the early morning chill, while on the seat ahead of her, Sydney took selfie after selfie, trying to get the perfect shot with her brown hair whipping in the wind.

Jordan had been ready to go right back to work, and sure he should, until Beto stopped him.

"Damn it, boss, take at least twenty-four hours off," his chief deputy had told him over the phone as Jordan rolled over the county line the evening before. "I've got this. Things have been downright quiet since the circus left town. A few more sightseers than usual but nothing we can't handle."

Grateful, Jordan had agreed. Several days before, a brief but unseasonably heavy rain had knocked out the remaining fires, and today the skies were a perfect California blue. Last night, his wife and daughter had promised him breakfast in bed and a day doing whatever he wanted, "even though we already know what you're going to say."

Amber didn't like to fish or eat fish, and Sydney hadn't wetted a line since she was twelve, but they both feigned enthusiasm so believably it made his heart ache.

He didn't care if he caught a thing today. He just wanted to be unreachable. He'd left his own phone in the glove box of his truck.

In a minor miracle, Bree had started talking sometime around the time Jordan found Cara Campbell in the urban canyon. According to Sydney, her friend's first words were, "Where's my phone?"

Speech was still an effort for her, and she wouldn't walk for months. Chronic pain seemed likely. But she would survive, and her personality seemed intact.

And Jordan, come this time next year, would still be doing the job he loved while Silverman continued his real estate hustles, most likely from Montecito. While he hadn't formally withdrawn from the race, his Facebook page had been deleted, which Jordan took to mean he'd stopped campaigning. The news that he'd accidentally shot Dylan Danvers as part of a plot to entrap Cara Campbell had been leaked to the media by a friendly source.

Jordan suspected Wen, who'd shared in his win—he'd given a statement praising her work—and would be back in good graces at her job.

The icing on the cake was the Silverman meme making the rounds with an unauthorized push from Gracia and the Madera Sheriff's social media. Silverman had repeated his defense within earshot of someone with a phone: *It was an accident.*

A campaign slogan worthy of its candidate.

Amber looked over her shoulder and smiled at Jordan. "All good?"

Holding the tiller steady, he leaned forward and kissed her. "All good."

ONE HUNDRED AND TEN
CARA

To those who say you never get a second chance to make a good first impression, I say: REBRAND.
—*@margiesmarketingmecca*

Taylor hadn't formally apologized to Cara, but she did send word through Aunt Evelyn that she had no plans to list the house. *Not for the foreseeable future, anyway.*

For now, that was more than enough.

Cara had a place to live rent free, even if she couldn't *foresee* living there very long. There were too many memories—wonderful, nightmarish, and bittersweet—to sleep soundly. Not to mention the lookie-loos driving by at all hours of the day and night. Some left flowers, stuffed animals, or notes wishing her well. Others shouted her name, hoping she would appear in the window. A carful of fraternity pledges had even piled out of their Jeep and onto her front steps to belt out the refrain of Kanye West's "Gold Digger."

The video went viral instantly.

After the charges were formally dropped and Cara's phone was returned, she began to read her endless messages. Almost all of them were left by former friends proclaiming they'd *believed you all along,* that she'd been *unimaginably brave,* and they were *proud to call her a friend.*

Stephanie—who'd approached Porsche corporate in the hope of leveraging her experience as the driver of the Beverly Hills getaway car into an endorsement deal—didn't need to pretend.

Nor did the throngs of strangers who sent DMs on every account Cara had ever created, even LinkedIn. Some messages were rebukes: *this woulda never happened if you weren't ho'in in the first place.* Others were praising: *I'm nine months pregnant and I'm naming her after you!* Cara liked the messages with advice the most: *Don't disband. Rebrand.*

Reading each and every message and thanking its sender for reaching out proved oddly therapeutic.

Cara was about to compose a polite thanks, but no thanks, to someone named Clyde who'd written, *I've got money and I've had some legal troubles, but I was exonerated, too. Want to meet?* when her doorbell rang.

Through the glass she saw Alan Segura, the producer who lived at the end of the cul-de-sac.

"I'm really sorry about all the people driving by," she said as she opened the door, assuming he'd come by to complain. "I hope it will die down soon. If it doesn't I'll—"

"I have a dynamite idea," he said, straightening his Moscot glasses. "For a project about you."

"As a gold digger, a wrongly convicted murderer, a prisoner, or an escaped convict racing to solve her husband's murder?"

"We'll have to hire a writer to flesh it out, but all of the above."

Cara laughed out loud.

ACKNOWLEDGMENTS

We are grateful to James L'Etoile for his insights on prisoner transport, law enforcement, and interagency cooperation—any errors that remain are ours and not his. Thanks also to Frank Sennett for reading an early draft and providing excellent feedback on stakes and pacing.

Editor Celia Johnson is every author's dream and one of the best in the business. This book is so much better because of her enthusiasm, insight, and sharp-eyed suggestions. Our sincere thanks to Addi Wright for bringing us back to Blackstone for another book, and to everyone at Blackstone for helping Cara Campbell find her way through the wilds. Lydia Rogue improved our sentences and caught several key mistakes.

Deepest gratitude to our friend and loyal agent, Josh Getzler; his assistant, Jillian Schelzi; and the whole team at HG Literary. (Let's go bowling!) We're so delighted to have Hilary Zaitz Michael in our corner at WME.

Mark Stevens deserves another standing ovation for his support, which always goes above and beyond. (Read his books!) And big hugs to Javier and Kristin Ramirez at Exile in Bookville in Chicago's beautiful Fine Arts Building.

We couldn't have done any of this without our families. Linda sends her love to Brandon, Andrew, Steph, Evan, Abby, and Eliza. Keir sends his to Marya, June, and Cosmo.